Texas Heat

Gertlett

shine

LYRICAL SHINE
Kensington Publishing Corp.
www.kensingtonbooks.com

LYRICAL SHINE BOOKS are published by

Kensington Publishing Corp.
119 West 40th Street
New York, NY 10018

All Kensington titles, imprints, and distributed lines are available at special quantity discounts for bulk purchases for sales promotion, premiums, fund-raising, educational, or institutional use.

Special book excerpts or customized printings can also be created to fit specific needs. For details, write or phone the office of the Kensington Sales Manager: Kensington Publishing Corp., 119 West 40th Street, New York, NY 10018. Attn. Sales Department. Phone: 1-800-221-2647.

Lyrical Shine and Lyrical Shine logo Reg. U.S. Pat. & TM Off.

First Electronic Edition: December 2016
eISBN-13: 978-1-60183-982-4
eISBN-10: 1-60183-982-0

First Print Edition: December 2016
ISBN-13: 978-1-60183-983-1
ISBN-10: 1-60183-983-9

Printed in the United States of America

*This book is dedicated to the memory of my dear friend Jean Dunn.
I finally wrote a Texas love story without a vampire for you.
I miss you, pal.*

ACKNOWLEDGMENTS:

Much love as always to my terrific critique partners Nina Bangs and Donna Maloy. Their patience is legendary. Thanks to super-agent Kimberly Whalen for steering my course to Kensington and to editor Esi Sogah, who proved to be great to work with. The team at Lyrical Shine came up with a sexy cover and my copy editor helped make this book come together with a minimum of pain.

I hope my fans will enjoy this visit to Texas, my home. I grew up in Houston and still live a few minutes away. If you've never come to the Lone Star State, give us a try. Everything's bigger and better here. Even the love stories.

Chapter 1

Cassidy Calhoun must have had worse days before, but she sure couldn't remember them. With the heat near 100, her car's AC giving out halfway to downtown Houston and the freeway in gridlock, she was going to be late. Plus, one jerk had almost killed her trying to move into her lane. Twice. Jeez. Her hands were still shaking.

This whole inheritance thing had better not be a scam. But then the man had tracked her down at work, handed her a business card from a fancy law firm, and claimed showing up at this lawyer's office today would be worth her while. That was an awful lot of trouble for a scam.

So she'd arranged for a personal day off from work. Why not? If some long-lost relative had left her enough money to trade in this hunk of junk and maybe pay down some bills, then this morning's drive would be worth every painful minute. Cass pulled into a parking garage with a twenty-dollar minimum. Great. It was as if someone had peeked into her purse. These people had better validate.

Minutes later she tried to smooth the wrinkles out of her dress. Black wasn't her color, but some poor soul had died, right? When she checked in the mirrored walls as the elevator took her up to the thirtieth floor she wasn't surprised to see she'd sweated off her makeup. Of course the heat had frizzed her hair from professional to Jane of the jungle. But her hopes rose with the elevator. This building was high-end. If she was the *right* Cassidy Calhoun and actually about to come into some money, her whole life could change.

Leaning against the cool mirror, Cass imagined what she could do with some extra money. Priority one? She'd get a place of her own without a horny roommate who was a screamer when her boyfriend stayed over. And speaking of boyfriends . . . The elevator door swished open and that thought vanished as she laid eyes on the most beautiful male specimen she'd seen outside the pages of a magazine ad. He had a cell phone to his ear.

"*Gorikai itadaki arigatōgozaimasu.*" He ended the call, then bowed. "Did I just do what I think I did?"

Cass couldn't resist. She bowed back.

He laughed a loud, from-the-belly laugh that was irresistibly infectious. Cass grinned and felt some of the tension that had started a headache behind her right eye ease a little. His laugh cut off abruptly, as if someone had turned the handle on a spigot, when his phone rang in his hand. "Shit." He leaned against the elevator door when it tried to shut on him.

Cass tucked her purse under her arm. Was this her floor? No, twenty-eight.

"Yeah, I just got through talking to them. The deal's still on." He listened for a moment. "No, you're not getting near the Japanese. I don't care if you do think they have their heads up their asses. I handled it and they sure as hell don't want to talk to you again." He stepped inside and glanced at the keypad next to the doors, then gave Cass a thorough inspection that made her brush her hair behind her ears, the less seen of it the better. "Listen, I'm going into a meeting and turning off my phone. I did my job, which should be enough to make you happy, Ed. Talk to you later." He made a point of shoving his phone in his breast pocket after shutting it down.

"You going to thirty too?" He kept his finger on the button that kept the doors open. The elevator had started buzzing while he'd been on the phone.

"No, thirty." Cass eased away from him into her own corner of the elevator. Not that he intimidated her with his expensive suit and the kind of confidence that *she* certainly didn't feel today.

"That's what I meant." He finally let the elevator do its thing and grinned, his whiter-than-white teeth perfect in his tanned face. "That's where I'm heading. Is there any chance you're Cassidy Calhoun?"

"Um, yes, I am. Cass." Cass blinked when he offered his hand. Clean, buffed nails, but calluses on his fingers. She clasped his hand. Firm handshake. Nice. None of that limp, pseudo-shake some men thought a woman expected or deserved.

"Mason MacKenzie." He gestured when the elevator doors opened again. "We're here."

"Are you one of the lawyers?" The business card had read *MacKenzie and Harper*. As she slid by the man and stepped into the spacious foyer with gleaming hardwood floors, she got a whiff of a subtle fragrance from him. Delicious. Almost as delicious as his broad shoulders in what had to be a custom-made Italian suit. She stumbled when her heel caught on the edge of the oriental rug in front of the receptionist's desk. He caught her elbow before she could hit the floor.

Cool move, Cass.

"Careful." He squeezed her arm, then let go when she was steady again. "No, not a lawyer. That's my brother Dylan. You'll meet him in a moment."

Cass noticed he wore shiny black cowboy boots with his suit. Interesting. He also had on a class ring from a Texas college she wished she could have afforded. His dark suit set off his dark hair and the pale blue tie could have been dyed to match his eyes. Which were also looking her over. Cass focused on the woman who'd shot out of her chair behind the chrome and glass desk centered under the name of the law firm. Killer shoes, dress-for-success suit in red and she was model-thin and tall. Cass hadn't looked that polished even before her ride from hell.

"Mr. MacKenzie! They're waiting for you in the big conference room. Is this Miss Calhoun? She's the last to arrive. Besides you, of course." The woman flushed, like she realized she'd just handed both of them a tardy slip. "Can I get either of you a water, or something stronger?" She said this last to Mason with a flirty look, practically dancing in her high heels.

"I'm fine, Amber. Yes, this is Ms. Calhoun. Cass?" Mason stayed by Cass's side, like he was ready to catch her if she stumbled again.

"Are we going to the same meeting? The reading of a will?" Cass looked up at him. He was awfully close, close enough that she could see the sweep of his thick, dark lashes as he nodded and took her elbow again.

"Oh, yes. I think you'll find it very interesting." Mason smiled and moved her forward. "It'll be down this hall."

"What about that water?" The receptionist kept pace with them, checking out Cass with a frown. "No offense, Ms. Calhoun, but you look like you're suffering from the heat."

"Cass? She's right." Mason stopped. "Your face is red."

"Car trouble—my AC went out. Water would be great. But like you said, we're late. Can you bring it to me in the conference room? Please?" Cass hated to ask, but she also hated to keep people waiting.

"Sure. Still or sparkling?"

Cass shook her head. "What?"

Mason started moving her down the hall again. "She means do you want water with or without bubbles."

"Oh. Without, please. And thank you." Now she felt like an idiot.

"Relax. The fun's just begun. Wait till you meet the rest of the Calhouns." Mason pushed open a door and conversation in the room suddenly stopped as the people inside turned to stare. "Everyone, this is Cassidy Calhoun. Goes by Cass. Be nice. She had car trouble and may pass out from heat exhaustion any minute." He held out a vacant chair. "The man at the end of the table is my brother Dylan, the lawyer who asked you to come here."

"You feel faint? Can't have that. Is someone getting you water?" This came from a middle-aged woman with pretty blond hair and sparkling blue eyes. "I'm Missy Calhoun, Connie's wife number two."

"Water. Yes, thank you." Cass settled into a comfortable leather armchair. Connie? She was about to ask when a girl who seemed several years younger than her own twenty-nine sat on the conference table in front of her.

"Why, she's the spittin' image of Daddy, isn't she, Mama?" The girl, who had the older woman's blond hair and blue eyes, bumped her mother with her knees and seemed determined to get into her space.

"I'll say. Dark hair and that unfortunate stubborn chin. Are you stubborn, girl?" Missy obviously didn't mince words.

"I've been known to be. Who do I look like?" *Daddy?* And there was nothing wrong with *her* chin, damn it. Except that it was square and tended to stick out when she was mad. Okay, so it was unfortunate. And stubborn.

"You don't know who I'm talking about?" The girl raised her eyebrows. "You've got to be kidding. Anyway, I'm Megan. This is my sister Shannon and that guy over there who won't quit texting is my brother Ethan." Megan smiled and left her perch on the table. "We had no idea Daddy had you first. It'll take some getting used to.

Don't know why it was a big secret all these years." She glanced around and the girl who looked a lot like her nodded. The boy, who also had Cass's unfortunate chin and dark hair, ignored them, more interested in his phone.

"Drink." Mason thrust a cold glass into her hand. The receptionist set a tray with a pitcher of ice water and more glasses on the table then hurriedly left the room, closing the door behind her.

Cass gulped the water gratefully. When she reached to refill her glass, her hand shook and she spilled water on the tray. She gave up and sat back.

"Relax, honey, we don't bite. I swear it." Missy Calhoun gave her a sympathetic smile, then touched her eyes with a hanky. "It's a sad day for us. Did your daddy ever come see you?"

"I don't know who or what you're talking about." Cass scanned the room. Mason had moved down the table to talk to his brother the lawyer. Now everyone stared at her. "I never knew my father and he sure as hell never came to see me. If that's who this is about, I'm out of here." She stood and her purse slid off her lap to hit the floor. Just her luck that her phone and wallet spilled out of it, along with a wad of tissues and her freaking keys.

"Hold it." Mason leaned down to shove everything back inside her black patent purse. Then he held it out of reach. "Are you telling us that your mother never told you Conrad Calhoun was your father?"

"She certainly didn't." Cass refused to jump for her purse. He was too damned tall and she was not going to look the fool in front of these well-dressed people who were examining her like she was a bug under a microscope. "My father abandoned her when she was pregnant, never gave her one dime of support. He left us to fend for ourselves. Why would I expect anything from him now?"

Mason put her purse in her hands but didn't release it. "Will you listen to my brother for a minute? And consider that maybe your mother didn't tell you the whole story? Or the *true* story?"

Missy took a glass of water. "Connie could be a mean son of a bitch, of course, but he loved his family. I can't believe he would abandon his wife and child." She glanced at the lawyer. "Maybe this is a mistake."

"I'm sure it is. He may have loved *this* family, but not mine." Cass gestured around the table. "If this Connie person claimed he was my father, then believe it, lady. He left us high and dry. I have thousands of dollars of student-loan debt to prove it. Hey, girls, did you have to work the McDonald's drive-through to help pay for college? Ever sleep through a test because you'd pulled the late-night shift at Hooters?" Oh, she shouldn't have said that. Now Ethan, the guy who was supposedly her brother, had looked up to check out her rack. Mason had already done that, but was giving it a second look. Dylan the lawyer did it automatically, then must have remembered he was supposed to be serious on this sad occasion. He cleared his throat and shuffled papers.

"It wasn't just a claim . . ." Dylan kept his eyes on hers.

"We're sorry, Cassidy." Megan's eyes filled with tears. "I'm sure if Daddy had known . . ."

"What makes you think he didn't?" Cass started toward the door. "And just didn't give a damn about me." Yes, her chin was doing its thing. Well, she was mad. Who were these people to talk about "Daddy" like he was someone they'd loved? She'd never had a father to love.

She faced the room and knew all of them were staring and judging her. "Hey, it's not like I lived in Siberia. If your 'Daddy' raised you here in Houston, then we were only about thirty minutes from each other. But I never heard his name before today. Never got so much as a birthday card from him." Cass gripped the doorknob, seconds from opening it and storming out. "I don't need this." But she couldn't open that door. High priced lawyer, well-dressed people. Conrad Calhoun. Where had she heard that name before?

She hesitated. All of this shouted *money*. Which meant there might, might be some of it coming her way. She wasn't so mad or so proud that she could afford to bolt and miss out on a chance to ease some of her debt burden. She was trying to figure out a way to back down from her dramatic exit line when Dylan stepped forward, a sheaf of papers in his hand.

"Wait. Please. Conrad had his reasons for ignoring you, Cassidy." He gestured toward the chair she'd abandoned. "Will you sit and listen? Give me five minutes. I can see you have your father's temper, but I promise that if you'll let me explain things, it will help you understand why he couldn't contact you. Or help you financially." The man who looked a lot like Mason stepped closer and held out a file folder. "Until now."

"I'm the lawyer Connie trusted with his estate and his private affairs after my father died. He and Dad were best friends. I have the paperwork from your parents' divorce right here." Dylan opened the folder. "Which prohibited him from contacting you. I'll sum it up for you, if you'll let me."

Cass sat. "Prohibited? That seems a little extreme." What could he have done that had made her mother refuse to let him see her? Contact her? Throw money at her? Cass looked around the room at her so-called sisters and brother, who were clearly hearing all of this for the first time if their expressions could be believed. Missy, wife number two, just pursed her lips, obviously not shocked at all. "Please, go ahead."

"All right, then." Dylan picked up the folder and began going through papers. "Your parents were married for a couple of years when your mother got pregnant with you. Apparently the marriage was rocky from the start. Then something happened and your mother sued for divorce. Conrad was willing to deal generously with her. His business had started to take off and he was already worth plenty. She could have had a settlement in the millions and as well as generous child support."

Cass held up her hand. "Wait. His business. What was it?" Conrad Calhoun. It rang a bell but she couldn't—

"Calhoun Petroleum, Cassidy. Maybe you've heard of it? It's worth billions today." This from another woman who was sipping a glass of white wine. She sat in a chair in one corner of the room, clearly not part of the other Calhoun family. She was beautiful, with carefully styled red hair and porcelain skin. Cass didn't need a fashion magazine to recognize that her elegant gray dress probably had a designer label.

"No one bothered to introduce me. I'm Alexandra, wife number three. No children with Conrad. We liked to travel and play." She smiled at Missy. "I'm the fun wife."

"Of course you are." Missy turned away from her. "I'm sorry you never knew your father, Cassidy. He was great with his children. Not so good with his wives." She glanced back at Alexandra. "I heard you were separated and he'd moved back to the house. You got lucky he kicked off before you had to deal with the prenup he made you sign."

"Poor Missy. Maybe if you'd had a facelift when you needed it, he wouldn't have dumped you for me." Alexandra flashed her enormous diamond ring. "Can we get on with this?"

"Getting on with it right now." Dylan looked ready to step between the two women, though neither of them had bothered to get out of their chairs.

"Daddy *was* a wonderful father." Megan patted Cass on the shoulder. "No matter what happened with your mama." She glanced at her mother. "Cutting you off from him, that's harsh. And not taking the money? That's awfully prideful."

"This is how it was stipulated in the divorce decree. Liz wouldn't take any money from Connie and he relinquished his parental rights, including the right to contact the child—you, Cassidy. He signed off on it without a fight and never would say why. His friends, including my own father, speculated that it was because he was sick of their fighting and he needed to be free to handle a bid for a hostile takeover going on at that time. He couldn't afford a big court battle then." Dylan shook his head. "I'm sorry."

"He gave me up for money? For business, I mean." Cassidy leaned her head back against the cool leather and tried not to let these strangers see how that hurt her.

"Maybe you're not really his. We should run a DNA test." Alexandra set down her wineglass. "I'm sure you're here because you're mentioned in the will. Isn't she, Dylan?"

"Yes, she is. That's why all of you are here." Dylan picked up a second set of papers.

Cass shivered. The room was cold, the AC obviously set at *arctic*. Mentioned in a billionaire's will. A man who hadn't wanted her. "Maybe you *should* run a DNA test. If I'm not his daughter, that would explain a lot. And I shouldn't take anything from him."

"You're his, Cassidy. It would be convenient if you weren't, but didn't my daughter just say you were the image of him?" Missy glanced at the lawyer. "And I'm sure Dylan checked that out already, if I know him."

"Yes. I'm not usually into such cloak-and-dagger stuff, but I had my detective, the one who tracked you down at work, Cassidy, steal your coffee cup from your desk. We ran a DNA test from the lipstick print on it. You are definitely Conrad's child." Dylan threw another piece of paper on the table. "The test results are here if anyone wants to see them."

Alexandra actually picked it up and studied it.

"I wondered where my favorite mug disappeared to. You can do that? Get DNA just from my lipstick on a ceramic cup?" Cass's fingers hurt and she realized she gripped her purse like it was a lifeline.

Ethan finally spoke. "You can. I just ran an Internet search and it's true. Three sisters. Great." He went back to his phone.

Cass swallowed, not sure she wasn't going to throw up that water. This was real. Her father was a famous oilman. A billionaire. Calhoun Petroleum. Who hadn't heard of that company? She wanted to pull out her own phone and call her mother right now. How could she have done this to her only child? Let her work so hard for so long? Her mom knew how desperate Cass had been for a father. No mention of this rich man in Houston.

Damn it. She looked up and hated the pity she saw in everyone's eyes. Yes, she and her mother were going to have a come-to-Jesus talk, if she could bring herself to ever speak to Elizabeth Calhoun ever again. And there was that. If her mother had hated Conrad so much, why keep his name? Only one person had those answers and she wasn't here. Cass took a breath and straightened in her chair.

"Okay, I'm Conrad Calhoun's daughter. So he died. Aren't we here for the reading of his will?" She looked around, meeting one pair of eyes after another, some sympathetic, one hostile, one bored. "I'm . . . um, sorry for your loss. Forgive me if I'm not feeling it. With this being news and all."

"We get it, Cassidy." Megan's sister—what was her name?— tossed her own phone on the table. "Welcome to the family. Now she's right, Dylan. Unless you've got some more secret siblings you want to spring on us, I say let's get on with it. I have a meeting of the rodeo committee later." She leaned on the table, focused on the lawyer. "Aren't you on the corporate-development committee too this year? Want to ride out there with me later? The meeting's at the Rocking R Ranch, you know."

"No more secret siblings." Dylan smiled. "And, yes, Shannon, I'm going out there too. Later." He got serious and flipped through his papers.

"So that explains why you're dressed in leather and lace, Shannon." Alexandra raised an elegant eyebrow. "Texans. Aren't you rushing things? I thought the rodeo didn't start until February. This is August."

"True. But we plan all year long. We work hard and party hard. Right, Dylan?" Shannon scooted her chair closer to the lawyer. "You are going to change clothes before we go, aren't you?" She slid her hand over his where he was rifling through a file.

"Of course. I'll put on my boots before we go. Unlike my brother, I don't wear them twenty-four-seven. Now we need to get down to business."

"Uptight lawyer." Mason had settled into one of the leather chairs. "The Japanese loved my boots and were disappointed I didn't have on my Stetson."

"I'm sure you played the good-old Texas boy to the hilt." Dylan ignored Mason's rude gesture. "Now, let's get back to the matter at hand." The lawyer sat at the head of the table and told them to look at the big-screen TV at the end of the room. "Conrad made a video of his last will and testament. Of course, I have all the necessary paperwork here to back up his last wishes. This is binding. So don't think you can wiggle out of any of his provisions."

"Provisions?" Ethan finally set down his phone. "What the hell did Daddy do this time? That man loved to tie strings to everything."

"You're right about that, son. You trying to scare us, Dylan?" Missy stalked over to the open bar and helped herself to a glass of red wine.

"No, just setting the scene." Dylan turned on the TV mounted on the wall and the screen came to life.

Cassidy gasped. He did look like her. He had the same dark hair, but with gray at his temples. And there was her jaw and the stubborn chin that served her well when she wanted to be taken seriously. His eyes were dark, not hazel. But she'd always known she had her mother's eyes. He was close to Mom's age, fifties or early sixties, maybe. Too young to be dead. She started to ask how he'd died when he spoke. His deep voice filled the room.

"Well, if you're seeing this, then I guess I've gone to meet my maker. Damn, but I'd hoped to live forever." His laugh boomed through the room. "Okay, guess you aren't in the mood to joke. I had a warning or two lately that my time was running out so I made this will. Seems like God has his own plans and I couldn't buy my way out of this one, though I sure as hell tried." Another laugh.

"I lived life the way I wanted, made my own rules." He shook his head. "I'm a sinner. I know that. So it's likely I'm burning in hell and

Lucifer's got me scraping out cesspools with a teaspoon while you're watching me in Dylan's office." His shoulders slumped and he picked up a coffee cup and took a sip. "No matter. I'm gone and you're still there. So I want to take care of you all." He looked straight into the camera and Cass felt like he was talking directly to her. Which was impossible because they'd never met.

She heard a sob and looked around. Shannon had Dylan's snowy handkerchief in her hands and leaned against his shoulder. Missy had tears running down her cheeks while Alexandra finished off her wine, then used her napkin to dab at her eyes. Megan reached out and gripped Cass's hand. Ethan watched the screen, his eyes bright with unshed tears.

"Now I expect Dylan's got you all together. You can trust him. He's good people. Missy, you and the kids are there. Alexandra, I'm sure you wouldn't miss this and I won't disappoint you. I hope he's managed to get Cassidy to this thing. I'm sorry, honey, that your mama is a stubborn bitch. I tried to watch over you all these years. Even wanted to arrange for your college to be paid for, but Liz would have none of it. So I know you suffered for her pride and her spite. I hope you haven't been poisoned by it. I wanted you. Wanted to help raise you, see you every weekend if she'd let me. But she had something on me—I won't say what—so I had to agree to her terms, even after you grew to adulthood." He looked older suddenly as he pressed a hand to his chest. "It's my biggest regret. But now I hope to make it up to you. So here's the deal."

He leaned forward, his elbows on his knees. He wore a navy-blue polo shirt and black slacks. There was a logo on the shirt that Cass realized was his oil-company symbol. She'd seen it on tanker trucks that had whizzed past her on the freeway. She wanted to believe him, this stranger who looked like her. That he'd wanted her. But if she'd had a child, no one could have kept her from him or her. She knew that in her gut. Anger kept her from shedding any tears. Why couldn't he have fought harder for her? How could he have let her go? She glanced again at his other three children. They'd had him all their lives. Not fair.

"I know what happens to kids of billionaires who don't have to work for their money. They end up druggies or no-accounts, sponging off their folks with no direction in their lives." He hit one knee with his fist. "I won't have that. So far I've been easy on the three of you I had with Missy. Gave you whatever you wanted. Didn't have the heart to put the hammer down like I should have. But that stops now."

Cass heard the three people in question move in their chairs. She could only envy them what must have been a wonderful childhood, indulged in every way.

"I made my way by myself, kids. I started with nothing and look what I had at the end. I want you to have that feeling of accomplishment. There's nothing like it. So you're each going to work in the business for one year."

There was a gasp around the room.

"Oh, not Missy and Alexandra. You two ladies earned your inheritance by putting up with me as a husband. Living with a workaholic couldn't have been fun. Missy, you sure bitched about it enough. So each of you gets twenty million, which will be held in trust by MacKenzie and Harper. That should provide you with a nice income for life. Upon your deaths, the remainder will be divided among my kids. Hope that makes you happy."

"Well, I expected a lot more than that." Alexandra picked up her designer bag and stood. "I've heard enough. I'll leave my address with your secretary, Dylan. I'll expect my first check by end of business Monday."

"Of course." Dylan hit *pause*. He escorted her to the door then sat again and glanced at Missy. "Any comment?"

"No, I'm satisfied. I got mine when we divorced. But I want to hear what else he has in store for my kids. Hit *play*, Dylan." She glanced at Mason. "And why is Mason here?"

"You'll see." He hit *play*.

"Now here's how it's going to be, kids. Oh, I know, you're all grown up now. But are you really? Never worked a day in your life, have you? But that will all change now. You'll find out what it's like to earn a living. Stick to a budget. Your credit cards are no good anymore and you will have to live on what you make at Calhoun Petroleum for the next year. I think that will do you a world of good." He picked up his coffee cup and took another sip. "Yes, Missy, there's bourbon in here. I think I deserve it, don't you? Because this is hard for me, believe it or not. Cutting the apron strings, so to speak."

Cass saw the other three Calhoun children giving each other wild-eyed stares.

"No credit cards? How can I even fill my car's tank?" Ethan stood and headed to the bar. He filled a glass while Dylan hit *pause* again.

"That's an exception. You'll have a gas card. But don't expect to get cash back on it. Connie was pretty clear with me on how this is to go." Dylan pulled out a stack of gas cards and set them on the table.

Shannon had her wallet out and Cass could see that she had credit cards for every exclusive retailer in town. There were Neiman, Saks, and little boutiques that Cass had certainly never visited.

"Are you saying he's cancelled every one of these?" She pulled them out and pressed them to her cheek.

"You can try them, but I think you'll be embarrassed when they're declined." Dylan wasn't very good at hiding his smile.

"You're enjoying this!" She jumped up and the cards scattered. "What's wrong with you?"

"It won't kill you to keep a budget, Shan. Now we have more to see." Dylan hit *play* again when Ethan sat down.

"Shannon, you have that marketing degree you've never used." Conrad smiled proudly and his daughter settled in her chair with a huff. "I can see you doing great things in Calhoun's public-relations department. So you'll work there for one year."

"Yes, Daddy, I'm great at PR." Shannon gave Dylan a look that promised she'd show him a thing or two as she gathered up her credit cards and stuffed them back into her wallet.

"Now, Megan, you need to learn more about my business from the ground up, so I'm putting you out in the field. You'll follow one of my engineers around and learn about my operations. I swear you'll find you have a talent for engineering if you'd give yourself a chance. I'd like you to go back to school and finish after that year of experience, but that'll be up to you." Conrad leaned back in his chair.

"Engineering?" Megan was up out of her seat this time.

Dylan paused the video. "Is that so bad? I seem to remember you were a whiz in math and science when you went to school."

Megan frowned, but settled back into her chair, waving her hand like he should hit *play* again.

"Ethan, are you listening or do you have your head in some video game? Well, son, it's time to put that computer shit to use. I'm placing you in the IT department. You'll either sink or swim with those computer geeks. I know you took classes, but you weren't focused in college. Now's your chance to prove you can handle a regular job in that field. Or not."

"I can hack it." Ethan had a wicked smile on his face as he sipped his drink. "Just wait and see what I can do with your stupid oil-company computers."

Dylan gave Ethan a hard look but didn't stop the video.

"And we're down to Cassidy. This child actually applied herself in college. Oh, yes, girl, I know exactly what you've been up to. I have my ways. You worked hard, got a degree in finance, and have been moving up in that little bank in Clear Lake. Earned your MBA while you were working full time and that got you promoted to vice president last year. Pissant little bank. Hands out titles instead of pay raises. I say good for you. But not good enough for the daughter of Conrad Calhoun. So I want you to quit that job and join the team in the accounting department of my company. As a vice president making a hell of a lot more than you were making at that bank. Sound good?" He laughed.

"I bet all of you are cursing me about now for trying to manage your lives. Well, there's a kicker, of course. And a reward. During the year, you'll be evaluated. By someone I trust. At the end of the period, he'll decide if you did a good job or not. Pulled your weight or goofed off." He aimed his finger at them and his dark eyes seemed to be looking right through the screen. "I'm serious about this, young'uns. Blow this and all you'll get is pocket change."

"Son of a bitch! I can't believe he's pulling this shit. Controlling us from the grave, that bastard." Megan stomped around the room. Ethan was texting like mad and Shannon had her eyes on Dylan, like she was plotting a strategy.

On screen Conrad laughed again and pounded one knee with his fist. "Watch your language, Meggie. Yes, I know you're calling me all kinds of names. You're too much like me, pumpkin, and I'm sure the idea of anyone forcing you to work for them is chapping your hide." He shook his head. "You're just going to have to get over it. All of you are. Because if you succeed in the position I picked out for you, if my guy says you tried your best, accomplished what I wanted you to—and he has a list from me, you can be sure of that—then you'll walk away with a cool three-hundred million dollars each. Free and clear at the end of twelve months. No trusts or loopholes like your mama, kids. Cassidy, of course your mother gets diddly-squat from me. That's the way she wanted it then and that's the way it'll be now."

He rubbed his left arm and grimaced. "And if the man evaluating you thinks you failed my test? Well, your millions go to charity. The Heart Institute in the Texas Medical Center. My ticker's been giving me some trouble lately and they have a top-notch crew there. I'm sure they'd be glad of the donation." He sat back with a groan.

"Now, I've got just one more thing to say: Work hard, work smart, but don't do what I did and put work first. I love my family but spent way too much time growing my business. I can't get back those hours I lost when I should have been at Ethan's robotics tournaments, Shannon's dance recitals, and Megan's horse-riding events. I'm sorry, kids. I love you more than anything and I didn't show it like I should have."

Megan sank down in her seat again. "Oh, crap, Daddy. We knew you loved us."

Shannon sobbed again.

"Now Cassidy . . ." He ran a hand over his face. "What your mama knew—knows—well, I was pretty ruthless back in the day. She can still hurt the business. It will be up to you to get her to hold her tongue or she'll blow what I've built sky-high. I'm sorry to leave you with that mess. Because I love you too. I tried to see you, baby, I did. I lurked in the audience when you graduated from high school top in your class. I was bursting with pride when you made that speech. And then to get through college like you did. You don't know it, but you served me coffee many a night at that drive-through." Conrad wiped his eyes.

"I'm hoping that your mama knows flappin' her yap now will hurt you, not me, and that it'll make her keep quiet." He blew his nose on a gray cotton handkerchief. "No guarantees with that woman, so good luck with that. Now I'll stop, 'cause this is getting sappy and I have things to do. Listen to Dylan bore you with the particulars." He held up his hand in a classic symbol and grinned. "Live long and prosper, family. I wish I could be around to see it. And, who knows, maybe I'm watching you right now to see how you handle things." The screen went dark.

Cass took a shuddery breath and wiped her eyes. How could she not have known she had a loving father? Her mother had a lot of explaining to do. And apparently was a blackmailer. Mason handed her a handkerchief and she took it gratefully. "Thanks."

Three hundred million dollars. She couldn't have heard right. It wasn't possible. And all she had to do was go to work for a year in a cushy job where she'd be paid a big salary. There had to be a catch. Cassidy Calhoun didn't have this kind of luck. She looked at the strangers who were supposed to be related to her. She wasn't like them. Her clothes came from the factory outlet and her roommate cut her hair. Her car in the parking garage was twelve years old. The purse she held in her lap had that twenty-dollar bill and maybe thirty cents inside and a debit card.

"Cassidy? I have one more important paper for you." Dylan stood next to her. "Conrad wanted to do this for you. Your mother won't approve but he arranged for it to happen upon his death so it doesn't violate their agreement."

Cass stared down at the sheet with the heading from the U.S. Department of Education. A quick scan made it clear that one Cassidy Jane Calhoun had her student loans paid in full.

Breathe. She tried. Really. But it wasn't happening.

"Cassidy? Are you all right?"

She heard the voice from far away. Because damn if she wasn't going to pass out for the first time in her life.

Chapter 2

Cass didn't want anyone to fuss, but Missy wasn't satisfied until there was a cool cloth on her forehead and she'd downed another full glass of water.

"Really. I'm okay, just a little overwhelmed."

"Guess so." Missy clucked and settled into her seat again. "I'm sorry your mama kept this all from you, honey. But now you have a new family. You need anything at all, just holler." She glanced at her children. "We'll be there for you, like your daddy surely would want us to be. Right?" She waited until she got nods all around.

"I'm fine now. Dylan, if you have more to tell us, please go on." No more student-loan debt. She couldn't process it. She kept her hand on the paper to make sure it was real.

"Well." Dylan cleared his throat. "I'm sure some of you have questions."

"When do we have to start?" Ethan asked that one. "I have a date for Comic Con coming up." He was surprisingly calm. Of course, the way he worked his phone made Cass think a job with computers would be no big stretch for him.

"The day after Labor Day. That'll give Cassidy time for two weeks' notice at her job."

"Oh, God, I really have to do that, don't I? Quit." Cass thought about how hard she'd worked to get that position and the friends she'd have to leave behind. But Conrad was right: The pay wasn't great, especially considering the responsibility she had. Three hundred million dollars. They didn't have even one single depositor at her bank with that much money. She glanced at the open bar. What would these people think if she poured herself a stiff drink too? No, she had a long drive home.

"Who's going to decide if we suck at this bogus job or not?" Megan's hands were fisted, like she was looking for someone to hit. "I'm going out in the field? I remember riding with Daddy out into those oil fields in his pickup. Filthy, noisy, and always in the middle of nowhere. This is my punishment because I didn't finish college." She glared first at Shannon, then at Cassidy. "He just made it clear how proud he was of his girls who did."

"Hey, I don't know about Cass, but I worked hard in college." Shannon smiled at Cass, who nodded.

"Hard? Kappa queen of the keggers and most likely to work her way through the football team?" Megan looked ready to jump across the table.

"What do you know about it?" Shannon put her elbows on the table and leaned in. "It won't kill you to apply yourself for a change, little sister. And excuse me—*didn't finish*? You flunked out twice before you gave up entirely. Now start figuring out how to make the best of this."

"The best?" Megan shrieked. "What could possibly be the best about the oil fields?"

"Admit it. You always liked being outside more than in. This job is perfect for you. So quit whining." Shannon smirked. "Frankly, I'm excited. Public relations. He didn't say, but I bet Daddy arranged for me to be a VP too, just like Cassidy. I'm so going to kick ass there." She fluffed her hair. "Dylan, are you going to be judging our performance?" She gave him a dazzling smile.

"No, Mason is." Dylan gestured to his brother.

"That's right, boy and girls." Mason grinned. "Since I know the oil business, Conrad thought I could judge whether you managed to get your shit together or not."

"What?" Ethan suddenly tuned in. "You work for one of our biggest competitors."

"Did Daddy lose his mind at the end? I bet this is grounds for having this whole bogus will thrown out. Isn't it, Dylan?" Megan's face had turned red.

"Conrad Calhoun was sharp as a tack until the day he died, Megan Louise Calhoun." Missy jumped to her feet and pulled her daughter up to face her. "Don't you dare question your father's sanity!" She looked Megan up and down, shaking her head. "I can't remember one damned thing you've stuck with for more than six months at a time. I bet that

outfit you have on came from the boutique you and your friend Chiq-
uita, or whatever the hell her name was, started last year."

"Yes, isn't it cute?" Megan held out the skirt. "The concho belt
was made by a Mexican artisan in Taxco. Do you like the matching
earrings?"

"Never mind that. What happened to that shop, Megan?" Missy
moved even closer. "I heard the name changed already."

"It's doing fine. Chica changed the name when I decided . . . um,
that I didn't want to mess with it anymore." Megan wouldn't look at
her mother.

"Because you got bored, didn't you?" Missy glanced over her
shoulder when Shannon giggled. "Damn it, Shannon's right. It won't
kill you to have to stick with something for a full year. Frankly, I'm
all for this plan of Connie's. He discussed it with me and I told him I
liked it. A lot." She took a breath and a tear trickled down her cheek.
"Didn't think it would happen this fast, though. Or that Cassidy was
part of it."

"You knew?" Shannon grabbed her mother's arm. "And you didn't
talk him out of it?"

Cass tried to tune out the family drama. Poor little rich kids, having to work for a living.

Megan whirled around to pull Cass into the argument. "Cass,
Mason's uncle runs Texas Star Oil and Gas. Mason is his second-in-
command. Those guys would like nothing better than to drive us out
of business. I don't know what Daddy was thinking, putting a Texas
Star spy in charge of this." Megan glared at Mason. "I'd think your
department would be a prime spot for him to snoop for inside information, Cass. Fair warning."

Cass turned to Mason. Corporate espionage? It did make her
wonder about her father's sanity. "Let me make it clear, then. I'll be
new to the oil business—not to balance sheets. If you think you can
get Calhoun company secrets from me, Mason, think again."

"Hold up." Mason moved to the head of the table. "Let me get
something straight right now: Calhoun Petroleum is in big trouble.
Conrad was a control freak and he left the company in chaos when he
died. The sharks are circling, people. He wanted you to work in the
business because he hoped one or more of you would figure out that
it's where you want to be." He gazed around the table, hitting each

Calhoun heir with a hard look. "That one of you would take the reins one day."

Cass kept her chin up when it was her turn, determined not to squirm under his laser focus. But she knew nothing about the oil business. How could she begin to work in it and be successful? Thank God, he moved on to Ethan before she wilted and stared down at the table, knowing she was over her head.

"I hope to hell that's what happens because you may not *have* an inheritance at the end of the year if your company falls apart in the meantime." He held up a thick folder. "Yes, there are plenty of assets that could be sold off to raise money, but I hope that won't be necessary. Your daddy built Calhoun Petroleum from nothing. For you." He nodded at Missy, who had a handkerchief to her eyes again. "Trust me or not, I don't give a damn, but if the only way to save it is to take it over myself? Well, then maybe that's what'll happen. That's my own fair warning."

"Now wait a damned minute." Dylan took the folder from his brother. "That wasn't Connie's intention."

"I said it would be a last resort." Mason faced his brother. "And I didn't ask for this. Did I, Dylan?"

"No, you didn't." Dylan frowned down at the pile of papers.

"But it's clear you're one of the sharks circling a dying company." The concept gave Cass a knot in the pit of her stomach. What if she worked her butt off all year for nothing? With the promise of millions in front of her and then . . . No, she couldn't start with negative thinking. Besides, she was already ahead. Debt free. The thought made her a little dizzy.

"Cass is right, Mason." Megan leaned back in her chair. "Rumor has it you'd do anything to get away from your uncle and Texas Star."

Mason didn't answer, although he didn't deny it.

Shannon glared at Cass, then Megan. "We've known Mason forever. He's a dear family friend. I'd sure rather have him evaluate my work than some cold-eyed stranger. And he'll help us save the company, I'm sure. Where's the trust, Meg?"

"Oh, here it comes, the suck-up." Megan leaned closer to Shannon. "Maybe I lost the trust when I got the news that I was going out to rigs in Hellhole, Texas with some geek of the week from the engineering department." Megan grabbed Shannon's purse and pulled out her platinum AmEx card. "And then there's my bad mood because of what we just heard about our finances." She bent the card in half, though it took some effort. "Won't be needing this, will you?"

"You bitch!" Shannon lunged and grabbed a handful of Megan's hair.

"Stop it, girls. You should know I won't let you suffer. I'll give each of you a gift card to tide you over." Missy put herself between them. "Meg, do not pull on Shannon's hair. That's an expensive weave."

"Mama!" Shannon glanced at Dylan while she carefully extracted Megan's fingers from *her* long blond hair. "A gift card? How much?"

Cass hid a smile. Sisters. She was going to have two of them now. After a lifetime as an only child it was a novelty she was a little excited to explore. She felt Mason's presence next to her. She wasn't sure about the trust thing and she'd never sucked up to anyone in her life, but she didn't want to antagonize him either.

"If you two will quit squabbling, I'd like to get a word in." He rested his hand on Cass's shoulder. "Cass doesn't know me, but you do. I won't be hovering over any of you 'evaluating'. You'll all have supervisors at Calhoun that I can ask about your performance. As for the business at Calhoun, I'll keep my eye on the situation." He looked down at Cass. "I can be a shark. In fact, I don't consider that an insult." His smile dazzled her for a moment. "But I want to see this family get what it deserves. So I'll hold off being an aggressor as long as no one else jumps in and tries to take over."

"That's a generous offer, people." Dylan knocked on the table. "More than most oilmen would give you."

"Okay, then. Now can we get the hell out of here?" Mason gestured toward the door.

"Wait a minute. I've got questions." Ethan put down his phone and leaned in. "Who gets the house in River Oaks, the cars, the ranch, for Christ's sake? There are other properties too."

"Good question." Dylan pulled out some papers and handed each of the Calhoun kids, as Cass was beginning to think of them, a copy. "Here's how it's going to be. You'll live together in the River Oaks house. It's big enough for all of you. I know Missy moved in when Conrad died. She has to move out, according to this, and back to her own place." He glanced at her. "Alexandra gets to keep the penthouse condo in the Tower on the Park. It was in the prenup."

"Really? He stipulated that I couldn't live with my own children?" Missy frowned when Dylan shook his head. "Fine. I prefer my home to that nightmare master suite anyway. I'll be gone by the weekend."

"Wait. The rest of us have to live together? Cassidy, you don't even know where the house is, do you?" Shannon quit studying the list long enough to look down the table at Cass.

"I may have grown up in the suburbs, but I know where River Oaks is. I assume it's much closer to Calhoun Petroleum headquarters than my apartment in Clear Lake." Cass glanced at the paper Dylan slid down to her and exhaled when she realized she'd been holding her breath. The address was in a part of Houston known for its really big mansions. "Okay. As long as we each get our own bedroom." She smiled.

"Our own cars too." Ethan grinned. "I have dibs on the Porsche. You girls can duke it out for the rest. Dad was a car buff. You'll see when you get there, Cassidy."

"None of the collectible cars. Conrad insisted they be auctioned off. He didn't want any of you driving them." Dylan ignored Ethan's curse. "We've arranged to lease cars for each of you. I'll let you decide what you want. The rest of the properties can't be disposed of until the end of the year—once we see how you fare in your evaluations. They may have to be sold to pay you your inheritance."

"Not what I wanted to hear, but I'll deal." Ethan had picked up his phone, his thumbs moving at warp speed. "Party tonight. To welcome Cassidy to the family. Too bad you won't be there, Shan. Try not to step in a cow pie at that ranch."

"Oh, yeah, I'm really sorry to miss one of *your* parties, little brother." Shannon barely looked up from the list she held in her hand. "Just don't drink the house dry."

"I won't be there either, Ethan. And if you trash the house this time, it comes out of your first paycheck." Megan jumped up from the table. "Mama, do something. The paper doesn't explain how we pay for stuff like food, maid service, laundry."

"I'm out of this. You're all adults. Let Dylan explain that." Missy nodded toward the lawyer.

"Housekeeping, food and utilities, all of the expenses for the upkeep of the house, are paid for by the estate." Dylan smiled around the table.

Cass couldn't believe it. What a sweet deal. She could live free for a year? It seemed too good to be true.

"Good news." Missy walked around the table and tapped Ethan on top of his head. "Though I'd dearly love to see my boy here on a riding mower, I don't think the neighbors would love the results."

"I guarantee they wouldn't." He swatted her hand when she made a grab for his phone. "I'll take one of those gift cards, though, Mama. This phone needs a serious upgrade."

"Never knew when it didn't." She shook her head. "Now I need to make some calls. I'll get movers over there this afternoon to clear my things out of the master suite." Missy smiled at Cassidy. "Draw the short straw, Cass, and it could be yours."

"Seriously? You're on her side?" Shannon jumped in on that. "It has the biggest closets." She smiled at Megan. "But then again . . ." The sisters laughed and looked at Cassidy. "Maybe we need to let our new sister have it."

Dreaming of living in a mansion, Cass tuned them out as they squabbled about rooms and cars. She jumped when she felt a warm hand land on her shoulder again.

"A little overwhelmed right now?" Mason asked quietly. "Can I give you a ride home? I doubt you want to hit the freeway in that un–air-conditioned heap you drove up in."

"A ride would be great." And who wouldn't want to spend more time with A) the hottest guy she'd seen in person in her entire life and B) what was probably a luxury vehicle with cold air on one of the city's worst freeways? And then there was the evaluator factor, which a smart woman would move right up to A). Cass stood and saw that her dress was a mass of wrinkles. Of course, her sisters looked perfect. Megan wore a white cotton skirt that hit mid-calf with an off-the-shoulder peasant blouse in turquoise and white that looked cool and expensive. Her Mexican silver accessories were gorgeous.

And then there was Shannon's cute leather skirt and vest. The outfit shouted *wealthy rancher*. She had on a red lace T-shirt under the vest that hugged her curvy figure. Red leather boots made the outfit perfect. A rodeo committee. Cass knew enough about the social scene in Houston to realize only wealthy socialites managed to get on those high-powered volunteer committees. Even Missy, the only one in mourning colors besides her, wore a black pantsuit that had a designer flair to it. Her silk tank top dipped low enough to show off her generous figure. Diamonds flashed on her fingers and at her wrists.

"Bring your paperwork." Mason handed Cass a thick folder. "It has details about your new position at the company and, of course, your new family." He waved to his brother, who was deep in conversation with Megan and Shannon. "Let's escape before they realize you're leaving. They might try to talk you into living somewhere else. Not happening."

"It's a strange request." Cass let him guide her toward the elevators again.

"Like I said, Connie was a control freak. He wanted you to get to know your brother and sisters. This was his way of making sure they had to give you a chance. And vice versa." He punched the *down* button. "You want me to arrange to have your car brought to you somewhere?"

"How about CarMax? I'm selling that hunk of junk. A leased car. A nice convertible. That would be my dream." Cass grinned. "Seems like I'll have something to drive while I'm at the house. And after . . ."

"You're taking for granted you'll pass Conrad's test." The elevator arrived and Mason stepped inside. "Confidence. Very attractive."

"Hmm. Why wouldn't I be confident? My father—" Cass took a breath. She'd never said those two words together before. "My father thought I could do it. So I'm going to jump in and prove him right."

"Well, then I'm sure you can." Mason moved in close and stared down at her, reaching out to brush one of her wayward strands back from her face. "I want you to succeed. You shouldn't have had to suffer like you did."

"Hey, I'm okay. I didn't suffer. I just worked hard." Cass put her hand on his chest, easing him back. "Don't pity me. Conrad was a self-made man. Well, I'm a self-made woman."

"I think that's sexy as hell." He slid his thumb down her cheek to her chin. "And for the record, this chin is anything but unfortunate."

"Well, thanks." Cass hurried past him as the elevator doors opened on the parking garage. "Which car is yours?"

He hit a key fob and the lights on a gleaming black four-door truck blinked. "There you go."

"Seriously?" Cass followed him to it. "I don't know why I'm surprised that a man who wears boots with his suits would drive a truck. Bet the Japanese loved it too."

"They did. Part of the Texas thing." He patted the side of the truck as he walked around to open the front passenger door.

"I just bet you have a ranch somewhere too. But this baby doesn't exactly look like it's used to take feed to cattle." Cass was grateful he had a sidestep as he helped her climb into the cab. This gleaming luxury vehicle couldn't seriously be called a pickup. She bet the most it had ever hauled had been luggage for a long weekend at a fancy hotel somewhere.

"There's a family ranch, true. My sister Sierra runs it. You should see what she drives. Looks like it's been in a demolition derby. But don't put down my ride, Cass. A man takes pride in his wheels and big trucks make us hard to take down on the freeways around here." His hand brushed her thigh when he set the packet of papers in her lap. "I can see that you're thinking I'm some kind of drugstore cowboy. Just wait. I'll take you out to the ranch sometime and show you that I can actually ride a horse, rope steers, do all the things a real cowboy can do. I spent a lot of time out there as a kid. It's still a great place to relax."

"I can just imagine." Boy, could she. This man in tight jeans and a Stetson? "Wouldn't that be cheating? If I get to know you outside of the evaluating thing?" Cass realized she'd been flirting but couldn't help it. This guy with the killer body and smile to match had started it.

"No. The rest of your family has an edge since we all grew up together." He shrugged out of his suit coat and laid it on the backseat. Then he loosened his tie before he slid into the driver's seat and started the truck with a roar. "It's only fair that you and I get acquainted. Believe me, the Calhouns will try bribery, blackmail, and bullying if it will get them an advantage." He grinned. "I'll let you guess which of your new siblings is an expert in each of those tactics."

"Hmm. And exactly how well do you know the Calhoun sisters?" Cass's cheeks went hot. Where had that stupid question come from?

He stopped the truck with a squeal of tires and took her chin in his hand. "You really want to know? Why? You planning to jump me when we get to your place? To even the playing field?"

Cass met his twinkling eyes. "Is that necessary for me to pass your test?"

"Well, now. I guess I'd better get this straight right now. No amount of sweet talk or special favors are going to get you to your millions." He leaned closer. "As for my relationship with your sisters? My daddy always told me that a gentleman is never supposed to kiss and tell." He brushed his lips over hers; once, twice. "Like that. Or this." He deepened the kiss and Cass grabbed his shoulders, ready to push him away. But then . . .

Oh, God almighty. As kisses went, this one was five stars, a home run—oh, screw it. Cass quit *her* evaluation and relaxed into it until a car horn jerked them apart. A glance through the back window made her sigh with relief. At least it wasn't one of her new family members.

"You shouldn't have done that." Cass fumbled with her seat belt.

"Had to."

"What? Why's that?" Cass knew she'd missed something when she saw his grin.

"I *have* seen both your sisters naked."

"Eww." She slapped his arm. "Don't count on seeing *me* naked any time soon." Cass aimed an air-conditioning vent at her face. "Now drive south down I-45 and prepare for traffic. I'll give you directions when you get close to Clear Lake City."

"Will do." He smoothed down his hair, then stepped on the gas. "Will it help my chances if I confess that the last time I saw the girls naked was skinny-dipping on the ranch way before any of us hit puberty?" He chuckled as he drove them out of the parking garage.

"You *have* no chances, Mason. But it's put a better picture in my head." Cass sat back, still trying to figure out that kiss. Why? Men didn't fall all over her at first sight. Though she had to admit she had no experience with men from his background. Rich men. Oil zillionaires. Men who looked good, smelled good and, oh Lordy, tasted good. This was not right. Just because she liked him and he seemed down-to-earth, not how she'd imagined someone like him would be, didn't mean she should have kissed him back. There were complications.

She ran her eyes over him from the comfort of the leather bucket seat. Eye candy. Gorgeous male looking even better without the suit coat. His white shirt had felt soft; Egyptian cotton. Gold cuff links gleamed on his wrists. She recognized the make of his gold and steel watch. Everything about him shouted money.

"Texas Star Oil and Gas."

"What about it?" He maneuvered skillfully through traffic. Driving a big-ass truck was definitely an advantage. Cars got out of his way.

Cass shivered, thinking about how close she'd come to taking a flying leap off an overpass earlier when a little car had tried to push in front of her. This big truck made her feel much safer.

"Your uncle owns it?" Cass adjusted her seat belt so she could lean against the door and watch him drive.

"He runs it. Our family owns it. My grandfather actually started the company. My dad liked the law better than the oil biz, but kept an interest. Now my brother, sister, and I own forty-nine percent. I help Uncle Ed, which can be a thankless job. Today's shit storm with the Japanese was a perfect example. My uncle doesn't know squat about negotiation unless it involves a shouting match and throwing money around. I'm the one who comes in when finesse is involved." He glanced over at Cass. "Sometimes that works, sometimes not."

"You must be good at languages. I suck at them."

"It's one of my talents." He gave her a scorching look. "Maybe you'll discover I have others."

Cass shifted in her seat, determined to steer the conversation away from where he seemed to be taking it. "Tell me more about your family and mine. Rivals, yet Conrad obviously trusted you."

"Dylan loves the law and inherited the law practice when Dad died." Mason got on the freeway, which was actually moving for a change. "Conrad knew Gramps first, but he was best friends with Dad. He trusted *him*, even though their companies were always going head-to-head in the marketplace. Conrad and Gramps were cordial. But Connie and Uncle Ed couldn't be in the same room with each other." He laughed.

"But then Ed makes enemies everywhere he goes. It's a matter of pride with him. Being tough is his calling card. Connie knew I would put our friendship first when it came to this evaluation thing." He gave her a quick glance. "I won't try to explain the ins and outs of the oil business while driving down the freeway, if you don't mind. It's way too complicated for that."

"I'm sure." Cass tried not to feel overwhelmed. "This is going to be different for me. *You* are different for me. You must be a billionaire too. Like my father was." Cass realized she was wrinkling the papers in her lap and dumped them on the floor. "I'm not used to thinking in amounts with more than three figures and change on a weekly paycheck after taxes. This sounds . . ." She leaned over again to straighten those papers, the seat belt cutting into her waist. That wasn't like her, to just drop such important documents.

"As you'll see once you get into the finances of it, this business is volatile. The price of oil determines everything. One day we're up, the next we're down." Mason patted her shoulder. "Oh, would you look at that. Hold on." He steered the truck over to the grassy shoulder and put on his emergency flashers after he parked behind a car. A woman stood staring into the empty trunk.

"What are you doing, Mason?"

"She's got a flat tire. Wait here. This shouldn't take long." When he saw a break in traffic he eased open his door and jumped out. He'd left the motor running and the AC blasting cold air.

Cass saw him talking to the woman, who pointed to the empty trunk. He calmly lifted the carpet and there was the jack and spare tire. Then he guided her to his truck and helped her into the backseat.

"You just get comfortable. I'll have you back on the road in a few minutes. This is Cass. Ms. Langley, Cass. Her cell phone's dead and you know it's hot as hell out there. I sure wish we had some cold water to give her." He winked and slammed the door.

"What a sweet man." The woman leaned back with a sigh. "I couldn't believe I forgot to charge my phone and then this happened. It's so hot out there!"

"It sure is." Cass jumped when there was a knock on her window. She rolled it down and Mason handed her his cuff links, then unbuttoned his shirt.

"Just stick those in the cup holder, will you?" He pulled his shirt out of his trousers, over his head, and then passed it through the open window. "I hope I'm done for the day, but you never know. So I'd better not get grease on my dress shirt."

Cass couldn't say a word. She just laid the shirt carefully on her lap and watched Mason stride back to the car and lift the tire out of the wheel well. Oh, my. His tanned back rippled with muscles. The lady hit the back of Cass's seat.

"You might want to roll your window up, hon. You're letting out all the cold air."

"Oh, yeah." Cass hit the button.

"Your husband is so nice and good-looking too."

"We're not married."

Cass felt another thump on her seat back.

"Put a ring on him, girl. That man's a keeper."

A battered pickup stopped and pulled in front of the lady's car. Soon Mason and another shirtless man dealt with the flat tire and had the car ready to go. The woman dug in her purse and opened the back door.

"Now you boys must take this. I insist. I just wish it was more." She waved two ten-dollar bills in her hand.

The other man took one and thanked her before getting in his truck and driving away. Mason smiled and helped the woman into her car. Cass tried to hear what he said to her. She noticed he stuffed the ten dollar bill back in her hand before he opened the back door again and pulled a sports bag toward him. His tanned body gleamed with sweat.

"You should have taken her money. She wanted you to." Cass watched him get a towel out of the bag and wipe off his chest and under his arms. Was he going to put on his shirt? No. She almost sighed when she realized he was going to drive without one.

He slammed the back door, laying the towel behind him after he dodged traffic to slip into the driver's seat again. "I told her to get herself a car charger so this couldn't happen to her again. I don't know if ten bucks will buy one or not."

"It might, at a dollar store."

"Good to know." He put the truck in *drive* and concentrated on easing them into the fast-moving traffic.

Cass couldn't look away from his bare shoulders. His suit hadn't lied. He was built. And now she knew he had a tattoo on his right bicep. *Sugar.* Who was she? The tat was beautiful, with colorful swirls surrounding the name. Was he still involved with a woman? He didn't wear a ring, but that didn't mean he wasn't married. Cass itched to get to her computer. Not only did she need to learn about her father and the oil business, but now she wanted to know a lot more about Mason MacKenzie. She could ask. No, she didn't want him to know it mattered. Which it shouldn't.

"That was nice of you. To stop and help that woman."

"My daddy would have whipped me good if I'd left a woman stranded on the side of the road." He had them safely on the freeway now and leaned back. "Did it win me any points with you?"

"I don't know why you care if I like you or not. You're in the driver's seat. Literally and figuratively."

"Hey, don't take what you heard in Dylan's office so seriously. I'll help you settle in at Calhoun and I'm sure your sisters and Ethan will help at the house." He grinned. "Wait till you see it. Connie didn't believe in underplaying his wealth. That is one huge spread. You may need a map to find your room at first. But if you like to swim, play tennis or billiards, it's all there. He has a putting green too, though I don't think Connie ever played a round of golf in his life. He was a worker and didn't play much."

Cass swallowed, the reality of what she was getting into hitting her hard. Did the people who lived there run around in ratty shorts and faded T-shirts? Did they drink beer? Eat burgers on a Friday night? Would there be servants to deal with? She felt panic begin to squeeze her lungs and pressed her hands to her cheeks.

"I can't believe this day. You know I can't move in right away, don't you? I have two more weeks with my job. Oh, hell. I need my car or I won't be able to get to work. You haven't had it towed yet, have you?"

"Hey, calm down. I'll help you figure things out." Mason reached over and dragged one of her hands from her face. "Remember, the company will pay for a car. What's your favorite color?"

"Red."

"Okay, then. And I'll get you some phone numbers so you can arrange things, like your move. On our dime. Connie didn't mean to stress you out over this transition." He kept his hand on hers as he shifted his eyes back to the road. As usual, Houston freeway traffic had slowed and he was watching for erratic lane changers.

"Hey, the Calhouns and the MacKenzies, we're people just like you. I like to kick back with friends and watch sports on TV with wings and margaritas." He winked. "And I'd have left a big tip if I'd seen you in your Hooters T-shirt."

"You *would* remember that." Cass had to admit his fingers wrapped around her hand made her feel better.

"Are you kidding? I'm obsessing over it." He shook his head. "Okay, I have to ask. Do you trust me yet?"

"Don't know why I should. I've known you—what? A couple of hours?"

"That can be enough. What does your gut tell you?" He slid their joined hands over her knee. Cass felt the heat of that all the way to her clenched thighs.

"My gut's not the one doing the talking." She jerked her hand from his. "Stop that. I'm trying to think."

"Sorry. Was I distracting you?" He put both hands on the steering wheel and hit a button. Suddenly music blasted from the radio. It was a country song that Cass liked and she laughed.

"Oh, please. Tell me you didn't have that programmed for a moment like this."

"Honey, I'm just lucky as hell. Now relax and think about what you want for lunch. I'm buying and you can take me to your favorite place." He hit the steering wheel and began singing along, his deep voice in perfect harmony. *"You know you want me and I'm going to make you say it."*

Cass shook her head and looked out the window. Lunch? Yeah, right. Oh, but this man was dangerous and she had no business reacting to him like a hormonal teenager. Her first priority should be figuring out how to make her old life work with her new one. It was enough to make her head swim. That had to be why she couldn't stop thinking about that kiss.

By the time Mason exited the freeway and followed her directions to her apartment, Cass was pretty sure she'd at least figured out how to handle *him*. He couldn't really be attracted to her. So he was a player. They'd stick to business or she'd send him on his way.

"Wait." He pulled into her parking lot. "Where are we having lunch?"

"Anywhere you want, if you really think that's necessary. But I'd like to change into something cooler first."

"I hope you'll let me use your shower. I'm sure you can smell me from there."

Cass just shook her head. "You can use our shower." Smell him? She'd inhaled as soon as he'd jumped back into the truck. There was something about a man who'd been in the sun. . . . He didn't stink. Far from it. He wore a combo of testosterone and sunshine that made her squirm in her seat.

"Good. I have shorts and a T-shirt in my bag so I can ditch the suit." He pulled into her assigned parking space when she pointed to it and looked around. "Nice complex."

"I share a two-bedroom with a friend. She'll still be at work. You don't have to go back to work now yourself?" Cass waited for him to walk around and help her down. No way could she get out of the high truck by herself without making a fool of herself. He opened the back door first and pulled out his sports bag, then came to her side.

"My uncle won't like it, but I'm taking the rest of the day off. So I'm all yours." He put his hands on her waist and swung her down from the cab, sliding her down his body. "Okay?"

"As long as we're clear what we're going for. I want to pick your brain about what lies ahead. If that's not what you have in mind, maybe you should just take off, Mason. I can grab a sandwich upstairs. Make some calls. We can get together another day." Cass pushed away from him and began to dig in her purse for her keys.

Looking around, Cass imagined what Mason really thought. This apartment complex where she'd lived for the past two years wasn't exactly luxurious. The few cars parked here during a workday were aging and bought for economy. Like hers, actually. The management kept the grounds neat and fixed things quickly, but the buildings weren't new and, when he got upstairs, he'd see that their carpet should have been replaced a decade ago.

"Hey, you do need to get more answers about what's going to happen now. Today your life changed forever. But you don't have to go through this alone. As an insider, I can help you get a handle on things. Be your guide, not just your evaluator." He grimaced. "Man, I hate that word. Forget it. I want to be your friend. Will you let me be there for you?" He moved in and took her keys out of her hand.

"All right then. I can use your help navigating this new life. Car first. After I look through these papers I'll have questions, I'm sure. About the Calhouns and their company. My father too. And of course, I don't know a thing about the oil business." She walked up the sidewalk toward the stairs and her second-floor apartment, then reached out for her keys. "I plan to take full advantage of your knowledge of the business. If you'll mentor me, then I should make it through the next year with no trouble at all. I'm sure you'll be fair and do the same for my sisters and brother." Cass knew she was rattling on, but wanted all of this clear.

"You left something out, Cass." His hand on her shoulder stopped her at the bottom of the stairs.

"What?"

"I told you I want us to be friends." He forced her to face him.

Some of the light had dimmed from his eyes. "So quit treating me like just a business associate."

"Don't rush me, Mason." Cass couldn't take his stare, so she made eye contact with his sleek tanned chest. Oh, God, but he was ripped. "I'm sure not going to bribe, bully, or blackmail you to get my money at the end of the year."

"I wouldn't mind a bribe." He leaned down and nudged her hair aside with his nose, his breath warm against her skin. "I liked you at first sight, Cassidy. Hair wild, looking like Conrad, but in a pretty, womanly way that threw me for a loop. And wary. Like it wouldn't take much to send you running. I could almost see you suck it up when you faced the Calhouns in that conference room. You sure looked like your daddy then." His thumb moved toward her lips. "I didn't need a DNA test to know who you were. But it was clear you went in thinking this whole thing with the lawyer might be a scam."

"Scam?" Cass moved up a step, out of reach. "Of course I did. No one drops millions on a girl like me. I'm still wondering if I'll wake up and find out I dreamed this. Or"—she glanced around at the landscaping—"maybe someone will jump out of the bushes and say I've been punked."

"Want me to pinch you?" He eyed her hips in her snug dress.

"Back off, Mason." Cass practically ran up the stairs. She couldn't figure this man out. And she sure didn't trust him. Did he think he could seduce his way into Calhoun company secrets? Whatever his motives, she couldn't handle his smooth talk right now.

He chuckled as he followed her up. "Oh, man, you are so much like your daddy it's scary. You'll give some of the folks at Calhoun Petroleum a start when they see you, that's for sure." He was right behind her when she fumbled getting her key in the lock. "You think I'm going too fast? So I'll slow my roll." He took the key from her and inserted it into the lock. "We can start out as friends, Cass. But I didn't imagine the spark between us when I kissed you. I could tell you felt it too." He opened the door and stepped aside. "Know that whatever does or doesn't happen between us won't help or hurt your case when it comes to the business. I'll make that clear to your brother and sisters too." Mason did his thing, which seemed to be to steer as he took her elbow and moved her into the cool, dark apartment.

Speechless, Cass let him, even nodded toward the hall bathroom while she went straight to her bedroom. There she dumped her hot dress and kicked off her heels. Thank God her roommate was a neatnik and had straightened the living room. Mason had barely glanced at it. Not that she blamed him. It really wasn't worth a second look. She and her roommate Ellie had furnished it with thrift-store finds, choosing things that were comfortable and a bargain. They called the look *eclectic*. She doubted any of it would have been good enough for the maid's room in the Calhoun house.

Mason MacKenzie and sparks. Oh, yeah. She hadn't seen or felt so much electricity since she and Susie Cantor had almost electrocuted themselves trying to jump-start Susie's car in high school. Right now he was pulling off that expensive suit in the hall bathroom. Briefs? Silk boxers? When she heard the shower start, she hit her own bathroom to run cold water over her hands, then splash her face. But it would take more than that to cool her off. What the hell was the matter with her?

Chapter 3

Cass found him studying the book collection on the shelves in the living room. He looked good, like a normal guy, in cargo shorts, a T-shirt, and leather flip-flops. Great muscled legs. No surprise there. His shirt hugged that amazing chest, which surely came from regular workouts. Was there any part of him that wasn't perfect?

Of course there was. He was arrogant and thought he could make a play for her and she'd fall at his feet. Then there was the way he steered her around like she couldn't make a move without his guidance. Hah! She was Cassidy Calhoun, the woman who'd worked her way through school without anyone's help. Certainly without a boatload of money. She was tough. More her father's daughter than anyone knew. And she'd prove it to all of them.

She stiffened her spine. She could resist Mason's charm and male beauty. If he thought he could steer her right into an affair and to be his inside woman at Calhoun Petroleum, he could think again.

"You want some water or a beer?" She might be tough, but she did have manners.

"No, I'm fine." He pulled a book from the shelf.

"Those books aren't mine. I haven't had much time for reading anything but business texts since high school." Which was sad but true.

He held up a self-help book on finding love. "You're not looking for love?"

"Nope." Cass grabbed her purse. Did he really think she was going to fall for that stale routine? "Let's go."

"Wait a minute. I don't believe you. I know women. They're always looking." He picked up his bag. "Seriously? Not interested?"

Cass gave him a scan. Yes, she just bet he knew women. They

probably threw themselves at him on a regular basis. "Not looking because I've already found it, Mason." Cass opened the door and stepped outside. "You met me and came after me hard without a thought about what I wanted. Maybe when you're after another notch on your bedpost it doesn't matter if the woman is in a relationship." She turned to face him. "Listen up. You're wasting your time hitting on me. I have a boyfriend who I love very much."

"No shit. That *is* a news flash. Surprised he didn't come with you today. To hear about your inheritance." He dropped his things outside her door.

"I told him not to. I was sure it would be a waste of his time when he has work to do. Rowdy takes his responsibilities seriously." Cass didn't like Mason's smile, as if he knew men and their motives too.

"Rowdy."

"Rowdy Baker. We've been going together a while now." Cass gripped the iron stair rail. Why had she been so vague? It was a lot more than "a while". But she hadn't given Rowdy much thought while she'd been in Mason's orbit. That had to stop. Clearly the shock of the will and the possibility of all that money coming her way had made her lose her mind.

"And you just now thought to mention him? Poor bastard." Mason shook his head.

"Stop it. Rowdy's great." She lifted her chin. It was the truth. "My love life is none of your damned business."

"It wouldn't be if you hadn't kissed me back." He held up a hand when she opened her mouth to argue with him. "Don't bother. You're seriously going to deny you kissed me like you didn't want to stop, Cass?" His steady stare made her glance away. "Were you thinking about Rowdy then?"

Cass wanted to lie and say exactly that. "You just caught me off guard and on a day when I'd been hit broadside by all that news." She looked up at the ceiling above her and counted ten cobwebs. Great place she lived in.

"Yeah, blame all that chemistry on shock." He chuckled and picked up his suit.

"Stop it. Rowdy is wonderful. All the man I'll ever need." Cass wanted to run down the stairs, but she had to get this settled.

"Yeah, right. So why'd you get into it?" He moved closer. "I tasted you, you tasted me. There were tongues involved, Cass. What about that?"

"Meant nothing." Cass turned and started down the stairs. This debate was stupid. *She'd* been stupid. "I wasn't in my right mind. I can't be held accountable for my actions. Leave me alone, Mason." Damn it, her cheeks were hot and probably bright red. She hurried toward his truck.

"Oh, Cass?" He still stood at the top of the steps. "Don't you think you should lock up?" Mason gestured toward the open apartment door. "Must be a really safe neighborhood." He looked around. "But I did notice the pepper spray on your key chain."

"Shut the hell up." Cass stomped back up the stairs to close the door and lock it. "You make me crazy. This *day* is making me crazy. Now I'm leaving my roommate in the lurch to move into a house with strangers. We have a lease. She'll have to find someone else to split the expenses."

"You're changing the subject." Mason followed her down the stairs. "Now, about that kiss—or was it kisses?"

"Quit making a big deal out of nothing." They were back at his truck. Cass waited for him to unlock it. And waited.

"Nothing?" He turned her around and pressed her against the metal door. "As an evaluation? That will not stand." He took her purse, dropped it on top of his bag, then grabbed her hands and raised them above her head. "Nobody dismisses my kisses as nothing. Now I have to prove I can do better."

"Give it up, Mason." Cass realized she was taunting him. Did she *want* him to kiss her again? Not a good idea. "If you're going to pout, I guess I could give you a satisfactory rating."

"Satisfactory? I won't settle for less than excellent. No, make that clearly outstanding." He adjusted his body against hers. Cass could feel hard muscle, solid and . . . interested.

"This is verging on harassment, Mason. Do you really want to go there?" Cass heard herself. Flirting? Oh, no.

"I want to go here." His thumbs moved over her palms like he was texting her. The message? *Look at me.* Cass raised her head again and licked her lips, undoubtedly sending her own message. His eyes narrowed. "Did you read me?"

"Don't." Her last effort to stop the insanity.

"If you really meant that, you'd shove me away." He gently bit her earlobe and Cass shuddered.

"This is a bad idea, Mason. Rowdy . . ." Cass realized the doubts she'd had lately about sticking with Rowdy were suddenly looming large. Mason was right. Kissing another man had made something clear to her.

"Fuck Rowdy." He shook his head. "Scratch that. Don't. Not ever again." He ran his lips over her cheek, skirting the edge of her lips, but not quite there. "Gonna push me away, Cass?"

"No. I need . . ." She turned her head until her lips met his, drawn to him. She needed to know . . . What? He jerked her arms down and around him as their mouths met and held. It was just a kiss. Or was it? She'd never had this kind of instant connection before, like she'd just learned to breathe.

The truck door handle dug into her back, but that didn't matter. All that mattered was this feeling—hot, wild, and desperate. In a good way. She'd spent forever tightly wound. Maybe finally losing control was what she *should* do. His hand slipped under the back of her shirt, tracing the edge of her bra. Cass twisted her fist into *his* shirt. No. This wasn't her. She didn't combust like this. Not even with—

She shoved him away, breathing hard, and saw a car slow down as it drove past, a neighbor watching the action. The truck door behind her unlocked and she turned to wrench it open, then awkwardly scrambled inside. His hand on her butt gave her a needed boost.

He dropped her purse into her lap. "Cass, I—"

"Shut up and get in the damned truck." She fumbled for a tissue and wiped her mouth. Lipstick everywhere. She glanced at him, then pulled out another tissue, wordlessly handing it to him when he slid into his seat. He wiped off his mouth without comment.

"Do up your seat belt," he ordered after he slammed the door. He tossed his bag over the console into the backseat before he started the engine. "Where are we going to lunch?"

"Maybe we shouldn't." She reached for the door handle.

"We're going." He hit the door locks.

"I don't care then. You pick." She fastened the belt, then pulled down the visor to fix her face. Disaster. Fresh lipstick did help, but her hair was so wild she pulled out a scrunchie and tamed it. Lunch? Her stomach rebelled at the thought. But she was locked in here with Mason. Could still taste him and smell him. Now he reeked of Ellie's

stupid herbal soap. She wanted to bury her nose in his shirt and forget . . . God, she needed therapy or a knock in the head. *Stop it. It was
just a kiss.*

He was watching her. "Are you all right?"

"No." Cass stared out the side window. "I shouldn't be kissing
you. Not while I'm with Rowdy."

"That kiss was pretty hot for a woman with another guy."

"*Shut. Up.*" Cass glanced over at him. If he grinned she was going
to hit him. Instead, he looked serious.

"Hey, it was just a kiss."

It was as if he'd read her mind. But hearing *him* say it made the
whole thing . . . hell. Cass knew her chin was out again, but she didn't
care. It pissed her off.

"Oh, great. All of that talk was just you being a dick. Good to
know. A billionaire player. Meant nothing." She would not cry. Her
tissue was still wadded up in her fist. Handy if she couldn't get this
under control.

"I didn't say that. But how long have you been going with this
guy?" He still hadn't backed out of the parking spot.

"Since high school. Off and on." She didn't add that they'd been
talking about taking another break. That they'd entered the friend
zone lately, their passion more fizzling than sizzling. No way was
she sharing *that* with this sexy stranger.

"All that time. You ever really dated anyone else? Seriously?
Was he your first?"

Cass could hear the amusement in his voice. Like he wanted to
mock her relationship with Rowdy. She wasn't letting him get away
with it. She faced him. Oh, yes, it was there in his eyes, amusement
and pity. Poor Cassidy. Doesn't know a thing about men, because
she never shopped around. There was knowledge too. Like he'd be
more than willing to fill in any gaps in her education when it came to
men. Shit. Here came that heat again. She couldn't give into it. Taking a breath, she kept her focus and dredged up some righteous in-
dignation.

"Look, Mason. What I have with Rowdy is none of your damned
business. But get this straight: I've dated other guys. He was away at
college while I had to stay here, so we took a break then. While he
did a stint in the Army we were apart for four years. But we always
come back to each other again. Because Rowdy's a great guy. A

wonderful guy. And he loves me. Loved me when I didn't have a dime to my name." Cass knew she was the one who should just shut up.

"True-blue Rowdy. Your high school sweetheart." He nodded, grinning now.

"That's right, he was." Cass stuffed the tissue into her purse. She wasn't about to cry. Mason wasn't worth it.

"Wait a minute—Rowdy Baker." Mason hit the steering wheel. "Did he play running back for the Aggies?"

"Yes. He got a full-ride football scholarship to A and M. Why?" Cass really didn't want to sit here forever with Mason in case another neighbor came by. "Would you start driving? If we have to eat lunch, let's do it far away from here. Okay?"

"You don't want him to see us together. I get that." Mason just kept on smiling.

"Drive, would you?" Cass suddenly felt exhausted.

"Rowdy Baker, Texas A and M. I was a senior at UT when he played as a sophomore. That son of a gun. He was tough." Mason backed out of the spot. "The Army. I figured he'd end up playing pro football."

"No, he was in the Corps of Cadets, so he felt like he had an obligation to serve. Then he got hurt in Afghanistan. That ended any football dreams he'd had." Cass sighed. It had ended dreams they'd both had.

"He was hurt over there? How seriously?" Mason got back on the freeway, heading south.

"I really don't want to talk about Rowdy with you." Cass leaned back against the seat and closed her eyes. "I didn't get much sleep last night. Wake me up when we get wherever we're going." She knew it was the coward's way, but it was the truth.

She was drained, overwhelmed. On top of finding out about her father, there was a new job, a new family; it seemed like the new list was endless. She had to discover not only who she was now, but who she wanted to be with as she started this new life. That kiss . . . Mistake or not, it had shaken her. Mason might be a flirt and a heartbreaker, but he was right about one thing—if she and Rowdy were still on again, what was she doing kissing a stranger like she never wanted to stop? Clearly she and Rowdy needed to end things if she was turned on this easily by a new man.

* * *

Mason glanced at Cass, sleeping peacefully as he drove them toward Galveston Island and a little seafood restaurant with a view of the water.

Conrad Calhoun's daughter. He was still reeling. Not because she looked like Connie. That would be creepy as hell. No, it was with relief, for one thing. He'd planned to make a play for her even if she'd looked like his old dog Tramp. When she'd turned out to be little, feisty, and hot? Well, some jobs were just too easy.

Of course this new wealth would change her. Bound to. It had been obvious, even before she'd told them off, that coming up struggling had made her tough. She was as far from the high-gloss, don't-mess-up-my-hair, Barbie dolls he was used to dating as a woman could be. That made the challenge of getting her to fall for him all the more exciting. It had taken her long enough to tell him she had a boyfriend. He'd take that as encouragement, but he wouldn't be surprised if that good old boy was going to be hard to pry loose once he learned his lady was about to hit the jackpot. Damn it.

She wanted him to go slow. Too bad. Because even now he wanted to reach over and release that wild mane of hers. Touch her soft cheek and taste those lips that, when she'd allowed herself to let go, had met his with a fire that had heated his blood. His seat vibrated under him, the warning that he was drifting out of his lane. He needed to keep his hands on the wheel and his mind on his driving. Even in the middle of the day the Gulf Freeway that led to Galveston had plenty of traffic.

Trust Conrad Calhoun to make a will that would complicate so many lives. The good news was it also gave Mason an opportunity to get away from his uncle and finally have a company to call his own. Connie had trusted him to make sure the Calhoun kids survived the next year and didn't run his company into the ground. Well, what if that wasn't possible? Could Mason really be blamed if three spoiled brats failed to deliver when thrust into the shark-infested waters of big oil?

Mason smiled, imagining the look on Shannon's face when she saw the cubicle she'd been assigned in the massive public relations office. And Megan was right about the conditions in the field. She'd look pretty cute in a hard hat and work boots, but totally out of her element. Then there was Ethan. If he thought he'd get a chance to hack anything more than a little data entry, he could think again.

Connie wanted to teach his kids a life lesson. No problem. Mason would make sure they all did a decent job or he'd kick their butts. Their end-of-the-year check might not be as big as they were counting on, but it should be enough to live on very comfortably. He'd see to that when he bought the company from them and changed the name to MacKenzie Oil.

But what about that bombshell Connie had dropped? What the hell did Cass's mother know that could blow Calhoun Petroleum apart? Mason had done a shitload of digging to get ready for this assignment and he hadn't found out anything about Elizabeth Calhoun and a secret. Whatever it was, he had to handle it, especially if he was going to take over Calhoun. No way did he want Connie's dirt to ruin his plans.

Enough conjecture. Cass suddenly stretched and opened her eyes. Mason noticed how her T-shirt molded her breasts. She'd kicked off her sandals and her bare toes caressed the floorboards. Damn, but she was sexy. He smiled.

"Welcome back."

"Where are we?" Her voice sounded rough and he had a sudden image of how it would be waking up next to her after a night of lovemaking. *Slow down, Mason.*

"Galveston. You like seafood?" He stopped at a red light and studied her sleepy eyes. They'd been pure gray when she'd been in that black suit. Now that she wore a snug blue shirt, they matched it. What color would they be when she was naked? He shifted in his seat. *Too soon.* But he'd sure like to see her wake up, then shake out her hair before she crawled on top of him.

"Love it. Fried shrimp. That's my favorite." She yawned and covered her mouth with her hand. Her nails were short and polished a pale pink, just like her toenails. No fancy manicure. He liked that. "I can't believe I conked out."

"Now that you're rested, maybe you'll tell me a little more about yourself." Mason smiled. "Dylan got a thick file on you from his detective. So I know about your schooling, job history, life of crime, stuff like that. Hell, even where you get your oil changed." He laughed at her expression. "Not really. That wasn't in there. Neither was Rowdy Baker."

"I have had no life of crime. And I'm glad at least my love life was off the table." She pulled open the vanity mirror on her side and reworked her hair with that stretchy thing. "God, I'm a mess."

"No, you're not." Mason figured his brother's law office needed a better firm doing their investigating. Stuff like her love life, especially a relationship that had lasted years, should have been in their report. What else had they missed? "Tell me this: If I gave you a hundred bucks right now, what would you do with it?"

"Hand it over and find out." She had a gleam in her eyes.

"Calling me on that, are you?" The light had changed and Mason dug out his wallet from his back pocket while he steered with his knee. "Fine." He pulled out a hundred-dollar bill and tossed it in her lap.

She tucked it into her bra. "Saving it. I'm not so sure about this inheritance thing yet. You'll find, Mason, that I'm conservative with money."

"A practical woman. I'm impressed." Mason parked next to the small restaurant. They spent the next hour enjoying a seafood lunch while Cass tried to learn as much as possible about the oil business and the Calhouns. Finally she sighed and wiped her mouth.

"I'm stuffed and that was delicious. Thanks, Mason."

"Not too late for dessert. I can always go for something chocolate." Mason signaled the waiter.

"Couldn't possibly." She sipped her iced tea.

"I hope you're not dieting. You're just right." Mason asked for the check instead. Cass had a rounded figure that most of his ex-girlfriends would have called "chubby" but he'd meant what he'd said. There wasn't too much of Cass anywhere. She had nice hips and those generous breasts. They'd felt great against him when he'd kissed her, definitely the real deal. Now he stared at her mouth as he tossed a credit card on the bill without looking at it.

"Stop it." She threw down her napkin.

"What?"

"You're thinking about that kiss." She frowned at him. "I made it clear I'm in a relationship."

"Your kisses said otherwise." He leaned back and watched her cheeks go pink.

"Let it go, Mason." She leaned over to collect her purse, clearly ready to leave. "Sign the check and take me home."

"Just promise to think about it, that's all. We connected. I felt it, you felt it." He held up a hand before he added a generous tip and signed the check. "Deny it all you want. Body language is just another language I speak fluently and yours was shouting *available* when we kissed." He laughed when she jumped up and headed for the door. Oh, but that woman did not want to admit she'd felt the fireworks between them. But he had. He watched her butt twitch in her snug shorts as she crossed the room. Then he had to order his body to calm the hell down. Patience. He had plenty of time to get this rolling. Plenty of time.

He got up and met her at the door.

"I do appreciate all the information you gave me over lunch, Mason. But now I have some difficult conversations to get through. You said you were arranging a car for me?"

"Did that while you were in the bathroom." He held open the door and hot air hit them. "Conversations?"

"I've got to go see my mother. I need to see if she'll finally open up about my father." She frowned. "I am so damned angry with her."

"I imagine so." He unlocked the truck and helped her in, then got inside and made sure the air was cooling them before he started probing. He needed her to trust him because he had to know what Elizabeth Calhoun had held over Connie's head all those years. It must be dynamite. Maybe even the very thing that could bring the company to him. "Wonder if she'll tell you what she had on old Conrad."

"I have no idea." Cass kicked off her sandals as he backed out of the parking space. "Whatever made her hate him shouldn't have cost me my father."

"What's your mother like?" Mason glanced at her. "Bitter? The bitch Connie described in the video?"

"No, but not particularly happy either. She loved me and worked hard to make sure I had as much as she could afford. I'll give her that." Cass studied her fingernails. "But she doesn't like men and never dated. I wondered why, but never had the nerve to ask." When she looked up her eyes glittered. "She lied to me my entire life, Mason, saying my father didn't want me. She has a lot to answer for."

"I'm sorry, Cass." Mason took a chance and grabbed her hand again. "But consider this: She must have had her reasons. To keep a child from her father and to give up millions of dollars?" He squeezed her fingers. "A woman would have to have powerful motivation to do that."

"I don't care what Conrad Calhoun did. Unless he was a pedophile. And that family sitting in the lawyer's office certainly didn't act like the man was abusive or a sicko. Was he?" Cassidy pinned him with a look that dared him to sugarcoat his answer.

"No, hell no." Mason dropped her hand. "If she claims that, then she's lying. Connie was mean as a snake in his business dealings, but he'd never raise a hand to a woman or mistreat a child. I grew up around him. He played with us—my brother, sister, and me—along with his kids. Taught me to swim and shoot. I never saw him lose his temper with either of his wives. The women were always the ones doing the yelling about how he worked too much. Connie just took it, then would disappear into his office." Mason gripped the steering wheel. Workaholics. He knew something about those. His tendency to work too much had played hell with his own relationships.

Cass squared her shoulders like she was preparing for a battle royale... and maybe she was. "I'm going to see her to give her a chance to explain. If she can't convince me it was in my best interests? Then we're through."

Mason got back on the freeway again. Cass wasn't the only one with something to do this afternoon. When he'd turned his phone back on to arrange that lease car, he'd found a bunch of missed calls from his uncle and a voice mail that amounted to an ass-chewing. Uncle Ed held the choke collar at Texas Star and didn't fail to remind his nephew of that on a daily basis. That was why Mason was determined to get free and clear of his uncle's authority. He hadn't bothered to call Ed back, just turned the phone off again. Hopefully his uncle was exaggerating the "emergency." It had happened before.

Mason gave Cass a few more tips about the oil business while they rode toward her apartment. She claimed she was on overload and finally begged him to put on some music. Progress. When he deliberately let his hand skim across her bare leg when he reached for a CD in the glove compartment, she didn't slap it. Better and better. He was going to make this evaluation thing work to his advantage in more ways than one. It was nice to have something to look forward to for a change besides rig counts and pump rates.

He pulled into her complex, then parked. "Cass, I want to make something clear."

"What is it?"

"I don't want to harass you. The job is the job. If you feel like I'm pushing you too hard about this personal thing between us, tell me to back off. Like you did a while ago. I can take it." He reached out, pleased when she actually took his hand. "I meant it when I said I want to be your friend. There's a lot of money on the line for you. I intend for you to get it." He wasn't lying. When he bought Calhoun Petroleum, he'd pay fair-market value for it and she'd have a great payday.

"Thanks, Mason. That means a lot to me." She squeezed his fingers, then gently pulled her hand away. "You've given me something to think about. I admit I kissed you back." She shook her head. "Which means I sent you a wrong signal." She sighed. "Truth is, Rowdy and I have been together a long time. I love him, don't get me wrong. But we're ... um ... comfortable together and that may not be good enough for either of us." She looked out the side window. "This news will change things, I know that. It already has. I'm thinking about a lot of things that I've let slide."

Comfortable. Mason wanted to pound the steering wheel. He could almost smell victory. "Yes, you need to think. So I'd appreciate it if you kept an open mind about me, us. Okay? You're worth taking the time to get to know so I'll try to be patient." He still didn't get out of the truck. "But that's not easy for me. Especially when I'm looking at a beautiful woman. I may slip up now and then." He grinned and ran his hand over her bare knee. "Oops, there I go. Sorry. Did I mention you have great legs?"

Cass just laughed and opened her door. "I've got to go." Okay, then. He had her right where he wanted her.

There was a gleaming red convertible in her parking spot at the apartment complex. The perks of a big company. No one had even asked Cass for her driver's license or proof of insurance. The keys were tucked in the visor, risky in this area where cars were broken into on a regular basis. There was paperwork in the glove compartment confirming that the car was leased by Calhoun Petroleum. The rate made Cass wince.

She wasn't in the mood to do more than thank Mason for arranging her dream car and send him on his way. He took her brush-off with good humor, putting his number in her phone before he left and got hers in exchange. He didn't try to kiss her again. Which was a good thing. Really.

Clearly she couldn't trust a man who was used to having women fall at his feet. Rowdy was different. He was solid, dependable, and he was the only guy she'd ever trusted completely. Of course he was sitting in her living room drinking a beer when she got inside her apartment. He was there for her on a day he knew she'd need him.

"Hey. I took off work early. Couldn't wait to hear about your 'inheritance.'" He pulled her close and kissed her. It was an easy hello kiss, nothing special. "Babe? You okay?"

"Why does everyone keep asking me that?" Cass wasn't going to analyze his kiss. This was Rowdy. She loved him. His kisses had made her knees weak since she was a sophomore in high school. He'd been a year ahead of her and had already made a name for himself on the football team when he'd asked her out. He had a single mom too and knew what it was like to struggle for every dime.

His ticket to college had been football. Hers had been academics. But her scholarships had been pitiful compared to the free ride he'd gotten to his dream school. So she'd been stuck living at home and going to the local college. Still, he'd always come home to her. Now he watched her, worried, as she settled next to him on the couch.

"What does that mean? Everyone asks you what?"

"Oh, I almost passed out at that meeting downtown."

"Shit!"

She squeezed his hand. "Relax. I just got a little woozy. That piece-of-crap car's air conditioner went out halfway to town and I got too hot."

"That does it. Let me loan you the money so you can go ahead and buy a new car." He strode into the kitchen and came out with a cold bottle of water. "You do look a little pale. Drink. You're probably dehydrated too."

Cass did take a drink, then laughed. "You won't believe it, Rowdy! Loan? I'm not going to need one. Because I got the most incredible, unbelievable news in that meeting." It was finally hitting her. This inheritance was real. If she played her cards right—and when had she not—she was going to wind up rich. A multimillionaire.

"Well, are you going to tell me or just sit there with a shit-eating grin on your face?" Rowdy took her hands. "This wasn't a scam?"

"No." Cass told him everything. Well, almost. She left out the kisses. Not important. He was silent when she got to the end and the red convertible in her parking spot.

"Conrad Calhoun is—was—your father." He grabbed his beer

and finished it off, then set the bottle on the coffee table—on a coaster, of course. Rowdy always did the right thing. "Did you know that CWC Industries, where I work, is a division of Calhoun Petroleum?"

"No, I had no idea." Cass decided maybe she'd like something stronger than water too. She figured Rowdy probably needed time to process her news anyway. She got up and opened a bottle of white wine, then poured herself a glass. She brought Rowdy a fresh beer too.

"Three hundred million dollars." Rowdy leaned back against the couch cushions. "You know what this means, don't you?"

"I don't have it yet. The man who will be evaluating me this next year could decide to flunk my ass." Cass took a sip and almost choked. This was Ellie's favorite and drier than she liked. "He's a MacKenzie, second-in-command at Texas Star Oil and Gas. Can you believe it? One of our biggest rivals. And he promises to be a pain in my backside."

"Why? You afraid he won't be fair?" Rowdy took the glass from her. "Why did your father pick someone like that?"

"He's a family friend. He says he's on our side, but I don't know." Cass leaned against Rowdy's firm shoulder, sighing when he wrapped his arm around her. "He's a little flirty."

"Do I need to whip his ass?" Rowdy pushed her away so he could look in her eyes. "What's that mean? Flirty? He's not harassing you, is he?"

His hands were gentle but his eyes were hard. She loved his thick sandy hair, cut close because he hated his natural curl. He was finally letting it grow out after she'd nagged him about it. She traced his strong jaw with a fingertip. If they had kids, they'd be all jaw, tough little soldiers. She'd always imagined them like that. She was the one who'd insisted they put off marriage. There was her heavy debt. Those student loans . . . She should tell him that good news. But she didn't. And now she knew why.

"Cass?"

"He made a move but I handled it." She kissed his evening scruff. "No big deal, Rowdy."

His dark eyes narrowed. "This asshole is supposed to evaluate you and he made a move? Sounds like harassment to me." Rowdy's hands had tightened on her shoulders. "You need to call that lawyer you met with and file a complaint. They should get someone else.

Someone impartial. You know you'll ace this job. Anyone with half a brain and who doesn't have a hidden agenda will see that and pass you with flying colors."

"Let up, Rowdy." Cass wiggled out of his tight grasp.

"Sorry." He released her. "Are you listening to me?"

"Yes. But the lawyer is the asshole's brother. And I said I handled it." Cass picked up the wineglass again. The second swallow tasted better than the first. "Now listen to this: I have to move into the Calhoun mansion with my new sisters and brother as part of the terms of the will. It's closer to the new job, near downtown. Ellie will have to find another roommate."

"That's strange. They're telling you where to live too?" Rowdy jumped to his feet, still worked up. "This father of yours sounds like a control freak. It's not going to be easy for us to see each other, living miles apart."

"Control freak, yes. Sounds familiar, doesn't it? He was a workaholic too. Just like me." Cass sighed. "I never met him, but we were alike in those ways. Crazy, isn't it?"

"Sure is. You have to do all this to get the money?"

"Yes." Cass patted the sofa beside her. "Sit. I have two weeks to finish my job at the bank and pack up my stuff."

"Ellie will be all right." Rowdy settled beside her again. "She and Manny are together almost every night anyway. I bet she just moves him in here." Rowdy looked toward her bedroom. "Yeah, having you downtown and in a house with a bunch of strangers will be a pain."

"I think . . ." Cass wasn't sure how to go on.

"What?" Rowdy jumped to his feet again, clearly nervous. "Are you thinking that now that you've come into money, maybe we should take a break?"

"The money has nothing to do with it, Rowdy. We've been talking about it for a while now." Cass got up to face him. "Maybe today's not the right time to discuss our relationship. This news. Finding out about my father. Frankly, I'm on overload."

"I'll bet you are. Don't decide today." Rowdy pulled her into his arms. "Three-hundred million dollars. I don't know how you can be so calm about it."

"I'm not calm!" Cass buried her face in his shirt. He smelled good, familiar. She'd given him the aftershave and he used it sparingly so it didn't overwhelm his clean, male scent. She took a shuddery breath before she looked up at him. "I'm in shock, if you want to know the truth. And, obviously, I need to talk to my mother."

"Yeah. She needs to come clean about this deal with your father." Rowdy put his hands on her shoulders. "Baby, I don't understand how she could have kept something this big from you all these years. Or why she didn't take money from the son of a bitch so you'd have had an easier life."

Cass's eyes filled with tears. "Neither do I." She leaned against him, sinking into his warm embrace. Yes, he was big, but gentle and very careful with her. But there was nowhere she felt safer, more treasured. "God, Rowdy. When I think what just a little of that money could have done for us. . . ."

"I know, baby. I know." He held her as she sobbed against his soft cotton shirt. He rubbed her back and drew her even closer. "And maybe he wasn't so bad. We know she has a temper and can hold a grudge. What a shame if she didn't let you know your father over a fight they had years ago."

"Now it's too late," Cass murmured against his shirt. "I saw a video." She looked up at this man who'd been the only important male in her life for so many years. "I look like him, Rowdy. So much." That had shocked her more than anything. Then over lunch Mason had told her what a great dad Conrad had been. Well, when he hadn't been making his billions. What would it have been like to have a man like that around when she was young? The tears wouldn't stop.

"Shit. That must have hurt." Rowdy kissed her wet cheeks, then picked her up. "You're exhausted. Bet you didn't sleep a wink last night thinking about today and what might happen. Come on. Let me put you to bed."

"I *am* tired." Cass sniffled, then held onto him as he walked her into the bedroom. He gently slipped off her sandals.

"You want me to come back later? Take you to dinner?" Rowdy stood next to the bed.

"No. I'll go see my mother later. See what she says. Maybe." Cass sighed. "Maybe we can meet tomorrow for breakfast and talk about our relationship." She saw his frown, knew she was hurting him. "We've been letting things slide, Rowdy. You know it and I know it."

"Cassie, don't make any snap decisions you might regret." He sat on the edge of the mattress and brushed back her hair. "I know we've been comfortable lately. That's on me. I travel too much in my job. I could ask for a transfer. A desk job. Stick around more and work on things with us."

Cass held onto his hand. "Tomorrow. We'll talk." He always called her Cassie and she loved it. It made her feel like a teenager again. Then she thought about Mason, teasing her because she was still with her high school sweetheart. Like she'd gone for safety, afraid to venture out and try deeper waters. She shivered. If ever there was a shark, it was Mason MacKenzie. He was circling already. And she'd bet a cool million of her soon-to-be fortune that he was only after her late daddy's company.

"Sure. All that money. I can see how your life is going to change, Cassie." He got up and walked to the door. "I'll try to be patient. But it won't be easy. I just have to wonder where I'm going to fit in." And with that he walked out the door.

Cass blinked back sudden tears. Money, a father she never knew, sisters and a brother. Trying to sort it all out *had* exhausted her. So she gave up and closed her eyes to let the world go away.

Chapter 4

"How was it today, boy?" Ed MacKenzie had his ostrich-skin boots on his wide mahogany desk as he leaned back and drew on a Cuban cigar.

Mason walked over and cracked open a window. Ed would call him a pansy, but he couldn't stand the smell.

"Interesting. The long-lost daughter is smart, pretty, and looks a lot like Connie. Can you believe it?" Mason headed for the bar built into one wall and poured himself a stiff one. At Ed's nod he made it two.

"You don't say." Ed laughed until he coughed. "Stubborn like her pa too?"

"Of course." Mason handed his uncle the glass. "Family trait. I was waiting for a show and I got one. You can imagine the surprise that Connie's firstborn is set to inherit some of Calhoun Petroleum. They all held it together like it was just fine and dandy. Then Missy's three kids found out they're going to have to work for a change." Mason chuckled. "You should have seen Shannon mourning her credit cards."

"Spoiled brats." Ed wore a sour expression. "Your daddy didn't raise *you* with no silver spoon in your mouth."

"No, he didn't." Mason thought about that. His dad had been strict, making sure all his kids had a work ethic. Conrad hadn't bothered. "Just wait. It's going to be interesting at Calhoun once Cassidy shows up and tries to do her job. None of Connie's other three kids like to share." Mason took a sip and savored the fine bourbon. "I figure there will be sabotage, tricks, you name it. Whatever will give them an advantage."

"It's what I'd do." Ed blew smoke across the desk. "Connie must have lost his mind at the end, putting his kids in charge. They'll have to cheat, 'cause not a one of them knows a drill bit from a rigger." He cackled, then took a drink. "That company'll be a bird's nest on the ground, boy. You can pick up some prime assets that would look real good with the Texas Star logo on them."

"I wouldn't count on picking up much. I've been running some numbers. The company's more solid than you'd think in this economy. Lots of cash, not much debt." Mason sat across from his uncle and loosened his tie. He'd put his suit back on as soon as he'd hit headquarters. He'd already been stopped twice while walking down the hall to straighten out problems his uncle had created. "Connie has some good people at the top. His children won't be in a position to do too much damage."

"Hold up. I've been asking around too. Calhoun Petroleum's been laying off people since before Connie died because investors started panicking when the price of oil plunged. The 'good people' in charge are looking around for other jobs. I hired one of them this afternoon."

Mason didn't have anything to say to that. Ed was coming after Calhoun hard. Damn it.

His uncle drained his glass. "Fix me a refill. Hell of a day here. First those damned Japanese. Notice I didn't say *Japs*." He smiled, proud of himself. "Then I had O'Riley in here on the carpet. He screwed up the contract on the pipeline through Odessa again."

"I know. I asked Lucille to bring in the paperwork." Mason had his temper under control, but barely. "If you didn't keep changing your mind, he wouldn't have to keep changing terms. Leave him to me, Ed. We'll get it worked out." Mason poured the drink and topped off his own. He knew what was coming. Ed had been talking about it ever since Connie died.

"Fine. Take care of that. And take care of Calhoun Petroleum." Ed took the glass and waved it at his nephew. "Bet that new daughter doesn't have a clue about oil either."

"I'm not going to talk about the family. Connie trusted me and I'm not betraying that trust." Mason sat again and took a sip, letting the bourbon warm him inside. But was he telling the truth? Wasn't it betraying Conrad to get cozy with his daughter for his own gain? While his uncle ranted about Conrad Calhoun for a good half hour, Mason wondered if he could really go through with it.

Oh, not for Ed or to push through his big plans for Texas Star.

Mason would be damned if he did one thing for the man who'd done nothing but treat him like a lackey when he owned part of this fucking business. His brother and sister had another good chunk of it. If the three of them sold their shares, they'd have enough money to buy out any business they wanted. Dylan and Sierra didn't give a damn about oil, but they'd help Mason if he asked. And this chance to have his own company wouldn't come along again anytime soon.

Calhoun Petroleum. Why not? It *was* ripe for the picking. And none of the Calhoun children acted like they wanted it or cared what happened to it. They'd each get their millions after the dust settled and he'd be able to run a company without having to deal with Ed. MacKenzie Oil. Not bad. The thought made him smile.

"See? You like the idea. You'll be right there, inside, won't you? And don't give me that bullshit about trust. We look out for number one around here." Ed snuffed out his cigar, then got up and refilled his glass. Mason joined him.

"It's not bullshit. I won't spy for you, Ed. That wouldn't be right." Mason suddenly found himself on the floor, his jaw throbbing. The son of a bitch had slugged him. Mason didn't get up right away, just stared at the man he realized he truly hated.

"Don't you go playing high and mighty with me, Mason MacKenzie. You've done dirty deals before and will again. Because you'll do what I tell you." Ed stood over him, rubbing the knuckles of his right hand.

Mason struggled to his feet and advanced on his uncle. "You hit me again, old man, and I'll put you down and you'll stay down. You hear me?"

There was a gasp from the doorway. Ed's longtime secretary stood there with a sheaf of papers in her hand.

"I have those Odessa contracts, Mason. You asked to see them." She looked from Mason to his uncle. "I'll just leave them out here on my desk. I'm heading home." She backed out.

"Thanks, Lucille." Mason focused on his uncle again.

Ed sank into his leather chair. Something in Mason's eyes must have convinced him that his nephew wasn't to be messed with. "Hey, I lost my head. You know I didn't mean—"

"Shut the fuck up. I'll say it again and you'd better listen this time. Connie trusted me to do what was best for his family and his company. That's my agenda there." Mason got a fresh glass, poured another drink, and drained it. If taking Calhoun Petroleum for himself was best, he was pretty sure Conrad the businessman would have agreed, as long as his kids got their payday. He turned back to Ed.

"I'm sick of your shit. I put up with it for my family. Because this company is our inheritance. Dad wouldn't work with you and neither would Dylan or Sierra, you son of a bitch. So it was either work here or stand by and watch you drive what Granddaddy started into a ditch." He walked over and hit Ed's barrel chest with his finger. "We sure as hell don't trust you not to cheat us either." He stepped back. "So I'm here to keep an eye on you."

"Why, you insolent little prick." Ed's face was red and he started to get out of his chair but obviously thought better of it when he saw Mason's hands fisted. His eyes narrowed as he aimed his own finger at Mason. "Tough talk, college boy. You think you're so smart with your engineering degree." Ed sneered. "I never needed college to teach me about oil, boy. Around here you're just the front man, the pretty face who goes out and closes the deals that *I* make. I'm the one who gets my hands dirty. Who knows how the real business is done." Ed's hand shook when he picked up his glass. "Your granddaddy and I *made* this business."

"That may be true." Mason nodded. "But you've been trying to ruin it ever since Granddaddy died. When I step away from here for good, I give you six months before Texas Star hits bankruptcy court." He stopped in the doorway and looked back. Ed still sat in his chair, an old man who brought nothing but misery to the people who had to work with him. His uncle fumbled when he reached for his cigar and lighter.

"What are you looking at?" Ed got the thing lit again and threw his gold lighter onto his desk. "You don't know shit, but you do still have that pretty face. Go use it to get some work done."

"No." Mason shook his head. "I'm out of here. Don't bother me over the weekend. I'm going to the ranch. You make any more messes, clean them up yourself."

Cass was glad her roommate wasn't home when she got up. She was going to keep her news from Ellie as long as she could. Time to confront her mother. Driving up in a shiny new car to the store Elizabeth Calhoun managed caused a little stir. Some of the regular customers recognized Cass as she climbed out of it.

"Cassidy Calhoun. What the hell have you done?" Her mother

stepped outside and met her on the sidewalk. "Did you buy a new car? And something so impractical and expensive! Have you lost your mind?"

"No, Mama. It's temporary. My old car's air went out." Cass took her mother's arm. "Can you leave for a while? We need to talk privately. I had that meeting today. With the lawyer."

"No, I can't leave." Elizabeth Calhoun looked tired. Her short, dark hair obviously hadn't been touched since she'd left her apartment early this morning and she hadn't bothered with lipstick. Her black slacks and white blouse, what she considered her uniform under her red apron, looked a little worse for wear. They also were loose, as if she'd lost some weight.

"We're swamped. Summer's almost over so we're running back-to-school specials. Look around, Cassidy." She pushed open the door and cold air hit Cass's face. "Do you see Betty Sue? She called in sick. You want to talk, you can put on an apron and get to work."

"Betty Sue's sick? I hope it isn't serious." The elderly clerk was like a grandmother to Cass. The feisty woman had been there for decades and had run register number one all that time. She'd always had a Band-Aid and a treat when Cass had needed one growing up.

"Just a summer cold, I think. She showed up anyway, the old fool, with her nose running like a faucet. I told her to go back home and get in bed before it turned into pneumonia." Elizabeth shook her head. "But it put me in a bind." She glanced back at the car. "She'd like a ride in that rig before you turn it in. She's crazy for red."

"I know." Cass laughed. "She wears those red sneakers with her apron, doesn't she? And then there's her hair."

Elizabeth chuckled. "Every woman over seventy who gets her hair dyed at the Chop Shoppe next door has that color. That's why I do mine myself out of a box." She held the door for a moment and took a breath before she pushed on inside.

"Are you all right, Mama?" Cass followed her mother into the Got-Yer-Dollar discount store. Her mother managed the store in the little town where Cass had grown up, down the freeway from Clear Lake City. The job was a big responsibility and one Elizabeth had earned after years of working her way up from stocking to clerk.

"I'm the same as always this time of year, Cassidy. Run ragged. What do you need?" Elizabeth didn't stop, constantly checking the aisles for customers. Her smiles were reserved for them and she stopped to help a woman pick out a backpack.

Cass waited until the customer moved on, then grabbed her mother's arm before she could get distracted again. "Mama, this is important. I know. About my father. Who he is, *was*. He's dead."

Elizabeth Calhoun's mouth tightened, but she didn't so much as stop as she pulled away and strode down an aisle crowded with school supplies. "I don't want to talk about him."

"Well, you're going to. I have questions. I think you owe me answers." Cass kept pace and pulled on her mother's arm again. "Please." Her voice cracked. "I have two sisters and a brother. A family."

Her mother whirled on her and grabbed her shoulders. "*I'm* your family, Cassidy Jane. Me. That son of a bitch who was your sperm donor is not your family and those strangers in Houston aren't either." She shook her daughter. "What did they do? Dangle money in front of you? Are you going to play the pretty little socialite like his pampered daughters?" She let Cass go and stared down at the brown tile floor. "You roasting in hell, Conrad? And now you're trying to take my daughter away from me. When I can't get to you? You always were a bastard."

"Mama, people are staring at you," Cass whispered.

"Too bad. I told you I was busy. We have to do this another time. Come back later. I should be available about ten. After closing." Elizabeth cupped Cass's cheek. "I'm sorry. I never wanted you to know that man. He was no good, Cassidy. It was better you grew up without him."

"Better?" Cass bit her lip. She looked around at the place where she'd had to make do her whole life. Clothes, shoes, food—hell, even her underwear had come from here. Dollar-store Cassidy. Kids could be cruel. But it had made her determined. To get an education and have a career that would get her as far away from this store as she could go. So she'd hit the books and worked her way through college. Her mother had done what she could to help, but that hadn't been much. What was wrong with child support?

"I can see your wheels turning, Cassidy Jane. It would be better for everyone if you'd just drop it. Let it go. Conrad's money too." Elizabeth sighed. "Money doesn't buy happiness. Surely I don't have to tell you that." Her mother automatically straightened a shelf of towels next to her, clearly anxious to get back to work.

"No, it wouldn't. But money could have bought me an education and a few other things that I had to work my tail off to get. I know you're tired. So am I." Cass picked a notebook up off the floor. She'd told Mason she hadn't suffered. Well, that had been a lie. "Maybe you should write down why you did what you did, Mama. I need to know. Your decision to take away my father had consequences. Do you get that?"

"Yes, Cassidy. It was for the best." Her mother stepped around her and headed to a cash register. "I sure miss Betty Sue." She waved her hand. "Laura, honey, those are a dollar each, not three for a dollar."

"Mama, listen to me." Cass stuck close to her mother, not about to let her get away. "Use this." She dropped the notebook in her mother's apron pocket, along with a dollar bill. "Mail me a letter. Do it, Mama. Because you owe me that much. I have to know why. Why you took my father away from me."

Elizabeth gave her a long look, then nodded. It was obviously all she was going to get, so Cass turned on her heel and walked out of the store. The red convertible gleamed in the late-summer sun. Calhoun Petroleum money had made it possible. Was she supposed to hate that? She looked back to see if her mother had followed her to the door. Of course not. Her mother was probably already immersed in her business, selling crayons and glue and notebook paper. Elizabeth Calhoun was tough and independent. Too independent. Her mother had made it clear to Cass many times that she had no use for men.

Conrad Calhoun must have loved her once and she'd loved him enough to marry him and give him a child. But then he'd done something Liz thought was so unforgivable that she'd kept his daughter from him. What could it have been? Right now the answer didn't matter as much as the fact that Cass had paid for it. Over and over again.

She got behind the wheel and punched buttons until the convertible top went down. The sun was sinking below the horizon in a beautiful pink and orange display and it had finally gotten cooler. She'd told Rowdy she'd call him tomorrow. Tonight she needed to read that packet of papers and figure out her future life.

First, she wanted to see her new home. A mansion in River Oaks.

Her new brother had sent her a text about his party. She programmed the address into the GPS. Why not?

With a last glance at the Got-Yer-Dollar, Cass backed out of the parking spot. She wouldn't be holding her breath for the letter. Maybe she'd never learn what her mother had on Conrad Calhoun. Right now she was interested in the future.

But when she thought she saw her mother step out on the sidewalk, she stopped. No, it wasn't Elizabeth, just another short brunette who worked at the store, a teenager, rolling out a cart with a display of colorful backpacks. How many summers had Cass done the same job? She hoped this girl had more waiting at home for her than canned soup and an empty apartment.

Cass fumbled for her sunglasses and followed directions as the soothing voice on the GPS told her to turn right out of the parking lot. Maybe getting with her new family was just what she needed to banish this feeling of having lost something. Ridiculous. Today she'd gained more than she could have ever imagined. It was definitely party time.

It was a freaking mansion. And there *was* a party going on. Valet parking with a security guard at the end of the gated driveway checked off a guest list. Her name was on it. Unreal.

Cass turned her keys over to the teenager in khaki shorts and a navy polo shirt and gazed up at the house that had all the charm of a McMansion on steroids. Wow. If Conrad liked to show off his wealth as Mason had said, then this was certainly doing the job. The three-story stone house had a portico that cars could drive through so you could arrive at the massive double doors in a rainstorm and not get wet. Those doors were a gleaming mahogany with shiny brass trim and doorknobs. It all screamed new money and lots of it.

Should she ring the doorbell? Walk on in? Since the text had said pool-party casual, Cass wore shorts and a tank top that were probably not quite as nice as the valet's outfit. Shoot. Was it too late to get her car back and run for home? She was actually turning around on the steps when one of the doors opened.

"Well, are you coming in, or not?" The middle-aged woman in the neat gray uniform with the white apron over it put her hands on her ample hips. "Cassidy Calhoun. Yep, you have to be her. Ethan said you might come." Her eyes sparkled with tears. "Girl, if you aren't the image of your daddy, I've never seen the like." She waved a hand. "Come on. Don't let these fancy digs scare you. It's just a house. Too big if you ask me, though no one did." She marched on down the steps and took Cass's arm.

"Please. I know I'm bossy. Don't take it personal. I boss all the kids. The party's out back. I'm Janie. Janie Schaumberg. Been housekeeping for Conrad since he got his first six-figure royalty check." She shook her head and gave Cass a nudge. "Come on, hon, you'll be fine."

Cass knew she had to say something, move. But this was reality crashing in on her, big-time. What had she fallen into? Another dimension? A coma? A daydream? She was going to *live* here?

"Okay, I get it. You don't know what to think." Janie began to ease her up the steps. "Come to the kitchen with me. Let's sit and talk before you face the crowd. Maybe I'll give you one of my special margaritas. Just to relax you. How does that sound?"

"Uh, thanks." Cass managed a smile. "That sounds great, actually."

"That's the girl." Janie was leading her through a maze of beautiful rooms that went by in a blur. "I know the first time Conrad showed me his dream home I just about fell out. I mean, how was I supposed to keep all of this clean?" She chuckled. "The man had such big ideas! But he hired me a staff. Can you believe it? Janie from Fredericksburg with a staff!" She pushed through a door into a gorgeous dining room with two enormous crystal chandeliers.

"Wow!" Cass had to stop for a minute.

"Beautiful, aren't they?" Janie gazed with pride around the room with the long, gleaming table and at least twenty chairs around it. "Connie and Missy built this house, then went to Europe to find the pretty stuff like those chandeliers. Too bad that man had a wandering eye. Blew that marriage right up. Guess your mama might have told you about that."

"Um." Cass wasn't going to admit her mother wasn't talking.

Janie didn't need any encouragement as she led the way into a huge gourmet kitchen. "Well, after the divorce he hooked up with that Alex creature. She didn't like his master bedroom or want to live with the kids. The young'uns always stayed here, before and after college. No, Alexandra wanted to live in a high-rise, in a penthouse." Janie raised her eyebrows and her voice, doing an imitation of a stuck-up woman, with her pinky finger held out just so.

Cass smiled and sat on a bar stool at the island when the house-keeper pointed to it. She knew she couldn't possibly belong here. Even the hand towels were finer than anything she owned. While she gazed around her like a country bumpkin, she listened, not about to interrupt this chance to learn a few things.

"Missy has her own home a few blocks away. It's big too, but not anywhere near this size." Janie went to work mixing a drink. "Now that Connie's gone, I guess things will change again. At least the witch—that's what we call Alex—won't be coming back. She and Connie had already separated before he died." She laughed. "He gave her that fancy penthouse as part of their prenup and then came back here to live. He liked being with his kids. Always tried to be a good father." She stopped and leaned against the counter, then looked at Cass. "Oh, I do rattle on, don't I? You never even knew your daddy. I'm real sorry about that."

"Me too. But there was a legal issue between him and my mother. I don't suppose you know what it was." Cass took the frosty glass Janie held out to her.

"Oh, no. That was all a big secret. I came to work for Conrad after that. He was already married to Missy and Shannon was a baby. They had a nice place out Memorial Drive back then. Plenty big, I thought." Janie nodded. "Taste that and tell me what you think."

Cass sipped. The tart margarita packed a punch, but it was deli-cious. She said as much. "I guess I should go say hello to Ethan." She finished the drink and felt it warm her insides. False courage, but it helped.

"I'd better warn you. Ethan is a good boy but he likes a fast crowd. Your sisters aren't home so it's mostly the young ones here tonight. And they've been hitting the alcohol hard." Janie frowned. "I'm sending out a lot more food to try to soak that up. Those people do have to drive later. Or I'm making sure we take keys and call Uber for them."

"Sounds like you're doing what a parent should do." Cass smiled and got to her feet. She'd been hearing music since she entered the house. There must be a massive sound system outside. "I assume they're all adults."

"They don't act like it. Wait and see." Janie poured herself a drink, which she claimed was a virgin margarita, then called a name. A woman in another uniform appeared and Janie started issuing orders about the caterer. "You run along, Cassidy. Just be careful when they start doing shots."

"Thanks, Janie." Cass stopped at the back door and looked out through the glass. At least two-dozen men and women in bathing suits, cargo shorts, and flip-flops were gathered around the pool. Okay, she wouldn't stick out like a sore thumb in what she was wearing. She took a breath, opened the door, and stepped outside.

The music was really loud and some people were dancing close to the edge of the pool. A few were swimming and the buffet was busy. All had drinks in their hands, even those in the water. Janie had been right about that. Cass looked around for her brother and finally spotted Ethan talking to a girl sitting on the diving board. He wasn't far from the DJ, who had set up huge speakers and seemed to be taking requests. When Ethan saw Cass he grabbed the DJ's microphone and the music stopped.

"Hey, everyone! Here she is, my new sister Cassidy. Say howdy!" Ethan waved at Cass and beckoned her over as everyone shouted "Howdy, Cassidy!"

Cass waved and smiled.

"Bring out the shots." Ethan grinned when there were hoots from the crowd. "New drinking game, y'all. Whenever anyone says her name, we all take a shot. Got it?"

Cheers all around. Waiters circulated through the crowd with loaded trays.

"Here's to family. Welcome home, Cassidy!" And Ethan downed a shot.

Cass had one shoved into her hand and had no choice but to join in. Tequila burned its way down her throat. She'd done shots before, back when she'd been younger and a heck of a lot more stupid. This was a much better quality drink.

She wanted to say no to the whole thing. But Ethan was grinning and introducing her to his girlfriend. Shot. Then he took her to a group of his former fraternity brothers. Shot. The evening began to blur after that.

Cass tried to keep up for Ethan's sake. She had a brother. That was cool and he was being friendly. The crowd got rowdier and a girl took off her bikini top before she fell into the pool, squealing. Maybe no one would notice if Cass slipped into the kitchen with Janie. Too bad the grounds around the pool were dark now except for pool lights. The music had slowed down to something that just begged for a partner and close dancing. Several couples were taking advantage.

The house had to be close by, but it was getting hard to focus. Cass stayed put, afraid a wrong move would land her in the pool. A hot guy had been circling her for the last half hour or so. Brad? Blake? Who cared? Cass grinned at him when he handed her yet another shot and called her name. Oh, she had to drink. She was putting it to her lips when a warm hand gripped the glass inches from her mouth.

"Step off, Bud. I'll take it from here." The deep voice near her ear made her shiver. The man took the shot glass and set it on the tray, then pulled her close. "Ready to go?"

"Mmm. Dance." She twined her arms around his neck and leaned against him. Great music. She swayed with him, liking the way his hard body fit with hers. She leaned her face on his chest and closed her eyes. They moved together just long enough for her to get revved up and press closer when he stepped away from her. "Hey!"

"That's enough. I think it's time for you to go." He gently steered them away from the noise of the crowd.

"Go where?" She balked and tried to open her eyes, couldn't manage it.

"You worried? Don't be. You're safe with me."

Stupid, but she believed him. That voice. Familiar. A gentleman. "Thanks."

"How many of those shots have you had?" The deep voice sounded amused.

"Lost count." Cass realized she was being helped into a car. Truck? Didn't matter. Quiet. Tried to look but couldn't focus, so she just closed her eyes again when her head hit soft leather.

"Are you okay?" He buckled her seat belt, then the seat buzzed back. Like a bed. Nice.

"Mmm. Late. Sleep now." Cass blinked and saw . . . Mason. He'd come to her party. Of course. He knew Ethan. All the Calhouns. He'd take her home. Good. No way could she drive.

"I'll wake you when we get there." He was laughing at her.

"Thanks, Mason. You're . . . um . . . sweet." Let him laugh. She'd take the ride. Uber to Clear Lake? Too expensive. Her head? Too heavy for her body. *Stay still or* . . . Cass swallowed. She could *not* be sick. Not in Mason's super-expensive truck. Oh. Lights out.

* * *

Mason had been on his way out to the ranch when he'd remembered that text from Ethan. A party for Cassidy. Would she go? Out
of curiosity, if nothing else? Ethan's crowd was a wild bunch and
younger, early twenties. He decided to just swing by on his way out
of town to see if she'd made an appearance.

Good thing. There she'd been, tossing back shots like she did it
every day and looking about cross-eyed from the punch of 110-proof
top-shelf tequila. He'd gotten her out of there just in time. Bikini tops
were flying off and he figured the orgy was about to start. Oh, hell no.

He'd had a bit of fun with Ethan after reminding him that the cost
of the DJ, catering, and valet parking would be coming out of his
meager (to Ethan's mind) Calhoun paychecks, not out of his family's
housing allowance. That had made the party break up early. Seems
that caterer's rate was steep enough to make little E think twice about
feeding his boozy friends into the night. Orgy interruptus.

Now Mason was headed out of town. Why not? It was a good opportunity. Cass would wake up with a hell of a hangover and the
ranch was a great place to recuperate. He'd let Sierra find her something to wear in the morning and then he'd have a chance to get to
know Cass better. He'd bet the woman had run straight to her mother
after he'd left her. Had she found out about the skeletons in Conrad's
closet? He really needed to know what they were.

Mason didn't like secrets, never had. Which meant he wasn't
crazy about this hidden agenda he had going on at Calhoun either.
Well, why should he keep it hidden? He'd lay his cards on the table
and let them know he wanted the company for himself. Would any of
the Calhouns care as long as they got their payout at the end of the
year?

Mason watched the traffic, but his mind was full of scenarios.
This was a tough time in the oil industry and he doubted Calhoun Petroleum was going to survive the way it was going. It needed someone experienced at the helm. For once his uncle was right. While
there were plenty of assets to make Calhoun a valuable commodity,
whatever secret Elizabeth Calhoun knew made it a risk for anyone to
take on, Mason included.

Cass started snoring softly and Mason smiled. She'd been cute as
hell when she'd been drunk and leaning on him as they'd left the
party. Dancing with her had been a pure pleasure too. He never took

advantage of a woman under the influence, but she sure had looked kissable. Their own personal orgy would have been a hell of a ride.

Would she be mad that he'd brought her out here instead of taking her home? Of course. And the stink she'd raise was just one more thing for Mason to look forward to. Who knew he liked difficult women? He must be losing his mind.

Chapter 5

"What the hell have you done, Mason?"

Cass heard the woman's voice but couldn't bear to open her eyes. She had the headache of the century and wasn't sure she wasn't going to hurl. It didn't help that she was being carried by someone whose stride bounced her just enough to make everything worse. She'd insist on being put down, but couldn't be sure she'd be able to stand on her own.

What *had* he done? Oh, yeah. Mason had rescued her from Ethan's party. That was all her brain could handle before her stomach took over.

"Put me down. Now! I'm going to be sick." She clapped her hands over her mouth and landed on the floor. Before she could help herself she leaned over and proved she hadn't been lying. Luckily, when she opened her eyes she'd hit a toilet bowl, seat up. God. Someone held back her hair. Please, please let it be that unknown girl, not Mason.

Her knees on the floor, she hugged the porcelain throne until her stomach was empty. A wet washcloth landed in her hand.

"Thanks." She used it to wipe off her face. She simply couldn't look at whoever was behind her.

"He's gone. I sent Mason out of here for a Coke. It always helps settle my stomach. You done?" At her nod, the girl helped Cass to her feet. "I'm Sierra, his sister." She smiled sympathetically. "You gonna live?"

"Not sure yet. Tequila shots." Cass staggered over to the marble sink and turned on the water, then rinsed out her mouth. She leaned against the counter and glanced in the mirror above it. Oh, hell. Mascara under her eyes, hair a wasp's nest, and God knew what that was on her tank top.

"Been there and lived to regret it. Stay put and I'll bring you a fresh shirt. We're about the same size." Sierra left the bathroom.

Cass noticed a new toothbrush and toothpaste next to the sink. Obviously, Sierra was a saint. Cass brushed her teeth, washed her face, and pulled her hair back with a thoughtfully provided hair band.

"Try this." Sierra was back and handed her a red T-shirt. "I'll be outside. Holler if you need me."

"Thanks." Cass jerked off the nasty tank and pulled on the shirt. It did fit perfectly. She'd been too focused on her own misery to pay much attention to Mason's sister, but her first impression was of a tanned and toned woman about her own age with a short haircut that emphasized big blue eyes men would fall into. Sierra had the kind of blond hair that was either highlighted from the sun or had cost big bucks.

Taking a steadying breath, Cass opened the bathroom door. Mason waited on the other side.

"Where am I?"

"My family's ranch. I was headed here anyway so I brought you with me." He handed Cass a Coke in a frosty bottle and a couple of aspirin. "For what ails you. You look like hammers are beating in your head."

"They are." Cass swallowed the pills and drank the cold soda gratefully. It did help. "You were supposed to take me home."

"You were in no shape to be left alone. And I didn't want to carry you up those stairs at your apartment and maybe come face-to-face with your boyfriend." Mason's smile made Cass think he was lying.

She bet he'd have loved to have shown up with her dead drunk in his arms to meet Rowdy for the first time. He'd have grinned like he was doing now and waited for the fallout. Maybe she should be grateful that bringing her here had suited him better, for some reason. Cass thought about arguing or probing for that reason, but didn't have the energy for it. Her stomach churned and her head was killing her as Mason led the way down a hall.

"Come sit for a minute. You've met Sierra. My mom would like to meet you too."

"Now? What time is it? And did you tell her?" Cass wondered how far this ranch was from the city and how long she'd been asleep.

"That I found you drunk on your ass?" Mason gripped her elbow when she almost plowed into a wall lined with photos. "No, just said

I wanted to bring you out here to relax for a while. You'd had a terrible shock at Dylan's office and needed time to get used to the news. No place better for chilling than our ranch. You'll see."

"Oh, thanks." Relax? When she had to meet the MacKenzie matriarch? First she'd heard of one. But then she knew a little of nothing about any of these people. She finger-combed her bangs. Hopeless. Bit her lips. Even worse. No makeup left. She shivered in the cool air-conditioning as they passed those framed photos. Happy family posed with horses, private planes, yachts, oil rigs. She was so out of her element here.

Would Mason's mother be a sophisticate like Alexandra, cool and condescending? Or more of the Missy type? Someone who came up from humble roots and might have some sympathy for Cass and her situation? No time to wonder about it as they walked into what seemed to be the family room. It was what Cass called *ranch-house chic*. She'd seen rooms done up like this in magazines. Trophy animal heads—ugh!—decorated several walls. There was lots of leather furniture and a large stone fireplace had green plants in the open hearth since it was still hot outside.

It took her a moment to notice the woman standing near the bar set up against one wall. She was blond like Sierra and had the same kind of trim figure. She was probably in her early fifties and had spent enough time in the sun that she had fine lines around her bright blue eyes. As soon as she saw them enter the room, she started forward, her hands outstretched.

"There you are. Why, you *do* look like your daddy! Welcome, Cassidy. I'm so glad to meet you." She pulled a speechless Cass in for a hug.

"Thank you, Mrs. MacKenzie." She did manage that.

"Mom, Cass has had a long, rough day. She probably wants to fall straight into bed." Mason steered Cass into a comfortable leather chair.

"Mason told me that you didn't even know Conrad was your father. I bet you have a million questions." His mother sat on the end of the couch facing Cass. Sierra was already perched on the other end.

"I guess I'm still in shock. Questions? Yes, ma'am."

"Call me Marjorie. Please. I hope we'll be like family. You can come here when things get stressful at the house. That man! Making you live with your sisters and brother who are strangers to you, of course, in the house in Houston." Marjorie sighed. "I'm sure the kids aren't going to make it easy for you. You were a shock to them too, I guess. Or were you? Mason?"

"Big surprise all around, Mama. But they took it pretty well. Or at least they pretended to." Mason stood next to Cass's chair. Moral support, maybe.

"I'm kind of excited to have a family. I grew up an only child." Cass couldn't help warming to Mason's mother. She was obviously sincere. Looking around the room, she could see that this was less a designer's dream and more of a home. There was a big-screen TV over the mantel and more family pictures scattered about. A book lay open on the end table. A big black dog got up from his plush dog bed and wandered over to sniff Cass's hand.

"Tramp, leave the girl alone!" Marjorie ordered. "Don't mind him. He's old and thinks he's in charge here. Don't let him jump up into your lap."

Cass scratched behind his ears and he laid his head on her knees. "He's sweet. I always wanted a dog, but Mom worked such long hours and in an apartment . . ."

Marjorie frowned. "I heard you had a hard upbringing but, I swear to God, to not even have a damned dog!" She glanced at Mason. "What the hell was the matter with Conrad? Why wasn't he paying child support all those years? It's the least he could have done."

"Calm down, Mama." Mason walked over to sit beside her. "You don't know the whole story."

"None of us do, Marjorie. All I know is that my mother is a proud woman. She wouldn't let him give us a dime while I was growing up." Cass sighed. "I'd love to know why I grew up in a tiny apartment when my billionaire father had a second family living high in Houston." She felt the dog's wet tongue on her hand. Comfort from a dog. Damn it. Once she started making good money at her new job, she just might get herself a puppy.

"Your mama won't tell you why she didn't take Conrad's money?" Marjorie leaned forward.

"No. It's some kind of big secret. I hope she'll tell me now that my father's dead, but I'm not wasting time worrying about it. I've got a new future ahead of me and I'm going to focus on that." Cass stood and the room dipped and spun around her.

"You okay?" Mason was suddenly right there, holding onto her. "She's exhausted, Mama. Let Cassidy go on to bed."

"He's right, Marjorie." Cass leaned against him, not ashamed to let him hold her up. There was something so solid and comforting about him. She smiled or tried to anyway. "I'm sorry, but I've got a terrible headache too. Would you be upset if I went to bed now?"

"No, of course not. We can talk tomorrow." Marjorie got to her feet too. "Sierra will show you where the guest room is. Mason, get Cassidy's suitcase out of the truck." She moved in for another hug. "I won't pry. I promise. You're overwhelmed by all this hitting you today. I can see that. Just know that you can always talk to me if you need a shoulder. Okay?"

"Thanks. Sounds good." Cass blinked back tears. This sweet-smelling stranger was treating her like a daughter. She couldn't take it and was glad when Sierra eased the dog out of the way and took Mason's place, grabbing Cass's elbow. It was as if she knew Cass wasn't sure she could make it out of the room without staggering.

"No suitcase, Mama. This trip was spur-of-the-moment. I thought Sierra could loan Cassidy some stuff for the weekend." Mason didn't blink as he told the lie.

"He kidnapped me, Marjorie." Cass finally managed a smile.

"Come on, Cass. I'll find you a nightgown." Sierra wagged a finger at her brother. "Mason, you're horrible. A woman at least needs her makeup bag. Right, Mom?"

"Right, honey. Run along. Despite everything, Cassidy, if you'd like to know more about your father, I have some old videos I can dig out to show you. From when these two were little." Marjorie smiled when Mason and Sierra groaned. "I don't want to hear it. You two were cute as bugs."

"I'm sure that would be nice." Cass heard Marjorie fussing at Mason about "kidnapping" as she made her way back down that hallway. Coming here this weekend might not have been such a bad thing. She was in no hurry to take on big decisions like her future with Rowdy or to drop the news about living arrangements that would leave her roommate in a bind.

The guest room was nice and it was no surprise that it was after midnight. Sierra was happy to answer questions, including exactly where this ranch was located. It was two hours west of Houston, not far from Austin. If it hadn't been dark, Cass could have noticed that they were in the hill country now, not the flatlands that surrounded Houston.

By the time she was settled into bed and closed her eyes, Cass realized she *was* exhausted. Her body, anyway. But she couldn't turn off her mind. She had a million questions and no answers. Billionaires. Ranches. Big oil. Where did ordinary, barely making the rent, Cassidy Calhoun fit into any of that? Obviously, she wasn't going to solve that riddle tonight. So she sighed and settled into the most comfortable bed she'd ever enjoyed and drifted off to sleep. Tomorrow she'd tackle the details.

Her buzzing cell phone woke her. She groped for it on the nightstand. Rowdy. Of course. He expected to take her out to breakfast this morning. She braced herself and answered.

"Where the hell are you?"

"Good morning to you too, Rowdy." Cass lay back on her pillow. Oh, how she wished she hadn't plugged her dying phone into the conveniently provided charger last night.

"Cass? Are you all right?"

"That's better." Cass sighed. She did love Rowdy and teasing him wasn't right. "I'm sorry. Are you at the apartment?"

"Hell, yes. And it's obvious that you spent the night somewhere else."

"I went to see the new digs in River Oaks last night and drank too much when I got there. It was a welcome-to-the-family party. You know I couldn't drive under the influence."

"River Oaks. Big mansion, I guess. So you coming home now?"

"Uh, not exactly." Cass eyed the bottle of water and pair of aspirin Sierra had kindly left on the nightstand. Oh, yeah. Her headache was back in force. "Hang on a minute." She didn't wait for Rowdy to say anything, just set down the phone and opened the water bottle, then tossed back the pills. "Sorry, I have a hangover. Took a couple of aspirin."

"What do you mean, *not exactly*? When are you coming home? Or do you need me to pick you up? I'd like to see that place anyway. Then we could go out to breakfast around there. Do one of those fancy brunches you like." Rowdy was making an effort. He hated brunch. Didn't even like to say the word.

"That would be fun, except I didn't stay at the mansion last night." The silence on the other end of the line made Cass take another gulp of water. "Rowdy?"

"Yeah, I'm here. Waiting for the punch line."

"Well, I couldn't drive so Mason . . . uh, MacKenzie gave me a ride."

"The mentor, or evaluator or whatever the hell you want to call him?" Rowdy took such a deep breath Cass could hear it hit the phone when he let it out. "You're not here, so where did he take you, Cassidy? Are you in his bed?"

"No, hell no!" Cass sat up straight and her feet hit the floor. "I wouldn't . . . You listen to me, Rowdy Baker! You know me better than that. I don't fall in the sack with just anyone."

"So where the fuck are you?"

Cass calmed herself down. Playing offended hadn't worked. Time to get it all out there. "He was supposed to take me home. But I passed out in his truck. He took advantage of that fact and drove me all the way to his ranch. The MacKenzie ranch."

"You're shittin' me."

"Rowdy, calm down. He saved me from making a fool of myself. I was drunk on my butt. Everyone at the party was doing tequila shots and you know I can't handle those. He got me out of there before I fell in the pool or did something else stupid."

"This is getting better and better."

"Nothing happened with Mason. Nothing's going to happen. Mason's mother and sister are with us. His mother is going to tell me about my father. I need to know this stuff. Understand?" Cass pulled some pillows together and sat up against the padded headboard.

"I understand you're at some fancy-ass ranch while I'm sitting here waiting for you." Rowdy still sounded pissed. "We had a date this morning. Not that I can compete with the high living you're getting used to."

"We didn't have a date exactly, but I'm sorry. It's not like I planned this." Cass sighed. Putting off "the talk" was just going to make it harder. "Don't be difficult about this, please?"

"Difficult? Suddenly you're with this guy who thinks nothing of taking you off to some plush ranch and you think I'm irrational because I don't like it?" Rowdy made a sound that could have been a curse. "Sorry, but I already got the message yesterday that things are changing for you. New job. Place to live. Fancy car to drive. Maybe I'm not going to fit into this new lifestyle."

"Rowdy, I never said that. But I can't come home either. Not right now." Cass stared up at the ceiling. He was jealous and she understood why. But she really didn't need this right now. It *was* pressure. "Please don't make things hard for me. I've got so much to think about, so much that's new . . ."

"Sounds like shucking off the old would make it easier for you. Is that it?" More deep breathing. "If you loved me, Cassie, you wouldn't have to think twice about it. It would be, 'Baby, we're going to be together forever, no matter what comes.' That's what I'm feeling. That's what I've always felt."

Cass blinked back tears. "You're pressuring me. Please don't do that."

"What I just said was *pressure*?" He was silent for a long moment. "I guess I just got my answer. I love you. Too bad that's not enough." He ended the call.

Cass threw the phone down on the bed. It bounced and hit the floor. She rolled over and buried her face in her pillow. Rowdy. She did love him, but not the way he wanted her to. They were more friends than lovers lately and she had a feeling he knew it but didn't want to face it. She hated that this was hurting him and the fact that defining their relationship was coming to a head just when this deal with her father's will had hit too. If only he could have been patient and waited for her to adjust to the inheritance and what it meant. Overwhelmed, she had an ugly cry, glad that no one came to her door and interrupted her. Finally, she grabbed a tissue from the box next to the bed and blew her nose.

A trip to the connecting bathroom showed her just what an ugly cry it had been. Sierra must have come in while she'd been asleep, because there was another outfit of shorts and T-shirt and even a brand-new bra and panties, still with the tags from a department store, stacked on the granite counter. As a bonus there was a full makeup bag waiting for her. Fresh tears filled her eyes at the thoughtfulness. No, she wasn't giving into them. Instead, she jumped in the roomy shower, bathed, and washed her hair. Pressing a cool washcloth over her eyes helped her look presentable again. She hoped so, anyway.

It still took everything in her to saunter out to the den like she was fine and dandy. The smell of frying bacon hit her hard but she swallowed and kept going into a huge gourmet kitchen. Marjorie nodded toward a bar stool when she saw Cass hesitate in the doorway. No cook, no maid. You'd never know these people were oil-rich. Cass relaxed and sat, able to smile for the first time since waking.

"Coffee?" Marjorie didn't wait for Cass to nod, just filled a mug then slid sugar, artificial sweeteners, and a cream pitcher toward her. "You look better. Guess you found Sierra's things."

"Yes. That was so kind of her." Cass decided black coffee might settle her stomach. And the bacon did smell pretty good. There were fluffy scrambled eggs in a pan too. A plate with a stack of buttered toast landed next to her left hand. "Where's everyone else?"

"Outside." Marjorie put her elbows on the counter across from her and gave her a sharp look. "Mason confessed the truth about last night. That boy never could keep a secret from his mama. So—Ethan had one of his out-of-control parties?"

"Yes. I got in over my head." Cass took a bite of toast. "I'm not used to so much drinking."

"Which is a good thing." Marjorie nodded. "I'm glad Mason went by to check on you. That Ethan needs a firm hand. Conrad didn't bother and Missy just indulged him. He's her baby. Now that he'll have to work for a living maybe he'll finally grow up."

"Working sure helped me become responsible." Cass decided black coffee wasn't going to help and stirred in sweetener and cream.

"Yes, Mason told me more about what your life has been like. Working your way through school and all. Conrad must have been very proud of what you've accomplished on your own." Marjorie spooned eggs and bacon onto a plate and pushed it in front of Cass. "See if you can eat a little. It will help settle your stomach."

"Thanks." Cass picked up a fork. "Yes, he said he was proud of me in a video will he made. I'm going to have to work in his company too. Learn the oil business from the ground up. It's . . . intimidating."

"Well, you're obviously a smart girl. You'll handle it. And Mason says he's going to help you learn." Marjorie picked up her own cup of coffee. "The kids are out dealing with a ranch issue, but Mason wants to take you for a ride later. Show you the ranch."

Cass put down her fork. "A ride? On a horse?"

"Why, sure. We have sweet mares out in the barn if you're out of practice. They won't give you a bit of trouble." Marjorie sat on the stool next to Cass and began to tell her about the Bar M, the MacKenzie ranch. They raised horses, which Sierra trained. She'd been a champion barrel racer as a teenager, but had retired after a serious fall during a competition.

"I don't mind telling you I was glad she decided to stop that foolishness." Marjorie leaned closer. "You won't notice it now, but she still limps a little when there's a cold front coming in."

"I remember barrel racing. When I went to the Houston Rodeo once. The riders go so fast." Cass played with her food and nodded while Marjorie went on about their beef cattle and the oil rigs on part of their land. But Cass's mind was on what was coming after breakfast.

Mason expected her to go riding with him. Of course. She was a Texas girl. All the women he knew probably had their own horses—hell, their own ranches. Well, guess what? Cassidy Calhoun had never been close enough to even pat a horse. Some of the kids in high school had been in Future Farmers and had done stuff like raise a hog or a cow for a project. But Cass had spent all her time studying, desperate for academic scholarships so she could go to college. She *had* been to the rodeo once, but that had been all about the famous country singer featured there.

By the time Mason breezed in, smelling of the outdoors and animal, Cass was wondering if she should claim a return of her headache and go back to bed. He looked hunky in snug jeans that molded his strong legs and a snap-front shirt in pale blue that matched his eyes. He kissed his mother on the cheek, then looked at Cass's messy plate.

"Still not feeling well?" He actually looked concerned.

"I'm okay." So much for a manufactured excuse. Cass hopped off the bar stool. "But I have a confession to make." If she was going to become part of this crew—and Marjorie made her want to be part of it—then she needed to learn a few things. "I've never ridden a horse in my life."

"No!" Marjorie looked as if Cass had just confessed to devil worship. "You're teasing us."

"Afraid not." Cass smiled at her. "Not in the budget growing up." She looked up at Mason. "But if you've got a gentle pony or something, I'd like to learn."

He laughed and slung his arm around her shoulders. "Honey,

you're too big for a pony. But I'm sure Sierra has a horse that'll work for you. One that's slow and steady."

"Very slow, turtle slow." Cass felt his warm hand on her back as he guided her toward the door. It seemed like he was always touching her. Did he do that with all the women he knew?

"I'll keep her safe, Ma. See you for lunch."

"You'd better. I'm fixin' your favorites." She waved them off. "Good luck, Cassidy. Don't break a leg."

"Oh, now why did you have to mention that?" After they were outside, Cass eased away from Mason. "Would you stop doing that?"

"What?" He did stop then. "What are you talking about?"

"You steer me, guide me, everywhere. I'm perfectly capable of walking wherever we go. Just point and I'll follow you. Okay?"

"Fine. We're headed to that barn over there. There's a paddock with some horses. See it?" Mason shook his head. "I'm being a gentleman. My mother taught me to take care of women. You don't like it? You're on your own."

"Thank you." Cass stomped after him. "Mason." She stopped next to a gleaming swimming pool. Flashback. If Mason hadn't rescued her last night. . . . Yes, she'd been so drunk that she'd really been close to pulling off her top and joining the skinny-dippers. God.

"What, Cass?" Mason leaned against the brick barbecue pit next to that pool. He was in cowboy garb from head to toe—well-worn boots, those jeans that fit so, so well, and a black cowboy hat that shaded his eyes.

"Sorry, I'm obviously in a mood. And look at me. Am I dressed right for this riding thing?" Cass knew she wasn't. She remembered those riders at the rodeo and was pretty sure, as dirt slid between her toes, that her flip-flops would fall off when she tried to get on a— God help her—horse. He grinned at her, clearly okay with her mood, and shook his head as he looked her over, slowly, his eyes skimming down her body until Cass wiggled her toes self-consciously. "Mason?"

"It's a shame to cover up those great legs," he said as he moved close enough to bump one of her knees with his, "But, no, now that you mention it, you don't want to get chafed. Wait here." He jogged over to the barn. "Sierra! You got something for Cass to wear when we go riding?"

"Oh, great. Your sister is going to be sick of me." Cass realized she was talking to herself. She shook her head and looked around.

The house was a sprawling one-story place but not a mansion by any means. Marjorie had admitted there was usually a cook-housekeeper around to keep things in order, but she was visiting a sick sister in San Antonio.

Bottom line: Rowdy had been off base with his fancy-ranch comment. He would actually love it here. He'd had buddies from college who'd come from a ranch background and he had spent weekends learning to ride from them. But she'd never been invited along. Had she thrown a fit about it? No, hadn't even let him know how jealous she'd been that his scholarships had given him that kind of freedom when she'd been stuck serving burgers on late-night weekend shifts.

So here was her chance to try something new. Cass walked over to the paddock and studied the horses. They were big. Too big. If she fell off one it would hurt, maybe break something. She couldn't afford that with the new job ahead. Now Mason and Sierra were coming toward her.

"I've changed my mind. Forget riding. Bad idea." Cass didn't like the way they grinned at her.

"Nerves." Mason elbowed his sister.

"We can tie you on so you won't fall off." Sierra hooked an arm through Cass's. "Kidding. Now, let's get you into some jeans and boots. Then you'll be ready to ride."

"Seriously, this doesn't need to be in my skill set." Cass complained all the way into the house. "Your boots will never fit me." But they did. The jeans were a little snug, but Sierra just grinned and teased Cass that Mason would probably like them that way.

When they got back to the paddock, Mason did give her butt a good, long look. He stood next to the two horses he'd saddled. His was an enormous black creature named Geronimo. Hers was Joe, brown with a white muzzle and sad eyes.

"Joe, wouldn't you like to go back to the barn?" Cass started to pat him on his rear.

"Stop!" Mason snatched Cass off her feet and pulled her against him. "Stay away from a horse's back feet. Joe is safe, but a strange horse could kick the hell out of you." He'd wrapped his arms around her, his solid chest against her back as he held her tight.

"Gee, thanks. Sorry if I scared you." She wiggled loose. "You see? This isn't going to work."

"Yes, it is. Quit trying to weasel out of this." Mason urged her forward when she did make an attempt to step around him. "Now put your left foot in the stirrup, grab his mane and the back of the saddle, then hop up and swing your other leg over." He stayed right behind her, his hand on her butt to give her a boost when her hop was less than enthusiastic. He wasn't going to give her time to think about backing out.

Before she knew it, Cass was on the horse, looking down. A long way down. "Did you have to give me such a tall horse?"

Mason and Sierra laughed as he adjusted her stirrups so that her boots fit just right. He patted her leg, then mounted Geronimo.

"You can do it, Cass. Have fun!" Mason's sister headed back to the barn.

"Cass, just press your legs against his sides and he'll move out. He'll follow Geronimo. We'll go nice and easy."

"Wait. Where are we going?" Cass felt paralyzed. Squeeze? She wasn't about to start this thing moving.

"I'd hoped for a tour of the ranch, but that was before I knew you were a novice." Mason straightened his cowboy hat. "How about a short walk to the mailbox and back down this road?"

Cass peered down the gravel track. No mailbox in sight. "How far is it?"

"A mile, more or less." Mason shook his head. "Come on. Give him a nudge." He just watched while she didn't move an inch. "You know, I'd hoped this ride would be over before sunset."

"Jerk. I should say something to him, shouldn't I? Like *giddy-up*?" Cass held the reins and saddle horn in a death grip. Sierra had told her this was called a Western saddle, whatever that meant.

"You've been watching cowboy movies, haven't you?" Mason couldn't quit grinning.

"Rowdy likes them."

"Horses don't care if you say anything. They're not like dogs. Now I'm heading out—follow or not." He turned his horse's head and started down the road.

"I don't believe him, Joe. Good horse. Now be nice and walk slowly." Cass squeezed and squealed when Joe suddenly stepped out, following Mason's horse. It took a few minutes to adjust to the movement but she finally could relax enough to look around. There were fences on both sides of the road and cattle grazing in the pastures. In the distance she could see an oil well pumping. There was a small pond opposite the well where several cows had made a muddy mess.

"Look at you. Riding." Mason came up beside her. He tipped his hat. "Mighty nice, ma'am."

Sierra had slapped a straw cowboy hat on Cass's head but she didn't dare let go of the saddle horn or reins to tip hers back. Instead, she smiled. She had a feeling Mason was itching to ride faster, go somewhere besides this pitiful little hike to the mailbox at the main road and back. When the box came in sight, he stopped.

"We're here." Mason got off his horse and dropped the reins to the ground.

"I see that. What?" Cass looked down at him.

"Come here, Cassidy." He reached for her. "Swing your leg over and slide into my arms. Toss your reins over Joe's head. He won't move."

Before she could overthink it, Cass did just that and ended up sliding down his body to face him. The horse did move a little bit and Joe ended up bumping her even closer to Mason, if that was possible.

"Won't they run away?" She sounded breathless, her hands against Mason's chest as he held her close.

"Nope. They've been trained to stay put. It's called *ground tied*." Mason shoved her hat back so he could look into her eyes. "You did good. How'd you like the riding?"

"Mmm. It was okay." Cass felt every inch of him against every inch of her. He was so solidly masculine, but the smell of horse was overpowering. She said as much.

He laughed, his white teeth gleaming in the sunlight. "I don't think we're going to make a cowgirl out of you, are we?"

"Doubt it." Cass let her hands slide up to his shoulders. "Is that a deal breaker with you?" Oh, God, where had that come from?

"Sierra owns the ranch. I chose the oil business for a reason." Mason's own hands had drifted down her back and now rested near the base of her spine. "This is fine for a weekend, but I'd go crazy if I had to stay here all the time. I like the action of the business world." He leaned down and brushed her cheek with his lips. "And deal breaker? What are we talking about, Cassidy? You think I have a list of what I want in a woman?" He nibbled his way to her ear, knocking her hat to the ground.

"None of my business. Don't know why I said that." Cass made a lame attempt to push him away. "My hat."

"I'll pick it up in a minute." He bit gently on her earlobe. "No earrings? I'm sure that's one more thing you would have packed if we'd planned to come out here."

"Yes." Cass sighed. Damn, but he felt good against her. She let one of her hands drift up to touch the back of his head. His hair was as soft as it looked. Pure meanness made her knock his hat off too.

"Well, now you've done it." He leaned back and stared into her eyes. "Woman, you don't mess with a man's hat."

"Really? You started it." Cass grinned. "What are you going to do about it?"

He didn't answer, just leaned down and took her mouth with his. Oh, Lordy, but he could kiss and the sparks that flew made Cass go up on her tiptoes to get every bit of his clever, clever mouth. She gripped that soft hair of his and moaned into his mouth when he jerked her closer. The kiss deepened and seemed to go on forever. Her breasts burned against his hard chest and she slid one arm under his to hold him even tighter. Madness. This was the kind of chemistry that could cause explosions.

When she was hit from behind, Cass lurched into Mason and they both staggered and broke apart.

"What the hell?" Mason turned to look down the road. "Mail truck. Joe doesn't like noisy motor vehicles. He's well trained, but he's letting you know to get back on and get the hell out of here."

Cass's face tingled and was undoubtedly red as she snatched her hat and stuck it on her head again. "Uh, left foot in the stirrup, grab the reins and saddle . . ." She managed to get back on the horse with Mason's push on her butt again.

He didn't seem embarrassed being caught kissing as he stopped to talk to the mail carrier. He took a large stack of mail and a package that he shoved into a pouch he'd tied on the back of his saddle. Cass couldn't wait for him when Joe started to move under her, so she squeezed her legs. Joe trotted faster than he'd gone before, down the road away from the noisy mail truck. She looked back over her shoulder and saw Mason slap the mailman on the back before he mounted Geronimo and urged him forward.

That kiss. Have mercy. What had it meant, if anything? He'd kissed her before, almost as soon as he met her. They had an attraction between them that was undeniable. But he'd just admitted he was all about the oil business. Did he have a hidden agenda? Was her Calhoun connection important enough that he'd make a play for her to get inside information once she started her new job?

Cass realized she'd quit worrying about being on a horse because that kiss had taken her mind to an entirely different place. Maybe that had been his intention and nothing else.

"Hey, slow up, cowgirl." Mason had rescued his hat and he laughed, clearly in high spirits as he rode alongside her on the way back to the barn.

Cass relaxed in the saddle, admitting to herself that this riding thing *was* turning out to be fun. The sun was warm but there was a breeze and this ranch was pretty, with the rolling hills and a few trees to give the cattle shade.

Wait till she told...Who? Her mother? Whose mouth would purse in disapproval at her fraternization with those rich folks? Rowdy? Who would hate that it was Mason riding alongside her and teasing her about her insistence on talking to Joe? And of course there'd been the kiss, which would make Rowdy insane and rightly so. What about her roommate? She'd probably think Cass was bragging about hobnobbing with the rich folks.

Cass suddenly felt more alone that she'd ever felt in her life. Damn it. This should be a happy time for her. She had more money than she'd ever imagined coming her way. Her enormous debt had disappeared as if by magic and she had a shiny red convertible waiting for her in Houston. Life was good. So why did she feel on the verge of tears?

Chapter 6

Mason knew he'd railroaded Cass into this weekend and that it was time to pull the plug. She'd been a pretty good sport about it. Even though the horses had freaked her out, she'd managed to ride to the front gate and back and had even looked disappointed when they arrived back at the barn. The way she'd kept chattering to old Joe had been hilarious. No one had conversations with the horses, but he could have sworn Joe had been listening to her sweet talk.

That kiss had confirmed what he'd known the first time he'd seen her. He wanted her. She was full of fire and had fit against him like she was made for him. Better yet, she was his ticket into Calhoun Petroleum. But that might not be the smart play. There was still time to figure that out.

"We've got to go back to Houston, Mama," Mason announced right after lunch.

"No, we're just getting started. I want to tell Cassidy about her daddy." His mother looked ready to do battle.

Cass was on the couch and Tramp had managed to crawl into her lap as soon as Cass had sat down. The old hound was snoring and probably drooling on her borrowed jeans, but she just kept stroking his floppy ears.

"You spent all of lunch bending her ear about Connie, Mama." Mason smiled. "After giving her the secret recipe for your chicken-fried steak."

"Everything was delicious, Marjorie. But Mason's right. I need to get back home too." Cass was carefully untangling herself from the dog. "I have a lot of things to deal with there."

"But Harvey's coming up and I was hoping we could barbecue

tonight out by the pool." Marjorie glared at Mason, who was dragging himself out of the leather recliner that had been his dad's favorite chair. It had taken him about five years after his father died before he'd had the nerve to appropriate it as his own.

"We're not leaving because of Harvey." He turned to Cass. "Mama's boyfriend. And he'll be a lot more comfortable sneaking into your bedroom, Mama, if I'm not here."

"Mason Alexander MacKenzie! Why, I never!" Marjorie turned red and stared down at her feet.

"Yes, you have, Mama. Don't bother denying it." Mason walked over and put his arm around her. "Do we have to have a conversation about safe sex?"

She hit his arm with her fist. "Shut your sassy mouth. Where's your sister? I don't want her to hear this."

"You think Sierra's not aware? Who do you think put this flea in my ear?" Mason laughed when Marjorie's mouth fell open. "She's gone to town to pick up something. Now relax and have a nice time tonight. But I did kidnap Cassidy and I should let her get back."

"Did he cause you problems, Cassidy?" Marjorie sat back down and picked up her glass of iced tea.

"My, um, boyfriend didn't like Mason bringing me out here. We were supposed to meet up." Cass gently moved Tramp's head out of her lap and stood.

"You have a boyfriend?" Marjorie looked from Mason to Cass. "What's he like? What does he do for a living?"

"He used to play football for A and M, Mama. Big guy, isn't he, Cass?" Mason wanted to picture some beefy guy running to fat. Competition? Somehow the boy had held onto Cass for all these years, so he must have something to offer her. But was it enough now that she was moving into the big leagues as part of Calhoun Petroleum? She hadn't kissed like she was taken. He grinned and caught Cass's eye. She flushed. Ah, guilt. He could work with that.

"Yes, he's big and smart too. He's an engineer for one of my father's companies. A real coincidence." Cass edged toward the door. "I hope he doesn't lose his job in this oil downturn."

"This downturn's a worry for all of us. The royalties from the wells are way down." Marjorie frowned at Mason. "We need to talk about that, son. I live on that money and my income has dropped by half since last year. Is there hope of that coming up any time soon?" She glanced at Cass. "Although maybe we shouldn't talk about this in front of company."

"I'll go change into my own clothes so I can leave Sierra's here." Cass smiled. "As for the oil business? We all hope things improve and soon." Cass disappeared down the hall.

"How serious is it, Mama? I thought you were left with plenty of money after Daddy died." Mason sat down again.

"I've got an interest in the law firm. That's a steady income because your brother does a good job there. But I signed the ranch over to Sierra. She gets the income from this place. It was your daddy's wish and I was happy to do it." Marjorie sighed. "I'm going to have to sell the house in Houston. It's too big and the property taxes are eating me alive."

"Don't do that. I can help you." Mason knew his mother loved that place. She'd planted the elaborate garden herself. It had been on the garden-club tour held each spring at least twice.

"No, I've lost interest in keeping up the yard. It's just too much work and I can't afford to pay an army of gardeners anymore." His mother smiled. "Besides, I won't need the house much longer. I know you don't like the idea, but I'm thinking I'll marry Harvey."

"Shit." Mason had been afraid that was the way the wind blew.

"Hush your mouth. Harvey's a fine man. I'm not desperately in love with him like I was with your father, but he's good company. He's well fixed and his money isn't in oil, thank the Lord. He likes to travel and we have fun together. I don't want to sneak around or openly live in sin, Mason, and I'm tired of living alone." She wouldn't look at him and played with her tea glass. It wasn't like his mother to be cold-blooded, so maybe she did love the man and didn't want to hurt her son's feelings by admitting it. Damn.

"I wouldn't object to you living in sin. Go for it." Mason was going to call his brother the lawyer as soon as he got some privacy. Credit check. Prenup. Whatever needed doing.

"Well, I won't do it. I'm old-fashioned enough to want a ring on my finger. And it had better be a big one." Marjorie stood, clearly through discussing it. "Weren't you in a hurry to leave? Cassidy is probably ready to go. And speaking of sin, I see the way you've been eyeing that girl. Now I find out she's already got a boyfriend. Are you planning to come between them? Blow up a good relationship because you want in her pants?"

"Mama, you shock me with your frank talk." Mason walked over to give her a hug. He did love his feisty mama.

"You started it. Now answer me. Because if all you're after is a roll in the hay with that girl, then you'd better leave her the hell alone, boy." Marjorie poked his chest. "That's what your daddy would tell you, isn't it?"

"Yes, Mama, it is." He kissed her on the cheek. "I'll stay out of your business if you stay out of mine." It was the best he could offer her. Leave Cass alone? No promises there.

"You're hedging. Don't think you can fool me, darling boy." Marjorie squeezed his arm, then gave him a pinch. "I like that girl and she's had a rough start to life. She deserves to be happy now. You do your little love-'em-and-leave-'em thing with her and it'll surely kill her."

"You give me too much credit, Mama. I think I might be the one wounded if this thing between us goes any further." Mason heard flip-flops coming down the hall. "She's got something . . . I don't know." He shook his head. He was telling the truth. "I just know I want it. Ouch!" His mother had pinched a damned hole in his arm.

"I hope that makes a bruise. Look at it in the shower and remember that she's off limits, son. Now scoot." Marjorie turned to Cass. "Come again, any time. Bring that boyfriend out here and we'll have a nice barbecue. Mason said you did real well on the horse. Sierra can fix up you and your friends with rides and we can take a picnic out to one of the lakes if you'd like."

"Okay, Mama, Cassidy gets the message. She's welcome out here." Mason pointed to the hall. "Let's go. I'll give you her cell-phone number so you two can make arrangements for all this partying. Obviously I'm not included in these plans." Mason rubbed his arm.

Cass looked at him curiously, then ran back to hug his mother. "I'd like that. All of it. Thanks again, Marjorie. And thank Sierra for me too, please." She followed him out to his truck.

"Still mad at me for kidnapping you and dragging you out here?" Mason pulled open the passenger door.

Cass grinned. "How could I be? I love your family and they couldn't have been more welcoming." She laid her hand on his chest. It felt warm and reminded him of how she'd kissed him back. He started to lean in for another one when she turned and pointed. "There's Joe! I actually rode a horse today! I still can't believe it."

"That isn't Joe. I think you need to work on identifying horses." Mason wanted to kiss her pout. He even reached for her. Damn, but he needed to feel her against him.

"Honey, you forgot your care package!" His mother stepped onto the back porch and waved an insulated bag.

"Thanks. Be right there." He settled for helping Cass navigate that steep climb into the truck. Then he slammed the door.

"Two steak sandwiches for later." His mother pulled him in for a hug. "I'm sorry I was hard on you about Cassidy," she whispered. "Maybe that boy isn't good enough for her. Keep an eye out. You might be the best thing that ever happened to her, you know."

"I have your permission?" Mason patted Tramp, who had followed the smell of steak and was sticking to his mother's side. "Thanks, Mama. But maybe you're right. I'm a dog. Sorry, Tramp. My history speaks for itself."

His mother's eyes filled with tears. "Damn it, boy. You deserve a sweet girl like her." She blinked and waved at Cass, who was waiting patiently in the truck and couldn't hear them. "I won't have you put yourself down. Ever. Maybe it's not her, but it's high time you got settled. So I'm just saying . . ."

"Good-bye, Mama." He grabbed the sack and kissed her cheek. "Don't do anything I wouldn't do. And don't be in any hurry to marry Harvey. Oil will come back. I'm counting on it!" He wrenched open the truck door.

"Drive safe!" His mother held onto Tramp's collar when the dog tried to follow the steak. "Love you!"

"Right back at you." He started the truck with a roar. Permission. How about that?

"We have to get my car from the mansion." Cass reminded Mason when they reached the outskirts of Houston. As usual, the traffic on the freeway going into town was heavy and it was slow going.

"I remembered." Mason turned down the radio. "You realize you always fall asleep when you're in my truck? Is that on purpose? So you don't have to talk to me?"

Cass stared out the window. Was it? She finally looked at him.

"Sorry about that. We've had strange circumstances, that's all. I'd rather not do a rehash. But this time it was because I was in a coma from your mother's lunch. Lots of carbs will do that."

"I know. I had to work to keep my eyes open too." He pulled off the freeway. "I'm hitting a drive-through for a soda. Need the caffeine. Want something?"

"Sure." Cass relaxed. Mason was actually easy to be with. In a few minutes they were both sipping big sodas.

"That helps. We should be there in about thirty minutes." Mason set his drink in the cup holder between them. "So your boyfriend didn't like your being at the ranch with me? Threw a jealous fit, did he?"

"Do you blame him? He gets to my place for a planned Saturday-morning breakfast and I'm not there. My bed hadn't been slept in either. What would you think if your girlfriend pulled something like that?" Cass leaned against the door.

"I hope I'd trust her and wait to hear what she had to say." Mason smiled. "Doesn't Rowdy trust you?"

"Sure he does." She flushed. "Maybe he shouldn't." She glanced at him through her lashes. "I shouldn't have kissed you, Mason. I'm going to have to be honest with Rowdy."

"Break up with him?" Mason looked like he'd just won the lotto.

"Not because of the kiss. But because of the inheritance. He said some things that made me think. He's worried I'll have my head turned by all that money and a new lifestyle. It's a valid concern." Cass frowned down at her drink. "I should have handled it better."

"Maybe he should have handled *you* better." Mason reached over and patted her bare knee. "This is all new. Twenty-four hours ago you didn't have a clue your life was changing. Rowdy needs to back the hell off and let you absorb what's happening."

"That's what I said!" Cass lifted Mason's hand off her leg. Yes, it was shorts weather, but she didn't like the way the heat of his hand had felt so intimate on her thigh. Or rather, she'd liked it way too much. He moved too fast and she'd let him. Breaking up with Rowdy had been in the back of her mind for a while, but the timing sucked. Rowdy would blame it on the money and Mason would take credit because of those hot kisses. Maybe they'd both be a little right. Which was ridiculous. Or was it? Cass wanted to bang her head against the window next to her.

"You want me to follow you home from River Oaks? Make sure he's not waiting for you at your apartment to give you a hard time?" Both of Mason's hands were on the steering wheel now, but his eyes had drifted back to hers. "Does he have a temper?"

"He can get mad but he'd never, ever hurt me. You can forget riding to my rescue, Mason." Cass smiled at the idea of Mason—who was a big guy but no match for bulky Rowdy—getting into it over her. No, not funny. Rowdy *did* have a temper. He would never touch her but he'd like it way too much if he had a chance to wipe that grin off of Mason's handsome face. So she changed the subject. Sports. Mason was like most men and football kept them talking until they were close to the Calhoun property.

"There it is." Cass put her empty drink in the other cup holder between the seats. "I have to go inside. I need to find a bathroom and my car keys."

"I'll go in with you. See who's hanging around. And find a bathroom too." Mason parked in the circular driveway. It was late afternoon but the sun was still bright. There were two other cars in the driveway, both fancy sports cars.

Mason came around the truck to help Cass down from the high step. She took his hand gratefully. "Thanks. I know I reamed you out earlier for helping me all the time, but your mama did do a good job of raising you to be a gentleman."

"A compliment? I'll pass that along to Mama." Mason still wore his cowboy gear and tipped his hat again. He walked on ahead and rang the doorbell. "If we're lucky, we won't have to deal with the Calhouns, just Janie."

The door opened and it *was* Janie who greeted them. "Well, glad to see you're still alive, Cassidy." She pulled Cass in by the hand. "When you disappeared, I was worried until Ethan confessed that Mason had taken you out of here." She smiled at him. "Thanks for that, sugar."

"My pleasure, Janie." He kissed her on the cheek. "The others around?"

"Out by the pool. Two out of three are hungover and drinking the hair of the dog. Megan is griping about the will. Still. You can avoid them if you want." She dug in a basket by the door. "Here are your car keys, Cassidy. The car's out back in the garage. Mason can show you where and here's a remote for the door opener." She passed her the electronic remote.

"Thanks, Janie. I'm sorry you were worried." Cass looked toward the French doors that gave her a glimpse of the pool. She couldn't see her new siblings. Should she make an effort to greet them? Snubbing them didn't seem right.

"I'm just the hired help, as the trio out there reminded me a while ago." Janie raised an eyebrow. "I got a pitcher of Bloody Marys going. You going out there to speak or try to slip away unnoticed? I got to warn you, they'll hear the garage door open when you hit that remote."

"That settles it. I can't be rude. I'll just stop and at least say hi." Cass straightened her shoulders. Three against one. Did they hate her? If they were griping about the will, it might be because there was a long-lost daughter taking a cut of their inheritance. Despite Ethan's attempt to welcome her, she knew there had to be resentment that she'd been a surprise from their father's past. But then having to work for a change had hit them hard too.

She felt a warm hand land on her back and turned to smile at him. "Oh, Mason. You can take off if you have things to do." *Please don't leave me alone to face these people.*

"Wouldn't miss this for the world. I'm sure Cass could use one of those Bloody Marys." Mason smiled. "Make mine a Corona. Thanks, Janie." He pointed out the powder room. "You first, Cass." When she came out, he darted inside.

Cass stalled, pretending to study the remote until Mason joined her. He started to take Cass's elbow, then must have thought better of it. "You lead the way."

"Caught yourself, didn't you?" Cass laughed and laid her hand on his arm. "I really am sorry that I jumped you earlier, Mason. Go ahead, drive me like a car. I don't care. I may need your moral support if they give me a hard time out there."

"You've got it." Mason covered her hand with his. "If they start something ugly, I'll finish it. Count on it." He kept her close as he moved them toward the French doors, gently steering her like he always did.

Cass shivered. He could do that to her. Just a touch and she was thinking all sorts of things she shouldn't. No time for that. Not when she had to step out onto the patio and face the nest of Calhouns who turned as one and stared at her like she'd brought them a contagious disease.

"Well, look who's here. Our new sister." Ethan rose to his feet and actually gave her a hug. "You were a good sport last night, sis. Ladies, you should have seen her toss back those shots. Didn't blink when Bitsy Byers dropped her top and fell into the pool."

"God, Ethan. Your parties are so predictable." Shannon sipped a tall Bloody Mary.

Ethan glared at Mason. "Now that I know I have to pay for my own food, booze, and DJ, my wild party days are over. At least at this house. My friends will have to pony up for their own shindigs from now on."

"About time too." Shannon did a finger wave. "Hi, Mason."

"Shannon. Have you managed to bag my brother yet?" Mason settled on a lounge chair and took a frosty bottle of beer from Janie.

"No. Dylan is playing hard to get. But we did have a good time at the rodeo-committee meeting. He makes a handy designated driver." Shannon waved a celery stick at Janie. "I could use another of these drinks—and put some booze in it this time."

Janie handed Cass her own glass. "Haven't you figured out what causes those hangovers yet, girl?"

"I could drink a dozen of these and wouldn't even feel a buzz." Shannon gave her the empty glass. "Double up on the vodka this time."

"Alcoholic," Megan muttered, ignoring Shannon's one-finger salute. "We were just talking about you, Cassidy. Discussing which bedroom to give you here at the house. Unbelievable that Daddy is making us all live here like we're students in a dorm or something."

"It is a strange request, but I guess we're stuck with it." Cass sipped her drink. It didn't taste weak to her. She glanced at Mason. "Aren't there plenty of bedrooms to go around? This house seems enormous. What's the problem?"

"No problem exactly." Megan hadn't touched her drink. Her smile seemed oddly calculating. "It's like this: We want to stay in the bedrooms we already have and the guest rooms are small. Not suitable for our, um, sister." She looked at Shannon and Ethan and they nodded. "We think, since Daddy was so proud of you, you should take his old room. The master suite. Mama didn't stay in it, at least not this time. Besides, she moved out yesterday, as ordered by the will." Megan finally grinned and Ethan and Shannon looked like they were fighting laughter. "You should take it. It's an honor. Trust me."

"An honor?" Cass had a feeling there was a joke here she was missing. "I guess. Surely it's bigger than any of yours."

"What the devil are you up to?" Janie arrived back on the patio and gave Shannon her drink. "You're offering Cassidy Conrad's suite?"

"Sure, why not? That way she can be closer to Daddy." Shannon laughed, then sipped her drink. "Holy shit! That's strong, all right." She leaned back in her chair. "Thanks, Janie."

"Closer to Conrad." Janie shook her head. "Come with me, Cassidy. You too, Mason. I don't think you've ever seen the master bedroom here. It was Conrad's pride and joy."

Cass set down her drink and stood. "That sounds good, then."

"Just wait and see. Alexandra wouldn't sleep in it. I'll show you why." Janie marched toward the doors into the house. "You kids. Pure meanness. I blame your mama. Missy put you up to this? I heard her ranting and raving before she left here yesterday."

"Don't you be talking about our mama, Janie Schaumberg!" Megan jumped up from her chair. "Of course she was upset about the will." She glanced at Cass. "Parts of it, anyway. She hasn't been happy since she gave Daddy her best years and he dumped her for a new model."

"Hah!" Janie turned at the door. "Is that what she's saying? I know things . . . Never mind. You'll be working from now on. I think you'd best be paying attention to the business your daddy left you and less to the stories your mama will be telling you." Janie stomped on into the house.

Cass quickly followed her. Whatever that was about, it certainly didn't concern her. But what did was this master suite. How bad could it be? Masculine, probably. Mason was hot on her heels as they headed up a staircase that looked straight out of *Gone with the Wind*. The curving bannister was a gleaming mahogany, smooth under Cass's fingers. Fine paintings lined the stairs and an oriental runner ran up the treads. The effect was tasteful and stunning. At the top of the stairs you could turn right or left. Janie stopped and caught her breath.

"These stairs are getting harder for me every year. But I tell myself the exercise is good for me. At least I have help that cleans up here. Now if you go left, that's the other bedrooms. Ethan and each of the girls have their own large suites there. To the right, the entire section belongs to the master suite. Guest rooms are on the third floor. That's why no one wants to use them."

"Yes, that would be a lot of steps." Cass glanced at Mason. "The master must be huge. Who wouldn't want it?"

Janie laughed. "You'll see. It's all Conrad. What he liked. His wives had no say-so. Missy put up with it, though how she slept at night, I don't know. Alexandra said *no thanks* and pushed him out to that penthouse property. She must have had real talent in some department to get him to do that. I didn't ask and he didn't say." Janie winked and finally walked over to ornate double doors. She used a key to unlock them before she flung them open.

"Welcome to the big top." She stepped back so Cass and Mason could see inside.

"What do you mean? Like the circus?"

"Yes indeed." Janie smiled, obviously watching for their reactions.

Cass wondered if her father had hired a decorator for this. If so, maybe they could sue for malpractice. She walked into what had to be Conrad's home office. Well, at least there was a desk, of sorts. It was massive, but had once obviously been part of a wagon, a circus wagon. The sides were painted garish colors with gold-leaf trim. *Conrad Calhoun's Traveling Show* was emblazoned boldly across the front. A laptop and a pile of packages sat on the surface.

"I never knew this was up here." Mason had wandered over to the chair behind the desk. It resembled a throne with zebra-striped faux fur covering the seat and back. "Connie was into the circus?"

"Obsessed." Janie gestured to that stack of packages on the desk. "He was always on the computer, ordering more stuff for his collection. These are what have arrived since his passing." She smiled as she surveyed the room. "How do you like it?"

"Well, it's colorful." Cass was trying to focus on the details; hard since the walls were painted in stripes of red, purple, and gold. It almost made her dizzy. There were bookshelves full of framed flyers and posters from old shows, as well as books on the history of the circus. "Why the circus?"

"Conrad told me once, when he'd had too much bourbon, that he'd had a dream as a boy of running off and joining the circus. His old man had been a mean drunk and beat the shit out of Connie when he was in his cups. But kids grow up, life gets in the way, and Connie had to settle for collecting all things related to the circus." Janie laughed. "Here's a secret for you." She pushed a book on the shelf and it rotated, showing a hidden bar, fully stocked with top-shelf bottles and crystal glasses. "He wouldn't pour his booze into decanters. Connie was funny that way. But those are Baccarat tumblers."

Cass sat down on the zebra throne. "Wow. It's like something out of the movies."

Mason laughed. "The book you push is called *The Flying Circus*. Don't forget, Cass." He pushed it again and the bar rotated out of sight.

Janie chuckled. "Just wait till you see the bedroom. Come on and look where you'll be sleeping." She threw open yet another set of double doors.

"You've got to be kidding." Mason pulled Cass up out of the chair. She stopped dead in front of an ad for a two-headed goat.

"This stuff is creepy, Mason," Cass whispered before she looked up and saw one of the biggest beds she'd ever faced in her life. *"Oh. My. God."* The canopy over the more-than king-sized bed came to a center point like a tent. It was made of canvas and had painted gold stars scattered across it. The headboard stood at least eight feet high and featured a colorful carved clown head. Cass knew that leering face with the open red lips would give her nightmares.

"Hope you don't have anything against clowns. Connie loved them." Janie pointed around the room. Sure enough, they were everywhere. In paintings; on mannequins with masks for the heads and giant shoes on their feet. There was even a small car with half-a-dozen dummies in clown garb frozen in the act of stuffing themselves inside. Janie said it was a sculpture done by a famous artist.

"I'll never be able to sleep in here." Cass turned to Mason. "Can you believe this?"

"Have to admit this is a side of Connie I never knew existed." Mason was trying hard not to laugh, she could tell.

Janie gestured again. "There's a big closet here that used to hold Connie's regular clothes. You can use it for your things. We donated his duds to charity. This other closet is full of costumes. Some he wore, some are part of his collection. Can you believe he even went to clown school once? Told everyone he was in Argentina, looking for oil leases."

"I can't believe it." Mason sat on a silver chair, then jumped up when snakes popped up from the arms and back to hiss a warning. "What the hell?"

"You have to watch yourself in here. Nothing is what it seems." Janie walked over to push a button and the fake snakes disappeared again with a last hiss. "Sorry, Cassidy honey. If it was up to me, this would have been cleared out the instant Connie's casket went into the ground."

"Why wasn't it?" Cass didn't know where to look. All around her clowns gawked and leered at her. Posters advertising strange creatures from sideshows gave her the shudders. But the worst thing was that open mouth with the exaggerated red lips at the head of the bed. The crimson velvet bedspread had obviously been chosen because it matched. God.

"It's in Connie's will. I'm told you only saw the video. Conrad had lists of special bequests and such. Codicils. One specifies that the circus collection has to stay together. He wanted to eventually start a museum. Intended to set up a trust for it, I guess, but ran out of time. If I was you, I'd use my year working for the company to find money for that ASAP." Janie winked at Mason. "Ask his rich friends to donate. Surely some of them like the circus too."

Mason held up his hands. "Not me. I'm fighting the urge to run screaming out of here. I had a bad experience as a kid. A clown made me drop my cotton candy at the state fair."

"Oh, come on. You're supposed to mentor me, Mason. Surely you can help me, um, dispose of this." Cass touched the warm velvet spread. At least it felt comfortable. Sleep mask. Ambien. Something would have to be done.

There was a knock and Janie walked over to the hall door. "I called my husband as soon as I heard Megan's plotting. Come on in, Tommy." She opened the door and a tall, slim man with white hair pulled back into a ponytail walked in. He was deeply tanned and had an infectious grin. "This is Tommy, my husband. He's in charge of the cars and grounds here. He's also our handyman. He can fix just about anything that breaks."

"I'm pleased to meet you." He held out his hand. "We might be able to move some of this out to the storage area behind the garage, but I admit it'll be tricky. There's mechanisms in them that need to be set just right." He glanced around the room. "Must say, I don't dare work on them and, like Janie said, I can fix just about anything, Ms. Calhoun."

"Oh, call me Cass." She eyed the oddball things surrounding her. Surely she could at least get rid of some of the clown pictures. "Give me a few days and maybe we can shift some of these out of here."

"About the cars . . ." He glanced at Mason. "There are too many for the garage now, but there's a codicil in the will that says the exotic ones are to be sold at auction. Conrad really didn't want the kids driving them. Ethan's already been pestering me about using a Porsche before I let it go. If you're comfortable with that Beamer you're driving, I'd say stick with that and I'll arrange to have those fancy-ass—beg your pardon—ones shipped over to the auction house pronto so we can garage your car for you."

"Yes. I love the BMW. I wouldn't know how to drive anything exotic." Cass heard Mason groan.

"You're giving up the chance to drive a Lotus?" Mason rested his hand on her shoulder.

"I don't know what that is." Cass did, but she knew that would set him off and it did. He and Tommy spent ten minutes telling her about the fourth-fastest car in the world. "Fine. Before it goes you can take me for a drive in it, Tommy."

"Let Mason do it, Cass." Tommy grinned. "Clearly he's dying to drive the thing."

The men exchanged high fives. Cass realized Janie had been quiet during all of this, just staring about the room.

"Janie? Does it make you sad to be in here?"

"Sure. I miss Conrad." The housekeeper exchanged looks with her husband. "He left Tommy and me a tidy sum. Enough for us to retire to our hometown and buy a nice little place. Plus we have a good chunk of Calhoun stock. Our dividends will allow us to have a comfortable retirement. But we had to agree to stay here for the year you kids are stuck living in the house."

"Oh. And after the year's up?" Cass kept her back to that giant clown headboard and ignored Mason, who kept grinning like he was trying to imagine her sleeping under the circus tent.

"Then we'll leave and you kids will have to decide what to do with the house and all the rest of it." Janie sighed. She glanced at Mason. "It can be pretty spooky, trying to sleep in here."

"Why are you looking at me?" Mason shook his head. "I'm not her boyfriend. She's made that pretty clear. Cass? You okay with this as a place to stay? One of the small guest rooms probably wouldn't be that bad. Small here is probably bigger than your apartment bedroom."

Cass looked around the huge and truly strange room. It was a little overwhelming. There was even one of those fortune-telling booths next to what was probably a bathroom door. She walked over to it and fumbled in her purse for a quarter. The small crossbody bag that held her phone and not much else had been a lifesaver this weekend.

"I don't know how I'll ever sleep in here, but let's see what the future holds. And it *was* my father's. It's a way to get to know him." She dropped the coin in the slot and watched the crystal ball light up. Music played, the freakish-looking mechanical lady in the turban nodded her head, and bells rang. A pointer began rotating until a fortune appeared in the window at the bottom of the glass. Cass leaned over to read it.

"*Dark clouds can mean rain or a silver lining.*" She read out loud then shook her head. "What the heck does that mean?"

"Fortune-telling double-talk. Trust your gut. That's what I always say." Janie dipped into her apron pocket and held out a ring with several keys dangling from it. "It's up to you, Cassidy. But this is the biggest bedroom in the house and that bed's comfortable. Why not fool those troublemaking kids downstairs and take it?" Janie smiled when Cass nodded. "Good girl. Now come see your new bathroom. You won't believe what happens when you flush the toilet."

Mason slung his arm around Cass's shoulders and squeezed. "You have trouble sleeping here, call me. I'll brave the clowns to come over and help you relax."

Cass gave him an elbow, a picture of how that would work just a little too vivid for her peace of mind. "You want to help me relax? Start running numbers on what it would cost to open a circus museum." Just then she heard a flush and calliope music. "Oh, now that's too much."

Mason laughed and she couldn't help herself. She giggled until she ended up burying her face in her hands. Maybe she should look at a guest room. This was insane.

"Look, this is getting better and better." Mason turned her so they could see into the bathroom. "Janie, tell me that's not a clown face on the showerhead."

Chapter 7

Cass delivered the news to her stunned siblings that she was going to take the master suite before she retrieved her car from the six-car garage and headed for her apartment.

"You aren't really going to shleep in that circus tent, are you?" Shannon slurred her question.

"I'm going to try. Maybe I'll call your mother and ask her how she did it." Cass had already said good-bye to Mason, who'd fielded a call from an oil rig and had raced off to take care of a business emergency. It made her wonder who was taking care of Calhoun Petroleum emergencies if there were any.

"Mother told me she hated every minute in that bedroom. She actually slept in a guest room when she stayed here this time. That suite is one reason her marriage to Daddy didn't last." Megan had changed into a swimsuit and had been doing laps when Cass showed up again. She pulled herself out of the pool.

"That and the fact that Daddy had a wandering eye. You know that, Meg." Ethan headed for the garage. "I'm going out. Good luck with the bedroom, Cass. We have two weeks of freedom before we have to go to work and I plan to enjoy every minute."

"God, I dread that job. When are you moving in, Cassidy?" Shannon got up and staggered for a minute, then seemed to pull herself together. "I have a date later. Guess I better take a shower."

"Make it a cold one." Megan was frowning. "When, Cass?"

"I'm finishing out my time at the bank. I guess I'll wait till my last day there. So you'll see me a week from Friday." Cass sighed. "This is going to be strange. I hope"—she smiled—"I hope we can get along. I know you didn't want me to like that bedroom and it *is* a nightmare."

"Yeah, well, nobody said you can't stuff some of that shit into an extra closet somewhere in the house. Ask Dylan about it. There's room behind the garage too. Check into it." Megan wrapped a towel around herself. "Shannon, you're about to fall down. Let me help you get inside. I swear I'm checking you into rehab if you don't get hold of yourself."

"Don't start." Shannon slapped at Megan's hand, then let her help her to the French doors. Soon they were out of sight, sniping at each other all the way.

When Cass got home, she parked next to her roommate's ancient beater. A football game on TV blasted out of her apartment when she got to the top of the stairs. The neighbors would be complaining, except most of them were inside drinking beer and watching college football. Half-a-dozen men were sprawled on the floor, using the big pillows she and Ellie kept stacked in a corner for that purpose. Ellie walked out of the kitchen with a bowl of dip and a couple of bags of chips dangling from one hand. She smiled at Cass.

"Just in time. I'm about to run to the store for some more beer. Can you give me a ride? My car is acting up again." She tapped Manny on his shoulder. He'd staked out the couch. "Hand me a twenty, baby."

"Oh, sure." Cass knew that as soon as Ellie saw her ride it would become obvious she had news. Better to deliver it one-on-one than in this crowd. The guys yelled as a team scored. She was surprised Rowdy wasn't here, since his college team was playing. He and Manny were friends from college. That was how she'd met Ellie. Male pride had probably kept him away. He'd figure she'd be gone all weekend to that "fancy ranch" and wouldn't show up here when he would have to explain why she wasn't home.

Ellie dropped the snacks on the coffee table and grabbed the cash. Two of the other guys came up with money and orders for their favorite brands. In moments, Cass and Ellie were on their way out the door. At the bottom of the stairs her roommate stopped and put her hands on her hips.

"Now who in the hell parked in your spot, Cass? Damn, that makes me mad." She walked over, clearly about to kick the bumper.

"Stop! That's my car. My junker's AC died when I went downtown today and I decided to let it go." Cass hit the remote and the lights came on.

"Oh, baby!" Ellie ran her hand lovingly over the fender. "You're kidding me. Is this a rental? Lease? All this just to avoid a little sweat?" She opened the passenger door, careful not to bump it against her own car. "I can't believe it. Must have cost a fortune." She froze in the act of buckling her seat belt, then stared at Cass. "Holy shit. Did that lawyer thing turn legit? Are you actually coming into some money?"

"Seems like it." Cass grinned and punched the button to lower the convertible top. "There are some hoops to jump through. But, Ellie"—She grabbed her friend's hand. "I found out that I had a father all this time who wanted to do right by me. He, he owned Calhoun Petroleum."

Ellie fell back against the leather seat. "No! Who hasn't heard of them? I mean that company must be worth"—she squeezed Cass's hand—"billions!"

"It was, before the price of oil sank like a stone." Cass had already figured out that much.

"So he left you money? Cass! Tell me." Ellie sat up again. "I swear to God, girl, if you are now an oil heiress I will pee my pants."

"Not in my new car you won't." Cass laughed and accepted a hug. Finally someone was glad for her. "And it's not that simple. I have to work in the company for a year. Live with—can you believe it—my two new sisters and a brother in this huge house in town. Prove myself to a guy who'll make sure I do a good job. All of that before I'm in line to inherit part of the Calhoun money."

"Wow. I mean, this is unreal. The job. Pays good?" Ellie was studying the car. "I mean, this car just shouts top dollar. The company spring for this?"

"Yes. The salary's a lot more than I'm making now. I have to quit the bank."

"Screw the bank. A year goes by quick." Ellie bounced in her seat. "Start the car. Let's take a ride. The boys can wait for their beer. I want to hear the sound system in this baby." She hit the button for the radio as soon as Cass cranked the engine. "Satellite. I knew it."

Cass backed out. "I'll have to move out of the apartment in two weeks. I don't know what we'll do about my half of the rent."

Ellie eyed her. "How much money are we talking about at the end of this year?"

Cass knew this moment was important. She loved Ellie like a sister. Certainly more than her new sisters, who were strangers. "Three-hundred million dollars." She didn't want to see her friend's face, so she just drove, navigating out of the parking lot, which had its share of treacherous potholes.

No response. Finally, as they got on the freeway for a quick ride down to the closest discount liquor store, she couldn't stand it.

"Ellie? Say something."

"I don't know what to say. That's so much money I can't wrap my head around it." Ellie stared out the side window. "But I'm thinking. Would it be awful of me if I asked for a favor? Now and even after the year is over?"

"Why? What is it?" Cass felt her stomach turn. She'd been dreading this. Was Ellie going to want money from her? Is this how it would be? Like one of those lotto winners who had to fight off leeches coming out of the woodwork? Would everyone she knew want something from her? She saw her exit and left the freeway, then stopped at a red light. "Come on, spit it out."

"You probably thought I'd hit you up for money, didn't you?" Ellie finally looked at her.

"I don't know what to think. This is new to me. Rowdy and I are already fighting about it. We had issues before this came up. Now that I'm starting a new life, I realized I'd been drifting with him. Letting things slide when I should have . . . well, forget that for now." Cass heard a car honk and realized the light had turned green. "What do you want, Elle? After my year is over?"

"It's about your hair. I think I do a pretty good job with it." She was twisting her fingers together, a nervous habit she had.

"You do! I wish I could let you do more. Working at the bank . . ." Cass wondered where this was going. Did Ellie want her to set her up in her own salon? She did complain about the manager where she worked.

"Yeah, well, the bank's history. Not that I think you should go wild. Not when you're starting a new job." Ellie looked down, then flattened her hands on her thighs. "So here's the deal. No matter what those rich bitches tell you to do, I want you to let me keep doing your hair. Then tell them all who does it. Ellie, hair stylist to Cassidy Calhoun the oil heiress." This was framed in air quotes.

Cass laughed. "Seriously? That's what you want?"

"Well, and free rein." She grinned and grabbed one of Cass's curls that blew in wind as they entered a parking lot. "You call it conservative. I call it boring. You've had the same style for years. You need layers, my friend. And highlights. Show them you have what it takes to fit in when you go to work in that fancy office downtown."

"I can't believe all you want is to be my hair stylist." Cass parked in front of the huge discount liquor store and turned off the engine. "What about the apartment rent?"

"Manny wants to move in. I guess I'll let him." She grinned. "I do love the guy and he's coming close to offering me a ring. This may push him over the edge."

"Really? That's great!" Cass lunged across the console to give Ellie a hug. "You sure you don't want your own salon? I could do that. After my year is up."

"No way. I don't want all that responsibility. Business stuff, the things that you groove on, makes me nuts. Just let me do *my* thing and make me famous. Send some rich clients my way. Big tippers." Ellie reached for the door handle. "We'd better get the beer. That crowd gets ugly if they run out." She stopped and gave Cass a serious look. "I'm sorry about Rowdy, but I had a feeling you guys were running on fumes."

"Did he say something to Manny?" Cass knew breaking up was the right thing to do, but the timing . . .

"No, of course not. If those guys discuss more than football scores, I've never heard it. But I've got eyes and ears, girlfriend." She patted Cass's hand. "You both need to look for someone new. Someone who'll put the sparkle back in your eyes and get Rowdy off the couch and into a suit once in a while. I know a habit when I see one and that's what you two have turned into. Am I right?"

Cass sighed. "I'm afraid so. This change was coming, but it's hard for both of us. I've loved Rowdy since high school. He'll always be one of my best friends—if he doesn't come out of this hating me."

"He won't. He's one of the good guys. Like my Manny. Now come on or—" Ellie's phone chimed. "A text. Where the hell are we?" She laughed.

"Then we'd better get with it." Cass got out to help. By the time they headed back to the apartment they had a plan. Ellie had the keys to her salon and they would spend Sunday afternoon giving Cass a makeover while Manny figured out what was wrong with Ellie's car.

Cass agreed to put herself in Ellie's hands, something she'd never done before. Because Rowdy liked her hair long and natural. Well, Cass didn't have to please Rowdy now. That thought made her a little sad, but not enough to stop the makeover. They were both overdue for a change.

She ended up sitting on the other side of Manny on the couch and keeping quiet when the other team beat the stuffing out of Rowdy's alma mater. She felt bad that he missed the day with his friends. And she actually missed him when she went to bed and thought about all the good times they'd had over the years. So much history. She was going to have to reach out to him. Tomorrow.

But her text to Rowdy went unanswered. So she spent the day getting a makeover and worrying about what to wear to break the news to her boss at the bank. Manny had picked up Ellie and they were at the movies. She was about to nuke a TV dinner when the doorbell rang that evening. She peeked and saw Rowdy on the porch. Great.

"You didn't answer my text." She gasped when she saw the vase of pink roses in his arms. "What have you done?"

His eyes narrowed as he checked out her new hairdo. "What have *you* done? What's up with your hair? You cut it off to spite me?"

"Don't be ridiculous. I was ready for a change." She gestured for him to come in. Pink roses, her favorite. "Are those for me? They're beautiful."

"Yeah. I realized I was an asshole. I shouldn't have yelled at you like that." He thrust them into her arms.

"My favorite." She inhaled the sweet fragrance. "But you shouldn't have. You can't afford—"

"Don't say it, Cassidy." He frowned. "Seriously. Are we going to let money come between us?"

"I didn't mean . . ." What could she say to him that wouldn't hurt his pride? "Look. They're lovely. Thank you." She set the vase on the coffee table. "We obviously need to talk."

"You know how much I hate those words?" He dropped down on the couch. "Sit here and hit me with it." He patted the seat beside him. "You spent the weekend with the billionaire. Did you get your head turned? You want that kind of life now? Fancy ranches, cars, money to burn?"

"You're jumping to all kinds of conclusions, Rowdy." Cass sat but left some room between them. "Mason's a nice guy. His family is nice too. You'd never know they were rich, if you could hang out with them."

"Not likely, is it? I'm a working guy. I don't run with that crowd. But you'll be part of it from now on." He leaned forward, his elbows on his knees. "Check you out, changing already. You look—what's the word—oh yeah: *sophisticated*."

"Ellie did this. She wanted me to update my appearance and I was ready for it." Cass touched her short and tamed hair self-consciously. "I like it. Don't you?"

"You don't look like yourself. Not like my girl anymore." He ran a thumb over her cheek. "And what's with all the makeup? I like you natural. You're beautiful without all that stuff."

"We were playing at the salon. Got a little carried away, I guess." Cass took his hand. "Honestly, Rowdy, I'm not fifteen. I should have done something with my hair a long time ago. And you're crazy if you think I don't put on makeup every day."

"Okay. Fine. You want to look nice for the Calhouns. Fit in. I get it. But I'm also getting the message that you want me to give you space. That you need time to figure out this new life." His hand landed back on his knee. "That's what you said on the phone."

"I know. I didn't think you heard me." Cass sighed. Here it came. Did she really want Rowdy to back off? To leave her so she could navigate her way through this minefield that was ahead of her alone? He'd been her rock for, oh God, fifteen years!

"Trust me, I heard you all right. I just didn't want to understand what you were saying." He skimmed a finger across one of her carefully painted lips, then looked down at his pink finger. "This is where you're supposed to say you didn't mean it. Throw yourself at me and say you're sorry." He smiled. "But I'm not stupid. This break was inevitable, wasn't it? I've known it for a few months now. You've been busy, I've been busy." He shrugged. "I guess we could work on this, but maybe that's not what you want."

Cass felt tears prick her eyelids. "I *am* sorry. But . . ." Part of her needed to cut him loose or she'd have to start lying to him. Next he'd be asking about Mason. What could she say? That they were just friends, hanging out? But then there'd been those kisses. And, damn her, but she knew she'd kiss Mason again if he looked at her just right. Shoot, Rowdy was staring at her and seeing way too much.

"I get it." Rowdy stood. "I'll always be your best friend, Cassie." His eyes swept the room like he was telling it good-bye. "Call me when you're ready to move. I figure Manny and I can take whatever you need in the back of my pickup. Unless that's too tacky for the River Oaks crowd. Wouldn't want to embarrass you."

"You could never do that. I'd appreciate it." Cass followed him to the door. "Is this it? Are we really breaking up?"

"That's up to you. I told you. I love you. But I won't stand in your way if being Conrad Calhoun's daughter gives you opportunities you never had before." Rowdy suddenly pulled her into his arms. "Shit. I don't want to lose you. Baby, I can't imagine life without you. But I'd be a selfish bastard if I held you back. I know that." He looked into her eyes and cleared his throat. "Kiss me good-bye and make it a good one."

"Rowdy." Her voice broke, so she just stretched up to touch her lips to his. His mouth opened and they shared a long, desperate kiss that only ended when he wrenched open the door and stepped outside, closing it behind him.

Cass leaned against it. He was really gone. Of course she loved him. He was a good man and what he'd just done proved it. He'd given her freedom. It was the right thing to do, but damn, did it feel lonely.

Cass sat at her desk in the bank and stalled for a good half hour before she finally headed to the president's office to tell him her news. She had decided not to share the details, just say that she'd had an offer for a new job with Calhoun Petroleum.

"Are you crazy? Don't you read the newspaper? Listen to the news? The oil business is laying off people left and right. That's a stupid move in this economy, Cassidy." Jim Raymond almost jumped out of his chair. He restrained himself at the last minute. "If this is a ploy for a raise, your timing is poor. I've just been told by corporate to lay off two people here."

"It's not about money, Jim." Cass fidgeted with her skirt. In the back of her mind, there was the chance, just a chance, that at the end of the year she might have to go back to banking. This man would be her reference. She needed his good opinion when she left here. She was going to have to tell him the rest, or at least part of it, because she wasn't going to have anyone think going to Calhoun was a stupid move.

"Well, what is it, Cassidy?" He leaned forward, staring at her as if trying to read her mind.

Cass smoothed her skirt over her knees. "I just found out I'm related to Conrad Calhoun. I have to work at the company to gain an inheritance."

"You're kidding. What do you mean, you found out? Didn't you know you were part of the oil Calhouns before?" Jim's eyes narrowed and he typed something into his desktop computer. "The net worth of that company is in the billions, Cassidy."

"Yes, I know. But I grew up without any idea I had a connection to the family. My mother never told me that Conrad was . . ."

"Was what?" Jim hadn't risen to president by being stupid. "Cassidy?"

"My father." Cass raised her chin. "I found out on Friday that he was my father and that he named me in his will."

Jim fell back in his chair. "I see." He rocked for a moment. "Named in the will of a billionaire. You don't hear that every day." He leaned forward and tapped on that computer again. "No chance you'd be bringing money to us. First Capital has that account sewn up nicely." He threw down his reading glasses. "No wonder you're quitting. Have to say, it's been nice knowing you, Cassidy." He stood and walked around the desk, his hand outstretched. "You remember who treated you well here, Cassidy. First Capital is a big bank, impersonal." He smiled and patted her shoulder. "If you do decide to bank with us in the future, you know we'll always give you the best service possible. Blue-chip service as a valued customer."

Cass jumped to her feet. "Sure, Jim. You always treated me fairly. I won't forget it. But I wasn't planning on leaving just yet. I thought I was giving you my two weeks' notice."

"Don't be silly. Why would a woman about to come into millions, maybe billions, work another minute in this little bank? And you've solved one problem for me, haven't you?" He wagged a playful finger in her face. "I know you've figured that out already, clever girl. Now I'll only have to lay off one person."

"Yes, I guess that's a good thing." Cass shook his hand and let him lead her to his door. Clearly he was already trying to decide who was going to get the ax.

"Of course it is. Now you run clear out your desk." Jim was already snatching up those readers and picking up a file folder. "Yes, this will work out perfectly. Paula can slide right into your position. She doesn't have your educational background, so I won't have to give her your title or your money, just your responsibilities." He was openly grinning now. "Love how it's coming together. Corporate is going to be happy. Saving money. A win for the bank."

"You want me to leave today? Shouldn't I train her?" Cass knew she'd said the wrong thing when he frowned and tossed down his glasses again.

"Why waste time? I'm sure you're eager to move on to your new life and Paula will land on her feet. She's been hankering for your job for some time now." Jim tapped the papers in front of him. "I'll have to keep an eye on her, sure. But she's competent enough. Not you, of course." He laughed heartily and waved her toward the door. "Go. Let us know how you do. Calhoun Petroleum." He shook his head. "You're a very lucky girl." He punched a button on his phone. "Hope you don't mind if we skip the going-away party. Budget concerns." He picked up the receiver. "Darryl, find a box for Cassidy. She's leaving us for big things. Big things. And ask Paula to come in here." He hung up. "Bye now. Shut the door behind you, would you? I've got to call corporate. This news does change a few things."

"What's going on, Cassidy?" Darryl the teller met her outside the office with an empty paper box.

"I'm leaving. Got a job downtown." Cass saw Paula head into the president's office. The woman would be over the moon when she got the news. Word spread fast and Cass was ambushed when she went to the break room to get her personal coffee cup.

"What the hell, Cass? What new job? And why are you leaving so quickly?" Angela, one of her good friends at the bank, appeared with her own coffee cup. "Tell."

"It's complicated. Jim told me to go today. Not to bother working two weeks more like I planned when I gave my notice." Cass stared down at her stained and chipped cup and decided to toss it. "He said there are going to be layoffs here, so I saved someone's job."

"Oh, my God! Did he say who was going?" Angela was a single mom with a five-year-old.

"Just that Paula was taking over my job." Cass realized she was forgotten as Angela rushed out of the break room. Of course self-preservation had to trump friendship. She did stop to say good-bye to a few other people on her way out the door. Paula got to her before she could leave.

"Dumping us for better things? Jim said you just found out you're one of the oil-rich Calhouns." She nodded toward the red convertible. "That your new car?"

Cass smiled. "Leased. Congratulations on the promotion, Paula."

"Some promotion. I get your workload but not the raise or the title." Paula pushed open the door, hot air hitting them both. She nodded, as if encouraging Cass to go ahead and leave.

"I'm sure you'll get them soon. Jim's facing budget cuts right now." Cass shifted her box. Not that it was heavy. There wasn't much in it. "Maybe if you finally went back to school . . ."

"You and your fancy degrees. I don't want to hear it. You always thought you were so smart. Well, I can do the job without all of that education and Jim knows it." She turned when she heard her name called. "Coming, Jim. Just telling Cassidy good-bye." Her bright smile was so fake, Cass wanted to punch it.

"Good luck, Paula. Call me if you need help." Cass pasted on her own smile.

"Not likely. Just watch yourself, Cassidy. The way oil's going, I won't be surprised if you end up back here someday, begging for your job back." Paula let the door shut in Cass's face.

By the time Cass got to her car, she was fully depressed. A glance at the clock there made it even worse. She was out of work with nothing to do and it was only 9:45 in the morning. A look back at the bank showed her that Paula was staring at her through the glass. The woman had good reason to be upset. More work and no raise or title bump. But blaming the person leaving hadn't been smart. One thing Cass had learned in business was not to burn her bridges. Paula needed to remember that. If Cass did end up back here someday, guess who'd slide right in above Paula, thanks to that education?

Oh, well, as Ellie had said, screw the bank. Time to look ahead. Cass had always relied on her own hard work to get her what she wanted. This inheritance was a crazy possibility that she still couldn't quite believe. And Paula's dire prediction about oil had a ring of truth—and echoed what she'd been hearing from everyone since this all started. Cass needed to learn as much as she could about the oil business.

* * *

"I learned a lesson today." Cass was going through her clothes. Some she wouldn't bother taking to the new place. There was a donate pile and a toss pile of clothes. Her rich sisters would probably toss them all.

"What was that, Cass?" Ellie sat on the end of the bed. She examined everything Cass threw into the donate pile and had started a stack for herself.

"I worked hard at that bank. Killed myself getting my MBA so I could get promoted and you know what?" Cass collapsed next to Ellie, the bitter truth of what she'd figured out making her madder at herself than at the system. No, maybe both.

"What?" Ellie frowned at a sparkly tank top. "Why are you getting rid of this? It's cute."

"Too low-cut. I look trashy in it and desperate." Cass realized she was wasting her breath talking to Ellie about this. Her roommate worked in an entirely different environment. She complained about bitchiness at her beauty salon, but it seemed more out in the open, not hidden behind the polite smiles of the banking world.

"Put it on." Ellie wasn't taking *no* for an answer.

"Fine. But you have to promise to listen to my epiphany." Cass pulled off her T-shirt and tugged the sequined tank over her head. She stood in front of the mirror. Okay, so maybe *trashy* had been too harsh. The silver made her eyes sparkle, especially with the new haircut and highlights. And displaying cleavage did show her figure off to advantage. With the shorts she had on, she looked ready for one of Ethan's pool parties.

"Cute. And you've never looked desperate in your life." Ellie nodded. "That's a keep. Now what happened at the bank?"

"They're giving my job to someone who is totally underqualified. They'll train her on the fly and she'll probably do okay because she's smart." Cass took a breath. "I could have saved myself all that time and money if . . . Never mind. Things have changed since I started. The economy has made budget cuts necessary and my MBA became a liability because it meant I expected more in salary."

"Well, you won't have to worry about that anymore. Your name got you *this* job." Ellie jumped up when Cass frowned. "Whew. Saved by the doorbell. Don't hit me. I'm just telling the truth."

"I know. And that's what the people at Calhoun will hate me for."

"Don't stress over it. I've known you for years. Epiphany or not, you'll work your butt off because that's who you are. And didn't you say that Mason guy is going to be evaluating your performance? So you'll make sure he's as impressed as hell."

The doorbell rang again. Cass followed Ellie to the door. "Everyone else we know is at work today, so who could it be?"

"Maybe Rowdy is sending you more flowers." Ellie grinned. "He's changed his mind and wants you back already."

"Don't start. I'm sad but a little relieved. I think we both needed this break. Are we a habit or forever? Sometimes I wondered that even before this will thing came up. Even Rowdy all but admitted it at the end." Cass waited while Ellie looked through the peephole before she opened the door. Her roommate's salon was closed on Mondays and everyone else they knew was at work. It made the apartment complex a ghost town.

"Hello, handsome." Ellie turned to Cass. "Peek out there and tell me if you recognize this guy."

Cass put her eye to the peephole. "Oh, it's Mason."

"Cass, are you in there?" He leaned on the doorbell. "I come bearing gifts." He waved two brown envelopes in his hand.

Cass unlocked the door and threw it open. "Hi. Come in." She smiled. "Gifts?"

"You'll see." Mason grinned at Ellie and held out his hand, introducing himself. "Is this your roommate?"

"Eleanora Rodriguez or Elle, hairdresser to the rich and famous." Ellie nudged Cass. "Come. Sit down. Tell us about the gifts."

"One for each of you." Mason handed Cass one of the envelopes. "Money to compensate you for the moving expenses. Ellie, you have a check for the rent Cass would have been paying until the end of your lease."

"Wow, thanks a lot." Ellie tore into her envelope. "This takes care of some concerns. I think I'll just take off and go deposit this right now. Excuse me, you two? Nice to meet you, Mason." She grabbed her purse and was out the door before Cass could stop her.

"Not subtle, is she?" Cass laughed and pulled out her own check. "I have to echo her *wow*. The estate is pretty generous with my father's money. You realize all my stuff will fit into the back of a pickup truck?"

"No need to tell them that." Mason glanced around the room.

"You want to go somewhere for lunch? They said at the bank that you quit and you're done there. No two weeks' notice, I guess."

"Nope." Cass looked down at her sparkly top. Mason looked yummy in his black business suit, white shirt, and red tie. "Let me change into something less comfortable and I'd love lunch. Could we do something after that?"

"Don't change. I love your outfit. You look like you want to go dancing. Turn on the radio and I'll show you some of my moves." He seemed to glide closer. "How's that for something?" He gave her one of his hot looks and Cass shoved him back.

"I want to see Calhoun Petroleum. The offices. Maybe you could take me there, show me around?" She smiled at his exaggerated crestfallen look.

"There goes my dream of an afternoon delight." He toyed with the thin strap of the tank top. "At least for now." He let his finger trace the edge until Cass grabbed it.

"I'll be right back. Check the refrigerator if you're thirsty. I'll hurry."

"I'm taking off my tie. Don't get too formal. You're not on the Calhoun payroll yet," Mason yelled as Cass shut the door.

She leaned against it and fanned her face. Just being in the same room with him, his finger on her skin . . . Enough. She needed to focus on her future and learning the business was priority one. She threw on the dress and jacket she'd worn just that morning and slipped on her navy pumps. It was a boring outfit, but professional. The white jacket was cool and crisp and the dress was a navy-and-white print that had held up well over several seasons. By the time she'd checked her makeup and run a brush through her hair, Cass realized she'd made him wait fifteen minutes. When she stepped into the living room she found Mason on the couch, sound asleep.

She grabbed a bottle of water out of the refrigerator and sat down beside him. Why was he so tired? Late nights? Working or playing? She dug her phone out of her purse and spent a few minutes checking her email. Finally, his phone buzzed and he woke suddenly to pull it out of his pocket.

"MacKenzie." He listened for a few minutes. "Yes, tell him I'll have to see him later. I'm in a business meeting. That's right. Don't disturb me until about four." He ended the call, then turned to Cass. "I fell asleep. Sorry."

"You were obviously exhausted." Cass stuck her own phone in her purse. "We can cancel if you need to be somewhere else."

"No, I'm all yours." Mason grabbed her water bottle and drained it. "Late nights have caught up with me. Problems with oil rigs, money, you name it. But it's all good. A power nap always does the trick." He yawned, then got to his feet. "Now, last time I took you for seafood. How do you feel about steak?"

"Love it." Cass let him talk and do his thing guiding her as they left the apartment and got into a black sports car. "Not your truck?"

"No. I think you figured out when I talked to Tommy about that Lotus that I like fast cars. This is mine." Mason helped her climb into the low-slung car with a prancing horse on the front. He leaned over her and touched her earlobe with its simple pearl earring. "Like the new hairdo. You look hot." Then he slammed the car door and walked around the car, whistling. He turned out to be a car collector like her father had been. He drove them into Houston, telling her about car auctions that he'd attended with Conrad. They ended up at a nice restaurant near the baseball park downtown and he explained that both Texas Star and Calhoun had season tickets for the Astros games.

"You know some of those perks are going to have to be trimmed if oil keeps dropping in price," Mason said after they ordered steaks and salads. "You sure you don't want a glass of wine with lunch?"

"Then I'd be the one falling asleep." Cass gazed around the paneled room. The tables were covered with white clothes and there were waiters hovering nearby. The prices on the menu were ridiculous. It made Rowdy's comments about high living echo in her head. Their own dinner dates were usually pizza and beer. Lunch was a drive-through burger and fries.

"Tell me more about what I'll be facing at Calhoun." She kept her hands in her lap, determined to keep this a business lunch.

"You'll see soon enough. Connie put you in the accounting department. The numbers will speak for themselves. My mother mentioned the royalties going down. That's the bottom line. Income from drilling is suffering as we shut down more wells. The rig count is the lowest it's ever been. Oil companies have lines of credit with banks and they help us stay afloat. You know a lot about credit, I'm sure."

"It was something I dealt with every day." Cass felt confident about her banking knowledge.

"Well, rumor has it that Calhoun's credit rating is about to be downgraded." Mason shifted his silverware around. "The one at Texas Star too."

"That's serious, Mason. If the cost of borrowing money goes up, you could get into a real bind if you need new equipment or if you have a disaster like an oil spill that needs a cash outlay." Cass reached out to him, not even thinking about it.

"Listen to you, getting the hang of it already." Mason covered her hand with his. "It's damned serious. That's why I'm always on the run, burning the midnight oil, so to speak, to try to keep the company afloat. There have to be people at Calhoun doing the same thing."

"I wonder who they are." Cass turned her hand over and let him hold it. She realized that while she could crunch numbers all day long, she'd have no idea what those numbers meant at Calhoun. It was terrifying. She knew mortgages and loans—but oil? She was afraid she was going to be totally lost in this new job.

"You'll have to find out." Mason squeezed her fingers. "And I have to warn you. Other companies have been poaching your best people since Connie died. It's what happens. Connie was a control freak who liked to handle the reins himself. There's a power vacuum at Calhoun and that's the perfect time for someone to come in and scoop up the company at a bargain price."

"Someone like you, Mason?" Cass pulled her hand back into her lap. "Don't think that hasn't occurred to me."

"It could be me. But Texas Star is drowning in debt right now. My own holdings are suffering and I'm not sure I could get the money together to make a run on Calhoun. If it was even a safe bet." Mason smiled as the waiter set their salads down in front of them. "How's that for honesty?"

"I appreciate it." Cass picked up her fork. "Obviously my sisters and brother won't be much help with this either."

"No, they won't. They don't have clue one about what's going on with the company." Mason picked up his glass of iced tea and took a swallow. "After lunch we'll go over to Calhoun and try to find someone who can help you. Let's hope we're successful."

Cass picked up her water. "I'll drink to that." But when she tried to swallow, she had trouble doing it. Mason acted open and above-board. But was he really? They ate lunch and chatted about local happenings. But the flirting, the banter, was just a little too easy. Men like

Mason, powerful men who moved in circles that included billionaires and sports stars like the one who stopped by the table and did a fist bump with him, didn't go for women like Cassidy Calhoun.

And if she didn't figure out a way to keep this company in the black over this next year she could end up right back where she started. Only in worse shape. Because, while Rowdy would mock it, lunches like this and riding in fancy cars with good air-conditioning was a lifestyle she would hate to give up, now that she was experiencing it. She cut into the sinfully tender steak and decided to live for the moment. Because she couldn't see the future at all.

Chapter 8

The offices at Calhoun Petroleum were busy. Cass took that as a good sign. The company leased a good chunk of a high-rise in downtown Houston. She didn't want to think what the overhead might be.

"Accounting occupies all of the twenty-third floor, according to the person I talked to," Mason said. "There's the head honcho's office." He pointed to where a woman held court in front of a suite of offices. He pushed open the glass door.

"May I help you?" The woman smiled.

"We'd like to see your boss, John Hardcastle." Mason didn't give Cass a chance to say anything.

The woman hit some keys on her computer and frowned. "He doesn't have any appointments scheduled and doesn't want to be disturbed. Can I set you up for later in the week? If you'll give me your name . . ." She smiled to take the sting out.

"I'm Cassidy Calhoun, Conrad's daughter." Cass gave Mason a look when he tried to take over again. He just smiled and stepped back. "This is Mason MacKenzie. We'd really like to see Mr. Hardcastle today."

The woman jumped to her feet. "Oh, sorry if I was rude. It's just that he's running numbers." She shook hands with both of them. "Glad to meet you. I'm Holly Rogers, Mr. Hardcastle's assistant. Let me see if he can be disturbed. I know he's looking forward to working with you, Ms. Calhoun." The woman hurried over to a door with a name on it in gold. "He doesn't like me to call him on the phone. Give me a minute. I have to stand there until he's ready to look up." She quietly tapped on the door, then stepped inside.

"He's got her well-trained. There's nothing worse than being interrupted when you're concentrating on a long string of numbers." Cass shook her head. "At the bank it was impossible to finish anything without someone butting in at just the wrong time."

"Here he comes." Mason leaned in. "John Hardcastle. He's the CFO."

"Ms. Calhoun. Didn't expect you so soon." He held out his hand. "And Mr. MacKenzie. This is a surprise." He raised an eyebrow. "Am I to understand that you'll have access to our financials here at Calhoun as well? As chief financial officer here, I have to say I'm reluctant to put certain facts into the hands of one of our biggest competitors."

"Of course. No need to worry about that. I'm only here to evaluate the performances of the Calhoun heirs. I'll trust you to keep me informed of Cassidy's progress." Mason had on his best professional smile. "I won't have to see the nuts and bolts of your operation."

"That's a relief." The man waved them into his office. He was middle-aged with salt-and-pepper hair and well dressed in a gray suit with a white shirt and striped tie. Cass thought of it as an accountant's uniform. He had the serious and solid look of a man who knew his business. "Come in, sit for a minute. Holly can fetch us some coffee or water."

"Not necessary, but thanks. We just had a big lunch." Cass waited until the assistant had shut the door. "I wanted to meet you and let you know I'm ready to go to work whenever you need me." She settled into the chair he indicated in front of his desk. Behind him there was a wall of windows with a breathtaking view of downtown Houston. "I gave my notice at my former job and they were kind enough to release me right away."

Hardcastle leaned back in his chair. "The bank where you worked. Layoffs looming there?"

"Afraid so." Cass glanced at Mason. He was letting her handle this and she appreciated it. "So about that starting date . . ."

"Of course. Next week will be fine. I've even got some homework for you. So you can hit the ground running, so to speak. The lawyer—I believe he's your brother, Mr. MacKenzie—sent over your résumé." Hardcastle punched in some keys on his desktop keyboard. "I have to say it was a relief to see your background." He smiled. "So I'm giving you an important task to start with. One you should be able to handle easily."

"Thank you. I want to be useful. Prove myself and help Calhoun stay afloat in these tough economic times." Cass leaned forward. "What do you have in mind?"

Hardcastle got up and walked over to a stack of file folders. "These *are* tough economic times. So we need to cut expenses. Income is down, thanks to the price of oil." He nodded to Mason. "I'm sure Mr. MacKenzie has explained how this business works."

"She's getting the hang of it." Mason didn't smile and Cass had the feeling he was not happy about what was happening here. "Would you like me to leave before you tell Cass about this assignment?"

"No, I don't think it's a secret that we're laying off people. I'm sure Texas Star is doing the same." Hardcastle waited until Mason nodded. "Just as I thought. No surprise, then, that our department is one of the places where we have to make cuts. We have thirty-six people on the payroll here. Yes, we have a lot of accounting to do, but we'll just have to consolidate the workload." He picked up the folders and handed them to Cass.

"What's this?" She was terribly afraid she already knew. Her stomach cramped and she regretted that big lunch.

"Personnel files for all the people we've got working here in accounting—except for you and me, of course." He finally smiled. "Those files have everything you'll need to know—performance reviews, salary, and background." He quit smiling and strolled back around his desk. "It'll be up to you to cut that number by a third. I don't have to tell you that the generous salary your late father arranged for you made sure two of the low men or women on the totem pole had to go."

"Oh, no!" Cass dropped the heavy folders onto her lap. She was a numbers person. To have to ruin people's lives . . .

"Not your fault, Cass." Mason frowned. "You sure this should be her first assignment, Hardcastle?"

"Trial by fire, MacKenzie." The man leaned back again. "She can prove herself here right away. I'd like to say there was another way to cut the budget in this department, but I simply can't see how. People will have to go." He tapped a few keys on his computer. "Once you're working here, Cassidy, maybe you can find other ways to save money. But for now, layoffs will improve our bottom line. Of course, I can give this to someone else if you don't have the stomach for it." He quit typing and leaned back, steepling his fingers as he studied her.

Cass noticed she'd already dropped to a first-name basis. The stomach for ruining people's lives? She'd rather sit at a desk and run numbers. Count money or paper clips. Both Mason and Hardcastle were waiting for her to admit she didn't want to do this. That she wasn't up for the job. Her new boss would probably gloat and pass word to his cronies in upper management that Conrad Calhoun's daughter was nothing like him. She was weak and bound to fail. He probably couldn't wait to see her in tears after she had to conduct her first exit interview.

She sucked it up and thought for the first time: *What would my father do?* She stood, hugging the folders against her chest.

"No need to pass this on, John. I'll get right on it. See you early Monday. I'll start working full-time then and bring you the list of people who must go." She swept her gaze around the room, then let it linger on his massive desk and that incredible view behind it. "I hope my office is as nice as this." She raised the chin everyone said was just like Conrad's. "I know my daddy would have expected it." She turned to Mason. "Ready to go?"

"By all means." He took her elbow. "I expect a fair report, Hardcastle, on Ms. Calhoun's performance. And you won't be the only source of my information, of course." He walked over to the door, which Cass had already opened for herself.

She turned back to Hardcastle. "I like Holly. I hope you assign an assistant like her to me. Or I'll take her." Cass walked through the door.

When she and Mason were in the elevator and the doors closed, Cass smiled. She'd done it. Faced off against a man who was clearly a bully. Then it hit her. Was she crazy spouting off to her new boss like that? She knew how business worked. Her evaluator stood right beside her. Hardcastle could decide that nothing she did from here on out was worth a damn, no matter how hard she tried. Her hands were shaking when she wiped a sweaty palm on her skirt.

"What do you think, Mason? Did I blow it with Hardcastle? Playing the daddy card?"

"Not at all. You handled him perfectly. He was sizing you up and hoping he could run you off and not have to deal with you." Mason squeezed her shoulders. "Look at the job he gave you. He wants you to go down in flames and make enemies."

"I hate to lay off people." Cass fingered the file folders. There were three dozen of them. These were people, with families to support. Losing their jobs would be devastating.

"It's something that we all have to do now. He was right about that." Mason punched the button for the parking garage below them and the elevator lurched into action. "I was proud of you. You set Hardcastle straight that you won't be intimidated."

"It was pure bluff." Cass sighed and moved away from Mason. "He was right about one thing. You can't be privy to any company secrets. Our financials have to stay in-house."

"Of course." Mason took her elbow and guided her out as the elevator stopped on their floor. "But wouldn't it be fun if I tried to pry secrets out of you?" He stopped next to his car and trapped her against the hard metal. "Can you resist me, Cassidy? When I do this?" He nibbled her neck where her new short hairstyle exposed her throat. "Or this?" He slid his hands up her rib cage, under her jacket and just close enough to her aching breasts to make her want to lean in to them.

"I'll never share company secrets with you." Cass's voice sounded throaty and she cleared it, faking a laugh. "You wouldn't try that, would you? My father trusted you."

"Maybe he was a fool." Mason kissed along her jawline. "Or maybe I'm just desperate enough in these hard economic times to do something out of character."

"Stop it, Mason." Cass pushed him back. "People will see." She remembered to look around when she heard the elevator chime. Sure enough, it must be time for a shift change because there were a half-dozen women getting off the elevator, Holly among them. She waved at Cass, then turned to say something to her friends. They all turned to look.

"Now you've done it. Secretaries and assistants have a pipeline. It'll be all over the company tomorrow that I'm involved with a MacKenzie." Cass reached behind her and tried to open the car door. It was locked, of course. "Open the door, Mason."

He hit the fob and the car unlocked. "I like the idea that they'll think you're off-limits."

"But it's not true." Cass slid into the car. "I'm not taken, involved. Any of that. For the first time in a long while, I'm free as a bird." She smiled up at him, then grabbed the handle and slammed the door shut in his handsome face. Wow. It was true.

The group of women next to the elevator dispersed, but more than one of them gave Mason a long look as he strode around the car. Of course he was look-worthy. Tall, good-looking, sexy as hell, and rich. Hmm. There was a Taylor Swift song in there, wasn't there? No matter. He got in the car and just grinned at her, in a good mood as he started the car with a roar. He thought she was announcing she was available for *him*. Huh. Was she? She looked down at the folders in her lap. It seemed wrong to even think about something as frivolous as an affair when she was about to ruin lives.

When he stopped to pay the parking attendant, Mason reached over and touched her cheek. "Don't take this hatchet job personally, Cass. As they say, you'll just be the messenger."

"Yeah. But sometimes the messenger bears all the blame and takes the shots." She leaned back, hating how true that was.

The helicopter swooped low over the choppy waters of the Gulf of Mexico.

If Mason didn't know better, he'd think the pilot was testing him when he did a 360 around Big Tex to give his passenger a good look at the deepwater oil rig before he landed. You'd have to waterboard Mason before he'd confess heights scared the shit out of him. So he studied the giant structure below them like it was just another day at the office and hoped to hell he didn't puke.

"Aw, man, that doesn't look good." The pilot hovered over the helipad before landing. "The thing's not level."

"I know. That's why I had to come out here. Wait for me. Shouldn't be here long. They're already working on a fix." Mason unlatched his seat belt as soon as the engines cut off. One of the men on the ground pulled open the door.

"Glad to see you, Mason. We're pumping as fast as we can, but you can see we're still not plumb. Thanks for coming out." Deke Rawlins, the head man on the rig, clasped his hand as soon as Mason's feet landed on the pad. "I wouldn't have bothered you if I could have gotten satisfaction from anyone else at Texas Star."

"I promised you when you took this job that I'd have your back and I will." Mason looked around and judged the rig was listing at about a 20-degree angle. Holy shit. "You say there's a crack in the ballast tank?"

"Yeah. Must have happened after that big blow a few weeks ago. We've already got it repaired but we have to pump until the rig is stabilized." Deke led Mason to the building where he had his headquarters. It wasn't an easy walk with the wind whipping up and the odd tilt.

"Evacuating for Hurricane Clarice cost us a pretty penny. Now this." Mason was glad when they were inside and he could finally hear himself think. His mind was running numbers and none of them were good.

"Fucking weathermen. Screaming dire predictions so we'd evacuate when we really could have sat it out right here." Deke motioned Mason to a chair in front of a computer monitor. "Let me show you what's going on. We've lowered extra cameras down there. Did it as soon as we got back and saw Big Tex wasn't right."

"So tell me first. What is it now?" Mason put on his game face. He'd been so proud that they were majority stakeholders in this rig. No oil company could afford to put one out here on their own but, with partners, Texas Star had managed to get together 1.5 billion dollars from investors and it had just begun to pay off when the price of oil dropped. They sure didn't need any problems right now. It was barely cost-effective to keep the deepwater wells pumping. He listened intently and watched the screen as Deke walked him through the technical issues. The first part was being handled and he started to relax. But it soon became clear that the news wasn't all good.

"During repairs we realized the welds on the pipes down there are bad. None of them should have passed inspection. They'll all have to be done over. If a real hurricane hits, we could have a rupture and an oil spill that could cost more money than I want to think about." Deke hit a button and the camera zoomed in on where one pipe joined another. "And don't get me started about the environmental issues."

"You're kidding me." Mason clenched and unclenched his fists. "Who was the inspector, Deke?"

"Take a guess." Deke got up from his chair and put some space between himself and his boss. "I didn't like it, but I had no choice. Your uncle sent Bailey out here. He was drunk most of the time and had an assistant do what passed for work on the job." Deke must have seen murder in Mason's eyes. "I'm just the messenger, Mason. Got the paperwork that says we passed, that's all I needed."

Mason took a calming breath. The helicopter was waiting and it was a rental. Cost cuts meant he'd had to sell the one with the company logo. The jet was next. Now wasting money here when he had a shit ton of expenses staring him in the face already . . . One more snafu and he'd have to make a hard call and shut the rig down completely. He'd already put out feelers about a shutdown with the partners. Their screams had made his ears ring. He knew Ed was going to blow a gasket.

"Call the welders. Get started on it right away." Underwater welding. More big bucks.

Deke sank down into a chair. "You authorizing the expense? Your uncle wouldn't even talk to me about it."

"Do it. Call me directly from now on. Ed's my problem." Mason got up and headed for the door. "Use an inspector you trust this time. Not Bailey." Bailey was Ed's buddy, a good old boy. Mason suspected he was paid to overlook anything that might cost the company extra. Mason should have put a stop to it years ago, but hadn't wanted to deal with the fallout from Ed over it. Now they were paying the price.

"If it was up to me I never would have let Bailey on this rig." Deke walked him out. "You have my sympathy, working for an asshole like Ed MacKenzie."

"Yeah, well. I've had it with his shit." Mason frowned at the angle of the rig. "You feel this is safe now? As it is? Or should we evacuate again?" Mason signaled and the pilot started the engine.

"We're okay. We've got the generators going twenty-four-seven for electricity and such. But we can't start pumping oil until we're right."

"Of course." Mason clasped Deke's hand. "Burning fuel, not drilling it. But that's what happens when you cut corners. Sending Bailey out here! I fucking want to kill Ed for this." He turned and ducked under the helicopter blades. Damn it all to hell. Just one more example of why he needed out from under his uncle's thumb. If he could only buy Ed out before Texas Star landed in bankruptcy court. He watched the rig disappear over the horizon while he gripped the armrests. Not showing fear.

"There's a beer in the cooler near your feet, Mr. MacKenzie. Help yourself." The pilot was frowning and listening to someone on his headset.

"I hope to hell you haven't been drinking this." Mason pulled out a cold one and popped the top.

"No, sir. That's for the customers." The pilot nodded. "There's some weather ahead. Hang on. It's going to get rough."

More weather? Just what they needed. Mason took a deep swallow and counted how many of the rigs below them were idle. Storm damage on some, but he'd heard their competitors were shutting down and there was the proof. Drilling wasn't cost-effective right now. He pulled his tablet out of the bag next to his feet and started a search. It would take his mind off his queasy stomach and help him figure out what to do about their own rig. Maybe if they'd just trimmed the size of the crew . . . Layoffs. Too bad he always thought about the people that effected. He took another swallow of beer as the helicopter dipped suddenly in the wind.

"Sorry, Mr. MacKenzie. It's going to be like this until we get to Houston." The pilot had both hands gripping the controls.

Mason put away the tablet and finished the beer. He hoped he didn't lose it all over his shoes as his stomach lurched. *Think about something else.*

Cassidy. Their lunch had lasted hours. He'd found himself spilling his guts to her, concerns about his business he never would have shared on a date. Because he'd always kept his social life separate from the grind of business. But she'd understood, listened, and even helped him clarify some things in his head. She'd looked at him with those big eyes and he'd found himself wanting to kiss her again.

By the time they'd hit Calhoun headquarters, he'd been determined to make sure she was treated right there. But that asshole Hardcastle had stuck her with layoffs and Mason couldn't do a damned thing about it. A Calhoun coming in with a new job—as a VP, no less—was enough to make anyone resent her and her boss clearly wasn't immune to that resentment. Cass was going to have an uphill battle trying to survive the year there without making serious enemies.

Mason was coming to hate the oil business. It would take a damned miracle for Cass or any of those Calhouns to come out of the next year with more than pin money. He'd like to fix that, but Mason wondered if he'd end up any better off than the Calhouns if Big Tex had to be mothballed. They hit a really bad air pocket and the seat belt dug into his belly. Shit. Maybe he'd be better off tending cows on Sierra's ranch anyway.

Chapter 9

It was raining on moving day. Cass hadn't had any luck getting hold of Mason. He'd left a voice mail that he was tied up in a series of business emergencies. But she'd talked to Janie at the house and she'd said Cass could move in whenever she was ready. Saturday was best for Rowdy and Manny. Of course, Ellie was dying to see the mansion too, but Saturday was her busy day at the beauty salon. She pouted about it, but understood as they loaded the back of the truck and threw a waterproof tarp over everything.

Cass gave Rowdy directions and he followed her in the truck. The closer they got to the big house, the more nervous she felt. She'd thought about telling him to forget it. That she'd hire movers to take her stuff. But she knew he wouldn't have taken that well. His pride was really bruised and she hadn't even told him about the big check she'd received for expenses. She didn't dare offer to reimburse him for gas. Manny had no problem with her offer to buy them lunch afterwards. Of course, he'd been filled in by Ellie about her windfall, then sworn to secrecy.

There wasn't much to move when all was said and done. Clothes, of course; her TV and DVD player that she'd used in her bedroom, and her personal stereo. A few mementos and photos. It was pitiful, actually, since she'd decided to leave her furniture in her old bedroom. Obviously she wouldn't need it in that freakish master suite.

She pulled in under the overhang, then eased forward so Rowdy's truck would be protected from the rain when they unloaded.

"You weren't kidding. This place *is* a mansion." Rowdy got out of the truck and pocketed his keys.

"Didn't you land in the honey pot, *chica*." Manny grabbed Cass and twirled her around. "I'm happy for you."

"Thanks, Manny." Cass laughed and ran up the steps to ring the bell. "I have a key but I want to alert the housekeeper we're here." The door flew open.

It wasn't Janie in the doorway, unfortunately, but Shannon. "What the hell is this?" She stared in dismay at Rowdy's four-door truck. "You moved in a pickup truck?" She sounded as if Cass had driven up in a hay wagon.

"Yes, Shannon." Cass smiled. "This is Manny, my roommate's boyfriend, and Rowdy, my, um, friend."

Rowdy stopped in the middle of pulling off the wet tarp and gave Cass a wounded look. Well, what had he expected her to call him?

"Nice to meet you." Manny shook Shannon's hand and gave her a wide smile.

Rowdy just nodded. Fine, he was going to be sullen.

"Can you hurry up? I'm expecting more company." Shannon glanced over her shoulder. "Ladies auxiliary from the Fine Arts Museum. We're planning a fund-raising gala."

"Oh, well, excuse us." Cass rushed to the back of the truck. "There's not that much to bring in. Then we'll get the vehicles out of the way." Fine Arts Museum. A gala. What would it be like to plan something like that? She'd read about those things in the newspaper. The beautiful people did fund-raisers all the time, while dressed in designer gowns and dancing to music provided by famous DJs.

"Earth to Cassidy: Take a box and show us where your bedroom is." Rowdy pushed it into her arms.

"Oh, there you are." Janie hurried down the front steps. "I didn't realize you'd arrived. I was serving refreshments to Shannon's group in the living room." She smiled. "Who are these handsome young men, Cassidy?"

Cass made the introductions. "We need to hurry. Shannon says more ladies are arriving and our cars are in the way."

"Let's see if it will all fit into the elevator and take it up that way." Janie directed the men and soon had her things packed inside an elevator Cass hadn't known existed. "Now if you'll move the cars, then come on back into the house, I've fixed a nice spread for you in the kitchen. Got to have fuel before you unload the elevator. Right, boys?"

Rowdy and Manny grinned, obviously responding to Janie's warmth. Cass tossed her car keys to Manny and followed Janie to the kitchen.

"Thanks for making this so easy. I was afraid Shannon was going to turn us away." Cass leaned against the counter and watched the housekeeper get busy.

"Nonsense. She's just in a bad mood. Has been for the last month since her daddy died. She took it hard. We all did." Janie began pulling plates of cold cuts and salads out of the huge refrigerators. "And then there's the big birthday staring her in the face." Janie laughed. "I told her, 'Honey, wait till you hit sixty, then you can come crying to me. Thirty? You're just hitting your prime.'" Janie walked over to the pantry. "You'd better meet the boys at the door and show them to the kitchen. They might get lost finding us."

"Yeah, sure." Cass felt like she'd been blindsided. "Janie. When exactly is Shannon's birthday?" She stopped in the doorway.

"Next week. September fifth. Why, honey?" Janie set a stack of plates on the granite countertop.

"No reason." But there *was* a reason, a big one. Cass headed for the entry and found Rowdy and Manny shaking rain off of their shoulders. "Back here, guys. Janie's laid out a feast."

The men followed her through the house, muttering comments and stopping cold, just like she had, in that gorgeous dining room with the crystal chandeliers.

"Come, fix you a plate." Janie pushed open the door to the kitchen. "I bet you boys are hungry."

Manny grinned and went right into the kitchen.

"Just a minute. Stay here and talk to me." Rowdy grabbed Cass's elbow before she could follow Manny into the kitchen. "What's the matter? You're upset. I can see it. Did that sister of yours say something?"

"No, not that." Cass pulled out a dining chair and practically fell into it. It couldn't be. But then maybe it explained something.

"What is it then? Cass?" Rowdy pulled out his own chair and sat facing her, then picked up her hand. "I know when you're upset. Tell me. You look like you're about to throw up or cry."

"It's something Janie just told me." Cass took a shuddery breath. "About Shannon. Her birthday."

"What about it?" Rowdy squeezed her fingers. "Shit. When is it, Cass? I know yours is next week. The big three-O. I'd already bought you a present before you found out about all this." He gestured toward the crystal chandeliers like they explained everything. "Seems kind of

pitiful now, but I'm still giving it to you, even though we're not together anymore."

"Oh, Rowdy." Tears. Damn it. He was the kind of man who never
forgot a special occasion. And she'd thrown him away. Had it been a
mistake? He stared at her, waiting.

"Dry up and spit it out, Cass. What about Shannon has you
upset?"

Cass took a deep breath. "Her birthday is next week too. And
she'll be thirty."

"Oh, man." Rowdy got up and pulled Cass into his arms, holding
her until she settled down. He could do that, make her feel calm
when nothing else could. "That means . . ."

"That my father got another woman pregnant while he was married to my mother. That was probably why they divorced." Cass
leaned back. "Shannon and I were born the same week. Daddy must
have married her mother, Missy, as soon as he was free."

"It happens, Cass." Rowdy rubbed his thumbs over her damp
cheeks. "You think that's the big secret your mother held? Doesn't
seem like enough to make him give up parental rights or her to refuse
child support, though."

"No. But it left my mother bitter about men." Cass sighed and
leaned in for just one more minute. "In his video will my father said
something about a big secret that could ruin his company. Infidelity,
while bad, doesn't seem like it could do that."

"You can confront your mother with this. Ask her if that's all
there is to it." Rowdy turned when the kitchen door swung open
again, his hands on her shoulders. "We're coming. Sorry if we kept
you waiting."

"Not at all." Janie smiled. "Didn't mean to interrupt. Thought I'd
see what you wanted to drink."

"Iced tea, if you have it." Cass didn't look at Rowdy as she
stepped back from him and wiped away any trace of her tears. "I got a
little emotional for a minute. Big changes in my life. Rowdy's a good
friend and was comforting me."

"This house can overwhelm you, that's for sure." Janie nodded.
"Well, come eat, you two, then we'll see about putting your things
away. Can I get you a beer, Rowdy?"

"Yes, ma'am. That would hit the spot." Rowdy followed Cass
into the kitchen. His back was stiff and Cass realized she'd hurt him

yet again. She was trying to think of something to say to make it better when the back door blew open and Megan ran inside, shaking out a wet umbrella.

"There's a tropical storm brewing in the Gulf again. I hope it doesn't turn into another hurricane." She looked up and smiled. "Well, hello."

"Megan, this is Rowdy and Manny. Guys, my sister Megan." Cass finished putting together her sandwich and settled on a bar stool. "Manny is my roommate Ellie's boyfriend. Rowdy and I went to high school together." There. Maybe that was better than just calling him a friend, or was it?

"Is this moving day?" Megan dropped her umbrella into a porcelain stand by the back door and went to the sink to wash her hands. She laughed. "What did you think of Cassidy's new bedroom, guys?"

"We haven't seen it yet." Rowdy dropped a pickle on his plate. "That's next, after lunch."

"Oh, you'll find it very interesting. Right, Cassidy?" Megan pulled up a bar stool next to Rowdy and grabbed a plate. "I can't believe she hasn't told you about it."

"We haven't spoken all week." Rowdy gave her a raised eyebrow. "Why don't you tell me about it, Megan?" And he proceeded to flirt with her while he ate two huge sandwiches and a piece of pecan pie.

Cass wasn't about to let him see her notice. Megan shot a look her way from time to time, but Cass would just turn to Manny and tell him about the research she'd been doing on the oil business. Finally, it was time to head upstairs.

"Like I told you, Daddy had this thing for the circus." Megan laughed and held on to Rowdy's arm as they walked up the stairs. "I didn't exaggerate. Just wait till you see."

"Cass, I remember how you used to be at a carnival. Clowns freaked you out." Rowdy was right beside her when they got to the double doors.

Cass pulled out her new key and put it into the lock. Janie had explained that it was kept locked because of the valuable collection inside. The housekeeper supervised the cleaning crew when they needed access.

"Brace yourselves." Cass flung open the doors and there it was, just as she remembered. She didn't show off the hidden bar. The room by itself was impressive enough with its gaudy stripes and enormous desk.

"*Cristo*," Manny muttered.

"Oh, you haven't seen anything yet." Cass stepped past the painted desk to the next set of doors. "You'll love this. Rowdy, imagine me sleeping in this bed." Oops, maybe that hadn't been the thing to say. She saw his frown before he quickly masked it. She threw open the doors.

Megan laughed. "The clown headboard is my favorite. My mother said she used to cover it with a sheet when Daddy was out of town on business. It gave her nightmares leering down at her. Of course, Mama has sleep issues anyway, among other things." She walked over to sit on the velvet spread. "I'm not afraid of clowns. In fact, I can think of a little scenario with clown paint and nothing else . . ." She ran a finger down the middle of her T-shirt.

"You've got to be kidding." Cass wasn't in the mood to listen to that. "Rowdy, how hard do you think it would be to change out this showerhead?" She grabbed his hand and pulled him into the bathroom.

"Seriously?" He laughed, all sexy thoughts clearly washed away by the sight of that ridiculous clown in the shower. "I wonder where they found that."

"I'm sure Daddy had it custom-made. He was always doing stuff like that." Megan had crowded into the bathroom with them. "Listen to this." She flushed the calliope commode.

Rowdy and Manny doubled over with laughter and pounded each other on the back. It took three more flushes before they were satisfied.

"You sure you want to change out that showerhead?" Rowdy said when he got himself under control. "I think it's awesome."

"I'd give it to you if I was allowed to part with any of this stuff." Cass sighed. "I'll buy a plain one and we can arrange for you to come switch it out. Okay?"

"Cass, that's what Tommy is here for." Megan smiled. "He's our handyman, groundskeeper, you name it. Janie's husband." She turned to Cass. "Really, Cass. He'll buy the part and install it. All you have to do is mention it to him."

"Okay." Cass could see Rowdy was easing toward the door. "Guess I have a lot to learn about living here."

"We'd better get those boxes and bring them in. I'm sure there are other things you have to do today. I have stuff too." Rowdy gave Manny a signal. "Megan, where's the elevator?"

"This way. Follow me." She led them down the hall. "Cass, this is your stuff we're hauling. Right?"

"Right." Cass had been in a kind of daze, thinking about actually living in this room, sleeping here. Alone. Now she followed Megan, cute in her snug T-shirt and denim jean shorts that had obviously been ripped by a designer. She'd left her sandals by the back door and her pedicure was flawless. Rowdy and even Manny, who was devoted to Ellie, were obviously enjoying the way Megan's taut butt swayed down the hallway.

Cass saw her life summed up in a dozen boxes and a pile of stuff that didn't make a dent in the huge walk-in closet. Suddenly she realized everyone was about to leave her here. The guys set the last two boxes on the floor and looked toward the door.

"Why did you bring this tiny little thing?" Megan nudged the forty-inch TV with her foot.

"I like to watch TV in bed. I didn't see one in here." Cass knew she sounded defensive. Little? She'd saved for months to buy that TV.

"Oh, wow. You didn't know about this." Megan flounced over to the bed and one of the bedside tables. They were each half of an elephant. The left one was the head with a trunk, the right one was the rear with the tail. She pulled on an ear and a drawer popped out. "Secret drawer and all the remotes. Look." She hit a button and the gold velvet-covered bench at the end of the bed opened. A huge big-screen TV slowly rose from the bench, a DVD player and DVR on either side of it.

"Now that's what I call entertainment." Manny said something in Spanish and Megan answered him fluently in the same language. They both laughed.

"You've really got it made here, don't you, Cassie?" Rowdy pulled out another remote. "What's this for? To call for beer and peanuts?"

Megan sat on the bed suddenly, her shoulders slumping. "Yes. You'd get Janie and the kitchen. Anything you wanted." She bent over and put her face in her hands. "Daddy loved this stupid room." Her shoulders shook and they all realized she was crying.

Cass sat beside her and tried to comfort her, sliding an arm around her. Megan sprang from the bed like she'd been electrocuted.

"Leave me alone! I'm okay." She dashed into the bathroom and came out with a wad of toilet paper, blowing her nose. "You didn't know him, Cassidy. Too bad for you. Now you can enjoy his room. I've got to get out of here." And with that she practically ran out the double doors.

"Wow. Guess this was harder than she realized it would be." Cass sat on the side of the bed again.

"I felt sorry for her. She seems nice." Manny hit the remote and the huge TV sank back into the bench. It closed with a soft *click*. "That TV is something else."

"Guess we'll be on our way." Rowdy started forward, as if he was going to kiss Cass good-bye, then seemed to think better of it. "Talk to you."

"Thank Janie for our lunch." Manny did kiss Cass on the cheek. "Ellie is going to want to see this for herself. Call her, *chica*."

"Oh, I will." Cass glanced at the pile of her things in the closet. "Hey, Manny. You might as well take my 'tiny little TV' and DVD player with you. Obviously I won't be needing them and you can use them again in my old bedroom." Cass almost fell over when Manny leaped at her to give her a hug.

"Thanks, Cass. I was hoping you'd say that. I was planning to move in there tonight." He winked. "Rowdy, give me a hand, bro."

"Sure." Rowdy picked up the flat-screen and nodded. "Nice gesture. But then you can afford it." He didn't smile as he headed for the stairs.

Manny was left with cords and the DVD player. "Don't mind him, Cass. He's hurt. But he'll get over it." He looked around the room. "Enjoy all of this. I know your history. You deserve this and more. *La buena vida*." He grinned and followed Rowdy.

The good life. By the time Cass got to the front door, Rowdy's truck was disappearing down the long driveway. She felt like she was seeing more than just a pair of friends disappear into the gloom of a rainy afternoon. It was as if a part of her life was over.

She shut the door and looked up at the two-story ceiling, hand-painted with a scene from the Renaissance, Janie had said. She could hear the chatter and laughter of women from the formal living room off to her left and knew Shannon was still holding court there. No alcohol with this crowd, and her sister had looked lovely in a silk dress that had brought out the green in her eyes.

"Your phone was buzzing in your purse, Cassidy." Janie found her on her way up the stairs. "You left it on the kitchen counter, hon." She held out her bag. "Maybe they've left a message."

"Thanks, Janie. And thanks for the great lunch and making my friends feel so welcome." Cass dug her phone out of her purse, reluctant to go on up to her room and start unpacking.

"You want a soda? To take upstairs with you?" Janie studied her anxiously. "Or a piece of that pie? You didn't eat much of that 'great lunch'."

"Diet Coke?" Cass smiled. Mason had called her and left a message. "I'll be right in. Let me listen to this." She hit *voice mail*.

"Cass, Mason here. It's been the week from hell. I'm sorry I've been so busy with work that I've neglected you. I know you've had those files to go over this week and thought you might need a break or a sympathetic ear. If you don't have plans, I'd like to see you tonight. Text me if that's okay and where to pick you up. Seven. Dinner and then we'll see where it goes from there. Looking forward to seeing you again, Cass. It's been too long." That last was in a low tone that made Cass shiver.

If he did make a move, what should she do about it? She was a free agent. But Mason had mentioned those files. She'd spent hours and hours going over those things. Trying to figure out who should stay and who should go. She'd made a list of qualifications, deciding early that she couldn't let gender or the number of dependents sway her. If singles were the first to go, how fair would that be? But then she found she couldn't ignore the idea that a father of five might have trouble getting another job. Oh, God! She'd love to run her decisions past Mason.

When Cass saw the time on her phone she realized he hadn't given her much notice. She texted her answer, then hurried to the kitchen. She grabbed her drink and told Janie she wouldn't be home for dinner. That was new, having to let someone know not to fix her a meal. And she found herself babbling about Mason picking her up because she sure wouldn't be able to hear the doorbell from her room.

Back upstairs, she dug through her clothes, tossing things on the bed instead of hanging them in the closet like she should have. Did she have anything that could possibly be right for dinner with Mason? Men. Would it have killed him to give her a clue about specifics? Casual or dressy? And she wasn't about to call him back and ask. Because that would put too much importance on what might turn out to be just a business meeting. She knew she was being set up for failure and needed Mason to help her handle her new job, not complicate her life. Stupid to get all fluttery about seeing him again. If he started with the flirty kissing thing again, she'd just have to shut him down.

It was also stupid to close her eyes when she had to take a shower with that clown face gaping at her. Freak. She was laughing at herself by the time she got out and dug through her makeup bag. She had new war paint, as Ellie called it, thanks to that Sunday in the salon. Now she went to work applying it carefully. She was about to pull off her towel and go in search of her underwear when the bathroom door opened.

"What the hell?" She leaped back and almost tripped on the tiger-striped bath mat.

Shannon strolled in, her mouth a tight line. "I see you've moved right in. The bedroom looks like the hurricane hit already. You know there's one brewing in the Gulf."

"Oh, my clothes. Yes, I was in a hurry. I'll put them away when I get back." Cass stepped around her sister and walked into her new closet. Underwear. Something black and sexy. Because it made her feel confident. Not because anyone would see it, of course. She picked through the laundry basket where she'd packed her best underwear.

Shannon wasn't going away. "Janie says you have a date with Mason. What are you wearing?"

"Why do you care?" Cass managed to wiggle into her thong under her towel, then kept her back turned while she dropped it and put on her bra. Seriously? What had happened to privacy?

"I looked over your wardrobe." Shannon drifted over to the bed and picked up a dress Cass had been considering. It was a sundress that she'd always liked. "This is pitiful."

"Excuse me?" Cass grabbed the dress and held it in front of her. "What's wrong with this? It fits well and is cool and comfortable."

"Comfortable. What are you? Ninety?" Shannon turned and headed for the door. "Follow me."

"In my underwear?" Cass still held onto the dress.

"Ethan is out and Tommy never comes up without an invitation. Besides . . ." Shannon turned and looked her over, "You have a good body. Don't be ashamed of it. Now, come on." She walked down the hall toward the other bedrooms, then threw open the door to what must be her suite of rooms. The bedroom was done in gold and cream and was beautiful. The hardwood floors gleamed and the oriental rug was obviously an expensive silk. The hand-painted bed frame was Venetian, if Cass had to guess, and featured pastel flowers that were echoed in the colorful silk throw pillows piled on the cream silk bedspread.

"I love your bedroom." Cass just stood and stared. There was a collection of crystal perfume bottles that made her eyes widen. "It's like a fantasy."

"Thanks. Now, come to my closet. I have some things here with the tags still on them that I was going to give to charity. Personal mistakes. Maybe you'd better take them. We have a name in this town that I won't see disgraced by having you schlepping about looking like a bag lady." Shannon gestured to a chrome stand that stood in the middle of her massive closet. "You can have all of these."

"Are you serious? You insult me and then offer me this?" Cass was drawn in despite the urge to toss all of it in Shannon's bitchy face. "Bag lady?"

"What you wear every time I see you is not fit for our cleaning crew." Shannon pulled out a dark-green print sundress with a deep V bodice. "Here. This one never fit me right. I have bigger boobs than you do. Try it on. Mason will love you in this."

"Why do you care what Mason loves me in?" Cass stepped into the dress. Why not? It had a designer label and the fabric felt like heaven against her skin.

"He's our overlord. I want to see him happy. He's obviously taken a shine to you. We can use that. Keep him happy, Cassidy. For all our sakes. We need that money at the end of the year." Shannon zipped her up the back, then turned her and adjusted the front until her cleavage was popping up to her satisfaction. "Look at yourself. This is what I'm talking about."

"You're pimping me out?" Cass had to admire her reflection in the mirror at the end of the closet. The dress hugged her curves, making her waist look small and her hips generous but not too big. The skirt was just the right length to flatter her legs and her tan had held up well.

"Oh, please. As if doing Mason is such a hardship. The man is hot. You and Rowdy are 'just friends'." She rolled her eyes at Cass's surprised look. "Don't tell Janie anything that you don't want the world to know, just saying. And Megan says Rowdy is a cutie. So I'm thinking you must have a little thing for Mason to be dumping the hot guy who was obviously your old boyfriend like that."

"Well." Cass was speechless. "What time is it?" When Shannon told her, she realized she didn't have time to debate any of this. "He'll be here any minute. What I do or don't do with Mason isn't for you or any of my new siblings to worry about. Please pass that word." She wondered if she didn't take up the Mason challenge if either of her sisters would think it was their duty to give him a go. The thought made her chin come up. "But I'm on it."

Shannon grinned. "All right, then."

Cass looked down at her feet. "What size shoe do you wear?"

Shannon shook her head. "Ah, glad to see you aren't the Goody Two-shoes you pretend to be. Daddy would be proud. My feet are too big, but Megan's got a pair of killer heels that'll look great with that dress."

Cass wondered about that. Would her father be proud of his scheming daughters? But the thought of seeing Mason again and looking sexy in high heels and a low-cut dress sent any serious second-guesses right out of her head. There was a big payday at stake and she needed help getting to it. If keeping Mason happy was part of the deal . . . Oh, who was she kidding? All of those touches, kisses, flirty conversations. She wasn't immune to a handsome man who obviously wanted her. Yes, they'd talk business tonight, but then . . . Well, Mason might be in for a surprise.

Chapter 10

Mason was as edgy as a kid on his first date. He'd been running early but knew better than to show up for a date looking too eager. So he'd stalled. Topped off the gas tank and picked up a flower at a convenience store. It was cheesy, but he liked the color of the long-stemmed rose. Not orange, not pink. Special. Like Cassidy.

Fool.

When she came down those stairs, he couldn't catch his breath at the sight. What was wrong with him? But she looked so damned beautiful and eager. Glad to see him. He stretched out his arms and she walked into them like they'd been doing this for years.

"Can I hold you for a minute? This has been a hell of a week." He inhaled woman, clean and honest, with a hint of something he couldn't name that made him want to stay there and just breathe her in.

"Good to see you too." She laughed and leaned back. "I'm sorry about your week."

"Yeah, well. That's the oil business. Here." Mason handed her the rose he'd almost dropped.

"What a lovely color." She smiled and lifted it to her nose. "Mmm." She turned and found a vase that was brimming with other fresh flowers. "I'll stick it there until we get back. Then it's going up to my room so I can enjoy it. It'll make my whole bedroom smell sweet." She took his arm. "Still raining?"

"Yep. Don't worry. I'll keep you dry. Where we're going has covered parking." Mason waited while Cass threw a silky black shawl over her shoulders, then picked up her small purse and brief-case. He took the briefcase. "Business?"

"Afraid so. I've got a pretty good idea who has to go, but I'd like your opinion. If you don't mind." She made a face. "This is one of the hardest things I've ever had to do."

"I get it. We're talking about people's lives. You'd be heartless if it didn't bother you." He opened the front door. The weather was horrible, gusting rain from the tropical storm threatening the Texas coast.

"Where are we going?" She stumbled a little in her high heels as they walked down the steps toward his truck and he steadied her with a hand on her waist. "Oops. I'm not used to these shoes."

"Take them off if they're dangerous." Mason helped her climb into the truck. "Not saying they aren't sexy, though. You look beautiful." He leaned in and kissed her cheek. "Should have said that right away." He tucked in her full skirt and slammed the door, then ran around to get in the driver's seat. She was grinning as he got behind the wheel.

"Thanks, Mason. The shoes stay on. I'll figure them out." She looked out at the driving rain. "Maybe we should have postponed. This weather is only supposed to get worse, according to the weathermen."

"Alarmists. I doubt that hurricane comes anywhere close to here." Mason started the truck. "Sorry about bringing this vehicle, but the rain is filling up some of the streets. I didn't want to take a chance on hitting some flooding in a low-slung car."

"This is fine. Now are you going to tell me where we're going?" Cass fastened her seat belt. "Am I dressed right for the place?"

"You're dressed right for any place." More cheesy stuff. That line was older than his granddaddy's first drill bit. Cass just smiled and adjusted her skirt until it covered her knees. Trying to look prim and proper? Didn't work when her breasts were popping out of her top. And, hell, yeah, he was noticing. Mason jerked his eyes back to the road when they hit a speed bump going too fast and he beaned himself on the headliner above him.

He needed to slow down. And not just the truck. Why was he panting after her? Thinking with the head below his belt instead of the one on his shoulders? He was supposed to be getting close to her so he could pump her for information. Those files she carried might help him in his bid to take over Calhoun. His personal bid? Or his uncle's plan for Texas Star to take over Calhoun? Either way, if he used her, he'd ruin any chance he and Cass had of developing a real relationship.

Whoa, partner. Since when did real relationships even hit his radar? If anything, what should bother him was his conscience, since Conrad had trusted Mason to see his company through the next year into profit for his kids. God, he was screwed up. Mason steered around a stalled car and reached over to pick up Cass's hand. Right now, with the weather on the warpath and a warm woman beside him, he would like to put thinking on the back burner and leave it there.

"You okay?" he asked when a wind gust rocked the truck after they'd eased through the worst of the high water. "This weather *is* pretty rough."

"Fine. You seem to know how to handle this flooding. I feel safe in a truck, so high off the ground." Cass squeezed his hand. "Oh, look at that jackass, going too fast. He'll flood one of those little cars."

Mason leaned on the horn but it didn't slow down the jackass. "Idiot. The waves he's making are going to end up taking out his own engine, see if they don't." Sure enough, at the next intersection that same car was stalled, the angry driver pounding his steering wheel. Mason just slowly drove past him, careful not to make the situation worse. They could see him talking on his cell phone. He wouldn't be stranded long.

Mason was glad when they got to his high-rise and he pulled into the parking garage. No worries about flooding there. He pulled the truck into his assigned spot and jumped out to help Cass down.

"Where are we, Mason?" Cass looked around the concrete area.

"My place. I'm cooking you dinner." Mason pulled shopping bags from the backseat. "I swear I won't give you ptomaine."

"Hmm. If you say so." She took one of the bags from him and glanced inside. "Looks complicated—herbs, fresh pasta. The most a man ever cooked for me before was a steak and baked potato."

"Throwing a steak on the grill is for amateurs. Wait and be amazed." Mason walked her over to the elevators and pressed the *up* button. He wanted to show off for her, impress her. To loosen her up so she'd share company secrets? Even he had to admit she hadn't had time to learn any. And it was a relief to think about something besides the company—any company—tonight.

Admit it, MacKenzie. You want to loosen her up for something else entirely. Mason got close to her again, juggling his bags until he had a free arm to sling around her shoulders.

"Cold?"

"A little. The rain has made it chilly." She smiled up at him and pulled her shawl together, hiding her cleavage. Next she moved her purse from one shoulder to the other and fiddled with the strap of her leather briefcase. Yeah, she'd brought it in. Business.

"Am I making you nervous? You can say *no* to coming upstairs. I'll take you somewhere else. But the weather is probably making places shut down early. Or I could take you home." Mason stepped into the elevator. He held the door open. "Your call."

"You make me a little nervous. You have ever since I met you." Cass smiled. "But I'm not afraid to see your place. Let's go." Her finger hovered over the buttons on the elevator panel. "Which floor?"

"Six." She punched the button. The doors closed and the elevator lurched into action.

"No higher? I'd expect you to have the penthouse."

"Nope. If we have a fire, I only have to go down six flights of stairs to get out of here." The bell chimed and the doors opened. Mason walked her to the end of the hallway and used his key.

"That's true." Cass didn't say anything when he threw open his door. She did what all his visitors did and made straight for the sliding-glass doors. He owned half the floor and the living-dining area wrapped around one corner of the building. The wall of windows, despite being pretty fogged up, still gave them a view of driving rain and the terrace outside.

"Oh, you can see the park. This is like living right above the trees." She looked as if she really wanted to step outside, but the rain kept her from taking that chance.

"Yep." Mason headed for the kitchen and began unloading bags. He didn't go out on the balcony. If he could have put protective iron bars and razor wire up to the floor above, he would have. Damned condo association. He wouldn't live off the ground at all if he hadn't decided long ago that the amenities here made his life easier. He ignored the windows and pulled out a pot to fill with water for the pasta. "I hope you're not allergic to anything."

"No, I'm easy." She was flushed when she handed him the bag she carried and set it on the polished concrete counter.

Mason just grinned. Easy? He doubted it, but couldn't help wishing it were true.

"How can I help?" She leaned in. "What are you making, Mason?"

"Wait and see. Just sit and watch me work. Want a glass of wine first?" He turned to the refrigerator and pulled out a bottle of Chardonnay and one of Riesling. "Which do you prefer? Dry or on the sweet side?"

"The Riesling. Thanks." She sat on the bar stool and sipped wine while he threw dinner together. It was clear she was trying to keep things light and that she *was* a little nervous. She laughingly told him about her move and how she kept finding booby traps in her new bedroom.

"The idea of that clown looming over me when I sleep is freaking me out. Megan said her mother put a sheet over it. I'm going to try that tonight. This will be my first time to sleep there."

"I'll refill your glass. Enough wine and you won't care where you sleep." Mason put the finishing touches on the pasta with shrimp and carried the plates over to the dining-room table, where they had a view of the storm raging outside.

"I *always* care where I sleep." She had followed him to the table.

"Good to know." He turned on the gas logs in the fireplace, then pulled out a chair at the table he'd set earlier. His mother had insisted he own a set of dishes, so it looked pretty good. He even had cloth napkins. "Sit." He waited until she slid into the chair and set her wineglass on the table, then he headed back to the kitchen. Now *he* was nervous. Stupid.

"This smells wonderful." Cass watched him set a salad from the refrigerator on the table.

"Thanks." He turned down the lights so the flickering fireplace was the dominant light source except for the one coming from the hall.

"Do we need bread?" He stood behind her chair, looking things over.

"No, this is fine." She picked up her napkin. "What a romantic setting. Storm outside, delicious food inside." She leaned back and looked up at him. "Thank you. I had a week from hell too."

Mason couldn't resist. He took her chin in his hand and leaned down to kiss her. It started as just a simple thing, but he couldn't let her go. It built until he squatted next to her, holding her shoulders.

"Cassidy." He brushed her hair back behind her ears, his breathing harsh.

She laid a gentle hand in the middle of his chest and pressed. "We should eat before it gets cold, Mason." Her cheeks were rosy in the firelight. The lady wasn't immune. But she wasn't going to let him rush her either.

"Yeah. Guess so." Mason stood, sure she could see how that kiss had hit him. He wasn't such a wuss that he was going to hold his napkin in front of his zipper to hide how much he wanted her. He was tempted to speed through dinner and pull her toward his bedroom.

Slow down. He sat across from her and picked up his fork.

"Tell me about your decision-making process. On the layoffs." He was surprised his voice didn't crack from tension.

She speared a shrimp and then explained how she'd gone through the personnel files. Her thinking was sound but she took everything to heart. It said a lot about her nature that she cared so much, but it had made the process painful for her.

"So you've got the list of names ready for Hardcastle on Monday." Mason hoped he'd done a decent job on the pasta. He hadn't tasted a bite, though he'd plowed through it. He realized his plate was empty.

"A tentative list of who *might* be going." She blotted her lips with her napkin. "I hit human resources this past week. Filling out paperwork as a new hire. You know the drill."

"Sure." Mason couldn't look away from her lips, shiny from the olive oil he'd used on the pasta. They were begging to be kissed again.

"Anyway, while I was there I asked for an organizational chart for the accounting department." She leaned forward.

Mason quit breathing. Would that dress hold her? Not even a glimpse of nipple. Damn.

"Mason, Hardcastle really set me up to make enemies. There are four divisions and each one has at least one supervisor. I shouldn't be making these cuts, the supervisors should make the recommendations for who should go."

"Uh, huh." *Brilliant, MacKenzie.*

"And the place is really top-heavy. I called Holly, Hardcastle's assistant, and she emailed me some numbers. We spend more on supervisors than on all the other accountants combined." She tossed down her napkin with a look of triumph. "What do you think would happen if I suggested we lay off a half-dozen supervisors instead?"

Mason realized she was waiting for an answer. Oh, yeah. He was supposed to be giving her advice. Instead, all he could think about was whether or not she was wearing a bra. He kept the air-conditioning low and he could see the hard points of her nipples through the thin fabric of her dress. Yes, he was a dog. A horny dog.

"Sounds like you're way ahead of Hardcastle on this one. Go in on Monday and let him have it. See where it goes. He can't fire you, so he has to listen to you. You did what he asked and more. I'm impressed." Mason smiled.

"Well, thanks." She laid down her fork. "Dinner was delicious. I can't eat another bite."

"You sure?" Mason frowned until he realized she'd cleaned her plate. "I have more. And dessert. I picked up a fruit tart from a French bakery that makes great pastries."

"Later." She got up from the table. "Let me do the dishes, then we can go over my paperwork, if you don't mind."

"Forget the dishes. I'll set them in the sink for now." Mason jumped up and grabbed them. "Rinse them off and stick them in the dishwasher, if that makes you feel better." He wasn't about to waste time on dishes or discussing business when he was on fire for her. He refilled their wineglasses and chased her out of the kitchen. "Come to the living room. Let's sit in front of the fire."

"Do you ever sit out on the balcony? I bet the view's wonderful when the sky is clear." Cass had wandered over to the damned sliding doors again.

Thank God it was still raining too hard for her to be tempted to go out there.

"Not often. I work too much. I have a home office in one of the bedrooms. My computer is in there." Mason set their glasses on the coffee table. "Maybe you'd like a tour."

"Maybe." She smiled and walked up to him. "You're putting off business."

"Can you blame me? You look like dessert to me." Mason couldn't check himself. He pulled her close, his arms around her waist. "God, you smell good too."

"My sisters think I should seduce you. So we'll get good evaluations at the end of the year." She ran her hands up his chest, her eyes steady on his.

"Really?" Mason started to laugh, but realized she was probably serious. Of course, Shannon and Megan would think that a fine idea. "What about you? Willing to sacrifice yourself for the cause?"

"Would it work? If I throw myself at you, will that get me a good evaluation, no matter how I perform . . . at Calhoun?" She slid a fingertip inside the neckline of his knit polo shirt.

Mason didn't know whether to be mad or to thank the Lord that she was telling him this. But then she kissed the place where his shirt was open and licked a little path of fire up his neck with her tongue. Holy shit!

"Cassidy." Mason had to collect his thoughts, taking a breath to sort them out. "Throw yourself at me all you want. At the end of the year, your performance will be fairly evaluated. Whatever happens between us won't matter." Sounded good, but he was holding her tighter as she nibbled his earlobe. His train of thought ran off the rails again when her lips grazed his jaw. "Do what you want, when you want it. It's all good. I mean, we can get together or not. I won't hold it against you."

"Oh, please. Hold it against me." Cass grabbed his hair and kissed him then, her mouth open and her tongue playing with his.

He slid a hand down to land on her hip. The other one eased toward her breast. God, but she was hot. He kissed her back, starving for her. They stood like that for endless seconds, learning each other's geography. Finally, one or both of them pulled back, breathing hard.

"This is crazy." Cass pulled her hand out of his back pocket.

"You're not stopping now, are you?" Mason thought he'd die if she said she had to leave.

"Not stopping. Slowing down, maybe." She gazed around the room. "We could sit for a while."

"On the couch. Make out like teenagers?" Mason grinned. "That's hot."

She laughed. "I haven't done that in years." She pulled him over to the couch. "I hardly know you, Mason. Would it kill you to slow down?"

"Maybe." He sat beside her. "So as I remember from—oh, junior high—I put my arm around you, like it was an accident," He did that. "Then I lean over, just so." He did, smiling into her eyes. "Then I go in for the kiss. Push me back if I'm rushing you, Cass." He kissed her then, taking the lead this time. Oh, boy, but they fit and she tasted like that sweet wine and garlicky pasta. What could he say? He loved both of them. He pulled back, a little out of breath.

"So what's next in junior high?" She had her hands on his chest and he was sure she could feel his heart beating like crazy.

"I go for the bases. I can't remember which is first, second or third base." He laughed. "But my favorite is right here." He slid his hand over her breast. Oh, man, but it was plump, obviously real, and felt perfect in his palm. "Feel free to shove my hand away if you're not ready for that step."

"Am I pushing you away?" She grabbed his hair and pulled him down again. "Kiss me again. I really, really like the way you kiss."

Mason didn't need to be told twice. She kissed him back and leaned in when he played with her breast. Her nipple was hard and he rolled it between his fingers. She moaned into his mouth. This time when he leaned back, she was flushed.

"Next I'd try for a hand up your skirt. Like this." Mason slid a hand up her knee. "I can't tell you how glad I was when, back in the dark ages, women quit wearing panty hose."

"Mmm. Me too. Banks were the last to give them up." Cass leaned her head back on the edge of the sofa, her eyes at half-mast, when he toyed with the edge of her panties. "I should stop you."

"Why? Are you not feeling it?" Mason kissed the deep V where the dress was open between her breasts. It didn't take much to push the material aside. Black lacy bra. "Oh, man. You know what under-wear like this does to a man?"

She smiled and touched that bulge in his zipper. "I have an idea."

"Now you've done it. You punishing me, Cass? Going to make me beg?"

Cass sat up and kissed him, long and hungrily. "No. Guess I've decided. Why are we sitting in your living room when I bet you have a perfectly good bed somewhere?" She stood and grabbed his hand. "Show me."

"God, woman. You're incredible." Mason didn't hesitate. He just swung her up and into his arms, surprising a laugh out of her. "You sure?"

"No. Yes. I don't know" Cass looked up at him and traced his jaw with her palm. "Don't talk it to death, Mason. I'm trying to let myself be free here. Just let things happen."

"Free. Got it." Mason strode toward his bedroom. Yeah, he could talk too much. Think too much. Worry too much. He was the front man, the closer. Glib, the one always brought in to seal the deal. But he wasn't at work now. Cass had told him her agenda up front. Bribing the evaluator. He chose not to believe her. He'd known plenty of cold, calculating women and Cass wasn't one of them. She was willing and he wanted her. Forget business. This didn't have to be complicated. Just two consenting adults having fun. He dropped her on the bed, then fell down beside her.

"Last chance to change your mind." He reached for her.

"Shut up, Mason." Cass smiled and put her hand over his mouth.

Was she sure? Cass pulled Mason down on top of her and kissed him again. She refused to slow down and think. She just knew she liked this feeling. Free, she'd said. *Wild* was more like it. She tasted him and savored the heat of his mouth and the way his clever tongue stroked hers. He touched her breast again and she arched up into his palm.

She wanted him. Wanted to know what it felt like to be naked with him. To have him inside of her. Had she lost her mind? He was virtually a stranger. And yet he wasn't. She knew him. Knew that he was smart and kind and could make her laugh. He was so different from—No, she wasn't going to even think his name. This night was special. There was a storm raging outside, but inside she felt safe. Safe enough anyway to allow herself to let go. To do it all, feel it all. With Mason.

He rolled her over until she was on top of him and he could unzip her dress.

"There it is. That sexy bra." He smiled when he saw the lacy black.

Cass felt beautiful when he looked at her. When the dress hit the floor, all she had left was that bra and her ridiculous thong panties that matched. He kissed all around both of them until he handled the front clasp. She gasped as she felt cool air on her breasts.

"Ah, that's what I'm talking about. You're perfect." Mason fell on them like they were a feast, his mouth taking first one, then the other. His warm hands were busy too, his fingers plucking her nipples like a virtuoso handling the strings of a fine instrument.

"I want to feel you against me." Cass shivered and tried to work his shirt up and off of him.

"Let me." He sat up and wrenched it off. Then he rolled off the bed and dropped his pants, coming back to her on the bed like a prowling tiger. He grinned at the sight of her tiny panties and ran a finger along the narrow band.

"Sexy lady. Lose 'em." He didn't wait for her to do it, just slid them down her legs. Her shoes had dropped in the living room when he'd picked her up. He stripped off his own briefs and they were naked, against each other. At last. They paused.

"Mason." Cass leaned against him, taking a moment to just feel him, his heat, his hard body. She tangled her legs with his and ran her toes up and down his calves. Wonderful.

"This time *I'm* slowing down. I don't want to get to home plate without running the bases." He leaned back and looked her over so thoroughly Cass laughed against his shoulder, suddenly shy. That embarrassment fell away when he began to gently explore her. He had a light touch in some places, then firm where she needed it. His finger slid inside her and she knew he found her wet and ready. He kissed her body, front and back, whispering sweet words until she moaned his name.

"Say it again." He smiled against her stomach.

"Mason." Cass pushed him onto his back to trace the lines of his chest and kiss his nipples. She ran her tongue down his hair-roughened stomach. His erection was right there, proof she'd got him going. She grasped him and moved her hands until he stopped her.

"You're going to have me back in junior high school, disgracing myself, if you don't stop it." He smiled and shook his head. "You're not even near ready, lady. Patience." He crawled on top of her again to hold her arms out to the side and kiss her eyes closed.

Cass shuddered when he kept stroking her with his fingers, then his tongue. She knew when he left the bed for a moment to find protection and opened her eyes to let him know she was aware and glad.

"Yes." She opened her arms and sighed when he finally surged into her, the sigh turning into a gasp of satisfaction when he pressed harder, making sure she knew he wasn't some easygoing lover who was content to let her have all the fun. No, he was taking, taking, taking, until she cried out, trembling on the edge. He reached between them then and, with just the right touch, shoved her over so that she screamed his name and lost herself.

She clung to him, quivering, afraid to let go until she could pull herself together again. Not in . . . forever had she lost control so completely. She'd never been so wild, so free, so uninhibited. She'd always stopped before . . . Not this time. Not with Mason. He kissed her face, her nose, her lips. Rolled her on top of him again and held her until she could finally breathe without gasping.

She kissed him greedily, gratefully, and they started again. It was incredible and maybe she wanted to know if it was possible for it to happen again. Mason proved that it could and did. When she finally fell into an exhausted sleep, Cass was smiling.

When Mason woke up, he realized it was really, really dark. He glanced out the window and saw it was still raining hard. He didn't give a damn. He had a warm woman in his bed and she was stirring. Guess he'd woken her up.

"Mmm. What time is it?" She brushed her hand down his chest and he captured it against him.

"Why? You have someplace you'd rather be? An appointment?" He rolled her on top of him again. Man, but he liked the way they fit together, her breasts soft against him, her legs tangled between his. He was getting hard and hoped she was up for another round of mind-blowing sex.

"No." She must have smiled, but he'd be damned if he could see much more than the glimmer of her white teeth. "Why's it so dark?"

"No lights. Storm must have knocked out the electricity." Mason reluctantly set her aside. "I have candles." The decorator who'd put the finishing touches on his place had insisted his mantle needed a pair of fat ones in silver holders to "balance" things. He'd just written the check. "Wait here."

"Hurry. I'd like to find your bathroom without breaking a toe or something." Her voice was throaty and so damned sexy he wanted to forget light and—what she'd said finally hit him and he hurried.

"Shit." He'd found the corner of his dresser with his foot. "There went *my* toe."

"You okay?" She wasn't laughing, was she?

"I'll live. It's as dark as the bottom of a well in here. Give me a minute." Candles, yeah. And he had matches. In case that automatic starter on the fireplace went out. He groped his way to the living room. The light from the fire helped. Good thing gas logs didn't need electricity to keep going. Maybe he should move the action in here. He lit the candles and left one on the coffee table.

"Here you go. Can you see the bathroom door?" He grinned at her when he set the candle on the dresser. She had the sheet up to her chin. As if he hadn't explored every inch of her before. Seen it too with the light coming in from the hallway. "Not going shy on me now, are you?"

"Toss me your shirt." She had pink cheeks. "Allow me a little modesty."

"What's the fun in that?" But he tossed her the shirt anyway. She wiggled into it and then threw back the sheet, sprinting for the bathroom. He was sorry to see that the shirt covered her to the middle of her thighs. She was a little thing. Well, not all of her was little. Those breasts ... "You'll have to leave the door open or it'll be black as pitch in there. Or you can come back out here and get the candle." He laughed when he heard her curse. "Never mind. I'll be in the other room to preserve your modesty."

Mason decided it wouldn't hurt to make a trip to his other bathroom and freshen up a little. He pulled on a fresh pair of jockeys, then hit the head and rinsed out his mouth. He met Cass in the hallway.

"You okay?" He pulled her in for a kiss. "About this?" He ran his hand under the shirt to caress her bare butt, disappointed that she'd found that tiny excuse for a pair of panties.

"I'm fine with it. No regrets." She smiled and ran her fingers through his hair. "Didn't you say something about fruit tart? I seem to have worked up an appetite."

Mason laughed and pulled her to the living-room couch. "Sit, woman, and I'll serve you. You want coffee? Oh, scratch that. No coffee without electricity. More wine with it?" He figured the power would be restored soon. This kind of outage usually didn't last long. Unless the storm had turned into a full-blown hurricane. He had a battery-powered TV he could bring out or check an app on his phone. But he really didn't want reality to intrude just yet. He glanced at his watch. Dawn was still a couple of hours away. They'd worry about reality after the sun came up.

"How about water? I do want your advice on these files. I don't think it would break any rules if I showed you some numbers. You might be able to tell me if these salaries are out of line or not." Cass settled on the couch. "After dessert." She smiled. "You're really going to wait on me?"

"You bet." Mason got things together on the tray the decorator had insisted he needed and had never used before, then set it next to the candle. "Try this." He picked up a slice of tart and held it to Cass's lips. She took a bite, then licked her lips.

"Mmm. Decadent." She smiled. "So are you." She pulled him to her and kissed him, the taste sweet and sinful.

"You're a constant surprise to me, Cassidy Calhoun." Mason forgot all about the tart, tossing the piece back on the plate and taking her down on the couch to cover her body with his.

"What did you expect? Some shy banker type who would be in awe of the billionaire bad boy?" Cass laughed up at him. "I am. This sex-crazed woman isn't me." She slid her arms around him, then down under his elastic waistband. "I admit we seem to have this chemistry between us that makes all my common sense go right out the window."

"Good. Common sense is way overrated." Mason made quick work of the shirt she wore so he could feast on her incredible breasts. "So is thinking. I want you to feel, Cassidy. Live in the moment." Oops. He saw her smile disappear. "Not that I think this isn't important. I do. I feel the chemistry too."

"Is it just that, Mason?" She held him off, looking up at him with her big eyes.

Mason knew women. They liked the pretty stories about commitment and a future. He didn't lie to them. He hadn't been trapped before by spouting that shit and he wasn't about to be trapped now. Except . . .

"Cassidy, I don't know what the hell is going on here. That's the God's honest truth." He sat up and pulled her with him. "You're one of a kind for me. Does that make sense?"

"Sure." She crawled into his lap. "Mason, look at me. I'm not your usual type. You don't have to tell me that. I grew up poor and I have no clue about how to do the society stuff that your women live and breathe. Women like my sisters. But I do know what I want." She wiggled and her smile was wicked. "And what you want, mister."

Mason felt her warm bottom cradling his erection and ached, needing her again. "You're right. You're not like anyone else I've ever been with. Thank God for that. Are you teasing me? Or will you put me out of my misery?"

"You mean you're through talking?" Cass turned and straddled him. "Get rid of this underwear and I'll show you."

It didn't take much to shove that string of a panty aside and Mason ripped his own shorts getting to her. He was inside her in seconds and she rode him like she'd never get enough of him. She threw back her head and looked like she was having the time of her life. Mason was almost sorry she'd cut off her hair, but he liked the way she looked now too much to complain. She was beautiful, flushing with her orgasm and taking him with her as she tightened around him. He held her hips, surged into her hard and fast until she suddenly leaned forward and bit his shoulder.

"God almighty!" He came with such a rush he almost blacked out. He finally fell back on the couch, Cass draped over him like a blanket. They lay there for minutes or hours, he had no idea which. Finally she peeled herself off of him, strolled off to the bathroom, and he heard the shower going. He sprinted after her. She greeted him with open arms, not afraid to get her hair wet as they made love again. Damn it, he was falling for her so hard he felt dizzy.

Later, they went through her file folders while they finished off the fruit tart and drank milk to go with it. The sun was trying to shine but it was still raining.

"I discovered there were four divisions in accounting—payroll, royalties, accounts payable, and . . ." She went through the files like a professional.

Mason only listened with half an ear. Maybe there was stuff here he could use, but he honestly didn't want to think that way. Like a predator. Not when he was struggling with the idea that he might have found the one woman who could make him happy for the rest of his life.

No, this was crazy. She'd talked about chemistry. This was just really good sex. He was making too much of it. But he knew the difference between lust and love. Or did he? He sure as hell knew lust. He'd fucked plenty of women and done his best to leave them satisfied.

Love? His parents had loved each other. He'd seen a happy marriage up close and personal. They'd been partners, respected each other. Put each other first and supported each other through good times and bad. Created a family that was a haven for their kids and rock-solid. All Mason had to do was look around at his friends and their broken homes to know he'd never settle for less than what his mom and dad had found. That's why he'd never had a long-term thing with any of the women he'd been with before. They'd always disappointed him, bored him or proved to be after his money when all was said and done.

Now, as he listened to Cass lay out her plan for Calhoun, he realized he felt more than a grinding need to get inside her again. He wanted to *know* her. She was smart, funny, and as honest as any woman he'd ever met. She might not have grown up around a decent relationship, but she wanted one for herself. Why else would she have hung onto the old boyfriend like a security blanket for so long?

But could she deal with the fact that he'd be the one to tell her that her dreams of a big payday at the end of this year were probably just that—dreams? She'd hate him if he took her daddy's company away from her family. Or used what he learned as her mentor to raid Calhoun's assets. Could he do it now?

When the lights suddenly came on, Mason knew he had screwed himself into a hell of a corner. Did he choose business or his own happiness? He got mad and asked the universe: Why couldn't he have both?

Then his cell phone rang and so did hers. By the time they got off their phones he knew the universe was a bitch who was going to make sure he wouldn't get either.

Chapter 11

Cass couldn't believe the storm was finally over. It had swept through Houston and the surrounding areas, leaving high-water damage and trees downed. Then it had gone on to do the same to Louisiana before petering out east somewhere. While she'd been losing her mind in Mason's arms, the world had kept turning and lives had kept going. Some of them downhill.

Mason's call had been about trouble in the Gulf with his oil rig. He'd rushed to Texas Star headquarters as soon as they'd been able to leave the high-rise. He'd turned on the TV and they'd realized they were an island surrounded by road closures. Not even his big truck could get through until they'd finally gotten an all-clear on the news. He'd been really anxious by the time he'd left Cass at her door with a quick kiss. She knew his problems were serious by the look on his face, but he wouldn't say exactly what had happened.

Now she was home and on the phone.

"Manny and I were celebrating that he was living here now. I forgot all about how that parking lot floods." Ellie sounded upset. Of course she was. "By the time Manny ran out to move both our cars to a high spot, it was too late. His truck was okay, but my hunk of junk drowned. I'll have to buy a new one."

"I'm so sorry. What about insurance?" Cass sat at her desk in her master suite.

"I just had liability, Cass, so no help there. The beater was over ten years old and not worth the high premiums." Ellie sighed. "It's okay. That money I got for your rent will give me a solid down payment and I wanted a new car anyway. It's just hard to be forced into this."

"I know. Can I help? I didn't need my moving money."

"No, I'm okay. Let me know how work goes tomorrow. Call me if you want to meet for drinks afterward. I should have a new car by then."

"I will." Cass looked up when the outer doors opened. "Good luck." She hung up and waited for Shannon and Megan to state their business. By the way they were staring at her, they had questions. Then Ethan came up behind them. He was grinning.

"Spent the night with Mason, sis? I'd say operation 'Seduce the Evaluator' is going full-speed ahead." He walked up and offered his fist for a bump.

Cass ignored it. "There was a hurricane outside. Power outage. What makes you think I seduced him?"

"Let's see." Shannon pushed her brother out of the way and stepped to Cass's side. "Whisker burn on your neck, maybe." She laughed. "Oh, look at her blush. I've heard Mason MacKenzie is hot in the sack. Any truth to that?"

"I don't think that's any of your business." Cass opened her laptop. "I have work to do. I start my new job at Calhoun tomorrow."

"No!" Ethan fell into a chair. It made a noise like it had a built-in whoopee cushion in the seat so he jumped back up. He glared at it before he turned back to Cass. "Daddy had the stupidest stuff in here. I'm almost sorry we set you up to live with it. But Cassidy, what the hell? You're starting work a week early? Are you trying to make us look bad? Does Mason know?"

"Of course he knows. It was pillow talk." Cass laughed when Ethan moaned and put his head in his hands. "Oh, get over it. You're going to have to work in our father's company too. If I were you I'd get busy learning about the job. Mason is pretty chill about this thing and swears he's going to be basing his assessment on how our supervisors rate us. That's not exactly good news, folks. Especially if you don't know what in the hell you're doing." She frowned at an email from John Hardcastle. Had he found out Holly had sent her those names and numbers? Was he going to slap Cass's hand? Fire Holly?

"My job is with computers. Piece of cake." Ethan smiled at his sisters. "These two? Listen up, girls. Maybe Cassidy is on to something."

Megan and Shannon were whispering together. Finally Megan spoke up.

"Well, I'm not in any hurry to put on a hard hat and go to work. I could study my brains out and not learn what I need to know in the oil fields. That's a job you learn as you go." She glanced at Shannon. "I say enjoy your week's head start, Cass. We don't have to jump on the bandwagon." She headed for the bookcase and hit the book for the hidden bar. When it swung out, she turned to her sister and brother. "Name your poison, kids. Our sister is buying."

"Now you're talking. I'll be in public relations. That's the kind of thing I do for my charities all the time. I'm a natural. If I can't bull-shit my way through that job, then I'm not Conrad Calhoun's daughter." Shannon studied the various liquor bottles and picked out one to carry to the desk. She stopped next to Cass and peered over her shoulder.

Cass ignored her. She'd opened that email from Hardcastle.

"Cassidy, what's wrong?" Shannon paused in the act of filling her crystal tumbler. "You look like you're reading an obituary."

"Might as well be." Cass stood, almost knocking over her chair. "Pour me one of those, Megan. I'll try our daddy's favorite bourbon."

Megan gave her a splash from a bottle with a label Cass had never heard of. "Okay, tell us the bad news. Shan's right. You look freaked out."

"I just got a letter of resignation from our CFO."

"What's that?" Megan gave herself two fingers of bourbon too.

"Chief financial officer. My boss in accounting. He's the man who keeps the financial side of Calhoun together. Without him, we're screwed." Cass sipped the alcohol and felt the smooth burn all the way down her throat.

"So he's quitting. Isn't that stupid? Where's he getting another job like that in this economy?" Ethan pulled open a mini-fridge built into the bar and grabbed a soda. "No alcohol for me. I'm supposed to go help a friend fix his laptop later."

"He's been hired by another big oil company. Apparently he was promised a raise and perks. The best perk, in his opinion? He won't have to deal with me."

Shannon gasped. She was reading the email. "That bastard! Listen to what he says about Cassidy: *I wouldn't use your pitiful excuse for a résumé to wipe my ass.* Can you believe he said that? About a Calhoun?" She took a deep swallow of her drink. "Why, Daddy would wipe the floor of the company with that man's insolent ass." She gave Cass a hug. "I'm sorry, Cass."

"So am I. He's using vacation time so he won't be back at all. That leaves us totally in the lurch." Cass looked longingly at the rest of the bourbon in her glass. She'd never had liquor that strong or that smooth before. No, the last thing she needed now was cloudy judgment.

"Good riddance, I say. Can you imagine how he'd have evaluated you? And he obviously would have done nothing to help you." Shannon poured herself another double vodka.

Megan stomped around the room. "No kidding. I wonder if we can all expect this kind of hostility at Calhoun. Any idea what you can do?" She picked up the poster of the two-headed goat, then turned it to face the wall. "God, Daddy liked creepy stuff." She faced Cass again. "You dodged a bullet there, sis."

Cass sighed. "Not a clue. As for what you'll find, I can only hope most people would have the good sense to think about the family connection and tread carefully. We're already doing layoffs."

"Yeah." Ethan sipped his soda. "Mason will protect us. That's what he's there for. If this CFO wasn't already gone, he would see about straightening him out." At that, her sisters and brother relaxed, clearly reassured. They went back to their drinks and discussing the tree on the property that had fallen during the storm the night before.

"People, please. Listen to me. That hurricane was nothing compared to what Hardcastle just did to all of us by leaving the company."

Well, that got their attention. They stopped talking and looked at her. "He was the numbers man. In charge of making decisions that affect our bottom line at Calhoun. Now that he's gone, guess who's going to have to do that? Our father made me Hardcastle's number two in the office." Cass's stomach rolled just saying that.

"So?" Ethan sat on the edge of the desk. "You can crunch numbers. Despite what that man said about your résumé, don't you have a fancy business degree and banking experience? How hard can it be?"

Cass sank into her chair again, fighting hysterical laughter. Sitting there in her outrageous zebra-striped chair, she almost wished she could turn back time. To her safe but comfortable world where she knew what in the hell she was doing. Now she had to go into the office on Monday and pretend to run a business that she knew next to nothing about. She had a gas card and could fill her own tank. Whoopee! As if that qualified her to deal with oil and gas royalties, leases and futures, not to mention the cost of the equipment they needed. Oh, and they had a pipeline division. The more she'd studied, the more complicated it became and the more lost she felt.

She let her head drop to the desk. She was tempted to keep banging it against the painted wood until she blacked out.

"Cass? Talk to us." Megan stood on one side, Shannon on the other. "Tell us why this is so bad."

"Okay." Cass sat up and gently closed the laptop. She needed to think and staring at the names of people to lay off just made it worse. "My experience doesn't qualify me to do Hardcastle's job." She looked straight ahead at a poster for one of the classic acts in the circus.

"It's like asking the guy who cleans the cages to step in and take over as lion tamer. The lions will gobble him up because they'll sense his fear. And if he does survive, he sure as hell won't be able to put on a successful show. Understand?" She closed her eyes. Yes, she'd make a tasty meal for any one of the executives who had reported to Hardcastle. They'd see right through her lack of knowledge and laugh her out of there tomorrow. God.

"Understand? Not really, but Hardcastle sounds like an asshole. Who hired him away from us?" Megan and Ethan jockeyed for position, shoving each other until Megan won and she sat on the edge of the desk.

"Texas Star." Cass picked up her glass and drained it.

Mason was so mad at first, he'd avoided his uncle, almost afraid of what he'd do when he saw him. But of course he got over that. He stormed into Ed's office past Lucille, who jumped to her feet, clearly frightened by what she saw on Mason's face. Yeah, he was in a mood to kill the son of a bitch.

Ed was on the phone, boots on the desk as usual. He frowned at Mason, but didn't hang up. "Yes, we're all over it. Mason went out there last week and found out what the problem was. We were on the way to fixing it when the fucking storm hit and those welds didn't hold. Cleanup crew is on their way. EPA is on our asses, you can be sure of that, but we'll deal with them like we always do. Pay a fine. You know how it goes." He listened, his feet hitting the floor as he sat up straight. "Now listen here. We're partners in this. There's any fines, we *all* pay them. Equal shares." He was gripping the phone hard now. "I don't have to listen to this. We have lawyers too, C.L. So don't try to pull that shit on me." He hung up.

Mason waited. It wasn't easy. He wanted to go ahead and tear into Ed himself. But he needed to hear the bad news first. C.L. Hunter was head of the other major partner on Big Tex. Which was spilling oil into the Gulf. No surprise. There hadn't been time to repair even half of the pipes on the well. He'd been on the phone all afternoon ordering more men out there and sending out the cleanup crews. It was a clusterfuck and he'd already tried to talk to their bankers about the cost. They were playing hardball, not willing to loan money in this economy without high rates of interest. It was his worst nightmare.

"What are you looking at? Progress report." Ed reached for a cigar.

"You first. What did C.L. say?" Mason couldn't sit down and didn't want a drink. He had too much to do. So he paced back and forth in front of that huge desk his uncle used as a shield against any and everyone who tried to get to him.

"He's blaming this on us. Trying to make us pay all the freight." Ed lit the cigar and puffed until he was satisfied he had it going good. "You heard me. I won't put up with that shit. We're in this together."

"Until he gets us in court and hears that it was your handpicked inspector's negligence that put us in this mess." Mason stopped and faced his uncle, his fists on the mahogany. "Goddamn it, Ed. This is our fault. No, *your* fault. Your cost-cutting and sleazy dealings made this happen."

"If called to testify, boy, you will lie your ass off." Ed waved that cigar. "You'll have amnesia about that damned inspector. We keep information like that in the family. You hear me?"

"Did you care about the family when you hired that damned inspector? Hell, no! And now you've put what could be the nail in our coffin." Mason walked over to the window. "I won't be surprised if this is the deathblow for Granddaddy's company. The banks have already told me they won't extend our lines of credit at the rates we're used to getting. All while we're still bleeding money into the Gulf."

"Shut your mouth." Ed was on his feet, standing next to him. "We don't give up over a little oil leak."

"Little?" Mason felt his blood pressure rise.

"Keep your shirt on. At least the rig didn't blow up and kill anyone." Ed waved that damned cigar for emphasis, scattering ash on the carpet under their feet. "This company has to survive and it's your duty, boy, to make sure of it. Use your pretty face and sweet talk to get us that money at the right price. You know that's what you do." Ed slapped him on the back. "Come on now, get to work. You can handle this setback."

"Don't touch me again, Ed." Mason wheeled around to face him. "I mean it. Don't fucking ever lay a hand on me again. You may have just lost us Texas Star." He looked down at his fists, wondering if he really even cared any more. Double-dealing, fast-talking. That was all he did here. He was sick of it. Sick of being Ed's boy.

"If this is the end of the family business, it's on you." Mason took a breath, almost choking on his anger and the stench of Ed's expensive cigar. "The only reason I'll fight to keep it afloat is because we have people who depend on the money we make. I won't let us go down if there's any way to prevent it." He backed away, afraid of what he'd do if he had to be near Ed another minute. "I swear to God, if this company fails, I'll kill you."

He stalked out of the open door, pretty sure Lucille had heard every word of what had been said inside. He didn't care. He had to beg the bankers to give them one more loan. Or sell off property and equipment at a loss just to get cash. Those were desperate measures that would have sharks circling, smelling blood in the water and ready to take advantage. Maybe they'd even try for a takeover. It would be a smart play.

Mason was more than a little sick at the thought. Was it just a few hours ago that he'd let himself forget all about the oil business and lose himself in Cassidy's arms? He'd like to do that again. Forget reality and sink into a warm and welcoming woman. He wanted to pick up the phone and see how she was doing. Did she have regrets about last night? He sure didn't have any. Then the phone rang under his hand and he was soon neck-deep in negotiations. Damn it, his personal life would have to wait.

Bedtime. Cass knew she needed a good night's sleep if she was going to face the people at Calhoun tomorrow, but there was that gruesome clown headboard staring at her. She tried a sleep mask but it was uncomfortable and kept slipping. Finally, she threw an extra sheet over the giant, grinning face. It helped.

She'd sent a text to Mason, trying to convince herself that he wouldn't, couldn't have been behind hiring Hardcastle. The CFO's email had been sent before their date on Saturday. No man could have been that good at keeping a secret. Could he? If Mason was such a great liar, then Cass knew she'd made a huge mistake sleeping with him. But now that she was in that giant bed under the circus tent remembering how he'd made her feel and how they'd enjoyed each other in every way . . . Well, she just refused to believe he would deceive her like that.

He'd talked about his uncle, a man he hated but had to work with. It must have been Ed MacKenzie who had stolen Hardcastle from Calhoun. She tried to convince herself that was true as she tossed and turned.

Sleep wasn't coming. Because she'd discovered another annoyance in that bizarre bedroom. It was a miracle she hadn't noticed it before. But then she'd been so excited about her date with Mason. Oh, and she'd had the TV on the weather report. Anyway, the clock against one wall chimed the hour and half hour. No, it didn't chime. It honked. Like the toot of the horn in a clown car. Oh, God, could this place be more ridiculous?

It was close to one in the morning when Cass gave up and turned on the bedside-table lamp. The lamp was a merry-go-round and tinkled merrily before finally settling down to light her side of the bed.

"What next, a roller coaster in the closet? Daddy, you were a little crazy, you know that?" Cass jumped out of bed to study the tall clock. The swinging pendulum featured, naturally, a clown car. It was behind a glass door that she opened with a flick of a lever. If she could stop the pendulum, then surely the clock would stop too.

Cass put her finger on the pendulum. It resisted. *Honk! Honk! Honk!* It sounded in distress. No telling how valuable the stupid thing was. Cass was ready to pick up the ringmaster's whip that sat on top of the dresser and use it to smash the clock face anyway. Hopefully that would kill the mechanism. But then this was supposed to go to a museum someday. Damn it.

Her phone buzzed with a text message. This late? She picked it up from the nightstand. Mason.

I'm outside. Will you let me in?

Cass sighed. Should she? It *was* late and she was tired. But she wasn't going to sleep anyway. And she wanted answers. Did *he* hire

Hardcastle? Did he know about it when they'd made love? She texted him to wait while she came down to unlock the front door. Then she grabbed a robe and headed down the stairs.

"I saw your light on. Can't sleep?" He didn't wait for her to say anything when she opened the door, just pulled her into his arms. Just before the house alarms blared.

"Oh, damn it. I forgot." Cass quickly punched in the code Janie had given her. Nothing happened. "Oh, wait. I think I got it backwards." She punched again. "Shit. What was it?" The wailing sirens were joined by the house phone ringing in the entry.

"That's going to be your security company." Mason picked up the phone. "Do you know your safe word?"

"No. Got it!" Cass finally managed to hit the right combination of numbers and the siren went silent.

The alarm company was asking Mason for a special word to verify that there hadn't been a break-in before they sent the police.

"Give me that!" Megan stomped down the stairs, a gun in her hand, and grabbed the phone. "We're okay here. *Ringling Brothers.* Yes, thank you." She hung up then turned to Cass. "Think you can remember that?"

Cass slammed and locked the front door. "Yes, sure. You remember where I sleep? Or try to sleep?"

"Hi, Mason." Megan glanced down at her gun. "Glad I didn't shoot you."

"Me too. Nice gun. And outfit." He grinned at her.

"I don't have a guest tonight so I'm all about comfort." She wore a T-shirt from a rock concert and nothing else. "As for the gun, you know I can shoot. My daddy taught you and me both. Cass? Do I need to put a bullet in him? About that new hire at Texas Star?" Megan looked serious.

"Maybe later. I need to get some answers first." Cass nodded. "Appreciate the offer."

"Any time." Megan winked. "Oh, here come the troops. One of them, anyway." She shook her head when Ethan arrived at the top of the stairs. "Heavy sleeper. Show's over. Go back to bed. It's just our sister, doing her duty for the cause." She beckoned to Cass and leaned in to whisper in her ear: "Daddy's gun is in the drawer at the bottom of the fortune-teller's booth if you need it later. If Mason's hiring away our people, put a bullet in him." She glanced at Mason.

"We'll all testify it was self-defense. If he didn't do it, move on in the seduction phase of the program. I'm sure it's a big sacrifice." She patted Cass's shoulder, then grinned.

"I wouldn't, I'm not—" Cass knew she flushed. Didn't help that she hadn't tied her robe and her skimpy nightie was showing.

"Do what you gotta do, sis." Megan looked Mason over. "Looking a little rough there, Mason. Heard your well in the Gulf sprung a leak."

"Yes. Thanks for bringing that up." Mason moved closer to Cass. "We're making progress. Glad to see you're keeping up with what's going on in the oil industry, Meg. Maybe there's hope for you yet."

"It's all over the news. How could I miss it?" Megan's smile was friendly now, as if she remembered his role as evaluator. "Good luck with it."

"Thanks. I'm surprised Janie and her husband didn't show up with a shotgun when that alarm went off." Mason looked tired and he still had on the clothes he'd worn when she'd left him earlier. If he'd run a comb through his hair, you couldn't tell it and he needed a shave.

"One of us manages to set off that alarm at least once a week." Megan flipped on the safety on her handgun. "You've seen how Shannon drinks. It's usually her. Janie doesn't come in unless the alarm company calls her too and the cops show up." She put her foot on the bottom stair. "Well, it's been fun, but good night." Megan waved the gun and headed back upstairs, giving them a good view of her bare butt as she walked away.

"I'm sorry about that." Cass nodded toward the kitchen. "How about raiding the refrigerator? I couldn't sleep and now I'm hungry."

"Good. I'm starved. Skipped dinner." Mason slipped his arm around her. "Come here first." He pulled her in and kissed her. "There. That's better." Then he studied her. "Something wrong? What's that Megan said about Texas Star?"

"Let's talk about it over sandwiches. Janie has roast beef." Cass pushed back and headed for the kitchen. She managed to put off the serious stuff with a description of her battle with the oddball circus collectibles. Mason volunteered to take a look at the clock. Which meant he wanted to head to her bedroom as soon as they finished their snack.

"Maybe. But first tell me this: Did *you* hire John Hardcastle at Texas Star?" Cass wiped off the counter, then faced him.

"What?" Mason looked astonished. "The CFO at Calhoun? What are you talking about?"

"He emailed me, Mason. He's going to work at your company, starting immediately. And he won't be back to help me with the transition on Monday." Cass ran her hands through her hair, realizing it was probably wild. "It's sink or swim for me, starting tomorrow. I'm going to be in charge unless I can find a supervisor who seems qualified to take over."

"I'll be damned." Mason jumped up from the bar stool where he'd been sitting while he ate. "That son of a bitch."

"Who?" But Cass was pretty sure she knew. Mason's surprise had looked real to her.

"My uncle Ed. This is just the kind of stunt he likes to pull. He'll be pumping Hardcastle for all the financial weak spots at Calhoun. He wants us to raid your company for prime assets. Take it over if we can." Mason walked around the end of the bar. "Did you think I did this, Cassidy? That I'd make love to you while I was plotting to sabotage you like that?"

"I don't really know you, do I, Mason? The oil business is in desperate straits. I spent the afternoon and evening reading everything I could on it. Texas Star has a big problem out in the Gulf right now. If Calhoun has cash, you could sure use it to plug the hole you've got leaking money."

"Wow. You did understand what you read, didn't you?" Mason kept his hands off of her.

"I'm not stupid. I won't say I love getting into this business. It's not a natural interest for me. But I can figure things out when I have to. Put our two companies together and you'd be in much better shape. I have no idea how much trouble my company is in because I haven't had time to check the books. But it's obvious to me that yours is on a slippery slope toward bankruptcy." Cass hated to put it so bluntly, but it was what she'd learned from the dozens of articles she'd read.

"Thanks for pointing that out. Why do you think I've been having these weeks from hell?" Mason did approach her then. "I had no idea Ed was going to poach your guy. It's a dirty, underhanded move.

Yes, he'll learn what Hardcastle knows and expect me to use it to steal what assets we can from Calhoun." He jerked Cass against him. "Will I do it?" He rested his chin on her hair. "I'll try not to."

"Try?" Cass didn't like that word. She shoved back. "Are we at war, then?"

"Honestly? In business, I guess we are. I sure as hell don't want to be. But this is my family's company we're talking about. You heard my mother. She lives on her Texas Star royalties and dividends."

"Yes, well, I'm sorry, but I have to put Calhoun first." Cass hated to say it, but it was the truth. She had a family now and she liked the feeling too much to throw it away. "I'm sure there are people like your mother depending on our royalties and dividends too." She looked around the huge kitchen. "They're probably what keep this house going. Janie told me she's planning to retire on her Calhoun income."

"You see? It's a standoff." Mason touched her cheek. "Do we have to let this come between us? I like the way we are together. As a man and a woman. Fuck the business side. Can we just be two people who want each other? Like we were last night?"

"We were great last night. I admit it. I can't stop remembering how it was." Cass moved into his arms. "But how can we separate the two things? This business is going to consume me starting tomorrow. I know it will. I always take work seriously. It's what I do and who I am. I'm a type-A personality."

"Sure. I admire that about you. Me? I'm type-F." Mason opened her robe and smiled.

"F? What's that?" Cass kept her hands on his chest.

"Fuck the rules and go with the flow. I use my talents to get things done and I love a challenge. Sometimes I use my gift of gab. Sometimes I know things that can grease the wheels in negotiations. I love it when I can surprise people and make things turn around on a dime." He grinned and her robe slid to the floor.

"A challenge. Was that all I was? Or part of a strategy?" She'd always wondered that: How much of Mason's play for her had been part of a plan. "To get inside Calhoun?"

"Now, I wouldn't say that." He toyed with the straps on her gown. "Okay, so you challenged me. And getting inside Calhoun wouldn't be a bad thing."

He must have felt her stiffen in his arms. "Whoa. Then I got to know you and strategy went right out the window. You felt it. This thing between us. I know you did. So did I. It started fast, yes. But I like where it's going and I think you do too. Will we need to renegotiate in the future? Who knows? Tonight, can we just go upstairs and kill the clock so you and I can do what we know will be great?" He slid his hand under her short gown, cupping her butt and pulling her firmly against him. "Deal?"

"You drive a hard bargain, Mason MacKenzie." Cass knew she was letting her feelings take over the logical side of her brain. But being this close to him did that to her. She hooked a leg around one of his hard thighs and crawled up his body. "Deal." She kissed him then, pretty sure she'd regret being such a pushover later. Yes, he was a smooth talker. But so what? Feeling him against her, his hand warm on her skin, how could she regret anything?

Chapter 12

Mason didn't kill the clock; he simply slowed down the pendulum until it finally stopped. Then he turned to Cass.

"It's late. I know what I said, but I should probably leave so you can get some sleep. Big day tomorrow." He glanced at the sheet covering her headboard. "You think you can sleep now?"

"Not a chance." Cass sat on the edge of the bed. She'd thrown that robe on the floor. Scruff on his jaw, hair a little wild. Why did this man make her so hot and bothered and needy? "You promised once you'd help me relax if I couldn't sleep. You still willing?" She smiled when he moved in, his knees bumping hers apart.

"More than." He shoved her to her back, then ripped his shirt off over his head. His shoulders gleamed in the light from that silly merry-go-round lamp. "It'll take some work to get your mind off all these distractions." He didn't have to name them—they were obvious. The sheet was slipping off the clown headboard and that stupid clock gave one last honk. "But I think I'm up to the job."

Cass reached for his belt buckle. There was no denying the bulge below it. "More than? Oh, yeah." She tugged him down to her. "We both need sleep. I don't think we got more than a couple of hours last night and it's late." She ran her hands up his warm, firm stomach. "But I'm too wired to sleep. My brain won't turn off. So come here and do something about that."

"At your service." Mason fell on her, taking her mouth with his. He held her head in his hands and used his lips and tongue to coax a moan out of her. She was unzipping him and guiding him to her before he drew back. "Slow down, Cassidy. Let's make this last so long that we pass out afterwards. Not a thought in our heads but a dizzy sense of completion."

"Sounds . . . irresistible." Cass loved the feel of him, so strong, so all male. True to his word he didn't strip down right away. He just concentrated on kissing her like she was more delicious than the finest chocolate. He sipped, tasted, went deep with his tongue, then barely touched her lips until she wanted to grab his ears and pull him in for more. He laughed and unwrapped her then, easing off the straps of her pale blue nightgown.

"I love a woman who wears silk and lace to bed." He used his nose to push down the gown until he bared her nipples. "Megan's T-shirt didn't do it for me. But this . . ." he licked, then drew one aching bud into his mouth, the pressure so intense Cass felt its pull deep inside. He leaned back. "Yeah, this is perfect. Feminine. Inviting." He kept going south, his hand, then his lips working a path to her stomach.

Cass sucked in as he circled her navel. Her hands stayed in his hair. He was doing all the work and she let him. Relaxing? She was wound up and getting tighter the further down her body he traveled with his clever mouth.

"You're tickling me, Mason."

"Can't have that." He glanced up with a wicked grin. "This is no laughing matter." He eased the gown past her hips. "No panties. Now I'd say that meant you hoped I was coming by tonight."

"I never sleep in panties. It's"—oh, God, his tongue was dipping so close—"healthy to . . . never mind." He pushed her legs apart and raised her knees. "Mason?"

"Hmm?" He didn't answer, just kept looking her over. His warm breath touched her and she shivered. "Don't distract me, Cassidy, I just hit liquid gold."

Cass choked out a laugh. "Are you comparing me to drilling for oil?"

"That was a compliment, sweetheart." He looked up, winked, then dragged his tongue along the valley where she was wet and welcoming.

Oh, yes, she knew she was dying for him. Needed for him to get on with it. Her hands clenched in his hair. She had to stop that or she'd pull out some of it.

"Mason!" It was an urgent call. He ignored her and plunged his tongue inside, finding that place that made her arch off the bed. "Oh, please."

He pulled back, his eyes shining. "Please what? You want something?"

"You. I want you. Inside me." Cass gasped and tried to sit up, get to him so she could pull him where she wanted him. She grabbed his shoulders, tried to reach his hips, but couldn't. Damn it, she wanted him now.

"But I'm not finished with you yet, lady." He had the nerve to lift her legs and settle them on his shoulders. then put his mouth to her again.

"Oh my God!" Cass didn't think she could take much more of that and beat the bed with her fists. "Damn you, Mason MacKenzie. Quit torturing me." Those were the last words she could choke out as waves of pleasure-pain took over every bit of her body. She was dying, living, feeling more than she wanted to feel. He had to stop or she'd—God! When she broke, she screamed, sure the people in the rest of the house were probably reaching for their guns.

Abruptly, Mason dropped her back on the bed and shucked his pants. Then, while the tremors still rode her hard, he drove into her. Cass felt him moving inside her and gasped at the sensation, his cock touching off another firestorm that swept over her. She didn't think she could take another overwhelming feeling like that again, but the way he held her hips and rocked against her answered her body's call for completion. She shuddered and grabbed hold of him, dying a little as he plunged into her. It seemed like hours, but was probably only a few minutes before they both cried out and fell together.

He rolled her on top of him and lay there panting, his cheek resting against her hair. Cass tried to collect her thoughts. But he'd managed to do what he'd promised. She couldn't think, couldn't focus. He'd taken her out of herself, this place and this time, and left her dazed and ready to sleep. So she closed her eyes and passed out.

Hours later she woke to the shower running. Mason. She stretched and looked up to see that damned clown leering at her. The sheet must have slipped during the night, probably while they'd made vigorous use of the bed. Cass glanced at the clock on the nightstand. It was her own clock radio she'd brought from the apartment. She'd decided the ridiculous circus-themed one that had come with the bedroom wasn't going to cut it. Five in the morning. So Mason was leaving. Probably to get ready for work. It wouldn't hurt her to get a jump-start on the day too. On less than three hours' sleep. Yeah, she'd be sharp all day.

She got up and found her robe. Forget the gown—it had landed on the floor next to the bed. Mason was singing in the shower, a country hit that made her smile. He sounded happy. Cass was going to take credit for that. His company was in a mess so obviously their lovemaking was what made him sing this morning. Lovemaking? Well, sex, anyway. There'd been no love words spoken by either one of them.

She was brushing her teeth when the shower cut off and he opened the glass door. Cass spit out her toothpaste, then handed him a towel. She almost hated to do it. That body. And what it could do. She smiled. "Good morning."

He ran the towel over his hair and chest, then wrapped it around his hips. "Good morning to you." He pulled her to him and kissed her. He tasted like toothpaste too. Had he used her toothbrush? That thought didn't bother Cass as much as it should have.

"It's early." Cass tweaked his nipples. "In a hurry?" What was she thinking? Maybe she was turning into a sex addict.

"Not when there's this in front of me." Mason opened her robe and slid his hands over her breasts. "You okay?"

"Oh, yeah." Cass sighed when he thumbed her nipples. "I'm great, actually."

"We're good together, Cassidy." He slid one hand down and around her to cup her bottom. "Once I leave here today, it's war, re-member? So I guess we'd better take advantage of this time we've got." He lifted her up to the counter and opened her legs, then dropped his towel.

"War. I don't want to think that way. Surely we can figure out how to work together, Mason." Cass gasped when he slid inside her. God, he felt good. She held onto him, linking her ankles behind him. "Our companies essentially do the same thing. Pump and move oil and gas. It might be a good idea to join forces." She leaned against him as he rocked into her. The pressure was building again. Not as intense as last night—nothing could top that—but good, so good.

"You don't know what you're saying, Cass. And I won't hold you to that." Mason kissed her, then held her hips tight. He moved faster, deeper, his face serious as he seemed to claim her in that steamy bathroom. "War, Cassidy. We're at war in business and it's good for you to remember that." He picked her up and moved her to the wall.

The pressure of that hard surface against her back made a difference and Cass cried out as her orgasm hit her hard.

"Mason, please! I don't want—"

"To fight?" He dropped his head to her shoulder, his forehead damp. "It was inevitable. Texas Star is going down unless I can find a way to save it." He looked up, deadly serious. "I'll be as honest as I can with you. The only way may be to raid Calhoun assets." He gently set Cass on her feet, their connection broken in more ways than one. "By the time all is said and done, you'll probably hate me."

Cass touched his cheek. Hate him? She was very afraid she'd fallen in love with him. So now what? Could she put a job before a man who was possibly the love of her life? Yes, she'd loved Rowdy, but it had been a safe kind of love that had turned into a habit. What she felt for Mason was so much more.

Would it be selfish of her to put her feelings first? Before a company? But it wasn't just a company, was it? It was her future and the future of her new family at stake. A fortune that she'd never dreamed of, but that could make a huge difference in her life and the lives of a lot of people: stockholders, leaseholders. She'd learned through her research that there were a lot of ways that people depended on oil companies for income. Yes, the price of oil made that income fluctuate, but if a company went under, the cash stopped flowing entirely. People would suffer.

Cass pulled Mason's face down to kiss him. What could she say to make this right? Make him understand that she didn't want war? But clearly she had nothing to say. There were forces at work that she didn't understand yet. Maybe once she got to her job, she could find a way to fix things. As if. Mason knew the industry inside and out and he had sounded desperate. His kiss felt that way too. She leaned back with a sigh.

"War, then." She walked over to the shower stall. "I have to get ready for work. Big day today." She dropped her robe on the floor. "I hope yours goes well." She turned on the water, deliberately ignoring that damned clown showerhead.

Mason watched Cass step into the shower after pulling on a plastic shower cap to cover her hair. Well, he'd tried his best to warn her. She probably didn't even believe him. But the truth was, he might have to go for a Calhoun takeover. If Hardcastle had information that made Calhoun vulnerable, then all bets were off. Mason stalked into the bedroom and found his clothes. He'd have to go by his place and change before he headed to the office. There were so many problems to deal with he hardly knew where to start.

He was just putting on his boots when Cass's phone buzzed on the nightstand. She had a text and he reached for the phone. This early, it was probably important. He couldn't help himself and read what it said.

Happy birthday, baby. It was from her mother.

Mason looked at the date. Well, what do you know? Cass was turning thirty today. He knew that from the paperwork he'd studied before he'd even met her. But the date had sneaked up on him. He carried the phone into the steamy bathroom. She was just stepping out of the shower. She'd been clean and fresh when he'd gotten here last night so this had been a quick wash, getting rid of the smell of sex, of course. Too bad. He liked it on her. She wrapped a towel around her body and walked over to the mirror.

"You got a text." He handed her the phone. "You speaking to your mother now?"

She glanced at the phone. "Guess so. I'll call her."

"Happy birthday, Cassidy." Mason pulled her in for a kiss. "You have plans tonight?"

"Ellie said something about getting together for drinks after work. I forgot it was today with the work thing staring me in the face." She was gripping the phone hard as she eased away from him. "You want to join us?"

"Wouldn't miss it. Text me your plans and I'll meet you anywhere, anytime." He followed her to the bedroom. "Good luck with your mother."

"You can stay, if you want to. While I call her." Cass sat on the side of the bed. "Do. I'm a little nervous. I haven't talked to her since I yelled at her about keeping my father a secret."

"Okay, I'll stay." Mason sat beside her on the bed. "She must get an early start. It's just a little after six."

Cass took a breath then grabbed her towel, which had slipped. Mason noticed, of course. She should have told him to leave but his presence did calm her down. She was glad her mother had broken the silence between them. Her birthday. She'd forgotten in the rush of moving, the new job and, of course, this thing with Mason.

"Got-Yer-Dollar opens early and she always gets there before any of the employees do." Cass took a steadying breath. "Here goes." She punched a button. The phone rang once before a woman answered. "Mama?"

"Cassidy. I'm glad you called, honey. Happy birthday. This is a big one, isn't it?"

"Yes, Mama. Thanks for the text." Cass reached for Mason's hand. "How are you doing?"

"The usual. Still running those sales. Store's busy. Which is a good thing." Elizabeth coughed. "Caught that damned cold that was going around."

"Have you been to a doctor?" Cass leaned against Mason. Could he hear the conversation? Probably not.

"Don't have time. I'll be okay. Want you to know: I wrote that letter. Explaining things. Sent you a little something for your birthday too. Did you get it yet?" More coughing. Deep, like a smoker's cough.

Mason squeezed Cass's hand. He must have heard that cough. If his mother sounded like that, she knew he'd be taking her to the doctor himself. She'd seen how close they were.

"No. Where did you send it?" Cass sighed. "You'd better go to the doctor. I can take you, Mama. Make an appointment."

"Forget it, Cassidy. I won't waste my time or money on those quacks. I sent it to your apartment. Guess you're not still living there, but I didn't have the new address. Maybe you can go get it."

"Ellie will bring it to me. I'm seeing her tonight." Cass stood, too upset to sit. "I have the money for a doctor. And you have health insurance. Use it." This was so typical of her mother. Stubborn about everything.

"I won't take a damned dime of Calhoun money. Never have. Never will. So get that notion out of your head right now, Cassidy Jane. Once you read the letter I sent, we'll talk. And you'll understand why I'm so down on anything to do with Conrad Calhoun and his ill-gotten gains." Coughing again. "Happy birthday, baby. I've got to get ready to go to work now. Have a wonderful day with your friends. I love you. Always have, always will. I'll never regret giving birth to you, just sorry I picked the wrong sperm donor."

"Mama!" Cass blinked back the tears in her eyes.

"Got to hang up." And the line went dead.

Cass stared at the phone, then wiped her wet cheeks. "My mother. She's sick, but would rather die than spend a dime on her own health. I guarantee if I showed up and tried to wrestle her into the car for a doctor's appointment, she wouldn't go."

"God, Cassidy. I'm sorry." Mason pulled her to him and rubbed her back. "She called, though. To wish you a happy birthday."

"Yes. And she loves me. She wrote that letter, but sent it to the apartment. I'll text Ellie and get her to bring it tonight. Maybe we'll find out what she had on Conrad that he thought would hurt Calhoun Petroleum." Cass got up to walk to her closet. "Boy, did she hate my father."

"I don't know about you, but I need coffee. Why don't you get dressed and I'll see if I can find some in the kitchen." Mason kissed her cheek, then tightened her towel, even though he played with it like he'd have been happy to rip it off of her. But this wasn't the time for that kind of thing.

"Coffee. Yes, that'll help clear my head. I'll come down in a little while." She smiled and brushed his cheek with her fingertips. "Thanks. For being here. I know you and your mother have an entirely different relationship. It was just Mom and me for all those years and she had to be strong or we wouldn't have survived. She never shows vulnerability. Like with an illness." Cass walked to the bathroom door. "And she sure won't lean on anyone. Especially not me."

"Well, it's not a sin to ask for help. Keep that in mind, Cassidy. It's why I'm here, remember?" Mason watched her disappear into the bathroom, then headed downstairs. He really wanted to know what was in her mother's letter. Good thing he'd already asked to be part of the birthday celebration tonight. He'd get a front-row seat when Cass opened her mother's surprise package.

Downstairs, he smelled coffee and bacon. It seemed too good to be true as he headed for the kitchen.

"Janie, you sure do start early." He accepted a cup of coffee gratefully.

"Not usually. But I figured Cassidy would want an early start today. First day on the new job." Janie sat at the bar and invited Mason to help himself to bacon and eggs. "You two seem to have hit it off."

"Yes, we did." Mason realized he was hungry. He hated to start without Cass, but she might not be down until he had to leave.

"Oh, it's none of my business." Janie smiled. "But then again, Calhoun Petroleum is. I have quite a few shares."

"Do you?" Mason wondered where this was going.

"Conrad was generous with Tommy and me over the years. Gave us stock in Calhoun instead of Christmas bonuses when the company went public. And it's part of my retirement plan." Janie leaned closer. "I have concerns, Mason. These kids need to make good there at Calhoun or my dividends won't bring me enough to live on. Know what I mean?"

"Sure. I think they'll do okay." Mason didn't like the way Janie was eyeing him. She was sharp, he'd give her credit for that.

"They won't if they aren't steered along the right path." Janie pointed to the local newspaper on the end of the bar. "I read the papers. Business section. Every day. I know Texas Star is in trouble. I hope you don't think to take advantage of your new position as their evaluator to throw Texas Star a life raft with Calhoun's name on it."

"Who says Texas Star needs one?" Mason shoveled in the last of his egg. "I've got to go back upstairs. Cass needs a cup of coffee. Can you fix one for her?"

"Wait a minute." Janie stood up. "You're cozying up to Cassidy and I just read the CFO at Calhoun jumped ship and is on the Texas Star payroll now. Was in the paper today too. Sounds to me like you're getting ready to sabotage Calhoun. Those kids and all the stockholders like me may end up with jack turkey at the end of the year. Is that going to happen, Mason?"

"Listen, Janie. I truly hope that the kids—as you call them—get a good chunk of change at the end of the year. But the price of oil is too low for anyone to get the kind of payday Conrad thought they'd get. So don't blame me if there's not a huge fortune for them at the end of the year. Blame the economy."

"The economy is one thing. But dirty dealing is another. I think that's what Janie is worried about, Mason." Cass stood in the doorway.

"My hands are clean." Mason smiled and carried coffee to Cass. He was glad he could still make that claim. He turned to Janie. "Wish this girl a happy birthday, Janie. Thirty years old today. I say she's just hitting her prime, don't you?"

"Well, I'll be switched." Janie walked over to give Cass a hug. "I'm baking you a special cake tonight, hon. What's your favorite? Lemon? German chocolate?"

"German chocolate? Are you serious? That's my absolute favorite. Do you mind if I bring a few friends back here after cocktails to share it?" Cass was grinning, obviously delighted.

"Did I hear this right? Today is Cassidy's birthday? And she's thirty?" Shannon stood in the doorway, obviously just getting home after a really long night. She had her high heels in her hands and her hair was wild. Her burgundy cocktail dress looked like it might have spent the night on someone's bedroom floor.

"True. I guess we're closer than we knew, sis." Cass turned and looked Shannon over. "Rough night? Where's your date? He should have come in for breakfast."

"I left him at the curb. He ceased to be interesting hours ago." Shannon grabbed a cup and held it out for Janie to fill with coffee. "Seriously. You and I were born days apart?"

"Yep." Cass smiled. "Seems like your mother might have been the reason my parents divorced. You know anything about that?"

"All I know is that my mother was Daddy's secretary when they got together." Shannon sipped the coffee and made a face. "I need sugar, lots of it, and cream." She staggered over to the counter and sat.

"Guess it's one of those classic cases of the boss and his secretary." Mason put his arm around Cass's shoulder. "Too bad it broke apart a family."

"You can't break apart a family that's solid." Shannon stirred her coffee. "But I'm sorry, Cass. Not that we had anything to do with it."

"No, you're right." Cass slipped away from Mason and sat next to her sister. "The adults were responsible. And tonight I'll find out what made my mother deny my father his parental rights. It's got to be more than his affair with your mother. Those things go on all the time. A woman would have to be crazy to deny a man access to his child and the obligation to pay child support over a little extramarital hanky-panky."

"Well . . ." Shannon gave Cass a look. "I can tell you things about mine that would make your head spin. But we're talking about yours. Is your mother . . . ?"

"Crazy?" Cass held out her cup for a refill, which Janie was quick to provide. "Intense, hardheaded; yes. Crazy?" She glanced at Mason. "I don't think so. But I'll reserve judgement until I read the letter she sent me and see what evidence she provided."

"So tonight it all hits the fan." Shannon stared into her coffee cup. "And I thought turning thirty was bad enough."

Chapter 13

Cass parked in the place assigned to the CFO. Why not? Hardcastle was history and no one else would dare take his spot. So she whipped right into it. Tommy had put a decal on the front windshield that guaranteed free parking in the high-rise where the Calhoun offices were located, so she didn't even have to worry about paying when she left.

She'd texted Ellie and they were set up for drinks at eight tonight. Since her best friend wanted to see the house anyway, Cass invited everyone over there. Ellie texted her that Rowdy was riding with them. Of course he was—they were still friends and he'd bought her a gift and wanted to give it to her personally. Mason and Rowdy face-to-face. Cass tried not to let that bother her, but how could it end in anything but a pissing contest?

Janie was insisting on putting out a spread, so the evening was sounding more like dinner than just cocktails and dessert. If she didn't have such a horrific day here ahead of her, Cass could almost get excited about her birthday celebration. But there was a lot that had to happen before she would see her friends and, yes, Mason, again. Excitement, nerves. If she didn't have a meltdown from the stress, it would be a miracle.

She met Holly at the elevator. Her assistant apparently had radar or a network that warned her Cass was on her way up, because she greeted her as soon as she stepped off on her floor.

"I think you should take Hardcastle's office, Ms. Calhoun. Unless you've heard they're planning to replace him with someone else right away." Holly already had a stack of messages in her hands.

"Heard from whom?" Cass stared at the door leading to Hardcastle's office. It was like the parking spot. Why not?

"Board of directors. They call the shots. Didn't you know that?" Holly sorted the pink message slips into two piles. "Maybe you didn't. Calhoun is a corporation. Publicly traded on the stock exchange. We have a board and the CFO reports directly to them. I'm sure Mr. Hardcastle sent them his resignation." She flushed. "A much more polite version than he sent you." She put her hand on Cass's arm. "He copied that email to me. So crude and uncalled for."

"Well, he did have a point about my qualifications for this job." Cass nodded toward that big office. "But, okay, I'll set up in there until we hear someone else has a claim on it. I hope you won't mind working for me, Holly."

"No, I'll be honored." Holly threw open Hardcastle's door. "These calls came in even before we were open for business. I collected them from voice mail. There are some that are urgent." She waved the stack in her right hand. "The board members. We don't ignore them. Like I said, they will call the shots and pick Hardcastle's replacement. The rest of these can wait." She set them on the desk in two piles, the urgent next to the phone. "Any questions?"

"Only about a million of them. But here's the thing I want to do first." Cass dropped her purse and briefcase on the massive desk. She took a moment to turn and stare at the view of downtown Houston. This could be a dream job if she knew what in the hell she was doing. But she was the first to admit she didn't have a clue. She took a breath and turned around.

"I want to call a meeting of the department heads in accounting. I'm sending them an email now. Do we have a conference room where we can meet?"

"Sure. Right down the hall. I'll show you around when you're ready." Holly made a note in her tablet.

Cass sat down and hit *return* on the computer. It was protected by a password. "Oh. What's the password for Hardcastle's computer?"

"You're kidding? He locked you out?" Holly came around the desk. "He never does that. This was deliberate. He must have known when he left here Friday that he wasn't coming back." She pulled open a drawer. "Cleaned out and no sign of a password. I swear, that man!" She held her finger over her tablet computer. "Tell me what you want the email to say. I'll send it. Then I'll get someone up here from IT to unlock the damned thing." She frowned. "I'm so sorry."

"I know the board of directors will put someone else in charge as soon as they find a person who knows how to do the work." Cass leaned back in her chair. State-of-the-art and ergonomic. She'd enjoy it while she could. "But we can't just sit on our hands until then. We have to hit the ground running just to keep this place from going under. At least that's my take on things. Hardcastle told me to get together a list of people to lay off. I'm going forward with that."

"Of course he did. Then he left. What a mean move." Holly tapped on her tablet. "Now, that email . . ."

"I want it to ask—no, *tell*—the heads of the four divisions in accounting to make a list of at least three people in their areas who will be laid off as of this Friday. I need to have that by two this afternoon and they should bring it to the conference room." Cass saw Holly's eyes widen.

"Sorry, I know that's bad news." Cass started to say something reassuring, but what was the point? There would probably be friends of Holly's affected, but there was nothing she could do about it. "Second, I need an email to go out to the heads of all divisions in Calhoun, not just financial. I need for them to give me a budget with recommendations for ways to cut at least thirty percent from their current expenses. They can make that happen by reducing personnel, supplies or services, however they choose to do it. But I want it on my desk by noon, Friday. Got all that?"

"Wow, Ms. Calhoun. You're going to make some waves with that. You don't think you should wait for the board of directors to meet first?" Holly was tapping like crazy.

"If I can show them that I've instituted some positive cost-cutting measures, I'll have given them a reason to believe that a Calhoun can handle this job. Even if her résumé is not up to John Hardcastle's toilet-paper standards." Cass saw Holly bite her lip. "Oh, go ahead. It's funny."

"No, it's not. The man was crude and out of line." Holly frowned. "I got my own degree from our local college and I think I got a good education. He insulted all of us who can't afford an Ivy League school."

"Yes, he did." Cass smiled.

Holly walked to the door. "I'm sure the board will be impressed. The vice presidents who get these emails about the budget cuts?

Well, your phone is going to be ringing off the hook. I'll tell them you're in that meeting. Good luck, Ms. Calhoun. I'm calling the computer techs now."

"Oh, Holly?" Cass dragged open another drawer. It had been cleaned out too. Apparently the CFO had kept the office supplies.

"Yes?" Holly stood in the open door.

"Call me Cass. Beating the Calhoun name into the ground will only remind everyone around here that I'm a legacy. I'm hoping to prove myself in this job on my own merits." She smiled and tried one more drawer. Not even a paper clip.

"I have faith in you, Cass. You'll blow them away."

"Thanks! Now after you send those emails and make that phone call, would you find me a damned pen and paper? I can't believe Hardcastle even took the extra paper out of the printer drawer."

Holly laughed. "If you knew him better, you'd believe it. That man was so tight, he'd wash out his Starbucks cup and reuse it, except he didn't believe in those fancy coffees. He stopped at a fast-food restaurant on his way in and got the senior discount on his cup of joe."

"He didn't look old enough . . ."

"Oh, he isn't. Lied about his age. The man turned gray at thirty and has been getting the senior discount ever since." Holly chuckled and let the door close behind her.

Cass dug her cell out of her purse and rotated the chair so she could stare at her view as she hit speed dial.

"Cass, how's it going?"

"Why didn't you mention I'd have a board of directors to report to? That's quite a detail I had to learn from my assistant." She smiled, remembering his hungry good-bye kiss this morning. But the smile quickly disappeared. She was scared witless about this day and what was coming. "Mason, we should talk more and play less."

"What would be the fun in that?" He sounded like he was in a wind tunnel.

"Where are you, what are you doing?"

"I'm in a helicopter and hating every minute of it. Have to go check the progress on Big Tex. Remember the oil spill?"

"Oh, sure. Hope it's under control."

"Me too."

Cass rocked in her chair. "Will you be back tonight? For my birthday party?"

"I'll make a point of it. Now, about the board of directors." He made a noise. "Sorry. This pilot just did a dive that has my stomach in my throat. Son of a bitch. The weather is calm. No call for that."

"Holly says they'll probably have an emergency meeting this Friday."

"She's right. They'll call one to talk about Hardcastle leaving and filling the position. The company's in a bind, Cass. You're great, but I can't see you filling his shoes. Calhoun's already missing a CEO because of your father's death. The leadership void in the company has made it vulnerable to a takeover."

"From a company like Texas Star?" Cass had to ask that even though it made her stomach jump to her throat like Mason's was doing.

"I've got my hands full right now. But you aren't wrong." He was silent for a moment. "Tell me what you're doing now."

"I'm meeting with division heads and getting them to make budget-cut recommendations. Doing layoffs in my own department. Is there anything else I can do?" Cass *knew* she was over her head. It would probably be a relief for the board to name Hardcastle's replacement. It was only Calhoun pride that made her want to step into this job or at least show everyone here that she didn't need a Harvard MBA like the departed CFO to run this side of the company.

"No, that sounds like a solid start. I'm giving you an A for effort. As your evaluator." He said something, probably to the pilot. "We're getting ready to land. This is where I say my prayers, so I'd better get off the phone."

Cass laughed. "Are you afraid of flying, Mason?"

"Terrified. But it's part of my job. Your job is to hold down the fort and then email the board members and let them know what you're doing in the interim. Tell them you're awaiting their instructions on how to proceed. The layoffs should go forward, but don't mess with the budget yet. Just let the people who have been there for a while, those in a position to know what's what, help you out. Holly can probably steer you to people you can trust. Nothing like a good assistant to get you the inside scoop."

"She *is* good." Cass had looked up Holly's résumé at home over the weekend. "Holly's worked her way up here and been with the company for thirteen years."

"Excellent. She'll be a good resource if she's not still loyal to Hardcastle." There was a bang. "Shit. Hell of a hard landing."

"You okay?" Cass heard more cursing from his end.

"We made it. I still have to get back to solid ground after the inspection on this damned whirlybird. Wish me luck."

"Luck. And thanks for the advice, Mason. I'll be praying for you too." Cass ended the call with a smile.

Holly. She seemed happy to be rid of the CFO, but maybe Cass should keep an open mind about her.

Ten hours later and more phone conversations than she could count, Cass decided she had to leave or she'd be late for her own birthday party. She'd finally gotten into her computer and was wading through the last of the emails when she came to one that was actually addressed to her. Unusual, since most of what she'd dealt with had been intended for John Hardcastle. She vowed this would be the last item she'd deal with before she shut the computer down for the night.

She clicked it open. *Leave Calhoun Petroleum, Cassidy Calhoun, or you'll be sorry.* Cass stared at the email, her heart accelerating and her face flushing. A threat. Had word of the layoffs made this happen? Did people seriously think they were her idea?

She checked the return address, but it was a Gmail account with the name Daffy Duck. If she'd noticed that, she never would have opened it. She read it again. It was laughable, really. As if she'd leave here and the chance to gain her inheritance because of a stupid email. She was tempted to answer the thing. No, best to pretend it had gone into her spam folder and she'd never even seen it. She did save it, though. Then she shut down the computer and grabbed her purse. She'd been here so long she wasn't thinking straight and there were people coming to the house. It was her birthday, damn it.

Holly was still at her desk and Cass stopped and told her to go home. Her assistant had been invaluable all day. She'd printed out agendas for the two meetings that had been tense and yet productive. The key players knew things had to change and they saw Cass as a potential fall girl if someone had to take the blame when the company slid into bankruptcy.

Cass punched the *down* button, glad that Holly joined her as they waited.

"I have thirty minutes to get home and change before my friends arrive." Cass smiled. "It's my birthday today."

"Oh, wow. I wish I'd known sooner. We could have brought in lunch and cupcakes." Holly hugged Cass. "I hope you don't mind that I did that—hugged you—but I really admire the way you stepped in today and faced all those—yes, I'll say it and roll my eyes—men."

"The organization is a little testosterone-heavy, isn't it?" Cass soaked in the praise. She needed it. Facing down the skepticism from what had clearly been a good-old-boy network had taken a lot out of her. But she hadn't worked her way up in the bank without running across it before. She'd ignored the whispered asides and just dug into her agenda. They'd resisted the layoffs but had shown up with their lists. When she'd told them to add a supervisor and to mix up the genders—funny how they'd only laid off women—the atmosphere had turned glacial. But she hadn't backed down. Another meeting was set for tomorrow and they'd be bringing back a revised list.

"You were awesome." Holly had been there, taking notes. "And I couldn't help hearing how you handled the board member who came by in person today. Mr. Peterson was eating out of your hand when you walked him to the elevator." Holly held back the door when the elevator doors opened in front of them. "He was one of your dad's cronies, so I think he would really like to see a Calhoun sitting on the board again."

"I know. He told me that. He doesn't want Missy, my father's ex, to be the one either. I thought that was interesting." Cass punched in her number. She noticed Holly was on a different floor of the parking garage. Her own car was near the exit on the bottom floor, the perk of being an officer in the company.

"Missy—oh, I mean Mrs. Calhoun—isn't too popular around here. She wants the worker bees to buzz around her, like she's the queen. She has a temper too." Holly leaned close, like this was a secret. "Heard there was a lawsuit once when she slapped a secretary for messing up her royalty check."

"Seriously?" Cass couldn't imagine such out-of-control behavior from someone so rich over a check.

"I hope you don't have to deal with her." Holly shifted her purse as the elevator *ding*ed. "She used come by on a regular basis until

Mr. Calhoun put a stop to it. He was sweet to the people who worked for him. Down-to-earth." Holly smiled as the elevator doors opened. "See you tomorrow bright and early. Happy birthday, Cass."

"Thanks." Cass leaned against the wall until her floor came up. She didn't know how she was going to find the energy for a party. Her feet hurt, she was running on too little sleep, and she needed a shower or at least fresh makeup.

She was halfway to her car when she heard screeching tires coming down the ramp from above. Holly? But the car kept coming fast, not slowing down even when the driver should have seen that she was in the crosswalk.

Cass threw herself forward. The car brushed the back of her skirt, knocking her to the ground before it raced away. It left the garage and turned onto the street to disappear from sight. She lay on her face on the concrete, trying to catch her breath. Pain. Her knees had hit first. Cass tried to get up—but her hands! Shit. She lay back down. She needed a minute to catch her breath. God. She'd almost been run over. An accident? Or on purpose?

She heard another car coming and scrambled to her feet, ignoring the blood running down her legs to cower in front of the car parked in the first space. Her heart pounded as she waited. Would this one try to finish her off? But it was a silver Toyota, barely moving as it carefully rolled down the ramp. She saw Holly's black hair through the window and waved her stinging hand to get her attention. The car stopped next to her.

"Cass, what—" Holly rolled down her window, her eyes widening when she saw her boss's legs were bleeding. "What happened? Did you fall?"

Cass staggered to Holly's car and leaned against it. "Someone almost hit me. I-I think it was deliberate."

"You're kidding! Let me call security." Holly pulled her cell out of her purse.

"Too late. They left." Cass pointed at the exit. "Long gone." She kept breathing, trying not to panic. They *were* gone. "I'm shaky and afraid to drive. Would you mind taking me home?"

"Of course not." Holly put her car in *park* and jumped out. "Here. I've got paper towels in the backseat. Just a minute." She pulled out a roll and gently helped Cass wrap her bleeding legs. "Not that it would hurt this old car to get blood on it." She laughed nervously. "It's survived two teenagers and I don't know how much fast food, but I'm sure you don't want to get blood on that fabulous suit."

"Thanks, Holly." Cass hadn't given a thought to the stylish dark-green suit that was one of Shannon's castoffs. She was just thankful that blood spatter wouldn't be obvious on the dark color. She shook her head and realized she was a little dazed.

"Teenagers. You need to get home, Holly. Give me a minute or two and I can probably drive after all."

"No way." Holly slipped an arm around Cass's waist and helped her hobble over to the front seat of Holly's car. "I'll drive you. Maybe you'll feel like coming in tomorrow and maybe not. But there's bound to be someone at your house who can bring you to work. Or call me. I'll put my number into your cell. Should have already done it." Holly efficiently arranged Cass in the seat, belted her in, then gathered her purse and briefcase from where they'd hit the pavement and slid them into the backseat. "Mind if I dig out your cell now?"

"No, do it. I would appreciate having your phone number. I promise not to use it except in an emergency." Cass leaned back against the headrest. Was she being paranoid imagining that she'd almost been run down? She stared at her red palms, her eyes stinging with sudden tears that she blinked back.

"Speaking of emergencies, are you sure you want to go home? Maybe you need to see a doctor. I could take you to an emergency clinic. Get you looked over." Holly slammed the back door and walked around to get behind the wheel. "Your call."

"I have guests coming. And it's just scrapes. My legs and my—" Cass held up her hands—"palms." Oh, they were shaking. She settled them into her lap again.

"Oh, look at that! You must be miserable. And on your birthday too." Holly started the car moving. She might have been driving crates of eggs she was so careful. If she drove that slowly all the time, she'd have people honking and road-rage issues. One guy roared around them, shooting Holly the finger. Good thing they didn't need to take the freeway, because drivers would go insane if they were stuck behind her. Fortunately, the Calhoun house wasn't that far away.

They were stopped at a light when Holly glanced at Cass, a serious expression on her face. "You really think someone tried to deliberately run you down?"

"I don't know. The parking garage is well lit. I was in the cross-walk. I don't know how they couldn't see me. But they were driving really fast and had just come down the ramp. Maybe their brakes went out or they were distracted, talking on their phone. It happens." Cass would love to rationalize the near-miss as an accident. Too bad it hadn't felt like one.

"There's a lot of office buzz about the layoffs. You know who they're blaming." When the light turned green, Holly looked both ways, then stepped on the gas. Barely. The car behind them laid on the horn before passing them.

"It's not my fault. I'm just doing what's necessary. Given time to analyze costs, I'd have probably come to the same conclusion Hard-castle did. We need fewer people to do the jobs we have." Cass was glad to see that they were almost there. "Let's keep what happened in the parking garage between us. I'm saying my injuries were caused by my own clumsiness. Okay?"

"Is that what you're going to tell your family?" Holly was shak-ing her head. "If someone almost hit me, I'd want to be on my guard. You people, no offense, can afford bodyguards. Right?"

"I think that's a little extreme. It probably *was* an accident. I don't want to overreact."

"At least tell me what kind of car it was. Maybe I can ask around. See who it might belong to." Holly slowed even more when Cass told her where to turn.

"Silver compact car. Like a thousand others in that garage. No chance to narrow it down." Cass gestured. "There's the house, the huge one with all the cars in front. Looks like the party is about to start without me."

Holly pulled into the circular drive and parked behind a bright-yellow Volkswagen convertible. "Now that's a cute car. Soon as the boys are through college, I'm getting something fun like that."

"Bet my best friend bought that today." Cass opened the car door. Every bit of her ached and she wasn't sure her legs were going to take her up those steps. She didn't move.

Holly turned off her car and jumped out to run around and grab Cass's arm. "Wait a minute. You need assistance. Let me ring the bell before you try those stairs."

"Okay, I think I'll let you do that." Cass wondered who would come out. She'd recognized Mason's car and Rowdy's truck in that driveway. Guess Rowdy couldn't fit into that little yellow car with Ellie and Manny. She sat back and closed her eyes, refusing to think past the pain in her shins and her hands.

Loud voices made her open them again and look toward the front of the house. Mason and Rowdy were charging shoulder to shoulder down the steps. They both looked ready to rip the car door off its hinges to get to her first. Would she be a coward if she locked herself in?

Chapter 14

"Cassie!"
"Cass!"

Rowdy wrenched open the car door. Big mistake. That let Mason get to her first. He looked her over, his brow wrinkled with concern.

"What the hell happened, Cass? Holly said you were hurt and couldn't walk up the steps." He brushed her hair back from her face and reached for her hand.

"Oh, don't." Cass inhaled sharply when he touched her palm. "I fell and caught myself on my hands. They're scraped raw."

"Would you get out of my way?" Rowdy looked like he was ready to start a shoving match. "I can carry her up those steps."

Mason turned on him. "You think I can't? Step off, Baker. I've got this." To prove it, he slid his hands carefully around Cass and eased her out of the car.

"You drop her and I'll knock your teeth down your throat." Rowdy kept up with them after slamming the car door. "Cassie, they said a car almost ran you over. Are you all right?"

"I'm just a little banged up. My knee stiffened up, that's all. Thanks for coming to get me. Both of you." Cass let herself relax against Mason, even though that made Rowdy's jaw tighten. Couldn't be helped. She was exhausted and it felt good to be in Mason's arms.

"But about that car . . ." Mason looked down at her. He was close enough to kiss. No, not in front of Rowdy, who was shadowing them and then rushing to throw open the big front door.

"Fool came down the parking-garage ramp too fast to stop. I had to jump out of the way, tripped, and did a face plant. I'm a klutz. What can I say?" She tried for a laugh but couldn't manage it.

Mason nodded and Rowdy frowned.

"You're not a klutz, Cassie. It's those high heels. They could make anybody fall." Rowdy shut and locked the front door behind them.

"You sure that's all there is to it, Cassidy? Holly was pretty wound up. Said something about the layoffs putting everyone on edge." Mason stopped in the entry. "You think someone on the lay-off list might have been steamed and wouldn't have been sorry if that accident had taken you out?"

"Shit, Cassie. Could someone have deliberately tried to run you over?" Rowdy stared at her wrapped legs. The paper toweling didn't hold and hit the floor. Both men cursed when they saw the raw abrasions on her legs and knees.

"How do I know?" Cass blinked when tears pricked her eyelids. "The person—don't know if it was a man or woman because of dark-tinted windows—never slowed down. If I hadn't had good reflexes . . ." She sniffed. *Do not cry.* "Don't make a big deal out of this, okay? It's my birthday. Where is everybody?"

"In the living room." Mason gave Rowdy a look. "How about we get you cleaned up before you make an appearance. Janie has a hell of a first-aid kit in the kitchen. She's had to use it on me more than once in the past."

"Thanks, Mason." Cass relaxed again. She really didn't want to cause a stir and keep explaining about this. "Rowdy, would you tell Ellie and Manny I'll be in as soon as I get cleaned up? And make sure Holly goes on home. She has a family to see to there."

Rowdy hesitated, obviously not too happy to be put in the role of messenger. He reached out and touched her cheek. "You okay, Cassie? Besides the obvious?"

"Yes, thanks, Rowdy. And for coming. Give me a few minutes and I'll join you." Cass did muster up a smile.

"Okay, I'll do what you need me to do." He glanced at the closed double doors that led to the living room. "MacKenzie, you be careful with our girl." He nodded and walked over to open the door and step into the room.

"Protective, isn't he?" Mason strode through the dining room and on into the kitchen.

"Always has been." Cass realized Rowdy wasn't the only one protecting her. "You sure I'm not too heavy?"

"You're fine. But I'm wondering if Holly had the right idea. She said she wanted to take you to an emergency clinic to be looked over." He stopped in front of the kitchen door before he shouldered it open. "Your knee looks like it's swelling to me."

"I'll ice it. I can't afford to take time off for an injury and you know it, Mason. I'm pretty sure it's just minor. I could move it when I first got up, but it hurts like hell." Cass inhaled. "Delicious smells coming from the kitchen. Take me to Janie and I'm sure she'll fix me right up."

"Stubborn lady." He looked back. "Rowdy's out of sight now, so I'll do this." He leaned down and kissed her, a sweet but claiming kiss. When he pulled back, he smiled. "Didn't figure I should let your old boyfriend witness something like that. He was already on a short fuse. Don't want to spoil your birthday party with a fight."

"Thanks. He knows we're done, but I don't want to rub Rowdy's nose in the fact that I've moved on at what seems to be warp speed." Cass reached up and used just a fingertip to trace Mason's smile. "Thanks for sparing his feelings. I do still care for him and always will."

"Loyalty. It's a good thing. Hope you'll be as loyal to me when all is said and done." And with that disturbing comment, Mason carried her into the kitchen.

Janie exclaimed and pulled out a large tackle box filled with all kinds of first-aid supplies. She fussed and cleaned and bandaged Cass's legs and hands until Cass felt like a mummy. Then Janie handed her an ice pack for her knee. Seemed the right knee had taken the biggest hit in the fall.

"Now go join your friends in the living room. Your sisters and brother are there too. It's a nice party and I put out some serious snacks since I know you didn't get dinner."

"Thanks, Janie. I feel better already." Cass shook her head when Mason started to pick her up again. "I can walk now. I insist." She had ditched her high heels. Now she limped out of the kitchen toward the living room, Mason right behind—to catch her, he said.

"There's the birthday girl!" Ellie rushed to greet her at the door. "Look at you, wounded. Who knew that job would be so tough on you?"

"I should get combat pay." Cass laughed and hugged Ellie, then Manny. "Thanks for coming. And family! Thanks, guys, for being here."

Shannon waved a cocktail glass. "Wouldn't miss it. Not with Janie's German chocolate cake on the menu."

"Happy birthday, sis." Megan was sitting on one end of the same couch as Rowdy.

"Your first birthday with us. May there be many more." Ethan grinned and looked around the room. "But without the bandages."

"No kidding." Cass hobbled to a chair. Someone had put a stack of wrapped gifts on a small table next to it. "Is all this for me?"

"Of course. You haven't been here to know, but birthdays are a big deal in the Calhoun family. We always have parties and gifts." Shannon frowned. "I was going to have a big blowout for my three-oh this weekend, but now that I have to pay for it myself, maybe not."

"You and Cass are the same age?" Ellie looked from Cass to Shannon.

"Yes, it's no big deal." Megan was quick to speak up. "Let's see what everyone got you, Cassidy. Open the purple one first. That's from me."

So Cass got busy. She had a photo album from Megan with pictures of her father and the Calhoun kids growing up. It was a thoughtful gift and one she'd treasure. She tried to get up to hug her new sister, but Megan ran over to her instead.

"Watch that ice pack. I thought maybe you'd like to know more about your new family and Daddy. I'm glad you like it." Megan actually teared up a little and took a cocktail napkin from Rowdy, who smiled at her.

Shannon gave her a beautiful vintage perfume bottle to start her own collection. "I saw how you admired mine. Someday you'll be able to clear out the circus stuff and make that bedroom your own." She glanced at Mason. "Or have a new place, away from here."

Ethan gave her a new phone. "It's the latest model, almost. Well, I upgraded mine so it's my old one, but I'll transfer your stuff to it. I saw what you were using and couldn't believe it. That tech is years old!" He said this like Cass was calling people using a tin can and a string and everyone laughed.

"Thanks, Ethan. It's perfect." Cass saw Holly had brought in her purse and briefcase before she'd left and gave him permission to dig out her phone and start the process.

Next, Cass opened Rowdy's gift, a beautiful Mexican silver pendant set with turquoise. "I know you can afford better now, but I saw that months ago in a little shop when I was stuck at a site near the border. I hoped you'd like it." Rowdy sounded almost apologetic.

"I love it. It'll look great on my silver chain." Cass smiled at him, knowing he might have expected a kiss, but she couldn't move and he didn't get up to take one.

"Let me see." Shannon did get up and took it. "It's a signed piece. Excellent taste, Rowdy." She nodded approvingly.

"You go out to the well sites? Tell me about your job and who you work for." Megan turned to him and started interrogating him.

"Open mine next, Cass." Ellie handed her a package. "It's from Manny and me."

Cass ripped open what was really just a long envelope. "What's this? A round-trip ticket to Cancún?"

"Yes, we're getting married and you have to come be my maid of honor!" Ellie held out her left hand. "Look what I got for your birthday!" She had a sparkling engagement ring on her finger.

"Oh, wow!" Cass said all the appropriate things. How on earth could she tell Ellie that there was no way she could leave town now? "When?"

"Oh, relax. That ticket is open-ended. We're in no hurry. We'll coordinate and find a time when we can all miss work." Ellie laughed. "I'm going to enjoy being engaged for a while."

"Good. I was freaking out. You have no idea how much I have to do at Calhoun." Cass glanced at Mason. "My evaluator is probably going to give me bad marks for how I started today. I didn't even know we had a board of directors!"

"I'm sure you did fine." He'd pulled a chair close to her. Now he picked up one of the two packages left, a large one, and placed it in Cass's lap. "Happy birthday."

"When did you have time to shop? On an oil rig in the Gulf?" She laughed. "Or did you have an assistant run out and buy this?"

"I think you found out today how valuable a good assistant is. I knew what I wanted so I told my assistant to find it." Mason leaned back in his chair. "Open it."

"Okay." Cass tore off the gold paper. Inside was a beautiful leather briefcase made by a famous designer. Cass's initials were embossed in gold near the handle. She stroked the soft leather. "It's perfect."

"Your old one looked rough and I'm sure it wasn't helped by the scrape across the concrete tonight." Mason took it out of her lap and leaned over to kiss her on the lips. "Enjoy, Madame Vice President."

Cass was very aware that all eyes were on them. She carefully used her fingertips to push him back. "Thanks, Mason." She cleared her throat and looked around him toward the table. "What's this last package?"

"It's something your mother sent, Cass." Ellie got up and handed it to her. "There's another large one that goes with it, but open that one first. Looks like jewelry to me."

"It does." Cass was glad when Mason sat back down. At least he didn't give Rowdy a gloating look, but it was clear he'd staked his claim. She didn't know how she felt about that. Oh, who was she kidding? She stared down at the box her mother had sent, hiding her pleasure. Mason wanted everyone to know they had a relationship. It made her warm inside.

She tore the cheap wrapping paper off an old-fashioned jewelry box. She snapped it open. There were a pair of diamond earrings, sparkling studs of a good size. Could they be real? The jeweler's name on the box made her think they were. Shannon was on her feet again.

"Well, look at that." Shannon picked up the box. "Excellent quality and clarity. A karat, yes. Maybe more. I thought your mother didn't have money, Cassidy." The wrapping paper fell off. "Oh, here's a note with them." She handed it to Cass, then passed around the earrings for Megan and Ellie to admire.

Cass unfolded the notebook paper and read her mother's hen scratch. It was never easy to read at the best of times. Obviously, her mother had been upset or emotional when she'd written this because it was worse than usual.

Dear darling Cassidy Jane,
Your father gave me these earrings when his first well came in. He was so excited. Spent too much on them but that was Conrad. I never wore them but maybe you will. I don't like flashy, never did, but that's not why I wouldn't put them on. I was pregnant with you when I found out that he'd got

that oil lease through fraud. The man was so desperate to make it big, he'd resorted to signing names for people who were senile or just plain ignorant. He took their oil rights for pennies and never gave them dime one of what was owed them. He built his Calhoun Petroleum using crooked ways and lies. I couldn't live with those lies or him.

Maybe he changed after he got a good start. I have no idea. What I do know is that I had his secret and I used it to get rid of him before you were born. I made him sign over his parental rights because I couldn't have a man like that around my child. He was a liar and a cheater. Yes, he made his billions. So what? Money made like that is dirty money. I kept the proof of his dirty deeds, the papers that show who he cheated thirty years ago. Now that he's gone, you can make things right for those folks. Will you do it? Or did I waste my time and did you turn out to be your father's daughter after all? Guess we'll find out, won't we?

I'll always love you, no matter what, Cassidy Jane. I think we had a good life without him. Sorry if you don't feel that way. Call me if you have more questions.

Mama

Cass let the letter fall to the carpet. This was it. The bombshell that could blast Calhoun Petroleum apart. She saw Mason bend over to pick it up. When he looked at her for permission, she nodded before she thought better of it. Yes, she needed his advice, but she'd have to make sure he didn't use this information against Calhoun. Damn it. Why did Mason have to work for the competition? Her first instinct was to do the right thing. She had to pay those people back. Then it hit her: Thirty years' worth of oil royalties? How much could that cost? What would it take to pull that much money together? Was it even possible? She almost snatched the letter back. She needed to think.

"Cass?" Someone called her name.

She heard the voices around her from far away as she seemed to fall into a tunnel. No, she didn't have time for weakness. She had to stay alert, figure this out. But, damn it, she was going to faint for the second time in her life.

Mason's hand on her shoulder brought Cass to her senses. "Isn't it great? Cass and her mother have made up. Her mom sent her a text first thing this morning and then they got on the phone and got things straightened out. It's hard to be estranged from your family. Right, Cass?" Mason squeezed her shoulder.

Cass saw him holding that letter in his fist, crumpling it. The revelations there must have knocked him for a loop. But leave it to Mason to keep smiling, putting on a show for the group around them.

"That's right. I'm so glad Mama reached out." Cass took a breath, her brain fog clearing. No way was she going to give in and fall out now. "Did you say there was a big package with this one, Ellie?"

"Yes, it's here." Ellie gestured to a large mailer by the door. "It's heavy. Don't know what it could be."

"Just a bunch of old papers." Cass nodded. "The letter says they're documents Conrad had left with Mama. Oil business. I'll look them over later."

"Do they explain what the big secret was that Daddy mentioned in his video will, Cass?" Megan leaned forward. "Tell."

"Can we put this on hold for tonight?" Mason gestured toward the door. "Look, here's Janie with the birthday cake and candles! Four, Janie?"

Cass was grateful for the interruption. Janie set the cake with the lighted candles down in front of her on the now-empty table.

"One for each decade and one to grow on." Janie nodded toward Ethan and the Calhoun sisters. "That's kind of a family tradition. Always have to have an extra to grow on." She pulled a paper towel out of her apron pocket and wiped her eyes. "Oh, how Conrad would have loved this moment, all of his kids together like this." She blew her nose. "I'm so sorry we missed your other twenty-nine birthdays, Cassidy."

"But you're sure doing this one up right." Cassidy looked around the room. This one *was* special, in spite of the worry about that package and what it stood for. She and Mama hadn't made a fuss over birthdays. What was the point when you couldn't afford much more than a card and a cupcake? But she'd always known she was loved. Now she felt surrounded by even more love or at least affection. A real family. Would she be able to drag Mama here one day? Get her to accept Cassie's new sisters and brother and make her part of *this* family? Probably too much to hope for with Conrad's picture over the mantle and his name on everyone's lips.

"Make a wish, Cassie." Rowdy knew how she always did that. In the past she'd had too many things to choose from. Now?

She smiled at him. It almost seemed like tempting fate to ask for more at this point. Even with the bomb her mother had just dropped, she still had too many blessings to count now. She thought hard and deliberately avoided glancing at Mason, who was back in his chair as close to her as he could get. *Wish.* Forget business. She always made her wishes personal. Okay, it was probably premature, but she hoped that what she'd started with Mason would turn out to be a forever thing. That they could build a life together, a secure one. Was it possible? She closed her eyes, made her wish, and blew.

Everyone clapped, then Janie cut the cake and passed out generous pieces. Coffee came next and Cass went through the motions. It wasn't easy. She hurt all over and exhaustion suddenly hit her hard.

"I think Cassidy is sinking fast." Mason stood. "What do you say we call this a night?"

"He's right, *chica*. You were falling asleep over your cake plate." Ellie got in front of her for a gentle hug. "No, don't get up. I'm so glad I got to see the house and to come help celebrate your birthday. When things calm down, I'll come back for the full tour."

"Oh. I'm sorry." Cass realized her eyes had closed. How rude! "Yes, you have to come back. You haven't seen my bedroom yet."

Ellie laughed. "Manny told me all about it. No wonder you're tired. I don't see how you get a wink of sleep in that crazy place."

"It's not easy." Cass hugged Manny too. Then Rowdy stood in front of her. "Thanks for the beautiful pendant, Rowdy. You were right. I love it."

"Bought it a long time ago." He reached in for a hug and held her for a long minute. "Remember, I'll always be your friend." He moved back and glanced at Mason, who was walking Ellie and Manny to the front door. "The oilman is acting like he owns you. Little early for that, isn't it?"

"Don't overreact. He was just concerned when he saw I was hurt. We've been together a lot lately. He knows the business, I don't." Cass realized Mason was coming back toward them.

"I saw the way he looked at you, Cassie. Just be careful. You're a novelty to a rich guy like him. Take whatever lines he's throwing at you with a grain of salt." When Mason moved in and put a hand on Cass's arm, Rowdy scowled.

"Seriously, Baker? Warning her off me? What the fuck do you know about me and my relationship with Cassidy?" Mason moved that hand to touch Cass's hair. "I think this woman can make up her own mind about what and whom she wants."

Rowdy stepped closer to Mason, in the danger zone, as far as a man's space was concerned. Cass was pretty sure a shove would be next.

"Hold it, gentlemen. Yes, I can make up my own mind about things and I'm pretty sure I can't take any more drama tonight. So you guys just calm the hell down. Will someone help me to the elevator?" Cass saw Ethan across the room. "Hey, little brother. How about you? I don't think these two could take exception to you as my escort upstairs. And bring my new phone."

"Sure, sis. I'm on it." Ethan pushed between Rowdy and Mason and offered Cass his shoulder so she could pull herself up out of the chair. "Careful. I'd carry you but—"

"No! I can walk." To prove it, Cass shuffled over to what looked like a closet door but which she now knew belonged to the elevator. She pushed the button. "Thanks, Shannon, Megan, Ethan, for the wonderful gifts." She bit her lip. "I'm so happy to be part of your family now. You can't know what it means to me."

"We're glad to have you." Megan sidled up to Rowdy. "Why don't I walk you to your truck, Rowdy?" She tapped Mason on the shoulder. "You, I want to talk to later. Maybe tomorrow. About my job in the field. Did you know Rowdy here works for one of the Calhoun subsidiaries?"

Mason shook his head, watching Cassidy step into the elevator with Ethan's help. "No, I didn't. Fine, we'll talk tomorrow, Meg."

Shannon joined Ethan and Cass in the elevator. "You leaving now, Mason? Or do you want to ride up with us?" She winked when Rowdy stopped suddenly at the door leading to the entry hall. "Just to help us tuck Cassidy in bed. Maybe you'd like to bring that pack of papers her mother sent. I'm sure she'll want to look them over."

"Oh, yes!" Cass pointed to the thick envelope. "Please bring it for me. I do need to ask you some questions about the documents, Mason." She saw Rowdy turn to give her a look. "It's business. Seriously."

"No need to explain things to me, Cassidy." Rowdy nodded and took Megan's elbow. "Good night and happy birthday." And they disappeared from sight.

"You think that elevator can hold all four of us?" Mason had grabbed the package. He squeezed in next to Shannon. It was a tight fit.

"Let's see." Shannon pushed the button for the second floor and the car lurched upward with a groan. She turned to Cass. "Are you mad that I said that in front of Rowdy?"

"Said what?" Cass realized she was definitely not firing on all cylinders.

"About Mason tucking you in." Shannon laughed. "Oh, boy. I think you are definitely ready for bed."

Cass held on when the elevator came to a jerky stop. "It wouldn't hurt you to stop stirring up trouble." Cass focused on Mason. He held her mother's letter on top of that bulky package of documents. The significance of that letter was still sinking in. And then there was the pain. She couldn't think ahead, couldn't concentrate. When the elevator door opened, she almost fell out into the hall.

"Here, let me." Mason thrust the package into Shannon's hands, then picked up Cass again. "I'm really getting a workout here. No need for a gym and bench press."

Ethan laughed, then looked more closely at Cass. "Maybe we should call a doctor for you, sis. You don't look so hot."

"She could be in shock." Shannon followed them to the bedroom and pulled back the red bedspread.

Mason gently laid her on the bed. "I could call our family doctor. He'll come to the house."

"I'm fine. Just tired. No doctor. Promise me." Cass was glad to be in bed, even if it was in a horror show. She could swear the clown headboard was leaning now, as if it was going to fall on her.

Shannon looked her over and frowned. "You guys get out of here for a few minutes and let me help her undress. I'll holler when we're ready." She gave Mason those papers. "Go wait in her office and close the door. Ethan, you know where the bar is. See if Mason wants a drink."

"I wouldn't turn one down." Mason tore open the mailing envelope and started rifling through the documents. "Damn. These are contracts for mineral rights. She wasn't lying about that."

Cass heard Mason say that as the door shut between the bedroom and the office. She tried to think about what he'd said, but her mind was too muddled. Instead, she looked up at her sister, who was unbuttoning her jacket.

"You're being really nice to me, Shannon."

"Hey, it's what sisters do, sometimes. I can be a bitch too. Ask Megan." She helped Cass ease out of her jacket, then wiggle out of her straight skirt. "You looked great in this suit, Cass. Much better than I ever did. It gapped over my chest."

"I felt good too. Confident. Thanks a million for all the clothes. If I didn't say it before . . ." Cass sighed when Shannon helped her slip off her bra and pull on a nightgown. "That feels better."

"You thanked me about a dozen times already. It's no big deal. Really." She picked up the discarded clothes and took them into the closet, then looked around. "You ready for the boys to come back in?" She helped Cass pull the sheet up to her chin.

"Guess so." Cass wondered if she was really ready. She just wanted to close her eyes and let the world go away. But then the circus tent loomed over her and that damned clown . . . At least the clock was staying silent. She closed her eyes anyway.

"I've put Ethan to work on those oil leases." Mason sat on the edge of the bed.

Cass blinked her eyes open and yawned. Shannon and Ethan were gone.

"What? To work?"

"We need to know which leases panned out and which were dry wells. Thirty years of royalties on producing property could be a hell of a lot of money, Cass. It could bankrupt Calhoun. But there's no way of knowing how big a deal these documents represent. First thing we need to do is see what happened after Conrad got these owners to sign the contracts. Could be there isn't that much to it. Yes, there could be fraud involved, but we can offer some stock options to settle some of these claims if we handle it right." He smiled. "That's the kind of negotiating I'm good at."

"You make it sound like we could come out of this okay. But is this really part of your role, as evaluator?" Cass wanted to touch him. Too bad her hands were wrapped in layers of gauze over smears of pure aloe vera, freshly oozed from the broken limb of the plant outside the kitchen door and Janie's personal cure-all.

"Conrad trusted me to help the four of you get your inheritance.

Seems like settling this advantageously will be essential if that's going to happen." Mason smoothed back her hair. "Forget about it for now. Why get in an uproar until we know the facts? Ethan's a whiz with a computer and he actually got excited to be given something meaningful to do. Putting him to work is definitely in my job description." Mason leaned down and kissed her forehead. "You want me to leave?"

"No." She really didn't. "I'm not much use the way I am, but I'd love for you to hold me right now. I'm still feeling a little shaky."

"You don't have to be of use to me, Cassidy." Mason pulled off his boots, then his shirt. "I'd love to just lie beside you and hold you. Of course you're shaky. Some bastard almost killed you tonight." He stopped before he took off his pants, held her wrist, and looked into her eyes. "God, Cass, is it possible that car tried to run you down?"

"I—I don't know." Cass blinked when her eyes filled. Not crying. "Maybe I'm paranoid, but another silver car, like that one, tried to run me off the road on my way to the reading of the will. Coincidence? Or . . ."

"Why didn't you mention this before?" Mason pulled out his cell phone.

"Because I've driven on Houston streets since I was sixteen. You know how they are. I have near-misses all the time. I chalked it off to a crazy driver in a hurry. But now this with the same kind of car . . ." Cass put her hand over his phone. "What are you doing?"

"Calling the police." He looked grim.

"And telling them what, exactly? That I fell in the parking lot? That a silver car like a million others in Houston almost hit me? *Almost*, Mason. Won't impress them." She took a shuddery breath. "And I sure don't feel like talking to the police tonight."

"Fine. But I may hire someone to watch over you. A private detective. Bodyguard. Someone like that." He finally stepped out of his pants and slid into bed beside her. Very carefully, he took her into his arms. "Did you take anything for the pain?"

"Janie gave me some over-the-counter stuff in the kitchen. I guess you didn't notice." Cass leaned her cheek against his warm chest and finally relaxed. He was becoming important to her. Maybe too important. Because seeing Rowdy had reminded her that this new relationship with Mason was moving too fast. Sensible, steady Cassidy

Calhoun wasn't impulsive. She didn't lead with her heart, she decided things with her head. This thing with Mason was not only too fast, it was dangerously deep. Was this what a fling felt like, quick to start and just as quick to burn out? Or could it be the beginning of something real? On that thought, Cass let her heavy eyelids close and just dropped into her dreams.

Chapter 15

"Of course I came in to work. I'm sitting at my desk. Holly set me up with an ice bag, but my knee isn't that swollen today. My hands are looking good. I even took off the bandages. Don't you have hair to color or something, Ellie?" She gestured when Holly peeked in from the doorway. "Got to go, Holly needs me." Cass was on her birthday present. Thank goodness Ethan had had time to move her contacts over before she'd had to leave for work.

"I'm sorry to bother you, but I have someone here I want you to meet." Holly pulled a big man into the office. "This is my husband, Abraham."

Cass jumped to her feet and walked around her desk. "I'd shake hands, but I scraped mine last night and they're still a little tender. I'm happy to meet you. I hope you're not here to complain about Holly's late hours. I swear I'm sending her home early tonight, Mr. Rogers."

"It's Detective Rogers, but call me Abe." He gestured. "Please sit down, Ms. Calhoun. I don't dare complain about my wife's hours or she'd start complaining about mine."

Cass was happy to sit since her legs were still sore. And standing next to Abe, who was at least six foot five with broad shoulders, made her feel intimidated. Now she noticed he had an ID clipped to his suit pocket.

"Holly, did you tell Abe?"

"About your near-miss last night? I sure did. Come on, Cass. You and I were both worried that was no accident."

"Would you two please sit down?" Cass sighed as she leaned back in her chair. "I don't think we need a detective looking into it."

"Why not?" Abe settled into a chair that groaned under his weight.

"I've sent my partner over to building security and he's looking at the surveillance video from last night. Maybe we'll get lucky and see who did this. We're on private property, but I'd like to have a talk with the person who was so reckless coming down the ramp."

"Reckless driving. It was that." Cass smiled. She was feeling safer already. Should she tell him about the other incident? No, it was stupid. How many times had she been almost forced off the road by an erratic lane-changer on the freeway? Too many to count.

Abe's phone buzzed and he pulled it out of an inside coat pocket. When he did, Cass saw he wore a sidearm. She didn't know guns, but it looked dangerous to her. She glanced at Holly while Abe conversed quietly with the caller. Her assistant gripped the chair's armrests.

"This is okay, Holly, you were looking out for me."

"So you're not mad?" She laid her hand on Abe's arm. "He's doing this as a favor to me. You know detectives don't come out for something that might not even be deliberate."

Abe had ended his call. "That was Carl. Video didn't pick up anything. The upper floors only have a few cameras and, like you told Holly, there are way too many silver compact cars to pick out the right one. We've pinpointed the time it must have happened, but that didn't help. The perp must have parked in a part of the floor that isn't covered by cameras. The ramp isn't monitored at all except at the exit." Abe frowned. "Got the exit on video but the license plate was obscured. That's a red flag. Who bothers to cover their plate with mud unless they have something to hide?"

"Mud?" Cass got up when Abe stood. "We have had a lot of rain."

"Sure. Which makes mud. But to cover the plates? That's unusual. And a criminal's trick." Abe pulled Holly to him and kissed her cheek. "Got to go. You both be careful in that garage. I don't like the feel of this. Any thoughts about a bodyguard, Cass? Holly says these layoffs you're implementing have caused some rumbles here. Wouldn't be the first time an employee who lost his or her job lashed out."

"My evaluator suggested a bodyguard but I thought it was an overreaction." Cass limped around her desk. Damn it, she was going to shake his hand. "I'll look into it. And thanks, Abe, for coming by. I know it was beyond the call of duty."

"It made my lady happy. How could I say no?" He looked at Cass's hand and gently took it in his large one. "You took a nasty fall. Take this seriously and call me if anything else happens that you think is threatening." He pulled a business card out of his pocket. "Here are my numbers. Use them. I mean it."

"I will. And again, thank you." Cass looked at the business card. "Abraham. It's a nice biblical name."

He laughed. "My mother was a churchgoing woman. I'm the oldest and she started with the alphabet. Thank God she only got to Isaiah before Daddy said *enough*."

"That's a big family." Cass couldn't imagine it.

"All boys and all successful, Cass." Holly looked up at Abe, her love shining in her eyes. "Every one of them graduated from college and is doing well. That's quite an achievement for anyone, especially boys coming from where Abe grew up."

"Oh, where's that?" Cass followed them to the elevator. She was glad to see how happy Holly and Abe were. He had his arm around her shoulders and they made a handsome couple, both strong and capable.

"Inner-city Houston, Cass. Someplace a white woman like you probably would never drive through, even for the world's best barbecue. Mama and Daddy won't move and still live in the same house where I grew up. There are burglar bars on the doors and windows, which is a damn shame. But we're working on making the area safe and it's coming along." Abe punched the *down* button.

"Did you grow up there too, Holly?" Cass realized she knew very little about her assistant besides her education and that she was the mother of two teenagers.

"No. My dad's a doctor and we lived in an upscale part of Houston. When Daddy found out I was dating a man from Fifth Ward, he had a fit." Holly laughed. "Abe won him over eventually, but Daddy still doesn't like for me to take the boys to Sunday dinner at Abe's folks' house."

"Yes, we were very different when we met in college. I had a scholarship, Holly was a rich girl." Abe kissed her on the mouth when the elevator doors opened. "Now, ask Cass to send you home early, woman. I'm cooking tonight."

"Stop, you're embarrassing me." Holly swatted him on the shoulder.

"No, you *should* go home early. I'll make sure of it. Last night you were really late because of me, Holly." Cass smiled at both of them. "I wouldn't mind going home earlier myself."

"Okay, then. Abraham, please make me something healthy for a change. Fried okra doesn't count." Holly shoved her husband into the elevator.

"But it's a vegetable! And delicious." He winked as the doors shut.

"Nice man." Cass headed back toward her office, eager to get off her aching legs.

"Yes, he is. I knew when I met him that I had to have him. That ever happen to you?" Holly stayed beside her own desk.

Cass stopped in her tracks. "You know. It has." Mason. That's exactly how she'd felt the first time she'd seen him. "And this love at first sight? It worked out for you two?"

"Sure did. Oh, there were a lot of sparks flying. You think maybe it's just lust, you know?" Holly flushed, darkening her cheeks. "But after all the chemistry got out of the way and we really got to know each other, we realized we had something special. We genuinely liked each other. Guess we were lucky. It was the real deal. Been almost twenty years now. Our twins are sophomores at the University of Texas in Austin. That's why I'm driving an old car and Abe is picking up all the extra shifts he can handle."

"UT Austin. That was my dream school. But I couldn't afford it. You and I had to stay here." Cass shook her head. "No, wait. You didn't. Your daddy's a doctor and you probably could have gone anywhere. Why didn't you go away?"

"I was scared." Holly straightened her already tidy desk, lining up pens and her tablet. "I was a daddy's girl and he overprotected me. We did live in a nice part of town and I was one of the few black girls in my classes in school. The idea of going far away and knowing no one . . ." She looked up. "Well, I couldn't handle it and college too. So I lived at home and went to the University of Houston. Guess you could call it fate. Because Abe and I met in freshman math. I struggled, he didn't. He offered to tutor me and Daddy could pay him." Holly grinned. "Oh, did Daddy regret that!"

"Fate. Yes, I'm believing in it more and more." Cass sighed and went back to her desk and all the emails that were overwhelming her. The meeting this morning with the department heads had produced a list for the layoffs that she could live with. Friday, the pink slips would go out, but the supervisors were giving out the bad news today. Would that get her another near-miss? Her new personal phone was ringing as she approached her desk. It was Mason.

"Ethan called me a while ago. He's been hitting those documents hard. Seems there's one that stuck out. Thought you'd want to know this right away. Does the name Harmony Baker ring a bell?" Mason sounded grim. "Unusual name."

"Harmony Baker? Yes, that was Rowdy's grandmother. Oh, Mason, no! You aren't telling me Rowdy's grandmother was one of those defrauded, are you?" Please let him say it was a mistake. A joke.

"Afraid so. What do you know about her?"

"Damn it, I know she had early-onset Alzheimer's, Mason. One of Rowdy's greatest fears is that he's inherited the gene for it." Cass took a breath. "How bad is it? Do we owe Rowdy's family a ton of money?" If they did, the significance of the fraud stunned her. Oil royalties on a successful site could have totally changed Rowdy's life. His mother had struggled, been forced to put Harmony in a nursing home on Medicaid. The care had been limited, so Lisa had gone by the home daily, just to make sure her mother had been fed and kept clean. Harmony had finally died in her early sixties after years of not being able to recognize her own daughter.

Lisa so far hadn't shown any signs of the disease, but it was a specter hanging over the family's heads. Rowdy had also spent many hours at that nursing home as a child and he'd never forgotten it. He paid for expensive long-term care insurance for his mother for his own peace of mind.

"Cass, you still there?" Mason cleared his throat. "We can't tell any of the contract holders about this until we have a clear picture of the cost."

"Wait a damned minute. As soon as I know what Rowdy's family is owed, I want to pay them." Cass rolled around to face her desk, wincing when her knee bumped it.

"You don't have the authority to do that, Cass. I'm sorry, but that's the truth." Mason's voice was firm. "Right now you're an employee—a new hire, at that. The board of directors would have to approve a payout for these people."

"What about the stockholders? The Calhoun family owns the majority of the stock." Cass had done some research on this. Yes, she wasn't coming into her inheritance yet, but the will had set up a trust for the four Calhoun children. It was the stock that would determine her own payout at the end of the year. Right now that stock represented the majority stake in the company. "Who controls the stock now?"

"The trustee. That's Dylan, my brother. If you think he's going to strong-arm the board of directors into doing something that will likely bankrupt Calhoun, think again." Mason's voice had hardened. "Listen, this discussion is getting us nowhere. I told you about the Baker woman first, but Ethan isn't through yet. We can't panic or act until we have all the figures. You're a numbers woman, so surely you understand that we need the bottom line before we can act."

"What I am is a woman with integrity, Mason." Cass's hand hurt and she eased her grip on her new phone. "I'll see those victims paid if it's the last thing I do." Cass realized this *was* going nowhere and ended the call. Fighting with Mason. She didn't want to do that. Not when she'd just about decided that she loved him. Her phone rang in her hand. Him again. She thought about ignoring it. No.

"Yes?" Oh, but she sounded sweet.

"Let's not fight about this, Cassidy." He could sound sweet too.

"I don't want to."

"Good. Dinner tonight? I'll pick you up after work. What time do you think you'll be through? I don't like the idea of you walking into that parking garage alone."

"I promised to send Holly home early. Around here, five is early. Could you make it then?" Cass looked at the pile of phone messages on her desk. If she got serious, she could work her way through them by then.

"I'll make a point of it. We'll go out to a nice restaurant and have a real date. How does that sound?"

"Good. And let's not talk business. Like you said, Ethan needs to finish researching the documents first." Cass took a deep breath. She was dying to know what Rowdy's family was owed. "Can you have him send me what he has on Rowdy's family so I can figure out what they might have coming to them?"

"There's no point, Cass. We'll have to give this to an accountant who specializes in oil-royalty work. You want to help, look at who you've got on your payroll there and try to determine who you can trust with the job. After we have it all figured out you'll have to pre-sent the findings to the board." Mason cursed. "Sorry. My assistant just put a message in front of me. I've got a problem here with my uncle. Got to see him and straighten out this mess. See you at five. In your office. Don't go down to that parking garage without me. Okay?"

"Fine." Cass ended the call. Trust someone here with this? So far she'd been met with thinly veiled hostility. And she sure couldn't do the job herself. She'd already decided there was no way she could learn enough about oil without years on the job. Because the price of oil seemed to fluctuate daily. Up and down. It was crazy making. She laid down her new phone and picked up the office one. She grabbed the first message. A division vice president. She'd been soothing ruffled feathers ever since she got here. She put on a smile, a trick she'd learned in graduate school. It was always easier to stay pleasant to an irate person when you were smiling.

Mason texted Cass that he was running late but on his way, then got in the car and hit the accelerator. He wasn't tired, just discouraged. Would Ed ever change? What would it take to get him to see reason? He'd left his steaming uncle in the middle of a mess and more complications with the offshore rig. He had to put that shit out of his mind or he'd ruin his evening with Cass.

His phone buzzed with a text as he stopped at a light near Calhoun headquarters. He glanced at it. No way. Stubborn woman. She was coming down in the elevator before he got there and would wait close to the elevator bank. He texted back: *No, wait for me upstairs.* Would she do it? Surely she wasn't *that* stubborn.

The light took forever to change but there was cross traffic and he didn't dare move before he got a green. Of course, he was probably overreacting. A person would have to be damned stupid to use the same place twice to take out a target. But then, since when were criminals known for being smart? He revved the powerful motor, ready to take off when a son of a bitch ran the light and flew across in front of him. He hit the brakes just in time. He'd do no one any good if he became a statistic.

He drove into the garage. No sign of Cass. He breathed a sigh of relief. Good girl. He wheeled in and parked. The place was busy with people leaving at quitting time. He studied that ramp. Plenty of room for someone coming down to stop if they wanted to. No excuses worked. Someone had tried to run Cass down. Son of a bitch. It had been late when it had happened last night. He needed to get Cass down here while it was still busy and a normal time for people to get off work. Cass would be safer in a crowd.

He punched the elevator button, his mind back on his own business despite his good intentions. He couldn't just turn it off. Once again he and Ed had almost come to blows. Ed had promised Hardcastle a ridiculous salary to come over to Texas Star. They couldn't afford him. And to top that, the CFO was a jerk who wasn't worth the aggravation. So far the company secrets he'd spilled about Calhoun had been common knowledge. Yes, Conrad had kept good cash reserves and bought a lot of equipment on credit. No surprise there. And the credit rating at Calhoun was about to be downgraded. Just like at Texas Star. It was a problem all the major oil companies were dealing with. Big fucking deal.

The icing on the shit cake had been when Ed had brought in his so-called inspector to deny that any of the problems on the rig in the Gulf had been because of faulty welds. The two men had tried to get their stories straight, arguing with Mason that it must have been the storm, more severe than the weathermen had reported, which caused the leaks. With all the yelling and name-calling, it soon became clear that Ed had decided in midstream to make the inspector take the fall for the problems on Big Tex. The look on the inspector's face had been priceless when his coconspirator had turned on him. Mason would have laughed, except their mess had cost the company millions and a dozen lawsuits.

When he'd had enough, Mason stormed out of Ed's office, pretty sure the inspector was on his way to get his own lawyer. That was all they needed—one more fucking day in court.

"Cass." Mason called her name as he threw open her office door. No sign of her. Her neat-as-a-pin desk made his stomach twist. He must have just missed her. There was a bank of four elevators and he rushed back to see that two of them were heading down. One was already on the bottom floor of the parking garage. He looked around for Holly, but her desk was cleared for the day too. Damn it. He punched the *down* button, thinking about running downstairs. No, twenty-three flights took too long. He just hoped she stayed in the elevator when she got down there. He stepped into one going down and startled a pair of women who were already there by hitting the lowest-floor button hard. They got off two floors before him, whispering to each other. Yeah, Mason knew he looked a little crazed.

When the elevator doors finally opened on the bottom floor, he saw Cass actually waiting for him. He pulled a handgun out of a holster at his waist that had been hidden by his suit coat.

"What the hell? Mason!" Cass recoiled from the sight of it.

"I have a permit to carry. This is Texas, sweetheart. If anyone tries to run you down tonight, I'm shooting at them. Not to kill, but I can blow out a tire. That should scare them off." Mason scanned the almost deserted garage. Boy, the place had cleared out quickly. "Go ahead and hurry to your car. You have your keys out?" He was going to stay glued to her side.

"Just a minute." Cass fumbled in her purse as she walked toward the car. "You're making me nervous with that gun. I'm out of the crosswalk. Put it away."

Mason stayed behind her, in that damned crosswalk. His eyes were on that ramp when she dropped her keys. She stopped next to the pillar beside her car to pick them up. The concrete suddenly exploded above her head.

"Gunshots! Get down!" Mason's heart lurched. "Hide." Another bullet slammed into the side of her car. He saw a flash from the exit near the street and fired three shots in rapid succession. "Cass? Are you okay?" He didn't see her.

"I'm on the other side of the car. Mason?" Her voice was shaky.

"Call 9-1-1." Mason heard a car peel out. He ran toward the street, just in time to see taillights disappear around the corner. Small car. License plate impossible to read.

"Did you call them? They're gone." He kept his gun by his side.

"I called someone else. Holly's husband. I have his card. He's a detective with the Houston police department." Cass had opened her car door and sat in the driver's seat, but was hunched over behind the steering wheel, as if afraid to be seen through the front window.

Mason bent down and touched her shaking shoulders. "Good. Did he answer?"

"He's on his way. You said they're gone? Maybe I should call him back. He was cooking dinner, Mason. Now . . ." Tears filled her eyes. "Why is someone doing this? Is it the layoffs?"

"I can't imagine, Cass. But they clearly were aiming at you." Mason rubbed her back. "Baby, let's see what Holly's husband says. What's his name?"

"Abe. Abe Rogers." She took a shaky breath. "He was just looking into my near-miss as a favor to Holly."

"That's a good thing." Mason gently pulled her up beside him. "Come here. Let me hold you. You're shaking."

"There was a gunfight, Mason. I've never been in a gunfight in my life!" Cass leaned against him.

"It wasn't a gunfight. We didn't shoot at each other. He shot at you, I shot at him. Gunfights don't work that way." Mason realized he was talking nonsense. He continued to hold her until a plain black car drove into the parking garage. He set Cass back inside the car. "Stay put. Is this detective a giant black man in a good suit?"

"Yes, that sounds like Abe." Cass pulled a tissue from the door's side pocket and blew her nose. "Poor Holly."

"I don't know about that." Mason grinned when Cass hit his leg.

"I meant about her missed dinner."

"Okay. Stay put." Mason walked over to introduce himself and to give Abe the details of what had happened.

"You don't think this was a random drive-by?" Abe was writing everything down in a small notebook. "Lots of violence in Houston these days."

"No. I was in the open but all the shots were clearly aimed at Cass." Mason swallowed, thinking about it.

"Then she's lucky you were here with her and could warn the shooter off." Abe nodded toward Mason's gun, still visible at his waist. "How many shots did you fire? Can I see that permit to carry, Mr. MacKenzie?"

"Call me Mason." He pulled out his wallet and showed his permit, which was next to his driver's license. "The shooter was in the exit driveway. You can see where his slugs hit the concrete post there and the passenger door of Cass's car." He walked over to point to the places.

"And where did your return fire hit, Mason?" Abe followed him, his eyes intent as he drew a diagram in his notebook.

"Over here." Mason saw that only one of his rounds had hit the concrete exit post. He assumed that the other two had hit the pavement. "I don't think I hit the guy. And there's no broken glass. Guess I need to hit the range."

"You say *guy*. Did you see the perp? Get a visual?"

"No. Wish I had. I was aiming at a muzzle flash. The shooter stayed out of sight." Mason realized he wasn't being very helpful.

"And the car as it was driving away. Any help there?"

"No. License plate was blacked out by something. Couldn't even tell the color because it was dusk." Mason looked toward Cass in her car. "I'm sure you want to talk to Cassidy."

"In a minute. Did she tell you we came by today and ran surveillance video from the parking garage? Not much help, but there was mud covering the license plate. Goes along with what you just described." Abe pulled out his phone. "Give me a minute and I'll visit with Cass. Why don't you go over and talk to her, keep her calm?"

"Sure." Mason strode over to her. She hadn't mentioned talking to the police before. But then they hadn't had much of a conversation other than about Calhoun business, had they? He sat in the passenger seat and picked up her hand. She had her eyes closed and her head against the headrest.

"Everything okay?" She turned to look at him.

"Yes. He's making a phone call. Maybe he needs to tell someone where he is." Mason heard a distant siren. "That sounds like it's coming closer."

"Hope the building's not on fire." Cass summoned up a smile. "That would just cap this evening off perfectly. Burn Calhoun to the ground. Why not?"

"Mason, would you step over here for a minute?" Abe pulled open the passenger door. "Cass, you doing okay?"

"Guess so. Mason saved the day. My own personal gunslinger." She patted Mason's knee. "Don't keep him long. I need him back."

"No promises." Abe shook his head just as a white police cruiser pulled into the parking garage and abruptly cut off its siren.

"What's going on, Rogers? You going to search the parking structure? I told you the shooter took off." Mason flinched when Abe's heavy hand landed on his shoulder. "Cass told me the layoffs were announced today. Maybe you should check to see who on the list has a silver compact car. Could have been silver tonight. Like the one that almost ran her down last night."

"Already on that, Mason. May I see your gun?"

"Sure. I told you I fired it three times. The safety's on." Mason pulled it out of the holster and passed it to the detective, who raised it to his nose and sniffed.

"Yes, it has been fired recently." Abe nodded. "Mason MacKenzie, you have the right to remain silent. Anything . . ."

Mason heard the rest of the Miranda warning as if in a daze. What the fuck was this? He was turned around by a man in a patrol officer's uniform, his hands cuffed behind his back. He was frisked thoroughly before being pushed toward the patrol car.

He heard Cassidy cry out. She ran to his side when his head was pushed down so he could be placed in the back of the car.

"What is this? Why are you treating him like a criminal?" Cass tugged on Abe's arm. "He didn't shoot at me. Someone else did."

"This isn't about you, Cass. At approximately four-thirty this afternoon, Edward MacKenzie was found shot to death in his office at Texas Star Petroleum. Witnesses claim he was seen arguing with his nephew Mason MacKenzie just before then. An APB was put out for Mason, since he has been heard making death threats against his uncle. Now we see he's carrying a gun that has been recently fired. It will be up to a judge to determine if there is enough evidence to charge him and bind him over for trial. For now, he's being brought in for questioning in the suspected homicide." Abe started to pat Cass's shoulder, but she scooted out of reach. "I heard the APB on my way over here. I'm sorry, but I have to follow through on this."

"Mason, who should I call?" She stayed next to the police car.

Mason stared at Abe. Ed dead? He should feel . . . something. But all he could do was react to the panic on Cassidy's face. "My brother Dylan. You have his number. Because of the will."

"Yes, I have it." Cass ran back to her car and came back with her phone. Her hands were shaking. "What should I say?"

"Dylan doesn't do criminal law, but he'll know the right lawyer for the job." Mason gave her a long look. "I didn't do it, Cassidy. I hated the son of a bitch, but I'd never kill him. He was family. Please believe me."

"I do. I'll call Dylan. Don't worry. I know you couldn't kill anyone." Cass gasped, then disappeared behind tinted windows when Abe slammed the door and the car started moving.

Abe stared at Cass. "I would like to think he's telling the truth, Cass. But if there's one thing I've learned in this business, it's that anyone, pushed hard enough, can kill."

"Not Mason." Cass turned her back on Abe and searched her contact list until she found Dylan's number. Then she realized it wouldn't

214 • *Gerry Bartlett*

be a smart move to talk in front of the policeman. She turned around again. "Abe. Will this be your case? Ed MacKenzie's murder?"

"No, I wasn't called out on it." Abe shook his head. "I can't get involved, Cass. I know you and now I've met Mason. Detectives need to be objective and I wouldn't be now. Your heart was in your eyes when you looked at him. You think he's innocent just because he said so." Abe shrugged. "Hope it's true. I'll keep an eye on the investigation. Make sure no one cuts corners. That's about all I can do for you."

"That's good enough. Thanks. Now go home and see to your family." Cass started to make that call.

"Not until you're on your way home as well, my dear. My wife gave me strict orders." Abe took her elbow and walked her to her car. "Make your call after you get home. They'll take a while to process him. You've got time. They'll let him stew in an interview room and your man knows not to speak without counsel. Right?"

"Of course." Cass got back into her car. "Thanks, Abe. I do appreciate your coming. Though I know you called this in and reported that the infamous Mason MacKenzie was right here in my parking garage." She hit the steering wheel. "How's that for luck?"

"He was going to get caught, Cass. Better here than in an embarrassing situation with you, right?" Abe's smile made Cass want to smack him. And this was Holly's dream man?

"Right." She started her car, leaving Abe and the garage as quickly as possible. Mason! He wouldn't kill his uncle, but she knew how much he hated the man. Everyone knew it. God. How many people were convicted on circumstantial evidence? A gun recently fired. Gunshot residue on his hand. Threats made in public. It all added up.

Cass stopped at a red light and hit speed dial for Dylan. He'd better answer on the first ring because Mason needed the best lawyer money could buy and right now!

Chapter 16

"I can't believe they charged him with murder!" Cass wanted to scream, hit something, or at least see Mason and tell him she *knew* he didn't do it.

"It's all circumstantial evidence, of course." William P. Pagan sat in front of the group gathered in the living room and exuded confidence.

"That's exactly what I thought!" Cass liked the man, who'd told them to call him Billy, immediately. "I'll gladly testify that Mason used that gun in my presence. That's why he had gunshot residue on his hands."

"We may have to ask you to do that, Cassidy." Billy glanced at Shannon. "You have something to say, Shan?"

Cass looked at her sister. Shannon was fairly radiating hostility toward the lawyer who was known in Houston as the one to call if you got in trouble with the law. If you had big bucks, that is.

"No. Do your thing, Billy. Just get Mason out of this mess. We appreciate your coming by to fill us in." Shannon got up and poured vodka into her glass from a decanter on a tray.

"You sure you need that?" Billy's raised eyebrow said he didn't think so.

"Mind your own damned business. We need our evaluator free and clear. Like I said, do your job." As if to prove she had a mind of her own, Shannon threw back the drink and poured a refill, her third.

"Mature." Billy turned back to Cass. "Mason brought this on himself. He went around telling anyone who would listen how much he hated his uncle, so the police have to look hard at him. They've got a secretary who heard him say he wanted to kill Ed MacKenzie at least three times and several other very reliable witnesses who heard the same thing."

"But people say things they don't mean all the time when they're mad." Shannon smiled. "I've said I'd like to kill you a time or two, haven't I, Billy? But then I've never had the right weapon when I needed it."

"True enough. But Mason had the weapon and was there about the right time. The gun was the same make and model as Mason's, but it's a popular handgun for people who have a permit to carry. Ballistics should prove his gun wasn't the murder weapon, but that'll take a day or two."

"So he has to sit in jail until then?" Cass hated the thought of him going through that. In a cell with hardened criminals. Every violent show she'd seen on TV started running through her mind and she thought she might throw up.

"Now, now. Calm down. I'll get him out on bail quick as I can. He won't even have to spend the night. I know people." Billy had a reassuring smile for them all. "We're just waiting for a judge to sign the papers. Mason will have to surrender his passport, of course. Probably shouldn't even take a helicopter out to see his rig in the Gulf. It might look like he's fleeing." He chuckled as he got to his feet. "You see? I know all the angles. Now I'd better get back there and make sure it all goes smoothly."

Cass walked him to the door. His confidence was contagious and she felt better, sure Mason was in good hands. "Thanks so much for telling us all this. If you're going back to the jail now, can I come with you?"

"Absolutely not. Mason doesn't want anyone to see him there. Strict orders." Billy looked over his shoulder at Shannon. "By the way, now I have witnesses too. If I wind up dead, y'all heard her. Shannon's made threats." He laughed, then headed for the front door. "I'll tell him you're anxious to see him, Cassidy. He wanted me to re-assure you that he didn't do it. We're cooperating with the police to help them find some good suspects to take his place." He patted her shoulder. "Relax. This will go away soon or I'm not worth the for-tune his family is paying me."

Cass sagged as the door shut behind him. What a mess. And she still didn't have a clue who had tried to kill her tonight. She realized her sisters and brother still sat in the living room and she wanted to let them know about her mother's letter. Now was as good a time as any. If she could get them to agree to the idea of paying the wronged people back, that would help when Ethan had run down the owners of the oil leases and she'd gotten the accountant to figure the cost. Then just the board of directors would stand in their way. She walked back into the living room.

"I'm glad we're all together. I know you were wondering about my mother's revelation." Cass sat in a chair facing them. Last night? Seemed like forever since her birthday.

"I know all about it." Ethan poured himself a drink. "I've been working on those leases all day. Let me tell it. You look beat, Cass."

"I am. Go ahead, Ethan." Cass sat back and watched her sisters' reactions. Megan got a calculating look on her face. Like she realized this was going to be really complicated. Shannon immediately saw another angle.

"You can't go public with this!" She jumped to her feet, her glass hitting the table with a resounding *crack*. "Think what it'll do to Daddy's image."

"Yes, well, seems like *our* daddy was dishonest." Cass leaned forward. "Let me tell you about Harmony Baker." So she laid out the story of the Alzheimer's patient.

"No! Does Rowdy know?" Megan got to her feet this time.

"Of course not. We've got a lot of things to work out before we can tell anybody." Ethan stood and now all three of them were face-to-face-to-face. "I've been working my fingers to the bone, trying to find these people and figure if the wells were even drilled on the land or if they panned out. It's freaking complicated."

"Yes, yes, I can see that." Megan hit the bar and poured bourbon. When she offered, Cass shook her head. She was hoping Mason would come here when he was released and she wanted a clear head.

"If we pay one claim, we pay them all. That could not only bank-rupt us, it could be a public-relations nightmare. You mention fraud one time then everyone and everything Calhoun has done is tainted." Shannon sank to the sofa again. "Daddy may have had his reasons, but the bottom line is he perpetrated a fraud. We can dress up this pig and put a designer label on it, but it still says oink when all is said and done."

"Colorful, Shannon, but accurate." Cass sat on the sofa next to her sister. "I'm sorry. I know you guys had your father on a pedestal.

Me? I never had a father at all. But I'd hoped . . ." Her voice cracked. What had she hoped for? A terrific dad who'd never known about her, but would have been thrilled to discover her existence? But Conrad *had* known and had given her mother ammunition for blackmail. His greed had overridden his need to know his firstborn daughter. Then he'd lavished love and money on these three people. At least they seemed as horrified by the fraud as she was. They could have been raised to think it was fine and dandy to rob people of what was rightfully theirs.

No, they were reeling. Cass could see that. The man who'd taught them to swim and shoot and God knows what else, had suddenly become a stranger. He'd had another family first and harsh secrets. Secrets that could bring down the company that had given them this grand lifestyle. But doing the right thing wasn't simple. Paying off these debts could also hurt other innocent bystanders, the stockholders and people who held legitimate oil leases and depended on their royalties from Calhoun.

"Cass, you didn't cause this and neither did your mother. She needed to bring this to light, even if it's thirty years too late." Megan seemed to be the one taking the news the hardest, her eyes wet. "I wonder if Daddy were here right now, what he'd do? Would he try to silence your mother with money?" Megan choked out a laugh. "That sure wouldn't work. Or would he finally fix this?" She gazed around the group.

"We all loved Daddy, but Calhoun Petroleum meant the world to him. I'm not sure he would be able to stand to see it go down." Shannon sat on the other side of Cass and picked up her hand. "Daddy said in his video that he hoped you could keep your mama quiet. Think that's possible?"

"What?" Cass felt surrounded, closed in. Who had the most to lose if she insisted on paying these people who'd been defrauded? She realized Ethan was right in front of her. No exit.

"Listen, my mother left this in my hands. She's not saying anything. It's on my conscience now. If you think I can stand by and let this go, think again." Cass started to rise, but then decided to wait and see what these strangers who were now her family did.

"Hey, I can see what you're thinking. We're in this together." Ethan held out his hand. "We want to do the right thing, don't we?" He looked at Shannon and Megan and waited. "Girls?"

"Yes, of course. But I want to try to do it in such a way that Daddy's name isn't ruined. We can't have a PR Armageddon." Shannon patted Cass's knee. "Think. If we let this get out the wrong way, everything Calhoun Petroleum has done, every contract, will be put under a microscope. We might as well declare bankruptcy and close the doors then. Who would that help? No one would get paid if that happens. Not even the honest contract holders and shareholders." She stared around the circle as if waiting for some affirmation. She got nods from Ethan and Megan.

Cass kept her hands in her lap. What Shannon said made sense. But if they thought she was going to keep her mouth shut . . .

"I'm just saying this news shouldn't be leaked before we're ready. Got to spin this just right. Understand? But we're with you, Cass." Shannon patted her knee. "We're not doing anything about it yet. Ethan's not finished with his research, are you?"

"No, but I'm hurrying." Ethan was still standing in front of Cass. "Give me another day at least."

"And Cass, you had a rough day." Shannon actually looked sympathetic. "Tell us what happened tonight. Before they put Mason in the police car. Why did he shoot up that parking garage?"

Cass opened and closed her mouth, feeling a little overwhelmed by all this concern. Did they mean it? Or was it a front, designed to get her to keep a lid on this big family disgrace until they could silence her forever? She shuddered, trying to decide who to trust. She was her mother's daughter after all, raised to look at any stranger with a certain caution. She'd let Mason slip under her guard and still wasn't sure why. Because he had that smooth talk down to an art form? What chance did a girl from small-town Texas have against such a man?

Now these three strangers who shared a father with her wanted her to believe they were on her side too. It was a leap she was having a hard time making. Their lives had been so completely different from hers. The ease with which they'd accepted her made her wonder. Did they have a hidden agenda? Cass realized she was squeezing Meg's hand and frowning.

Megan dropped Cass's hand and gave her a hug. "Cass, relax. You can tell us anything. Is the stress getting to Mason? Did he lose his cool there? We've known Mason forever; we want to help him too. What's the deal?"

"Amen to that." Ethan sat across from them. "Now, why did Mason have to shoot his gun in that garage?"

So Cass told them. About the gunshots so close that she probably had bits of concrete in her hair. How Mason had shot at, then chased down that car, but it had gotten away. She even offered to show them the bullet hole in her new car's passenger door.

"Damn! Now who could have done that?" Megan was up pacing. "You really think this is all about a layoff? That's stupid. Killing you won't stop that."

"Exactly." Shannon stared at Megan. "Any other problems? Before the layoffs started?"

Cass decided to share the incident on the way to the reading of the will.

"Oh, that changes things." Ethan cleared his throat. "Who do we know that really doesn't want to share?"

"Stop it." Megan grabbed his arm. "You are not going there."

"I'm just saying I've been getting a lot of phone calls lately. And someone is off her meds."

Megan bit her lip and Shannon hit the bar again.

"What or who are you talking about?" Cass didn't like the way they seemed to be exchanging silent messages.

"Never mind. Look, you've got a text. It's from Mason." Ethan picked up Cass's phone from the coffee table. "What do you bet he's coming over? I say we clear out and revisit our problems at Calhoun later, when I have more information ready." He grabbed Megan's hand and hustled Shannon out ahead of him. "Ladies, you won't believe how good it feels to work for a change. I'm stoked to help figure out this shit. Just wait. Next Monday you may realize it's cool, working for our own company."

Cass read the text as the elevator went up. Mason was on his way. He had to stop at his place first to shower and change clothes. She quickly texted him back, letting him know that if he could get over his clown phobia, he was welcome to use her shower instead. She laughed when he texted back that he was on his way, phobia cured.

"The family meeting over?" Janie poked her head into the living room. "Mind if I clean up in here?"

"No, go ahead." Cass got up and stretched. "Mason is on his way over. Would you mind staying and answering the door? I'm going upstairs for a shower."

"Of course not, honey. Go ahead." Janie gathered used glasses on a tray. "So he's not in jail? Heard on the news that his uncle was killed and Mason was charged with the murder. A horrible thing!"

"He's got a great lawyer. Mason is out on bail, but the lawyer is pretty sure the charges will be dropped as soon as some tests are run on Mason's gun." Cass pushed the button for the elevator. "I know he didn't do it."

"I'm glad you're sure, Cassidy." Janie piled used napkins on top of the glasses. "But I know from experience that even the nicest people can snap when pushed."

"Oh." Cass studied Janie's solemn face. "Please don't think Mason did it. He's not a killer."

"If you say so." Janie turned around and headed for the kitchen. "You know where your daddy's gun is? Just in case?"

"In case of what?" Cass jumped when the elevator door opened in front of her.

"You need to defend yourself, honey. That's all. Forget I said anything. I'm just jumpy. I knew Ed MacKenzie. Yes, he was a son of a bitch, but he didn't deserve to die like that." She shook her head. "Better catch that elevator."

Cass stepped inside the car and pressed the button. Strange. As if she'd need to use a gun to defend herself from Mason. Impossible. Besides, she didn't know how to use a gun and didn't want to learn. She showered, so distracted she forgot to freak out over her clown showerhead. Maybe she was getting used to it.

She slipped on a black silk and lace nightgown and pulled back the bedspread. It had to be her imagination that the headboard was leaning over her a little more than usual. She gave it an experimental push, but it didn't move. Okay, then. She was too tired to pull out a sheet, but maybe Mason would cover it for her when he got here.

When he arrived in the doorway, she held out her arms, desperate to kiss him.

"No, don't touch me. I feel filthy. They threw me in a holding cell with a drunk and . . ." He shook his head. "You don't want to know." He stripped off his clothes, dropping his gym bag on the floor before stalking into the bathroom.

Cass settled back and waited. It seemed to take a long time for him to decide he'd scrubbed off the stench of jail. Finally the water turned off and he came out with a towel on his head and another around his waist.

"Are you all right?" Cass held out her arms again. "Will you kiss me now?"

"I'm not all right, but I'll kiss you." He threw off both towels and came to her naked. He slid beneath the spread and wrapped his arms around her. His kiss was hungry and he tasted like toothpaste. Finally he lay back and stared up at the tent above them.

"That's better. Can you believe they charged me with Ed's murder? On those bullshit pieces of evidence." He stretched and his hands touched the headboard. "What's up with this? I think it's going to come down on us."

"I thought I was paranoid." Cass sat up on one elbow. "Forget it. Look at me, Mason. How are you feeling? I know you hated Ed but he was family. Are you upset?"

"It's a mess, Cass." He pulled her down on top of him. "Upset? Yeah. Guilty too that I'm relieved. He was a miserable old man and I'd come to hate him, Cass." He closed his eyes. "I did want him dead." He opened them again, his eyes the blue of a clear Texas sky, glittering. "How's that for a confession?"

"But you didn't do it." Cass knew this in her heart.

"No, I didn't. I told the police they were welcome to polygraph me, whatever. He *was* family and he was someone I had to put up with because of that." Mason played with her hair. "Now his death leaves Texas Star without leadership." He ran his hands over her back. "I do like this gown. Silky. Like you. Trying to take my mind off my troubles?"

"Is it working?" She kissed his frown lines.

"Not yet." He rolled her under him. "My mind is pretty full of those troubles. Texas Star. You know the logical successor to Ed is me. Which is motive in the eyes of the police. I've made no secret of the fact that I want to take over and do things right in the family company." He slid her straps off her shoulders. "Forget that. Look at what I've got here." He kissed her shoulder, then pushed down her gown until he could see her breasts.

"Mason." Cass ran her fingers through his wet hair. "Make love to me. I need you."

"God, Cass. No more than I need you." He cupped a breast in his hand and took the nipple into his mouth. It was the start of tender lovemaking that left them both gasping. The bed made an ominous creaking sound when they finally lay still in each other's arms.

"Mason, watch out!" Cass shoved him off the bed, flinging herself after him to the floor when the giant clown headboard came crashing down. She looked at Mason. He looked at her. They burst out laughing.

"Did we do that?" Cass leaned against him. They were both naked and each time they laughed, the friction was pure pleasure.

"There were times when we could have, but just then? Hey, we were taking it pretty easy." Mason set her aside and got up to examine the broken base of the headboard. "Shit. This thing has been sawed almost completely through. All it took was a little movement for it to finally break all the way."

"What? Sabotage?" Cass joined him next to the headboard. There was no denying that this had been no accident. She glanced at the clock. After midnight. "Should we call Detective Rogers?"

"Probably. This was clearly another attempt on your life." Mason scratched his bare chest. "Damn, but I hate to see another cop tonight. But it's got to be done. This is a game changer. Someone with access to this room did this, Cass. Couldn't be an employee about to be laid off at Calhoun." He pulled her into his arms. "Who does that leave?"

"No, don't say it. My sisters and brother would not do this. We had a good talk earlier and I got a vibe . . . I think they have an idea who might be behind it. They wouldn't say, though." Cass walked over and checked the lock on the door. "We need to sleep somewhere else tonight. Why don't we get dressed and go to your place? I'm sure we'll be safe there. We can call Abe Rogers tomorrow. This thing," Cass bumped the edge of the bed, "isn't going anywhere until then."

"Okay. I appreciate that. I'm up to here with cops." Mason tapped his forehead, then pulled Cass against him for one more kiss. "Bring your work clothes for tomorrow. We need to act as if it's business as usual. Someone is trying to take you out of Calhoun for a reason. We need answers." He opened his sports bag. "Come on, get ready."

Cass kept staring at that headboard. It could have killed her, them. What kind of maniac had done this? And gotten past house security and the locked door to this room? Of course, money talked. The person behind this could have hired someone to scare her. To keep her from going public with Conrad Calhoun's fraud? To protect his reputation or to protect the company? Cass jumped when Mason touched her back.

"Honey, I know you're freaked out. Come on. I promise you won't have to spend another night in that bed if you don't want to. Now get dressed." He steered her toward her closet, then skimmed a hand down her backside. "Not that I don't love you like this. I do. But we need sleep. I know you're tired. So am I. Drama like this takes a lot out of you."

"Okay, I'm moving." Cass turned and rested her hand on his firm chest. "I love this view too." She almost said it then. That she loved him. But something held her back. The fear that he wasn't there with her, of course. But he looked at her with so much feeling that she hoped they were on the same page. Never have to sleep here again? If only. But the will had said . . . Oh, well. She wasn't going to bring that up now.

She pulled out a tote and began to dress. The future was uncertain. The best thing to do was to concentrate on now. Getting out of here sounded good. She started hurrying.

"Here's what I want to do." Cass had met Abe Rogers at the house before she headed to the office the next morning. Now she faced her siblings again in the living room, their place of choice for a family meeting. They'd spent ten minutes griping about the early hour before sitting down with a silver coffee service and bagels and agreeing to listen to her.

"Do about what?" Megan was the most wide awake and that wasn't saying much.

"That horrible clown headboard almost killed me last night." Cass waited for reaction. What she got was laughter all around. "I'm not kidding, folks. I just had the police here. It was sawed at the base so that it would break if the bed was jostled. Mason and I almost died in that damned bed."

"Too much action. Oooh." Ethan still wasn't getting it.

"Grow up, little brother. Didn't you hear her? She almost died." Shannon set down her coffee cup. "This is serious. That means . . ."

"Someone who could get into the house and into my locked bedroom did it." Cass wanted this clear. "So all of your secrets have to come out. Who could that be? Who doesn't want me to have part of the Calhoun inheritance?"

"Now, Cass, we're not sure. Maybe a maid got paid to do it. Then anyone could be behind it." Megan glanced at Shannon.

"Not an answer, Megan. Don't you think we thought of that? Detective Rogers is questioning Janie right now about who works here." Cass pleated her napkin.

"Janie wouldn't—" Shannon banged her spoon on the table. "You didn't suggest . . ."

"Of course not. But he has to interview everyone here. Tommy too." Cass hated that. She liked the couple. But then she knew they depended on Calhoun money and they might have heard what she was up to with the news from her mother. "Did you tell Janie about the fraud, Ethan?"

"What? No. But I didn't hide the papers. Anyone could have seen what I was working on. I left them out when I went to lunch yesterday with Mama." He stared into his cup. "This is bogus. No one we know would do this to our sister."

"I hope not." Cass decided to let the detective take it from there. "Detective Rogers will be questioning you guys next. But here's what I want to do to make sure I'm not the threat this person may think I am, at least about the fraud."

"What?" Shannon leaned forward again. "I told you, this could be a public-relations nightmare. It has to be handled just right or Daddy's reputation and the company's rep will be ruined."

"I'm aware of that, Shannon. Here's what I plan. I want to send a letter to the people who were victims of fraudulent documents, telling them that we're looking into old oil leases. That there may be an issue with them. We'll just inform them that we need updated information in case they might have royalties due. This doesn't admit liability and it will give us current information when we do have the numbers we need to make things right."

"That doesn't sound so bad." Ethan tapped his fingers on the table, then looked at Shannon and Megan. "Once that goes out, surely whoever wants to shut up Cass, will realize the cat is out of the bag. So there's no point in making any further attempts on her life."

"How many people are we talking about?" Megan drained her

cup. "I know you aren't doing money figures, but you do know how many families are involved, don't you, Ethan?"

"One hundred and twenty-three." Ethan threw his bagel on his plate and pushed away from the table. "Yeah, it's that bad. I'm ashamed of Daddy. There was no reason for him to screw over that many people."

"That's a hell of a lot." Megan bit her lip, a habit of hers when she was nervous. "Why? If he struck oil early, why'd he have to keep going on the bogus-lease scam? It doesn't make sense."

Shannon stood. "Make sense or not, we have to deal with it." She nodded. "Do it. Sounds like the sensible thing and may stop this person in their tracks." She smiled at Cass. "Don't you have to get to work, big sister?"

Cass looked at the clock and gasped. "Yes, I'm late. Okay, I'll get my assistant right on it. Ethan, you'll email me the list of names and contact information you have now, won't you?"

"Sure. I have that at least for half of them." He sat at a signal from Shannon. "Guess I'll have another cup of coffee." He reached for the silver pot. "Run along, Cass."

Cass realized they were going to meet without her. To discuss this mystery person they were protecting? She hoped Detective Rogers could pry it out of them. He was an expert at interviewing people. Cass didn't have time to worry about it, since she had to hit the office and do what she could to keep things together in her division. She decided to do one more thing before she left, though.

Cass headed upstairs to her bedroom. She needed more clothes for the week because she wasn't going to sleep here again if she could help it. That headboard still lay on the bed. Abe had told Tommy to leave it there until he could have someone examine it more thoroughly. She shivered and turned her back on it. The fortune-teller stared at her, all-knowing. Huh. Black clouds. Well, she'd had some rain all right, but her time with Mason had given her some rainbows. If Dylan couldn't find a loophole in the will so that she could spend time away from the house, then she'd have to move into a guest room.

Cass quickly filled a garment bag and a tote, then stopped again in front of that fortune-teller. She didn't know how to use it, but maybe having one to wave around would scare off anyone bold enough to come after her. So she pulled open the drawer at the bottom of that booth. Janie and Meg had both assured her that Conrad kept a handgun in there. The drawer was empty. A few rounds of ammunition were there, but no gun. Cass sighed, actually relieved. It had been a silly idea anyway. She hoped Abe would figure out who was stalking her and get this solved before another incident happened.

At least she didn't need to worry about Texas Star taking any more of their key employees. Mason was at the helm there now and had all he could do to keep that ship from sinking. Last she heard he was getting rid of Hardcastle. Seems the man hadn't signed a contract yet. Cass could only be glad that the bastard was getting his own pink slip.

Chapter 17

"You know, I didn't think we could get this done so fast, but you're a demon when you want to finish something." Holly put the stack of letters on Cass's desk. "Sign these and I'll put them in tomorrow's mail."

"Thanks. I'm not the only demon around here. I know you're exhausted." Cass realized it was late and the floor was deserted except for the two of them. "Go home. I'm sure Abe is waiting for you."

"He is." Holly smiled. "Promise you'll be right behind me?"

"Mason sent me a text a few minutes ago. He's on his way to pick me up. He won't hear of me hitting that parking garage without him." Cass pulled the letters toward her and grabbed a black pen. "Go. I'm fine. He'll text when he gets here."

"If you're sure . . ." Holly frowned at the letters. She knew what they represented. Cass had filled her in on the reason for them. "All the names except for a few have email addresses too. It's there on your desktop. You can send them that way if you wish. Though most people would think it's a scam if it didn't come on paper with a company logo too."

"True. This looks official. Excellent work." Cass signed her name with a flourish and set the first letter aside. "Tell Abe thanks for coming so quickly this morning. I'm staying at Mason's place until we know who was behind that accident with my headboard. Your husband grilled everyone in the house and seemed as frustrated as I am trying to figure out who could have tampered with that thing." Cass signed another letter.

"I'm horrified that you were attacked in your own home." Holly had her purse over her arm, clearly ready to leave.

"Me too. But it makes me feel better that someone I trust is all over it." Cass shooed Holly away. "Why are you still standing here?" Her assistant finally headed for the elevator.

Cass leaned back and finally took a moment to just breathe. Despite being impossibly busy all day, she'd been haunted by the thought that someone wanted her dead. So many near-misses. And she hadn't told anyone about those anonymous emails she'd been getting from Daffy Duck, Han Solo, and even Superman. They were vague threats. Stupid, really. Just warnings to "leave Calhoun Petroleum." As if she'd walk away from her inheritance. But the last one had made her forward them to Abe.

You'll regret what you're doing to Calhoun Petroleum. She had to take it seriously after those gunshots and that clown almost falling on her. Regret the layoffs? Or her attempts to right her father's wrongs? She heard the elevator open and stood with a smile. Mason. She could sign the rest of these letters in the morning.

But it wasn't Mason who walked into her office.

"What are you doing here?" Cass sat behind her desk again, her stomach churning at the look in the woman's eyes. This wasn't a social visit.

"I had to see it for myself. That you were really going through with it." Missy Calhoun, Conrad's ex-wife, strolled through the door and right up to Cass's desk. She hit the pile of letters with her fist. "Are these what I think they are?"

"What do you think they are?" Cass pulled her phone out of her purse with shaking hands. She'd left it next to her chair, on the floor where Missy couldn't see it.

"Letters to those idiots who lost their oil rights to Conrad and me all those years ago." Missy picked up the top letter and scanned it. "Of course. You just wouldn't let it go, would you?"

Cass glanced down and hit Mason's name on her speed dial. She prayed Missy wouldn't hear him answer. She slipped the phone into her jacket pocket and stood. Surely a little attitude would send this woman on her way.

"What are you talking about? You and Conrad? So you were in on it too? Forging signatures, taking advantage of people who had no idea what they might be signing." Cass walked around the desk, determined to put on a show of strength. She hoped Mason could hear this.

"Listen to me, Missy." Cass stepped closer, wanting to scream at

230 • *Gerry Bartlett*

the woman who stood there like she'd done nothing wrong. "That fraud cost me my father!"

"Oh, please. Not that ethical bullshit again." Missy opened her own designer bag and pulled out a pistol. "I heard enough of it from your mother back in the day."

"What the hell are you doing?" Cass jumped back, scurrying behind the desk again. "Are you crazy? Do you really think you can shoot me and get away with it?" She held onto her chair, trying to figure out if she could use it to defend herself.

"Crazy? You won't hang that label on me. It's not crazy to do what you can to take care of your kids and their inheritance." She began pacing and waving the gun. "I know what I'm doing. Some people don't have the guts to do what it takes to make things right. Well, no one will ever accuse Missy Calhoun of wimping out. They try to medicate me. Make me calm down." She leaned across the desk. "Screw their meds. I can't think on 'em. I know what's right and wrong and Conrad got it all wrong when he put you in his will. You're proving that with this shit right here." She hit the letters with her gun.

"The letters?" Cass kept the desk between them. "What kind of medicine, Missy? There's nothing wrong with taking a little something when you need to calm down."

"Calm? Fuck that. All calm gets you is a trip to the looney bin. Been there, done that. Now shut up and do what I say. You're not going to pay all those idiots who gave us their oil rights thirty years ago." Missy waved the gun. "Pick up those letters. I saw a shredder behind the desk out there where your secretary sits."

"She's an assistant, not a—"

"I don't care what the fuck her title is, do what I say!" Missy stalked around the desk and jammed the pistol into Cass's back. "Move!"

"Ow!" Cass gasped. She was afraid to move or the gun might go off. Best to pretend she was still hurt. "Go easy. I'm unsteady. Was it you who took shots at me in the parking garage the other night? Almost ran me down with a car?" Cass leaned against her desk, fumbling with her mouse and managing to highlight what she needed.

Missy laughed. "How stupid do you think I am? Why would I admit something like that to you?" She poked Cass again. "Straighten up, quit fooling around."

Cass pretended to reach for the papers, knocking the computer screen awry so Missy couldn't see what was on it. Damn it, if she did nothing else, she was going to give those people the notice they deserved. Cass clicked the mouse while she gathered the letters, her hands shaking so much it was easy to make a big deal out of it. There. No matter what happened, the emails were gone. At least ninety of them sent to email accounts that Ethan had found. Cat out of the bag, as her brother would say.

"Shredder? You really want me to shred them? Don't you know we can print more? Let me go. We can talk about this. Work out a compromise." Cass limped around the desk, exaggerating her hurt legs so she could try to knock into Missy. She had to figure out a way out of this.

"Compromise? Not necessary. When you're gone, my kids will get it all. Ethan doesn't know it, but he's going to give me the original leases and I'm going to destroy them. Without them, there's no proof of any fraud. You can't ruin my kids' inheritance then." Missy waved the gun again. "Now move it, bitch."

Cass started to tell her about the emails. Bad idea. Missy might shoot her out of rage and frustration. She needed to stall. Her heart in her throat, she looked down at the letters in her hands then tossed them up in the air, so they scattered. "Oops."

"Stupid bitch!" Missy drew back her arm as if to hit Cass with her pistol.

Cass lunged, grabbed the pistol, and fought for her life. The letters had made the floor slippery and they both went down hard. Her hip hit the floor and Cass gasped with pain. Missy pulled on the gun, trying to aim it at Cass's head.

"I'll show you who the stupid bitch is." Cass banged Missy's wrist on the edge of the desk. She hated this damned woman, hated her. She'd scared Cass and made her so mad she felt for the first time that she could kill. Cass tightened her grip and just kept hitting Missy's wrist against the desk, never stopping as long as Missy held the gun.

"Ow! Damn!" Missy's diamond bracelet cut into her wrist and she started bleeding. The large handbag dangling from her other wrist kept her from doing much more than pulling at Cass's upper arm.

Cass straddled her, her hurt legs crying out, but she wasn't about to give in as she held Missy down and finally wrestled the gun away from her. "I swear I'll shoot you if you move another muscle." She reared back, pretty sure she'd do it too. She was breathing hard, her heart pounding as she swatted at Missy's attempts to get the gun back again. "I mean it."

"Believe her, Missy. And if she doesn't, I will." Mason stood in the doorway, his gun pointed at Missy. "Move off of her, Cassidy." His face was grim and he looked as if he'd like to shoot anyway.

Cass held the gun as far from Missy as she could, not sure if she even had her finger on the trigger, as she crawled off the woman. She must have, because Missy's eyes were wide as they followed her movements. She would have sagged with relief, but she was too wired, still ready to follow through if Missy tested her. She even feigned a kick toward the woman. She'd done it. Beat that bitch down. If she hadn't felt like she was about to fall down herself, she'd do a victory lap around the desk.

"Mason, where did you come from? I didn't hear the elevator." Cass carefully laid the gun on Holly's desk, far away from Missy. Now that she looked at it, she felt a little sick. God, if it had gone off. . . . She shook her head and turned to Mason.

"Took the elevator to twenty-two and walked up a flight. I heard what was going on and didn't want to make her use that gun." Mason gestured with his gun. "Missy, get up. Stay away from the desk. Now."

"Oh, give it a rest. I wasn't really going to shoot her." Missy shook her head. "It isn't even loaded."

"I don't believe you." Mason held out his hand. "Come here, Cass."

"Did you call the police?" Cass ran to stand beside him and he put his arm around her. She was still shaking and wouldn't be surprised if her legs were bleeding again. Missy glared at both of them.

"Sure did. Abe will be here any minute."

"You think I care?" Missy frowned down at the papers all over the hardwood floor. "Stupid bitch. Why are you going to pay back all these ignorant people? It will take away your inheritance too. Don't you see that?" She stomped the letters with her black lizard heels. "It was bad enough when Conrad included you in the will. But now you're out to drain the company dry with your stupid high-and-mighty values. Oh, you're just like your tight-assed mother!" She kicked the letters, a furious figure in her elegant little black pantsuit.

"It's the right thing to do, Missy." Cass jumped when the elevator doors opened near them.

"Right? Did Elizabeth teach you that while you grew up in your squalid apartment with nothing? How'd it feel, Cassidy? Growing up poor, when you could have had the world at your feet and a loving father?" Missy patted her hair, like she was ready to play innocent. "Don't bother answering. I ended up with Elizabeth's husband and a mighty fine life when all was said and done. Conrad got struck with a conscience pretty soon after the first few contracts, but I straightened him out." She smiled as Abe stalked into the office area. "We made billions together. If you piss it all away, Cassidy, you'll be sorry."

"Did I just hear a threat?" Abe stalked over to Missy. "Mason says you had a gun. Where is it?"

"Why here, in my bag. Want to see my license to carry, Officer? I assume you are an officer." Missy batted her false eyelashes. "Cassidy is so jumpy. Seeing threats where there are none."

"No. Here's her gun right here." Mason pointed to the gun Missy had used.

"Cassidy had that gun." Suddenly Missy was all tears, collapsing into the chair next to the elevator. "Oh, God, I was terrified." Tears ran down her cheeks and she sobbed, her shoulders heaved.

"That's a lie! She threatened me with this one." Cass glared at Missy. "She must have brought two guns here."

Missy dug a hanky out of her pocket and wiped her eyes. "You can check it for her fingerprints. I have my own gun. That one looks like Conrad's gun. He kept it in his bedroom." Missy sobbed again. "I came up here to beg Cassidy to be sensible about the company. She's going to bankrupt it. Instead, she attacked me. I guess I'm going to need to press charges. She threatened to shoot me, Officer." More tears.

Abe showed her his identification. "Detective. And I've been investigating these threats against Ms. Calhoun. Let's go down to police headquarters. I have some questions for you, Mrs. Calhoun. We can talk about charges there." Abe was clearly skeptical.

"Not without my lawyer present." Missy opened her purse and carefully pulled out her phone and her wallet. "Here's my permit. Just so you know." She also handed over her gun.

Mason motioned to Abe. "You should have seen what I walked in on. Cass had her down on the floor. I also heard her threaten Cass through her phone. Cass dialed me when Missy arrived."

"Of course Mason will back her up. They're lovers." Missy pointed at Cass. "She hurt me. See? I'm bleeding." She held out her wrist.

Cass couldn't believe her ears. "She held that gun on me and threatened to shoot me with it. Then she claimed it wasn't loaded. I took it away from her after a struggle." Cass watched Abe check it. Her heart dropped when he pulled out bullets.

"It's loaded." He stared at Missy. She was on her cell, calling her lawyer.

Cass listened as Missy calmly told her lawyer she'd been in the office as a concerned stockholder in Calhoun Petroleum and of course she wasn't talking to the police without him. Her tears had dried up fast. Was Missy crazy? No wonder her siblings hadn't wanted to tell Cass who might be behind what had been happening to her. Abe reached for Missy's elbow to escort her to the elevator but she shrieked, making such a scene that he let her go and called for backup.

"Clearly this isn't going to be easy. I'll need a formal statement from both of you." Abe looked grim.

"I won't move a muscle until my attorney gets here." Missy stayed planted in the chair near the elevator. "You think I don't mean what I say? Try me." She pulled out her phone again and started going through her contacts. "If he's not here in five minutes, I'll just call another one."

"I'm going to let her wait. You two get out of here." Abe patted Cass's shoulder. "Don't worry, we'll get this sorted out. Your housekeeper said Mrs. Calhoun was supposed to turn in her key to the master suite. Of course, she could have kept a copy. And what do you bet she has access to a silver compact car?"

"Be careful, Abe." Cass walked with him to the elevator. "I have a feeling she'd like nothing better than to invent a charge of police brutality."

"Oh, I could see that right away." The detective looked around. "There are cameras out here, so I'm covered. Too bad there's no surveillance in your office, Cass."

Cass nodded, only too happy to leave Missy in Abe's hands. She and Mason got on the elevator. When the doors closed, Cass moved into Mason's arms. Feeling them close around her finally gave her

the sense of safety she needed. "I don't doubt Missy's been threatening me ever since I drove to the reading of my father's will. I can't
believe it!"

"I think you're right." Mason looked into her eyes. "Did you send
the letters? What was that all over the floor?"

"I sent emails. They'll make it impossible for her to stop us now."
Cass was glad that when the elevator doors opened, they saw a police
cruiser pulling into the garage. "Good. I hated to leave that woman
with Abe. She was just the type to cause him problems." She clutched
Mason's hand as they walked to his car. "But I need to make sure
Ethan doesn't give his mother the original documents for those oil
leases. He mentioned going to lunch with Missy yesterday. I'm sure
she's been pumping him for information."

"I think she'll be busy for a few hours. You can call him when we
get home. My gut feeling about Ethan is that he's mature and smart
enough to keep those documents safe and away from his mother."
Mason stopped next to his car. "Let's go to my place. You can ride
with me and I'll bring you to work in the morning."

"I have extra clothes in my car." Cass flushed, admitting that she'd
planned to spend the night with him bothering her a little. "I really
didn't want to go back to that freakish circus room."

"I don't want you back there either." Mason paused before he
opened the passenger door, then leaned her against it for a long kiss.
"Cass, God, Cassidy." He held her and she could feel his heart beating fast against her own chest. "Seeing you and Missy tussling over a
loaded gun . . . I'm the man who always knows what to say, but I—"
He shook his head and rested his cheek on her hair. "Cliché alert,
baby, but my heart stopped."

"I'm sorry." Cass pulled his face down to kiss him. She'd scared
him. What did that mean? She mattered to him. It made her want to
kiss him forever. Finally she pulled back and smoothed his hair back
from his face.

"Sorry? For what? You were brave. Awesome. And that woman
needs to be put away." Mason looked up when a black car entered
the garage and parked. "Her lawyer. He's famous; I recognize him.
Thank God it's not Billy." He helped Cass into the car. "Let's get out
of here."

"Yes. I'm beginning to hate this place." Cass settled into the
leather bucket seat, really glad to be off her feet at last. When Mason

got behind the wheel, she stared at him. "I was scared too. But I've always taken care of myself. Thank God, you came when you did. I'd come to an impasse. I don't know how long I could have sat on that woman with a gun I wasn't sure how to use. You came to my rescue." She ran her hand along his jawline. "You look tired. Rough day?"

"Yes. The first of many. You remember what I told you about my personality?" Mason started the powerful engine and backed out of the parking spot. "Well, it seems I found out something important as I tried to step into my uncle's shoes."

"What's that? Is a type-F man finding it hard to hold the reins of a *Fortune* 500 company?" Cass leaned back in the leather seat as Mason drove them through downtown traffic. She loved this, that they could talk about his day. That he could confide in her. He mattered to her too. So much. And she could have died today. She took a shaky breath and reached for his hand, but he was shifting gears. "You're smart, capable, you know you can do it. Hey, you always wanted this job, didn't you?"

"In theory. My own company. Large and in charge." He laughed. "Guess what? I'm not loving it. Not like I thought I would." He glanced at her. It was dark except for the glow of the dashboard lights. "You'd be much better at it."

"Get real, Mason. Me, running an oil company?" Now it was Cass's turn to laugh. "You really do know how to throw around the bullshit."

"Is that any way for a lady to talk?" Mason shifted gears again, then took Cass's hand. "Oh, you'd have some learning to do, but I can imagine you taking over that kind of job and just eating it up. Ordering people around, making those executive decisions, all the nitpicky things that are driving me batshit-crazy. I like troubleshooting, jumping in to fix problems or using my gift of gab—what you so elegantly call *bullshit*—to smooth things out."

"Well, then." Cass let go of his hand when she realized they were at his building and he needed it to shift gears again. He was right. About all of it. What she loved and what she was good at. And he was her opposite in so many ways. Ways that drew her. She loved his smooth talk and easy charm. Wished the things he could handle with ease were that easy for her. "What are you going to do?"

"What I have to. It's my family's company and my duty is to push on through. But I'm going to figure out a way to join forces . . ." He pulled into his parking spot and cut the engine. "Seems to me that we make a perfect pair, Cassidy Calhoun. You and me. A and F. We complement each other."

"In business?" Cass held her breath. If this was just about that, she was going to be very . . . *disappointed* was too mild a word.

"More than that." Mason got out of the car and came around to open her door. "Come here, woman. I guess what I'm trying to say is that I love you. I want you to be with me as a partner in every way. Maybe business someday, but definitely in pleasure. What do you say?"

"Say?" Cass threw her arms around him, sure her heart would burst before she could get the words out. "I love you, Mason. Your partner? I can't think of anything I'd want more."

Mason tried to stay out of it. Of course the three other Calhoun children didn't want their mother to go to jail. They'd been putting pressure on Cass for the past hour not to press charges against Missy. There were a variety of charges possible, but the only one where there had been a witness was the scene in her office. Mason would be happy to tell the world that the bitch had threatened Cass with a gun.

Of course, his recent history with the law didn't make him the best witness in the world. At least that murder charge against him had been dropped. Now the police were looking for Paul Bailey, the inspector who had also been arguing with Ed right before he'd been killed. Mason wouldn't be surprised if Bailey had done it and then fled the country.

"She was off her meds, Cass. We've checked Mama into a treatment center. She's been ill for quite a while. You don't know what that's like, living with mental illness." Megan blinked back tears.

"She shouldn't have been running around like that, then. Who's to say you won't let her sit in some swanky rehab facility somewhere for a token time period, then let her loose again to come after me?" Cass wasn't feeling sympathetic. "Isn't this the way rich people get out of every legal jam? Check into rehab. Sorry, people, but I'm just not buying it."

"It's not rehab, Cass, it's a mental-health facility. Hard core. She'll get therapy and they will get her meds straightened out." Ethan stared down at his feet. "We've known she had a problem for years. It isn't her first stay there."

Shannon patted her little brother's leg. "Ethan's right. Mama can't help herself. There's a diagnosis if you want to see it. It contributed to our parents' divorce. But you don't care about that, I'm sure." She looked at Megan and Ethan. "If you insist on pressing charges, her lawyer is pretty sure he can work a plea deal for her. She'll end up there anyway. But it would give her a record."

"A plea deal would at least make her stay a minimum amount of time." Mason couldn't stay out of this. "By then this oil-lease thing should be settled and you will all have what inheritance is left, coming to you. She'd have no reason to bother you then, Cass."

"If I don't press charges, I just let her get away with what she's done? And trust that she'll stay in treatment until she's—what—cured? She tried to kill me, Shannon." Cass walked over and helped herself to a glass of the fine bourbon kept in stock on the sideboard in the living room. Mason had to admire a woman who could drink that straight without flinching.

"I'd think you'd want to put this all behind you, Cass. Concentrate on getting this reparation thing through the board of directors. So far they like you and are letting you stay where you are, even trusting you to implement your budget cuts. Right?" Megan joined her at the bourbon. "We just lost our father, Cass. We don't want to lose our mother too."

"Don't pull that on me, Megan." Cass set down her empty glass and sat beside Mason again. "Detective Rogers discovered that your mother had access to a silver car like the one that almost killed me. She could have borrowed it from her gardener. They even found a bullet fragment in the rear bumper that matched the kind from Mason's gun."

Mason was glad his shooting wasn't as lame as he'd thought. He was getting tired of these Calhouns ganging up on Cass.

"She has the right to make your mother pay, people," he said. "That headboard could have seriously injured both of us."

"Mama told me she tried to cut that thing down years ago. It was just coincidence that it came down on you, Cass. Because of all the movement going on in that bed, maybe?" Ethan spoke up. "We all hated that headboard. She lived here and had to stare up at it for years. Mama got mad and took a saw to it while she was still married to Daddy and he was out of town. Who could blame her? I know you're glad to see it gone, Cass."

"Doesn't matter to me. I'm moving out if Dylan can figure out a way to get around that clause in Conrad's will." Cass leaned against Mason. "Mason asked me to move in with him and I'm already packing."

"Good for you." Shannon grinned. "See? You're going to be happy. Why mess up things for us? If Mama has to go to trial, think of the misery and bad publicity that will hit all of us."

"And we did say we would back you about the payoffs, didn't we? We'll be going before the board as a united front. Even though this will cost us a lot of our inheritance." Megan nodded. "Come on. Say you'll tell the detective you won't press those charges."

Shannon leaned against the bar, her face serious. "And while the lawyer says he can arrange a plea deal, we really don't want to have to rely on that promise. District attorneys can decide to play hardball on a whim and you know it. Too many rich people have gotten away with stuff in this town lately. Mama might end up paying the price for that. Then we'd have one of those nasty trials with the big headlines."

Cass looked at Mason. He could tell she just wanted this to go away. And he knew she didn't want to have to testify in court. Missy's lawyer had a reputation for tearing apart witnesses against his clients. Then there was the bad publicity. Oh, yes, it would be a shit storm.

"If you want to drop the charges, Cass, do it. Your family will be happy and you can forget this and move on." Cass nodded and Mason gave each Calhoun a stern look when they set up a cheer. "But keep in mind you said Missy is getting treatment. She must. And staying in that hospital until the royalties from thirty years ago are settled. That's the deal."

"Oh, she will. We've all threatened to cut off communication with her if she doesn't. Mama realizes now that we disapprove, strongly, of what she's done to Cass and of what she and Daddy did thirty years ago. She has to stay on her medication too. She's out of control without it." Shannon jumped up and gave Cass a hug. "Thank you, thank you! You won't regret this!"

"I hope not. You all start your new jobs on Monday. Are you ready?" Cass finally relaxed next to him.

"I'm ready." Megan got up and walked over for a refill. "Mason, did you tell her?"

"Tell her? Who? Me?" Cass turned to look at him. "What's going on?"

"Megan had a special request. About her new job." Mason eyed the decanter. Dutch courage? No, he'd done the right thing, arranging this. Of course he didn't feel guilty, taking Cassidy away from the good old boy.

"So why is it a big deal to tell me about it?" Cass squeezed his thigh.

"I asked him to partner me with Rowdy, Cass. I liked him and he has the kind of job Daddy wanted me to take on. So, as of Monday, I'm hitting the oil fields with Rowdy Baker." Megan took a swallow of bourbon. "How do you like that?"

Cass smiled. "I think it will be very interesting. For both of you." Then she turned to Mason. "And you didn't tell me this before because . . . ?"

"Slipped my mind." Mason knew that wasn't going to fly. "Well, okay, I thought maybe you wouldn't like it. Throwing your sister and your old boyfriend together like that."

Cass pinched his leg and Mason jumped. Damn it, why did his women always pinch him so hard? "What's not to like? But I have to warn you, Meg. When Rowdy finds out Calhoun may have robbed his family thirty years ago, he's going to be a very unhappy camper. And that's putting it mildly. So be aware."

"Oh, yeah. We have that to look forward to." Meg finished her drink. "You broke his heart too, Cass. Maybe this won't be the fun and games I think it might be."

Cass grinned. "I don't know. Rowdy's hot and can be a very good time." This time she jumped when Mason pinched her.

"All moved in. How does it feel?" Mason pushed back from the dining-room table. He'd cooked again but hoped Cass had some talent in the kitchen. He'd used up his skills with the pasta and now a stir-fry. Even so, he had to admit he liked having her here with him. He'd never had a woman living with him before. It felt good. Permanent.

"Great. But I want to go out on the balcony. We should have had dinner out there." Cass picked up her wineglass and opened the sliding-glass door. "It's perfect outside. Come on."

"I'm okay right here." Mason gathered the dirty dishes and set them in the sink.

"Seriously." Cass walked back inside and stood behind him to slide her arms around his waist. "You've got to come out to the balcony. There's a breeze and you can smell the roses from the rose garden in the park. I want you there beside me." She tugged on the back of his belt. "Please."

"Remember me in the helicopter?" He turned in her arms. "I hate heights."

"The balcony isn't moving." She kissed his chin. "I'll hold onto you. Promise."

"Why are you pushing this?" Mason let her pull him toward that freaking death trap.

"Are you going to let fear keep you from one of life's pleasures?" She let go and skipped out onto the terrace.

Yeah, it was an actual terrace, at least eight feet wide and paved-in slate. Logically, Mason knew the wrought-iron railings couldn't be loose, but when Cass leaned against one, his heart seemed to stop.

"Get back from there!" He took three steps toward her, then put on the brakes. "Come here." He hadn't seen this side of her before, the daredevil. She was laughing, the sun kissed her face, and she almost tempted him to take another step.

"Mason, I'm fine. Look at me." Cass held out her hands. She wasn't in danger. Logically he knew that. She did a little dance as she reached for her T-shirt and pulled it off over her head.

"People will see you." Mason's voice came out as a croak. God, he hated how fear made his knees weak. He sank into a chair the decorator had set out there. He'd never been in it before, but it was sturdy, a heavy iron, and made him feel grounded. Good. Now if he could just get Cass to leave this death trap.

"So? I have on a bra. Like a bathing-suit top. It's warm in the sun. I'm working on my tan. Take off your shirt. I like looking at you." She strolled over and stood in front of him. "Give." She held out a hand. She was tempting, he'd give her that. Everything about her tempted him. Oh, she wanted his shirt.

"Fine." He ripped off his shirt. With any luck they could move this inside. She wasn't an exhibitionist—not that he'd noticed yet anyway. He had a ring in the living room, a speech planned. He wanted to do the proposal right. She'd say yes; it was a formality. But he wanted it to be a moment they'd both look back on and have a nice story to tell their children someday.

He just hoped he wouldn't shed a tear. He loved her so damned much it made him nuts. Like maybe he'd do something stupid like that. He'd almost lost it when he'd seen her with Missy that night. With a gun that could have gone off . . . He still got choked up, thinking about how close he'd come to losing her. He grunted when she landed in his lap.

"What are you thinking? You are so intent, it makes me wonder if it's work. That's supposed to be off the table today." She rubbed his chest. "Quit worrying about it."

"No, not work. Children." He smiled as her eyes widened. Oh, he was going to fuck this up. Didn't matter. He had to get it out. "I was imagining *our* children. How many you want?"

"Two, at least. Being an only child was lonely." She leaned against him, her skin warm from the sun. "Mason, what are you saying?"

"You know I love you. I want us to get married. Do it up right. A big deal. Have the families there. Think your mother will come?"

"If I have to drag her there, kicking and screaming." She sat back, her eyes shining. "Do I get a chance to say yes or no?"

"Sure. Yes?" He kissed her tenderly. "Or no. Please, God, don't say no." He kissed her with a ferocious hunger that almost made the chair topple. His heart raced and he stood. "I've got to get off this fucking balcony." He carried her inside and sat on the couch. "Answer me, Cassidy, before I have some kind of meltdown."

"Yes." She said it firmly, no doubt in her voice in all.

"All right!" Mason pulled her to him for a kiss.

"Wait a minute!" She held him off. "I need to know something first." She traced his bicep, the one with the tattoo. "Tell me. Who was Sugar?"

"Are you jealous?" He smiled, loving it. He'd been waiting for her to ask. Women always did. She'd stared at it the day they'd met, when he'd taken off his shirt to change that flat tire.

"Damn right I am. Who was she? Do you still see her?" Cass sat up and looked him in the eyes.

"From time to time. You know a man never forgets his first." Mason laughed when she crossed her arms over her chest.

"What?" Her eyes flashed like she was ready to kill, either him or the mysterious Sugar.

Mason resisted the urge to keep it going. "Honey, Sugar was the first well I brought in on my own. I later brought in four more in that field. It was a proud day for my granddaddy." Mason laughed when Cass pushed him to his back and fell on top of him.

"You couldn't just say that, could you? Really, Mason. I guess I'd better marry you because no one else would have you." Cass's body was a sweet weight on top of him.

"Guess so. And remember, married or not, I'll still evaluate your performance at Calhoun fairly." Mason smiled up at her.

"Do your worst, Mason. And I'll do my best." Cass winked and slid down his body. "Just don't be surprised if I have you eating dinner on that balcony before all is said and done."

Mason groaned, figuring he'd probably jump off the damned thing if Cass wanted him to. He pulled her up and smiled into her eyes. "And I'll have you galloping on old Joe."

"Shut up, Mason." Cass leaned down and kissed him.

Like what you read?
Keep an eye out for
TEXAS FIRE
Available May 2017
From Lyrical Shine

ABOUT THE AUTHOR

Nationally best-selling author **Gerry Bartlett** is a native Texan who lives halfway between Houston and Galveston. She freely admits to a shopping addiction, which is why she has an antiques business on the historic Strand on Galveston Island. She used to be a gourmet cook but has decided it's more fun to indulge in gourmet eating instead.

You can visit Gerry on Facebook, Twitter or Instagram. You can also check out her latest releases on her website at gerrybartlett.com where you can sign up for her newsletter or read her articles with advice for aspiring writers, The Perils of Publishing.

CPSIA information can be obtained
at www.ICGtesting.com
Printed in the USA
LVOW08s1740080217
523625LV00002BA/273/P